LUNAR MARKED

(SKY BROOKS SERIES BOOK 4)

MCKENZIE HUNTER

McKenzie Hunter

Lunar Marked

© 2016, McKenzie Hunter

McKenzieHunter@McKenzieHunter.com

ISBN: 978-0-9903441-7-9

ACKNOWLEDGMENTS

~

Once again, I am humbled by the people that are willing to help me with this process. I am truly thankful for my mother, Tiffany Dix, Sheryl Cox and Stacy McCright.

I would also would like to thank Luann Reed Siegel, editor, and Nicole Anderson, my patient and very talented, cover artist.

Last but definitely not least, I would like that thank my readers for giving me the opportunity to entertain you with my books and choosing to follow Skylar through her journey. I really hope you enjoyed it.

CHAPTER 1

Quell slowly walked around the *Hidacus*, studying it, his face blank. His fingers ran lightly along the branches as though dealing with fractured glass. I stood a few inches away, looking at the odd plant as if it were the first time I'd seen it. Its thick, obtrusive trunk overtook the small, darkened greenhouse, willowy branches stretching out and swaying ever so gently. The slender stems of its leaves pumped with a constant rhythm like a pulse. Tiny buds filled with sappy fluid gave off the fragrance of fruit and metallic scent of blood.

The silence stretched as Quell periodically looked in my direction before returning his attention to the plant. His onyx eyes, which always seemed searching and distant, watched me with curiosity. With fondness I remembered it wasn't a year ago that distinctive green eyes looked back at me, which were a result of him feeding off Hidacus. It had become his brand; his mark, as well as a constant reminder of his past, when he felt he had betrayed humanity. A constant and explicit reminder of the abnegation of human blood and his disdain for humanity.

The silence remained as he approached me. Should I have expected anything more from Quell than silence and emotions so deeply hidden that at times he seemed elegiac? Naively I did. There was a part of me that had wanted some display of excitement from Quell when I'd told him I had a surprise for him. I'd been nearly bursting with excitement as I led him to the backyard to show him the greenhouse I had built for him.

Ten minutes had passed since I first showed him the greenhouse. He'd spent most of it examining the plant with a stolid expression. One moment he was near the plant; the next he was in front of me with his mouth slightly parted, but words wouldn't come freely.

"You did this for me?" he finally asked.

"Of course. I don't need it." I looked around the space and admired the plant again. I wished Steven would at least come out for a moment to see it, too, but he was in the house sulking as he had since I first asked him to help me with the greenhouse. He'd mumbled and griped in protest throughout the construction process, saying almost hourly, "Now we are building a little playhouse for your vampire?"

I guess in some odd sense Quell was my vampire. I felt responsible for him and wanted to keep him from killing others as he had before. When he had his first taste of human blood after years of abstaining, he'd killed five women. I still wore the burden of that guilt. If I hadn't forced him to feed from me, he wouldn't have done it. But after he was staked and it sent him into *reversion*, I needed to feed him to save his life.

I wanted to make sure Quell never killed like that again. He became my responsibility.

Like an elusive shadow he moved effortlessly throughout the room, regarding the plant. "You know Michaela has forbidden me to use it." Michaela, his creator, had destroyed the Hidacus that he once used to feed on in one of her many irrational fits of rage.

"No. You were forbidden from *having* the plant. It's *my* plant, at *my* house. Michaela doesn't have a say on what happens here," I said with a smile.

2

His movement was so quick I hardly had time to adjust to his presence in front of me. I would never get used to the way he looked at me—a combination of intrigue, adoration, and aversion. His touch was gentle as his hand ran along my arm. "I sometimes forget how beautiful you are," he said softly as his fingers continued to trail down my arm until it reached my wrist. His thumb rubbed rhythmically along the pulse there.

It was the first time he'd ever said anything like that, and I wasn't sure how to respond.

He moved even closer, his lips barely brushing mine before he pulled away and watched my reaction in silence. Then he kissed me again—longer, genteel, searching. When he moved away, there was a gentle sadness lingering on his face.

"You are leaving, aren't you?" he asked.

Quell was more perceptive than I gave him credit for. I nodded my head, barely committing to my assertion. But I owed him more than that. I owed him the truth. My life was getting complicated. Trying to find the Tre'ase that created Maya, a spirit shade whom I hosted and who was keeping me alive, was going to take me away from home longer than I expected. I wouldn't be there for him. There was a lot of guilt entwined in my gift. "No, I am not leaving, but I may not be around as much," I admitted.

He looked at the Hidacus and then at me again, his hold on my hand tightening to the point of becoming uncomfortable. Still close, he leaned forward and rested his forehead against mine, the palm was gentle as it rested against my face. He kissed me again, his lips firm against mine, unquenched desire seemed to have erupted in him as desperation melted into the kiss. When he pulled away abruptly, he presented me with the same emotionless look I had become used to. *Quella Perduta, the Lost One.* And nothing seemed more fitting.

After a long moment of silence, he spoke so softly it was barely audible. "I will miss you". Then he kissed me lightly on the forehead, and it felt vacant, cool, and sad.

3

"I would never leave without telling you. You know that, right? I'm coming back."

"Promise?" he whispered.

"Promise."

Steven cleared his throat. Quell barely gave him the pleasure of an extended glance before returning his attention to me.

"You should try the Hidacus," Steven suggested. "See if it is as you remember."

Quell brought my hand to his lips and kissed it.

Steven stepped farther into the greenhouse. "Go ahead, give it a try," he reminded Quell again, a little firmer this time. Usually his gentle features held a certain congenial warmth, but now they were hard and unwelcoming. Quell continued to hold my hand and made no effort to move.

"I will," he said, dismissing Steven, and within moments it seemed like he had forgotten Steven was there.

He guided me over to the plant. It wasn't as large and lavish as the ones he once had at his home, but its willowy presence overtook the small space. I became aware again of its fruity, metallic smell and the even pulse-like thumping of the nodes. The stems moved as though they were controlled by a light breeze. He broke off a stem and sank his teeth in it, extracting its sap, but he didn't drain it. Instead, he broke it apart, the sap welling to the surface, and then he pressed it to my lips. It tasted just like the one I'd tried at his house, a deep berry flavor with a hint of metal. A fruity version of blood.

I could still feel the cool tingle that Quell's lips left on mine and reluctantly admitted to myself that I wouldn't mind feeling it again. There was something intriguing and comforting about it.

Steven stayed, making his presence known, which made the prior effortless interaction between Quell and me become uncomfortable. Steven relaxed into the wall, like a shadow, his green eyes reflecting anger and disgust he wasn't able to mask.

"Is it as you remember?" he asked.

Quell nodded, his attention split between me and the Hidacus.

"From my calculations and the last time you visited Sky, you should spend some time getting better acquainted with it," he said with a smile that was strained but pleasant. It was forced because I never failed to comment on the scowl that always peeked through and overtook his face each time Quell visited.

Steven led me out of the greenhouse, his hand firmly on my elbow, and didn't say a word until he'd led me into the house. "What the hell is going on between you two?"

"Nothing."

"That didn't look like *nothing* to me."

"Don't make it into more than what it is. We're friends."

"*We* are friends," he asserted. "That wasn't a friend kiss. Please tell me the last time I kissed you like that?"

"Yesterday." I referred to the peck on the cheek he'd given me when I brought groceries in and he'd noticed I stocked up on his favorite snack. Fifteen bags of dill-flavored chips that he would mess up by adding hot sauce to it. I didn't know what was grosser, the smell of it or watching him eat it and claim it was a "southern thing," something I am sure he'd made up. Something no one from the south would willingly admit to eating or enjoying. "*That* was a very passionate kiss," I joked, trying to diffuse the situation.

"Quell's was hardly a friendly kiss on the cheek. He likes you, and please don't give me that 'we are friends' or 'he feels indebted to me' garbage. What I saw in there was intimate. Sky—" Frustrated, his hands washed over his face as he displayed a level of distress that was new to me. Based on how poorly he was handling the situation, it was new for him as well.

"You're making it a bigger deal than it is and reading far more into it," I said in a soft voice, as gold rolled over his eyes. I needed to rein this in.

"No, *your* vampire is becoming a problem". It was said with the same disdain that Ethan and Sebastian used when they spoke of most vampires.

"I'll handle it."

"You keep saying that, but when will he stop being something that you have to handle? One mistake—yes, saving him from reversion was a mistake—and now you feel eternally responsible for him. I call bullshit. Let him go, and whatever happens, happens."

"Even if you don't trust his intentions, trust mine. Somewhere in the middle of all this I started to care for him, and whether or not you think my obligation to him is foolish, you need to trust me. I would do whatever it takes to keep him safe—just as I would do with you."

Steven was like a younger brother and I hated fighting with him. The disagreements about Quell were getting redundant and becoming a constant obstacle between us. Our eyes locked for a long, tense moment. He raked his hand through his hair, the longest I'd ever seen it, loose ginger waves dangling just above his ears. "I can't just sit here and watch you make a mistake that can't be easily fixed without wanting to do something. You're tying my hands, and I don't know what to do."

His ragged, heavy sigh broke the silence that followed. "You are binding yourself to him with unwarranted loyalty, and you won't let me fix it," he said. His eyes had lost that gentle twinkle that I'd gotten used to.

"Because there's nothing to fix."

"Sky, I always want to fix things for you, and that won't change. When I see you putting yourself in a situation that will ultimately end badly for you, I don't know how to ignore it. Watching it happen is getting harder for me. This is going to end horribly."

He shook his head, and said, "I have to be away from it—from you. I'm moving out." He didn't give me a chance to respond. He went into his room and closed the door. That was a gut punch that I wasn't prepared for—couldn't be prepared for, didn't want to be prepared for. Long moments crept by as I stood staring at the door, hearing him move around, probably packing.

I waited longer than I should have for him to come out and our argument or whatever it was to end like it always did—with him running the tips of his fingers over my face then pressing his forehead against mine. Or I would do something like that to him. Real apologies never needed to be voiced. That was better than one. We understood it, and it worked for us. But we'd never had a fight like this.

The next day I worked with Josh in the pack's library as I tried not to think about Steven moving out despite hearing him packing his things as I left. Josh glanced up from his notes several times, studying me a little more each time and opening his mouth to speak but deciding against it.

In less than a week, Steven would be all moved out. Each time I thought about it, I got queasy. He was a constant when things seemed chaotic and his presence made things a little better. Less frenzied. Josh came to his feet, still watchful as he paced the large space, unable to resist looking over my shoulder at the book. The moment he did, the words vanished, leaving us with weathered vellum.

The closer he got to me the harder it was to ignore the changes in him. His outward appearance was the same. Carmel-colored hair was disheveled as usual; defined features and a strong jaw drew focus to the cerulean eyes. The soft fabric of his t-shirt silhouetted the muscles of his slender body, and intricate tattoos overlaid whatever skin was left uncovered. Just a few inches over six feet, he used to be unassuming despite being one of the most powerful witches on this side of the country. But things had changed. Magic was a muscle that he had ignored and deprived of constant exercise. He had become stagnant and relaxed in his skills, and a couple of months ago he was dominated again by another witch. One slight too many against his ego and he now seemed to be diligent about not allowing it to happen again.

He wasn't depriving his magic muscles anymore. Now his magic was obtrusive, an overbearing and uncomfortable force that made being around him different. It was a roaring wave instead of the gentle, soothing breeze it had once been. Is there such a thing as overusing magic? His miscreant smile was the same; his blue eyes were always gentle, the color like those of his brother, Ethan, the Beta of the Midwest Pack, but Ethan's held a hint of steel. The playfulness of Josh's wasn't enough to smooth off the sharpness that was there now. They were off—he was off.

Just like his brother, Josh wasn't unaware of his looks. Some described them as a quiet beauty—I had to disagree. They practically screamed, "You're welcome." But arrogance didn't accompany them the way it did in his brother. Ethan was *very* aware of his looks.

"What's the matter?" he finally asked, without looking up from the notepad that contained the spells that we had translated. For months he had tried to find a pattern in them, hoping to translate them without the third book. Samuel, a powerful witch who wanted to use the Clostra to rid the world of magic, had that book in his possession. It was a source of frustration for Josh but I was content with Samuel having it. I couldn't wait until Joan, the Alpha of the South, came to pick up one of the two we had. The books were dangerous and as far as I was concerned should be in different parts of the world and never in the same room again, like they were when we removed my death curse, which also removed every curse that had ever been performed. We still didn't know the extent of the damage that single act had done. I knew we had released the Tre'ase and they now were unrestricted by the ward that had kept them isolated in their homes. I lived with the guilt that we—the pack—had irreparably changed the world to help me.

"Nothing," I finally said.

He frowned as he appraised me. "So you look like you're carrying the weight of the world just because you think you look sexy brooding?" he asked, the glint in his eyes and kink in his lips a simple reminder of why the witch was just as charismatic as he was powerful.

I squeezed my own lips together in a duck face, narrowed my eyes, and slouched into a silly pose, arching my back and contorting my body. "You mean this isn't sexy?"

He laughed and pushed the notepad aside, running his fingers through his hair, which probably was the closest it came to being combed or styled today. Josh had always been a get up, shower, and go guy. "Seriously, what's wrong?"

"Everything," I admitted, but I wasn't ready to talk about Steven moving out because there was a part of me that hoped this was just a fight that went on too long. Hopefully, he would soon make the decision to stay. "We removed curses—I am not convinced that there will not be some consequences. Do you ever wonder how we changed this world? And Samuel, why has he been so quiet? People like him, who have a dogmatic agenda like his, just don't fade quietly into the night. They plot, plan, and wait for an opportunity to strike. Why hasn't he struck?"

"You were his plan. I don't think he had anything else. And we haven't been able to fix the Aufero, so the witches whose magic it's holding will not feel an obligation to become his allies because there isn't anything in it for them," he said.

I looked over at the Aufero, its odd coloring tarnished by magic from Ethan. An object that had endless potential, but Marcia had used it to harshly punish witches for minor infractions to ensure that the Creed were the most powerful among them.

"You think he's just at home wallowing in his failure?" I asked skeptically.

"Honestly, we have no idea what he's doing. He's disappeared," he said.

Someone like Samuel didn't just disappear into the night never to be heard from again. He was always steps ahead of us, so the fact that he had disappeared and we couldn't find him heightened my concerns. You don't want a powerful witch on the loose with an agenda to remove magic from the world—stopping were-animals from being able shift to their animal form, divesting elves and witches of the ability to use magic, and killing all vampires. Samuel believed that magic made people evil, and he was ready to execute his version of misguided vigilante justice to save us from ourselves. We should know the whereabouts of someone like Samuel at all times.

We needed to be on the offensive and figure out his next move. And we knew his next move. He wanted the Clostra. It didn't make me feel good knowing that we had two of the three in our possession in the same location. They needed to be separated.

They had a ward that prevented just anyone from reading them—that was good. Each spell was divided between the three books—that was also a good thing. But the spells could be performed by anyone strong enough to wield its magic—that was a bad thing. We didn't know if the books had to be together to work—and that was another bad thing.

Josh shrugged, but the stress of the question lingered and burdened his features. His brow furrowed and he started to bite into his nail bed, his "tell" that he was uncomfortable or nervous. He continued to look at his notes, perhaps thinking the same thing I was. Liam, the leader of Makellos, and Marcia were now allied, making things very complicated. The Makellos were considered the elven elite, a self-proclaimed title, because they were all "pure" and untainted by interbreeding with other groups in the otherworld or with something even worse—humans, which they considered the worst dilution.

To our favor, we were secretly allied with elves. Last month

Gideon had taken the position as leader of the elves. I'd openly showed my disgust but couldn't ignore or take comfort in the knowledge that the alliance between the Makellos and the Creed would soon be severed because of collusion between Sebastian and Abigail, Gideon's sister. She almost guaranteed that she would incite a civil war in an effort to bring them under one leadership, her brother's. A war of any kind would leave them fractured, and Sebastian was aware that Marcia would not maintain an alliance with a fractured power and would quickly sever ties once they were of little use to her. It was convoluted and calculated manipulation on Sebastian's part, and it made me realize that he was more than just compact and robust physical power but cunning as he worked the system to do whatever necessary to protect the pack and keep us strong.

Sebastian's stratagem was to be allied and have a leader of the elves indebted to him, for one reason only—to change their covenant regarding dark elves. Ethan was part dark elf and upon the death of his grandmother he inherited her magic. Based on the covenant, Ethan was supposed to be killed. We used the Aufero to divest him of the dark eleven magic, but since then, the Aufero had been too dangerous to use. If I used the magic from the Aufero and erected a protective field, the air would be siphoned out, suffocating the very person the field was supposed to protect. If touched, it pulled out your breath, and hammered your heart into arrhythmic behavior, which was why Josh and I were in the library trying hard to find a spell to correct it.

Josh had split his attention between trying to fix the Aufero and interpreting the remainder of the Clostra.

The Aufero was placed on the table, a burnt orange and pulsing in light beats, recovering from another spell that hadn't worked. Whenever Josh neared it expelled a burst of magic, as though it recognized Josh's power and wanted to protect itself.

"I can't believe you knew what my brother was before I did," Josh mumbled, glancing at me, as he stood a couple of feet from the Aufero. A combination of pain and anger managed its way to the surface. Ethan kept secrets. Lots of secrets. He and Sebastian seemed to take on the roles of not only Alpha and Beta but also guardians of the secrets and protectors of the skeletons that were effectively hidden in our closet. And when it came to this pack there were tons of both secrets and skeletons. Everything was on a need-to-know basis, and as far as they were concerned, most people didn't need to know. It was to protect the pack and its loved ones, but I believed that secrets caused more harm than good, especially between Josh and Ethan.

In an effort to assuage his feelings of betrayal, I said, "He was trying to protect you. You know the rules, if you knew, you were required to expose it. We all are or would be in violation of our covenant. The situation was supposed to be contained."

I hated that word, *contained*. It was their nice word for saying *murdered*. They contained dark elves because of their ability to kill someone with a mere touch. No one knew how to control their ability; consequently, an agreement was made by the leaders in the otherworld that dark elves would be destroyed. I felt it was a cruel act until Ethan nearly killed me during an argument just by touching me. I realize it might not be as malevolent as I thought if even Ethan couldn't control it. Something as casual as a touch could be the end of someone they loved, and part of me sometimes played with the idea that it might have been more of an act of benevolence than malice to end a life that had to be more misery than pleasure.

Josh's scowl didn't change. In fact, he looked troubled, which made me feel more uncomfortable about the other secret Ethan and I shared. I stared at the myriad of markings that formed a tapestry of sleeves on both of Josh's arms. But I concerned myself with the one on his leg that he thought was a birthmark. It was the only thing keeping him alive.

He was cursed, as punishment for something his mother had done. Ethan and Claudia, their godmother, had found a way to circumvent the curse. Now that we had removed all curses, I was sure he didn't have to worry about it. But I still wished Ethan would tell him. He asked that I keep his secret, but I only agreed after he promised he would tell Josh himself. I wished I had given him a specific time frame, because I'm sure Ethan's okay with holding on to it until he's on his deathbed.

"You have a birthmark, don't you?" I clamped my mouth shut the moment the words came out. *Why did I ask that?* I knew why— I wanted to tell him.

His half smiles always had an air of deviance. "Of course, you've seen it," he teased. Of course I had. Like his brother, he thought clothing was more of a hassle than he cared to have. Countless times I'd come to his home to practice magic, only to find that his clothing of choice was a pair of boxers and maybe a t-shirt. He would have stayed that way if I hadn't refused to come in until he was dressed.

"Do you want to see it again?" He winked.

"He actually has two birthmarks. But I don't think it is necessary for you to see them."

I looked over my shoulder at Ethan. I was met with an intense gunmetal gaze that I could feel on me even after I had turned back around. "Hi, Ethan."

He walked in and the smirk had eased; a challenge. "Did I interrupt anything?" he asked Josh, but his eyes shifted in my direction several times.

"Nope. Just working." Josh was short with Ethan, more than usual. I'd finally gotten used to their dynamics. Ethan was a powerful were-animal, the Beta of one of the strongest packs in the country and in any other pack he could easily be the Alpha. If he ever challenged Sebastian, I wasn't sure of the results. Ethan exuded a confidence, power, and primal grace that commanded compliance and subjugation, except when it came to his brother. They were always in a battle of wills over who was going to be the Alpha in their two-man pack. I wish I could say they dealt with it nonviolently all the time. Their sibling dynamics were often the source of entertainment for most people in the pack. "I called you several times," Ethan said, his eyes narrowing as he watched his brother, who was noticeably distant.

He shrugged. "Sorry, I must have left my phone at home."

Both Ethan and I looked at his phone on the table just a few inches from the notepad.

"Really." Ethan reached for it, picked it up, and displayed it for Josh to see.

Defiance shaded Josh's face, and his lips twisted into a moue that was the clear giveaway of his position as the younger brother. It wasn't an adult tantrum, well not really, but if there were such a thing, it was a man-pout. He might as well have stuck his tongue out after touting, "You're not the boss of me!"

Ethan inched closer to the Aufero and his brother, but the Aufero belched another violent burst of magic as it formed a cloudy field around itself, which it maintained until Ethan had moved several feet from it. Josh and I watched with interest.

"What?" he finally asked after noticing Josh continued to watch him.

Josh shook his head. "I needed a break," he said as he grabbed his jacket and headed out the door. Josh had taken a lot of breaks today, usually taking a ride on his Ducati, a guilt present from Ethan he gotten about two weeks ago. He accepted the gift but hung on to the anger.

Ethan sat down in Josh's chair, perusing the notes, only taking a break to look over at the Aufero which hadn't dropped the protective field it had formed around itself. There was always something off about Ethan, and the more I discovered about him the more there was to find out.

He sighed. "What is it, Skylar?" His tone was as sharp as the edges of his jaw. His defined features never seemed to soften, and I can't remember the last time his eyes were their natural vibrant cobalt color.

"Nothing."

"77 BPM."

Ugh, I hate when he does that. "Stop that!"

"I will when you start being completely honest with me. Don't tell me something isn't wrong, when something is." He rested back in his chair, his cool gaze boring into me.

"Really? *You* are giving me the 'you should be honest lecture'?" Ethan and Sebastian were liars by the strictest definition of the word and often did it to protect the pack. But of course they would never call what they did a lie. No, they considered it "getting people to see the reality you wish them to believe." Although the motives behind them doing so were understandable, the ability to detect lies by listening to the changes of the body, everything from the deviations in your respiration to the light uptick of your heart rate, were things that most were-animals had the ability to do. Ethan and Sebastian were masters at it. Which in turn gave them the exceptional ability to get you to "see the reality they wish you to believe" without anyone detecting otherwise. And no matter how they spun it, *that* was the behavior of a psychopath. Often I had to brush aside my rigid ethics and accept that the behaviors I hated about them were the very ones that had kept me alive. I had to learn that some things in the otherworld were gray.

"I don't like that you are keeping information from your brother, and I hate that I am part of it. You have to tell him." After a long pause, I added, "Or I will."

He stood and closed the distance between us in a long, graceful glide. Now that he was next to me, his faced relaxed, a smile tweaking at his lips. His tone was low and inquiring. "So you'll break the promise you made to me?"

I tried to think back to the conversation we had when I found out Ethan's secret. Did I promise? Part of it merged together with all the things that had occurred that day.

He moved closer and his lips lightly brushed mine when he

spoke. "You're a lot of things Skylar, but a person who would go back on her word isn't one of them."

He gave me a little space, but he was still too close.

"I will tell him when I am ready. I don't think it is necessary for him to know, so I will tell him when I damn well please. Let's have enough with the idle threats. I don't like it."

"I don't like keeping your secrets."

"Then forget that you know it," he suggested, his jaw set with the familiar tension that meant I wasn't going to get any further with the conversation and it was over.

"You have two days or I am going to tell him."

His smirk taunted me and my mind slipped back to the time I punched him in the face, the desire to do it resurfacing. Smug bastard.

"No threats. I will take as long as I need and will tell him when I am ready." He leaned forward and kissed me, a light peck on the nose. "Tell Josh to stop being such a jerk."

"If I can't convince you to stop being one, what makes you think I can persuade him?"

He chuckled, and I could hear the deep rumble as he made his way down the hall.

I was going to tell Josh.

But I promised.

I didn't care. I was going to do it.

Dammit. I promised I wouldn't.

Ugh, why doesn't he just wipe that smug grin off his face?

Josh took more than his usual twenty-minute break. I guess he wanted to make sure his brother was nowhere to be found when he returned.

"So how long do you plan on treating your brother like this?"

His shoulders sank with his sigh. "I don't know. It pisses me off that he treats me like—"

"He's treating you like the brother he will do anything to protect. He just does it really wrong. I don't think he knows how to love like a normal person," I asserted with a grin.

Josh laughed, and not because it was funny. It was true. The only relationship of Ethan's that I knew of was with Chris, former hunter who was turned into a vampire, and it was the epitome of dysfunction. It lacked commitment, and they would sacrifice each other for their own interest. Yet, that was his longest relationship. Ethan and I had a couple of moments, and we almost slept together, but then he stopped it. I'm not sure why, but I was glad he did. Having a relationship with Ethan was like playing with a bee and being shocked when it stung.

We settled down to our work, both of us actively trying to forget about his brother.

The time crept by and when I looked at my phone, it had been two hours and Josh and I were still sitting across from each other looking at the Aufero and its odd coloring, trying to figure out the magic that emanated off it, which was wrong—very wrong. Its new powers had a maladroit effect on my magic. Protective fields no longer protected me from anything; instead it converted the illuminant bubbles into gas chambers that slowly pulled the breath out of anyone enclosed in them. I'd destroyed several pieces of clothing while trying to use it to *travel*. Before Ethan had taken Ethos's magic from me, my mornings were lively shows as my clothing danced in front of me, whirling and twirling in a manner that made all of Disney's dancing silverware, clothing, and household appliances pale in comparison. Instead the clothes were mangled and destroyed at the mere use of the Aufero which made me more concerned about the magic that was in Ethan.

"Are you ready?" Josh asked, standing.

I hesitated before nodding. This appeared to be another act of futility, but he was convinced that if I borrowed his magic, as I had done on numerous occasions, I would be able to manipulate it. Converting natural magic to dark magic and vice versa was one of the gifts I possessed. Well, one that hosting Maya gave me. My mother was a witch, but since witches couldn't manipulate magic, I knew it wasn't a gift from my mother. Maya was something powerful, but we didn't know what. A little voice in my head was a constant pessimist and had convinced me that she was something terrible. When I first found out she was killed as a child, it bothered me—as infanticide would, it was the act of a monster. But what if it wasn't? What if what Maya was destined to be was a reason to prevent her from becoming it?

It had been a long time since I had borrowed Josh's magic, and this time I did it with reservation. He was different, stronger. His magic was coarse, no longer the gentle oceanic breeze it once was, but now a tumultuous wave overpowering the room and capable of unspeakable damage. I wasn't sure I would be able to control it. He stood closer, personal space being something he would never accept. His fingers lightly slid down my arm until they met with mine. He was too close, his warm breath bristling against my cheek as he spoke. Taking the knife in his other hand, he turned my hand over and sliced across it and then his. Once the blood welled, he took my hand in his and whispered the spell to bind us.

I wasn't sure what I expected, but definitely not the cataclysmic wave of magic that beat into me like a blistering cold—I felt it to my bones as it chilled me. I ignored the feeling. I had borrowed before and this was his magic, no matter how different it felt. I relaxed into him. With everything changing, it was comforting that at the core of things Josh was still the same. He gave me a light, chaste kiss on my forehead, stepped away, and with his familiar miscreant grin said, "You worry too much."

He winked.

Josh was one of the most perceptive people I'd encountered, but I doubt he needed to be very skilled when dealing with me. I wore my emotions on my face like a promotional sign.

Josh shuffled back a couple of steps and allowed me to work as I took hold of the Aufero.

It expanded, its odd coloring lightening. As Josh moved his lips frenetically, his eyes darkened to night as the strong magic took on a life of its own. The books in the library trembled on the shelves, and the Aufero continued to pulse at an erratic beat, expanding to the brink of destruction only to rebound and push us against the wall in retaliation. Bright orange burst from it like flames, and then the room calmed. Josh and I peeled ourselves from the wall and approached it with caution. Once drawn to me, it now seemed repelled by my presence, as if it had developed a mind of its own and didn't like Josh too much either anymore. It responded as it did to Ethan, burst of color and magical posturing before forming a dark, clouded ward around itself.

"Try it," Josh suggested in a weak voice. This was the third spell we had tried, and Josh was starting to show signs of fatigue.

I inched closer, the ward dropped, and I pulled the Aufero closer to me. Inhaling a small breath and preparing for the worst, I formed a protective field. Okay, things were better. Good. Once again, it became the orange illumination it had been prior to removing Ethan's magic. After removing the magic from Ethan it hadn't been the same. The field formed around me, my heart rate stayed the same, my breathing normal. And then things went wrong. Oxygen was quickly pulled out, and my heart thrashed so hard in my chest that it felt like it was trying to punch its way through. I tried to drop the field. It stayed firm. My mind became a fog as I tried to pull in whatever oxygen remained in the bubble.

It didn't feel like a field but more like a chamber. I was reduced to pounding my fist against it trying to break it. Josh placed his hand on it and it finally shattered, leaving remnants of magic that felt as poisonous as they smelled. Something was terribly wrong and I didn't know who was going to fix it.

I tossed the Aufero in the corner, no longer caring if I

destroyed it or not. This was the third time it had tried to kill me and I was starting to take offense.

Josh plopped into a chair, his hand scrubbing over the light hairs on his face that had gone past just a simple shadow. It was time for a shave, or maybe he was going to grow a beard. He'd do whichever was easiest. His hair was longer, and he had to keep raking it away each time it dipped into his face.

"I don't know what else to do Sky," he finally admitted.

We sat in silence for a long time until it became too uncomfortable for Josh and he took another break. I knew that although he left, his mind would be on this. It was a puzzle, and he wouldn't rest until it was solved.

While Josh was gone I flipped idly through a couple of the books we had on the table, looking for spells that would return the Aufero to normal. Every spell that I had tried turned into something draconian, pulling me into a state of darkness where I couldn't find an anchor. I'd learned quickly not to use it unless Josh was present.

Quickly becoming discouraged with the spells in the books we had searched, I grabbed the Clostra, reluctant to accept that the spell we needed was probably in it. To fix a protected object, we probably needed to use another one. If that was true, we would need Samuel again, and I doubted he would be willing to help. And if he was, the debt would be too high.

He seemed so repelled by were-animals that he would probably only agree if he was allowed to prevent us from changing into our were-half. Sebastian and Ethan would never want to lose their ability to shift into the animal half any more than Josh wanted to have his magic stripped away. I wished I had the same feeling. I had accepted my wolf—we were one—and magic was part of who I was, but sometimes I missed my old life—the oblivious state of ignorance before I was yanked into the otherworld.

However, before I was part of this world, I didn't have anyone except a handful of people who were casual acquaintances at best. Now I had people I cared about and who cared for me. Despite the pack's questionable ethics that bordered on psychosis and their love that was a cross between an overprotective father and a deranged stalker, I believed they wanted to protect, in their own way. I guess the pack didn't really know how to love, either.

The thoughts of the people in my life usually comforted me but I felt like I had one less person in it—Steven. He was leaving. I knew he was just moving out, but it felt like he was not only changing his address but also his position in my life. I hated that.

I shook off the thoughts and tried to focus on what seemed like a reversal spell, although I wasn't sure because the third part of it was missing. My Latin was much better but I still needed a little help, which is where Google Translate came in, becoming the most used option on my phone. If experience had taught me anything, there was always something to magic. Spells were so simple, but a string of words linked together could have devastating results. Josh was teaching me the rules. In the past, he slacked when it came to the rules, but after being dominated by Ethos and Samuel, he had become a savant with his skills.

"You don't think Kelly would just leave without telling us, do you?" said a voice from the corner of the library.

Don't show fear. I tensed, trying to keep myself from jumping to the other side of the room at the sound of Gavin's voice, the pack's fourth and resident problem child. Like a shadow, he withdrew from the wall and sat on the table next to me, moving with the lissome steps of an efficient and lethal predator. His tall, lean body, built for agility and speed, made him look all the more menacing. He was a skilled hunter with the temperament to match, and it was hard not to go into high alert when he was near. If I had to name someone in the pack as a nemesis, it was him. I was "wrong" and a danger to the pack, a belief he stood by and refused to change. He pricked at my defenses until they stood like a bastion ready to protect.

How long had he been there? When did he come in? But with Gavin you never knew; he moved in silence, his presence often unknown until he wanted it to be. And yet no one thought to make him wear a bell.

His sharp eyes seared through me with a force I don't think I will ever get used to. Brushing his midnight azure mass of too-long hair away from his face, he spoke again after a long moment of silence. "Do you really think Kelly would just leave without telling anyone?" His eyes were desperate and searching.

I guess he sensed my discomfort because he moved a couple of feet back. It was hard to get used to his predacious nature and the stealth of his movements. The sharp way he tracked movements, assessing a person, was always so intensely wound and ready to recoil. He never relaxed. It seemed like it would be tiring to be at high alarm all the time.

Taking a deep breath, I pushed aside the anxiety that afflicted me each time he and I were in a room together. "It would surprise me if she did," I admitted. Kelly wouldn't leave without telling us why. Even if it was because of something someone did, she wouldn't have a problem telling us. I had a feeling she wouldn't mind telling a choice few to go to hell and which route they should take to get there. She was a mouthy malcontent with an altruistic agenda who didn't mind violating pack rules to help someone. In the past she went against Ethan and Sebastian to help Chris when they had chosen to let her die rather than be changed into a vampire.

"Then tell Sebastian," he said. Requests from most were-animals always came off like well-worded commands that you dared not ignore. "We all should be looking for her. She's been missing for a while. I know she just wouldn't leave but he doesn't think so."

"Gavin, it's only been a couple of weeks."

"Sixteen days," he offered.

Gavin didn't like most people; Kelly was one of the lucky ones who had gained favor with him. But as with anything Gavin, his affections were as dysfunctional and unusual as he was. An odd mélange of paramour and hater, psycho and nobleman, protector and stalker, and it was all Kelly's. I was about to suggest that maybe his crazy brand of friendship was too much for her to handle and maybe she needed a break, but his overt concern restrained me.

"Will you go with me to look at her house? Maybe I missed something."

No, I will not. You hate me, remember? I had every intention on telling him no, but I'd never seen him so distressed. He was just three stops from crazyville.

I nodded.

CHAPTER 2

*B*y the time I arrived at Kelly's home, Gavin was already inside. Good, I wasn't present as he broke laws breaking into her home. But when I got closer, I noticed keys in his hand, and the door didn't look like it had been tampered with.

"Did she give you a set of keys to her place?" I ventured. I didn't allow my mind to go to a place of paranoia and suspect that he made a copy of them without her knowledge, although I wouldn't have put it past him. The affections and protection of the Midwest Pack seem sweet and comically overbearing from the outside looking in; but from the inside, it was a hostile takeover of your life where they violated and ignored your autonomy in the name of protecting you. What started off as a kind, sweet act of benevolence quickly turned into something ugly.

I asked again, and he simply gave me an odd look of censure, as though I had asked something ridiculous. I was left trying to figure out what was ridiculous—thinking she wouldn't give him a key or that there wasn't anything audacious and infringing about him making a key without her knowing.

Gavin's fingers slipped through his hair as I watched his crazy slowly unravel as he walked through her house. "She's at the pack's house from eight to three Monday through Friday." I didn't know that.

He continued through the house, and I followed him. "She has dance class on Tuesday, Thursday, and Saturday." He showed me her four pairs of shoes placed in order by the door; two pairs for jazz and another two for tap. I'd seen her performance last year and she was talented but didn't strike me as someone who considered it more than just a hobby. Missing class wouldn't be unreasonable.

Taking my arm, he guided me to her kitchen and then opened her refrigerator. "No grapes or strawberries and her apples have gone bad. She eats strawberries and grapes almost every day, and she goes to the grocery store on Sunday. There should be some in the fridge," he said. "Isn't that strange?"

There are a lot of strange thing going on, but the absence of fruit isn't one of them. I just looked at him. I didn't know anything more about her than she was a nurse, she danced, how she met Dr. Jeremy—which I found out just recently—and all her scrubs made me think of Skittles. And I also knew that Gavin had crossed the line from perceptive friend to possible stalker.

"She could have gone home, Gavin. What she went through was pretty bad; she probably just needed a break. Have you spoken to Dr. Jeremy?" If anyone knew anything it would be Dr. Jeremy. She was his protégée, and he treated her like the daughter he never had.

He nodded. "He's been strange since that happened to her. He blames himself and has been distant." He looked around the room.

"Maybe she went to Georgia, to visit her parents."

"No, I checked."

"You went to her parents' house?" Shock made my voice go up an octave.

His head tilted to the side and he looked at me as though I was the odd one. Then he said, "No, but she wouldn't go visit without luggage." I followed him to her closet, where all her plaid pink luggage was aligned at the bottom, her totes and overnight bags placed on the shelf by size and color from light pink to dark pink. All the colors, like her scrubs, could be found in a bag of Skittles.

"She was taken," he said.

Obviously I was missing something. Everything was meticulously placed, which fit Kelly's personality. The only thing that stood out were a few empty hangers and a shirt that was on the floor as though she had taken her clothes off in a hurry. All her shoes where in plastic shoe boxes, each with a picture of the shoe inside on the front. It didn't seem like any were missing out of them. Her bed was made with a plethora of decorative pillows and a fluffy teddy bear protecting them. I didn't want to say it because Gavin seemed to be convinced that she was taken, but it looked like the place of a person who had rushed home and packed her things to get the hell away from a world where she didn't belong.

"What do you think?" he asked. His dark eyes shone with hope and entreaty. He needed me to agree with him, but there wasn't enough evidence and he was on the edge.

"I don't know, but I will talk to Sebastian."

He nodded, and as I slipped out of the house behind him I got a glimpse of the Hermès Birkin bag that Dr. Jeremy had given her for her birthday a year ago. She'd squealed for what seemed like hours but had only been a few minutes. She'd carried it everywhere and the purse, which was the monetary equivalent of what I put down on my house, had become her most treasured possession. It was odd that she would leave it. Maybe it was symbolic, leaving the baggage of the Midwest Pack behind, but something about it didn't fit. I stared at the purse for a long time but didn't point it out to Gavin—he was already too intense. I had no idea what extreme he would go through to look for her if I gave him more to fixate on.

"She wouldn't just leave us," he said, voice low with resolve. He needed to believe that, and part of me needed to as well. It was about acceptance. If there were ever a time we were exposed there would always be people like her who didn't care. We were human —that's all she saw.

"Have you spoken to her parents?" I was just stalling.

"Not yet."

"She might have gone home. It's home, she might not have felt the need to pack a bag," I offered.

I'm not sure if he believed it, but he wanted to. It was better than her being taken but it was more hurtful. If she had indeed left in a rush, she was running from us—from him. I'd always considered her an adrenaline junkie, riding the wave of danger by affiliation. The rules changed when she was hurt because of her association with us and the people who dwell in this world.

He nodded. "Yeah, she might have. She said she missed her brother." He didn't seem any more convinced than I did.

Gavin's eyes narrowed as he raised his head, inhaling and slowly surveying the area. My focus landed on the jackal moments after his as it started to retreat back into the thicket, the spark of its eyes the only thing that shone through the dusk. Gavin darted, moving fast toward the animal, which turned and flitted around the trees. It was just barely seconds ahead of Gavin, whose speeds were faster than I had seen anyone run. Winter was fast—very fast—but Gavin seemed just as quick. That was another thing that I filed away along with his skill of moving in silence. Two things that didn't bring me any comfort.

I waited by the car, and when he returned, his breathing was heavy but substantially lighter than I would have expected after running at that distance and speed.

"Why did you go after it?" I asked.

"Were-jackal" was all he offered, as though it should have meant something. It didn't.

"So?"

"We've never had any around here. It's new. I think it was watching you."

Great, another person that seems to just watch me. Logan did it

27

often, but he didn't do anything. Just an odd demon, in whatever form he had chosen that day, staring at me—not staring, leering. Added to the list was a jackal.

"Why?"

"When it comes to you, who knows," he snipped.

There it was. His general disdain for me had reared its little head. He ducked into his car and I expected him to speed away, but instead he followed me home and waited until I was in the house before he left but not before doing a cursory look around my home, out the back, and in the greenhouse. He even searched near my neighbor David's home.

"That has to be exhausting," I mumbled, walking into the house.

"What has to be exhausting?" Steven asked from the couch. He must have parked in the garage because I hadn't seen his car. My heart jumped and I wanted to ask him if he'd changed his mind. But out of my peripheral vision I saw the packed boxes on his bed, and I felt that the world was too heavy. I tried to ignore them, but it was hard.

His feet were propped on the coffee table next to a bottle of hot sauce and a bag of dill-flavored potato chips. He had convinced me to try his little concoction that didn't seem fit for consumption by anyone. At what point in his life did he decide those two things should ever be near each other at any given time? But Steven considered it a genius idea, a culinary master-piece, and didn't take it kindly when I pointed out that whoever decided to make a cookie with M&Ms was a genius and what he created was an assault on the taste buds. He attributed his creation to being a "southern thing." I argued that there were a number of people living across the Mason-Dixon line who would take offense to being associated with that snack disaster.

"Being on high alert at all times. It just seems like a waste of energy to be prepared for some kind of apocalyptic danger at every given moment," I said.

"Who, Ethan or Sebastian?"

"Gavin."

He looked surprised and then frowned. "What were you doing with Gavin?" He moved over to give me room to sit on the sofa next to him. He put his bowl of yuck on the coffee table and grabbed my legs, and I turned my body with them to face him as he rested them over his legs. It was how we usually sat when we were going to watch a movie, which apparently we were because he turned the TV to Netflix.

I told him everything, even about Kelly's favorite bag being left behind. His mouth twisted as he rested back against the sofa, his fingers tapping against my leg. "I don't get her. I can't imagine she would leave something she loved so much behind, but I can see how she could. I don't blame her for leaving and needing some distance from us. It just seems like she would at least tell Gavin."

"Maybe she thought he would try to talk her out of it."

"Maybe. But if she needed to leave, I would hope he would care enough to respect her wishes," he said softly, but there was a weight to his words like a hidden meaning. Just as he expected from Gavin, he wanted me to respect his wishes about leaving. I wanted to, I really did, but the thought of him moving out just made me sad.

"What about the jackal?" I needed more to focus on, anything other than the boxes sitting on his bed. "He seemed very concerned about it, too."

He shrugged it off but didn't seem as unconcerned about it as he wanted me to believe.

"I should be concerned, shouldn't I?"

He sagged into a sigh. "We've always had small cliques of were-animals that consider themselves nonconformist and resist joining a larger pack. Refusing to bow down to 'the man.' Sebastian and Ethan usually don't bother with them because they usually stay to themselves and cause little trouble. Most have just three or four weres; we never give them a second thought. There are four that we keep a watch on. Two are so small they don't even have a name, there are about eight in each one. But there are two others; Worgen—"

"They sound scary."

Steven chuckled. "Not at all. They named themselves after a race in the World of Warcraft. The biggest threat they present is a cyberattack. They might hack into our computers and screw things up just to make a point. There are about twenty of them, very low-key. We've hired them a couple of times, and Sebastian keeps a watch on them. If they ever joined a real pack they would definitely take on submissive roles. Most of them were turned and they aren't as well adjusted as they should be and could benefit from more assistance, but they will not accept our help and declined joining us. I think they are afraid of us."

"Did Sebastian and Ethan go and show their scary 'I destroy everything in my path' face?"

"Yeah, all of us went to meet them, but they only seemed interested in Winter. They couldn't stop staring until she did that weird eye thing. Things went downhill from there." He shrugged it off. Vertical slits in pupils may not seem weird on a snake but seeing them on a human was off-putting. I hated when Winter did it to me. "The other group—Ares, yes, they named themselves after the Greek god of war—is just a minor pain in the ass. With a membership of just a little over one hundred they aren't as big of a threat as their leader, Anderson, would like them to be. But in the past two months they've seemed to be increasing their numbers at alarming rates."

"Is he making more? That can be dangerous." Temperament plays a big part in dealing with changed were-animals. Making a were-animal with the intent that they will be an ally is a foolish strategy. If they survive, they might hate you for what you've done to them. The only changed were-animal that I knew of was Steven. He was badly injured after killing a vampire. Joan, the Southern Pack Alpha, found him and had him changed by were-coyote in her pack in an effort to save his life. He was grateful to her and to the pack because they not only saved his life but also became his family.

"We'll have to look into it," he said, dismissing any more talk of it. He started scrolling through movies on Rotten Tomatoes reading the synopses to check out the star ratings. He finally settled on a movie with a two-star rating.

"We have to watch this one, it's terrible." He laughed as he pulled up the movie. We watched bad movies and not the ones that were subjectively awful—no, we went straight for the movies that most critics gave two stars or less. The type of movies that moviegoers and critics were so disgusted with that they couldn't even bear to write a complete critique. Movies so bad that people often walked out in the middle, but we never gave up. We generally talked through them, laughing at the plot, dialogue, and whatever else we could find to make fun of. He rested his dill pickle and hot sauce mess on the coffee table and settled back to watch the movie.

As we sat on the couch sharing a ritual as we had done many times over the past year, I pretended that his things hadn't disappeared from around the house. I ignored that his blankets were no longer thrown around the house, nor his jackets, which had never managed to make it into the closet. Most of all, I pushed away the thoughts of the packed boxes on his bed.

I had to, because if I hadn't, I wouldn't have made it through the movie.

CHAPTER 3

*S*leep was something that hadn't come easy in months, and this night wasn't any different. Steven and I continued to watch our movie, while I pretended that things were the same and he wasn't moving out. An hour had passed since the movie ended and we had said our good nights and retreated to our rooms. I was still trying to pretend things were normal, and the next morning I wouldn't have that feeling of emptiness that came over me each time I thought about him leaving. He would be out by the end of the month.

When I sat up in the bed, the odd-colored Aufero, its magic off, draconian, destroyed by whatever the hell was in Ethan, came to mind again. The moment I opened that door, everything bothering me starting flooding in and I tried to prioritize, but it all seemed important—fixing the Aufero, figuring out the Clostra, determining if Kelly had fled or was actually missing, understanding how we had changed things by removing my curse, and finding Samuel. I closed my eyes, waiting for my brain to just shut it all out for a minute. I just needed a moment to think about anything else but everything that was going on. But when I did, it wasn't darkness that I saw but an image of the boxes stacked on

Steven's bed. And more images of him adding to those boxes as he prepared to move out.

I blinked back the tears that started to form, and I wiped away the bugger that dared to escape as soon as I felt it.

I jerked at the sound of glass breaking. Steel bending and collapsing under great pressure whined in the darkness. I looked out the window to see small sparks, orange and red embers, coming from my backyard. I grabbed the fire extinguisher and ran toward the back door, the smell of necrotic tissue wafting in, strong and pungent. It was the odor I smelled when the Hidacus at Quell's home were burned. It tainted the air, making my nose burn. A halo of fire reached the sky, but as the damaged occurred, it slowly dimmed, to just a flicker. Destroying only the greenhouse and nothing else. Its single target and sole focus of destruction was just one thing—the greenhouse.

Like a phoenix Michaela emerged from the smoke, her loose-fitting t-shirt hanging off her waiflike frame and jeans clinging to her slim hips. Her long, dark hair was swept back, and a cynical smile twisted her lips, marring her pleasant features. She looked none the worse for the destruction she'd caused. I was trying so hard to rein in the anger and subdue it the best I could, but it was persistent, chaotic, and becoming hard to control.

Anger moved through me like a current and the desire to control it dwindled as Michaela stood among the refuse. A curve in her lips resembled a smirk more than a smile as she ran a tongue over her fangs. She had taken care not to destroy the neighborhood, not even the rest of the land, just the greenhouse. Just the thing I had worked on for weeks to make perfect for Quell.

And once she had taken a place in front of me my rage became unfettered, striking with ferocity. Gripping the extinguisher tighter, I closed my eyes for a second and inhaled a slow breath, but it didn't help. The scent of burned wood, necrosis, smoke, metal, and scorched fruit stained the air and heightened my anger.

It taunted me. A spiral of red ribbons whirled in my head obscuring any rational thoughts. The heat coming off my cheeks was enough to start another fire. My eyes narrowed, honing in on her. More anger, so intense it throbbed like an injury. A smirk of cruelty and unwarranted sense of entitlement laid effortlessly over her features. Seconds later, her opal eyes met mine, narrow lips perking into a smile as she stood inches from me.

"If you ever try to make Quell choose between us, you'll be the next thing destroyed," she said, her words as sharp as her fangs.

The tendril controlling my anger snapped. Fury raged and needed to be released. I smashed the extinguisher into her sending her back several feet where she didn't stay long. As soon as she hit the ground she was on her feet again. I descended upon her and punched her square in the face knocking her down with a thud. Slamming the palm of my hand into her nose, I felt the bones crush under it and tears fill her eyes before her fist struck me hard against my temple. The burst of dizziness was a reminder of vampire strength. Another punch cracked against my jaw, and blood shot into my mouth as I rolled my tongue over my teeth expecting to find some missing. When I crashed to the ground, I swiped her leg, bringing her down next to me.

Years of training with Winter and Krav Maga, and it all went out of my mind. This was a street fight. I wrapped my hand around her ridiculously long midnight-colored hair and dragged her across the ground, trailing her through the broken glass until I came to what I needed.

Grabbing my arms, she tossed me over her body. I collapsed next her. Her movements were like flashes of light as she came to her feet and kicked me in the ribs. They groaned at the impact and broke with the second sharp blow she delivered to them. Gritting my teeth, I rolled to my side in time to catch another thrashing kick in my back. But anger pushed me to unknown limits. I wanted to hurt her. No, I wanted to *kill* her.

The next time she drove her foot toward me, I grabbed it,

snatching it and yanking her to the ground. I struck hard, blood spurted. I drilled punch after punch until blood dampened and tinted my skin. I snatched up a long, thick glass shard and was about to imbed it in her chest when I heard Steven call my name. The cloud of anger was too much and I couldn't respond to him. I couldn't control the rage. He called my name again, but the only thing I could focus on was my desire to kill her. And I wouldn't stop until she was just dust in my backyard.

His hard coarse voice cut through the air, but I couldn't stop. The glass was clenched so tightly in my hands blood from the cuts ran down my arm as I prepared to drive the shard into her heart. A firm grasp encircled my wrist before I was yanked back. I snatched my arm from Steven, pushed him back, and started toward her again. He pulled me back harder and stood between us. Gold flooded his emerald eyes as they narrowed to meet mine. His lips pulled back in a snarl. "Back," he growled.

If I could have controlled it, I would have. But I couldn't. I tried to shove my way past him but he pushed me back with his shoulder, baring his teeth and growling an inhuman sound. I retreated back a couple of steps, and he looked over his shoulder. Michaela wilted into the ground after making several feeble and unsuccessful attempts to stand.

The more she struggled, the more I wanted to finish the job. *Kill. Her.* I'd never been so in touch with the predator that shared my body. It should have repulsed me and given me a moment of pause, but it didn't. I welcomed it, embracing the violence and anger with unbridled passion.

Perhaps Steven sensed my intentions because he placed a firm grip on my shoulder as he held me back.

"Calm down," he whispered. I took several shallow breaths but it didn't help. The anger was there—unfettered, vengeful, and ravenous. I looked at the burned ground, the scattered ruins of the greenhouse, and was revisited by the images of her destroying it. When she bared her fangs anger reasserted itself and I lunged at her. Steven took hold of me again. He held me—maybe it was supposed to be a hug, soothing and comforting—but his arms girdled around me, binding my arms to my sides and tightening each time I attempted to pull away. In this position he walked me back several more feet and spoke in a calming voice, making every effort to diffuse my anger.

The level of rage was new to me. I didn't think it was possible to hurt someone more than I wanted to hurt Michaela. She came to her feet straightening her clothing and stared hard across the distance that Steven had put between us. I may have wanted her dead, but there was a promise of revenge on her face. She wanted me dead just as much. She backed away and then disappeared into the darkness. I wasn't sure if she *traveled* or moved so fast that I wasn't able to process the movement.

Steven remained silent, and I didn't have anything I wanted to say. Instead I started to walk. I needed to expend the energy, go for a jog or a brisk walk. That was the lie I told myself as I secretly hoped I would run into Michaela again.

After a couple of minutes, the thirst for Michaela's blood and her demise was slowly leveling out. I took the scenic route, cutting through the back, hoping to avoid any looks from my neighbors. I could only imagine what I looked like. The adrenaline that had pulsed through me was tamping down. The pain was gone and I could feel every ache. I went quickly past my neighbor David's home, and his deep, ebullient voice cut into the silence that I so desperately needed in order to get to a place where I could find calm before the very image of Michaela sent me spiraling into another fit of anger.

"Hey kitten."

I cringed. I couldn't decide what was more jarring, the pain or his little nickname for me. He knew I was a wolf, but he kept calling me *kitten*, among other things. The cutesy little nicknames never stopped and could be anything from *butterscotch* to *cookie*, and somehow *muffin* had somehow found its way into rotation. But I liked him too much to let something like that change my mind about him. The frailty of humanity always seemed to wisp off him like a vapor. He was wholly human, without a shred of doubt, and there was something comforting about it. The fact that he still liked me and enjoyed being around me made me feel like I was still deeply rooted to the life I had before the pack entered it.

I started to turn and wave but the ache was a reminder of what I probably looked like. I didn't want him to see me like this.

"I can't talk right now," I said, keeping my back to him and picking up my pace. His heavy steps quickened behind me.

He purred the name *kitten* again. *Ugh.*

His steps came faster and I knew he was at a slow jog trying to catch up to me. When the sounds of the steps were just a few inches behind me, I stopped and turned. Wide-eyed, he gawked before blinking several times. He swallowed and took a moment to get his composure. My appearance must have been a sight, because David worked in public relations and often bragged that he had seen it all. This probably just gave that bar an uptick.

He took in the bruises, concentrating on some places more than others. Gently touching my shoulder, he said, "I've seen your face look prettier. Why don't you come in the house and clean up before you scare the neighbor children." It was after midnight—if they were still up, maybe they needed to be scared.

David started to back away, waiting for me to follow, and when I didn't his brow raised and he gave me a stern look. I knew he wasn't going to take no for an answer.

David's partner, Trent, didn't make an attempt to keep his poise. "Oh my, what happened to you! Oh my god! Oh my god! Who did this to you?"

My silence only made things worse. He had his phone in hand. "I am calling the police."

"Please hang up. I know who did this."

His horror was soon drowned by concern and speculation. I knew what he was going to ask before he said the words, "Did *he* do this to you? I can't believe he did this to you!"

I sighed, getting a glimpse of myself in the mirror near the door. My lips were swollen, and blood was smeared over my lips and cheeks, probably from attempting to wipe it away. A cut was near my eye and there was a patchwork of bruising on my cheek. It was only then that I noticed my shirt was torn. "Steven didn't do anything to me, and you know he would never touch me."

Trent was convinced that Steven was my boyfriend because "You don't let someone like that move into your house without making him yours." But his crush on Steven didn't overshadow his imputation toward "the boyfriend." "The boyfriend" was always his person of interest whenever we watched a criminal investigation or mystery. "It's always the boyfriend. Don't be fooled. If anything ever happens to me—David did it. Avenge me, honey. Avenge me," he would always joke in his lighthearted voice.

Trent's features were even more off-putting scowling as he assessed me. He wasn't unattractive by any means but his keen features were too angled and sharp. Wide expressive eyes were just a shade or two lighter than his umber-colored hair and complemented his olive skin. Despite his features he had a moppet appearance, and the light beard didn't improve it. His six-five frame, thin from his love of running, looked more coltish than sinewy and athletic. Many times I considered holding him down and force-feeding him cake and burgers, but he would like that, since that was how he ate most of the time.

David's appearance was the opposite. A little over forty, he was more than ten years older than his partner. David was classically handsome. Age had slightly diminished his strong, refined features, and the salt-and-pepper hair added to his distinguished appearance. The one thing they had in common was that for the two years I'd known them I hadn't seen either one in a pair of jeans or t-shirt. They preferred slacks and shirts or cashmere sweaters for lounging around the house.

"Okay, if it wasn't Steven, then whose ass am I kicking?" He grinned.

Smiling made my lips hurt, but I did it anyway. It was a sweet gesture, but he couldn't kick his own ass. As a person who had an adversarial relationship with jars and anything heavy, I doubted he would be an adequate match for Michaela.

"No one needs to get their ass kicked, it's over," I said. But I wasn't sure if it was.

Trent nodded slowly, unconvinced, before excusing himself to the bathroom. David stayed, keeping a careful eye on me, his arms crossed over his chest. Wide flat lips were drawn together in a disapproving pucker framed by small lines. I am sure he knew that there was more to it. He knew what I was and probably realized that if there were were-animals there were other, worse things that went bump in the night.

But before he could satisfy his curiosity, Trent returned with a warm towel. Gently he wiped my face, making an attempt to remove the blood. He wasn't ever going to get it off at this rate. I took the towel from him, and using the mirror on the wall behind him I started to wipe my face. It wasn't enough, so I went to the bathroom.

After great effort, I had removed the blood and took a moment to deal with the pain of my aching ribs. Broken ribs hurt like hell but I couldn't show pain while in front of David and Trent or they would worry, and things would escalate into something bigger. They would want the police involved.

I sucked in a deep breath and returned to the living room. It was safe to assume that in my absence they had let their imaginations get the best of them. Deep, assessing gazes continued to examine me and the strain on their faces grew harder by the second.

"It was just a fight," I said.

"Over what?" David asked.

"A guy." It was kind of the truth. I wished they would drop it, but I knew they wouldn't.

"Really!" Both responded almost simultaneously. I ignored the miscreant smiles of interest. I had successfully diminished this story into a drama-filled tale of two women fighting over a man. They wouldn't have to get their dose of it from a reality show. "Over who? The hot one that forgot how to smile?" Trent asked.

He was talking about Ethan, who they referred to as "sour face."

"Ethan. His name is Ethan."

"Well, Mr. Personality isn't worth ruining your face over."

"It wasn't Ethan."

"Is it the blond broody guy that lurks around your house at night? Mr. Broody. What's his deal anyway? Or is it the hot guy with all the tattoos? I'd fight over him," Trent continued with a big grin. "I'll kick your ass right now for him."

David laughed. "Yeah, will you be using your trademarked tactical techniques? You know, the one you used last month?" Then David turned to me. "While full of liquid courage, he decided to start a fight with a man who kept spilling his drink on him—"

"I won that fight," his partner interjected.

"No, you didn't win that fight. When you ducked your head down and started swinging your arms like a malfunctioning windmill, he was too busy laughing at you to fight. So I guess technically you did win," David said, chuckling.

Trent made a face and refocused on me. "So which one was it?"

"How often do you watch my house?" How much had he seen? Did he know more than he was letting on?

"We like to keep an eye on you to make sure you're okay."

"Eye? Stalking?" I shrugged. "I guess that's for the courts to decide, which is the appropriate term," I teased.

"No one's stalking you, silly. We just want to make sure you are safe. This area is going to hell. You know there was a burglary last week."

I knew that.

"Because of construction in that new subdivision behind us we are seeing an unusual number of wild animals, mostly coyotes, and I saw a wolf a couple of times. And I'm pretty sure I saw a jackal the other night. Trent is convinced he saw a large cat, a lynx," David said, holding my attention, and when Trent wasn't looking he winked. He knew Trent was probably right, but there wasn't an explanation he could give without betraying my secret. I'm sure the coyote was Steven—he changed more often than I did but I wasn't aware that he went on the neighbors' land. I assumed he just stayed in our area. But the lynx and the jackal were troubling. We didn't have either one in our pack, and if the jackal was the one from earlier today then Gavin was wrong. He wasn't watching the pack—he was probably watching me.

"Was the fight over Steven? He looks like a straying type. I see the way he looks at me. The boy-next-door looks just scream trouble."

"Is he giving you strange looks before or after you've hit on him?" David joked.

"Once again, Steven isn't my boyfriend and the fight was just a simple argument that escalated and got out of control." I steeled my voice hoping to put an end to this conversation. I didn't want to talk more about it because I could feel the heat of my anger over the situation starting to rekindle.

They both nodded, but the curiosity remained and I knew we would revisit this topic again.

"Fine, topic dropped, but I have to do something to your hair," Trent said, taking my hand and leading me to a chair in the kitchen. My hair was messy but nothing terrible. But the beauty school dropout had been trying to get me into his unlicensed chair since we met. Each new trend he saw on YouTube, E!, or the Style Network was on his to-do list for my hair. Sometimes I indulged him, but today I didn't want to. But he was as usual persistent and it was hard to say no, especially when he complained that none of his girlfriends kept their hair long. I was convinced they all chopped it off to keep from being his practice heads.

So while I sat in the chair, he brushed through my hair before he started doing whatever it was that he pulled up on YouTube. I think he was working on a fishtail braid.

I'd been at my neighbor's for an hour. It was a well-needed escape despite the fact that the awkward-looking braid I was sporting looked nothing like the one in the video. Trent seemed happy with himself so that was all that mattered. As I started to leave with David, who wanted to walk me home, Trent said, "My advice, honey, let her have him. Something just isn't right with him. I've seen him a couple of times waiting outside your door. He just stands there, as still as a statue, those odd dark eyes staring into the darkness seemingly preoccupied with his crazy thoughts. Stick with the sexy farm boy that keeps giving me the eye." After a few probing questions while I was sitting in his chair having my hair twisted and mangled he had come to the conclusion that the fight was over Quell.

"Once again. Steven's my housemate, not my boyfriend, and he's moving out anyway." It was the first time I had said it out loud, and as though I had just cast a spell it seemed to change the world around me. Despair—it licked at me worse than any of my bruises. That cold hard realization that at the end of the month, Steven would be gone.

I was in a good place and was glad for David's intrusion and for the short time with him as he walked me home. "We don't have to talk about it now, but I want to know the truth, Sky."

"It's not a lot different than the version I gave you," I admitted with a sigh. "But I promise, I will tell you everything."

That satisfied him enough. I had a feeling he didn't want to know everything. There had to be something comforting about living in a world of oblivion, unaware of all the strange things that existed in the otherworld. Unlike Kelly, I don't think David was curious about it.

"The jackal, when is the last time you saw it?" I asked.

He opened his mouth to answer but got distracted by the gray Hennessy Venom GT in my driveway. I hadn't heard of the car and probably would never have if it wasn't for Steven, who talked excessively about Ethan's new purchase. My lack of interest only seemed to fuel Steven's enthusiasm. After all, once I knew the engine size, horsepower, and how difficult it was to get one in the United States, only then could I truly appreciate it. He was wrong. I couldn't stress enough how much I didn't care, which only made him pull a picture up on his phone and show me. My disinterest didn't temper his fascination with it and he stared at the picture the way David was looking at the car now. Running his hand over the lines of it, David peeked through the window to look at the interior. He dropped down to examine the tires and the rims.

Oh come on! It's a car. David, you're better than this.

But he wasn't. He kept touching the car, appreciating it in a manner that obviously was beyond my reach. "I think when you ogle something like that, you should buy it dinner first," I teased.

"Sorry, it's gorgeous."

"Thank you," Ethan said from the door of my house. David jerked up and his eyes met Ethan's, but they didn't stay. Most people can't hold his gaze for very long: the intensity of it alone was hard, and there was always the threat of danger if you tried. It was subtle but still there.

David hugged me before he left and squeezed too hard. I had to bite back a groan as he pressed into my ribs. I watched him as he disappeared into the darkness toward his home, needing the extra minutes before I had to deal with Ethan.

I walked into the house with purpose, ready for a battle that I was hell-bent on winning. Ethan leaned against the kitchen counter, a genial smile leveling his usual stern features.

"Hi," he said in a low, gentle tone as he pushed up from the counter and approached me. Carefully, he lifted my chin and examined me closely. His eyes narrowed, gunmetal drowning out any hints of the blue of his natural eyes.

"Where's Steven?"

"Gone. I wanted us to be alone."

Standing in front of me, he was quiet for a long time and would have continued so until I blurted, "She started it." *Nice. Real mature, Sky. Do you have a tantrum you want to throw, too?*

He nodded slowly, the light smile remaining as he slowly circled me. When he was in front of me again, he said, *"Você está machucado?"*

He was speaking Portuguese. Since my mother's death, I spoke it so infrequently that it took a moment for me to translate. *Are you hurt?*

Portuguese was the language I shared only with my mother, it was private, intimate—special to us. It didn't feel right sharing it with anyone else, especially Ethan.

I shook my head. "Probably a broken rib," I responded in English. I raised my shirt, exposing the raspberry marks that spread and wrapped around my side. I knew exactly what broken ribs felt like because Winter had accidentally broken mine twice while sparring. It was a painful reminder why Winter was third in the pack, that I needed to get better and avoid a real fight with her at all costs.

He gently pressed his hand on my right side, the wrong one. I moved his hand to my left side.

44

Languid fingers roamed over my ribs; the warmth of his touch didn't feel as good as ice would have. When he applied a little pressure, I hissed at the pain. His scowl turned to a little smirk that vanished quickly under my glare.

"Você quer um pouco de gelo?" Do you want ice?

I didn't answer, but instead continued to look at him as though I hadn't understood.

He frowned at my passive display of defiance. He circled me, in slow easy strides. He was too calm, and I was waiting for the storm he presented after the calm. His gentle timbre of voice didn't reveal any perils in sight. Since I had removed the dark elven magic from him, there was an odd connection between us: I could feel his emotions as raw and true as if they were my own. He was angry; it was an explosion brewing, ready to blow but he was working to suppress it.

"Do you want me to get you some ice?"

"No."

He nodded. "Do you need anything?"

"No, I'm fine."

"Good." His voice was low and serene. It made me nervous. Ethan was a tidal wave of emotions, coiled and poorly controlled, and there wasn't anything quiescent about him. His countenance bothered me.

"Okay, let's talk then." Gently taking my wrist, he guided me toward the living room, and took a seat in the oversized chair across from the sofa that I sat on.

As he sank into the chair his lucid pewter gaze fastened on me. "So at what point of the day did you decide that your life wasn't complicated enough and you needed to start a war between us and the vampires?" His words were chilled by his tone.

"She destroyed my property!"

The slight smile barely made it to his eyes, but they were much kinder than his tone. "Did she? Or did she destroy something of

Quell's? You don't require a greenhouse nor do you have a use for Hidacus, do you?"

Who the hell invited logic to this party? I wanted irrational anger to run this conversation. "It was something on my property for Quell. She destroyed my property. How can you all just allow her to behave like this? She does whatever she wants with impunity and everyone just turns their heads because it's Michaela, the otherworld's psycho bitch, and she gets a pass. Well I am not going to give her a pass."

"She's also the Mistress of the North and responsible for creating the most vicious of her kind. Yes, she warrants certain consideration. But you didn't answer my question, what exactly did she do to *you?*"

If my teeth didn't release their grip on my lips, I was eventually going to bite right through them.

Ethan's movements were too fast and stealthy for someone his size and he'd quickly moved out of the chair to the ottoman in front of me before I had time to really consider the question. "Skylar, answer me. What did she do to *you?*"

That was the million-dollar question. She hadn't done anything to me per se, it was to Quell, and my property was just collateral damage.

Ethan's voice held a hint of revulsion and anger. "What exactly are you doing with him?"

"What do you mean?"

Silence. But his eyes held mine with an intensity that made it hard to maintain focus. "I want a real answer, Sky."

"We're friends, nothing more, nothing less," I admitted.

Ethan sighed as he stood. "If he is your friend then you need to make better decisions to ensure that he stays alive—or whatever vampires are. You've played your hand. She knows how much you care for him. Michaela would rip off her own nose to spite her face and isn't above killing him just to get back at you."

He was right. The more I tried to fix things the worse I seemed to make them. I felt feckless as the problems escalated like a wild-fire out of control. Was it best to leave Quell alone? I felt like I was his anchor, keeping him grounded into somewhat humane behavior. If I turned my back on him, then what happened to him?

"Okay." But I wasn't sure what I was agreeing to.

Ethan headed for the door, but stopped with his back to me and said, "If you have another one built, you won't have to worry about Michaela destroying it, I will."

He left before I could respond and I had a perfect one ready for him; granted there weren't any actual words involved just a lot of name-calling and cursing.

CHAPTER 4

*T*ry to kill *one* vampire Mistress and life becomes a series of meetings and getting a good "talking to."

When Sebastian asked me to join him for dinner, I knew exactly what it was about. I wanted to decline, but like his invitation, which was cursory, my agreement to it was tacit. Anything that came out of Sebastian's mouth wasn't a request as much as it was a nicely worded command.

When he picked me up for dinner, it was weird. Sitting across from him in a posh restaurant in downtown Chicago was even weirder. The large windows with the thin taupe sheers provided a beautiful view as the lights of the city came alive while offering some privacy from the outside. The wave-shaped lighting was dimmed, soft and ambient. The white table linen, offset by chartreuse napkins, was a beautiful contrast to the black and white leather seating. It was a wonderfully opulent restaurant that I should have enjoyed, but I was too focused on the many shades of odd that this so-called simple dinner was. My attention quickly went to the art on the wall as I thought about how I could make this go as quickly as possible.

Sebastian's smile blossomed, unfolding into something that

was enchanting and charming, one of the more lethal and unassuming weapons in the arsenal the pack used. When necessary they were so charming that you were lured into a trap you'd be unlikely to escape. Being a were-animal didn't make me immune. I returned the smile.

He was quite handsome, but it was his presence that was the most enthralling. His confidence and power were as refined and tailored to him as the clothes he wore. You couldn't be meek and demure if you wanted to command the most powerful pack in the country. He wore it well, and people noticed. Flawless mocha skin, well-deep oval amber eyes, an imposing presence you never got used to. Instead, you remained acutely aware that he was a well-dressed, attractive predator.

The stock smile stayed on my face, my muscles fixed into a curve that simply displayed a pseudo pleasantry that I just didn't feel. The situation was made no less strange when he ordered a bottle of wine and dinner: filet mignon, rare; roasted red potatoes and asparagus. Then he ordered the chocolate ganache and grinned at me when he asked the waiter to bring the dessert first.

I am a dessert first type of woman, and it seemed like everyone knew it.

"Who's spreading these rumors about me?"

"Do you want me to change it?"

"No, I don't want to be a bother." I smiled.

We sipped on wine while I tried not to drink the whole bottle. It was a delightful white, crisp with a hint of peach that lingered on the palate. I didn't bother finding out the name because based on the decorum of the place, I doubt I was willing to pay to taste it again.

I tried to focus on the woman standing in front of the piano, her expressive eyes closing occasionally as an emphasis to the soulfully intense sorrow that lingered over her words. Her crooning was a roller coaster of immense pleasure and intense pain and every emotion that existed in between. It was a soulful sound, with enough sorrow, seduction, and joy to tug at the emotions and entrance the spirit. She was a siren, enthralling the audience, forcing them to deny their hunger in search of something that fed them more intensely. Her voice, beyond her years, wailed a deep sultry melody over the crowd. If she was twenty-five, she was barely, but she seemed like she should have been born in a different era. She was dressed in a simple white shirt with cap lace sleeves and a long A-line skirt that clung to her body, moving as gently as she did during the song. Short layered dark bangs swept across her brow, held back by a small flower, drawing attention to thickly lined smoky eyes. Peach gloss accented her full lips. Her poise and mannerisms reminded me of a movie my mother loved, *Lady Sings the Blues*. I changed my mind several times about whether or not I would visit the place again. Maybe I would come for dessert or appetizers—which cost the equivalent of a meal at most restaurants. I would come back if only to hear her again.

"Beautiful isn't it?" Sebastian pulled me from my trance.

"I don't know if I would describe it as beautiful. Elegiac? Its peculiar combination of sorrow and happiness and all the variations in between."

I watched him as he watched the songstress.

"You hear sorrow?" he asked, frowning. Then he directed his attention to me. "*Hmm*, you hear sorrow where there is beauty."

He considered me in silence for a long time.

A bottomless pit of deep browns with a hint of amber continued to assess me but they were quickly forgotten when the waiter brought the ganache. The rich, decadent flavors dominated my attention.

"Skylar, how are you?" Sebastian finally asked.

"I am eating chocolate pie; how do you think I am—I'm great!"

"It's a ganache."

"Yeah, that's just restaurant trickery that they use in order to charge you quadruple the price of pie."

The gentle curve of his lips made it easy to forget that he commanded a pack of over five hundred predatory animals.

He leaned back in his chair. "Seriously, how are things, Skylar?"

Good, an opening. "Weird."

His brows furrowed. "Weird?"

"Yep, weird. Nothing about this"—I moved my hand back and forth between the two of us—"is normal. It is weird." I hate that I couldn't think of a word more fitting. *Yep, weird is all I have.* Sitting across from him in a fancy restaurant with a songstress baring her soul was weird. Behaving as though this was just a casual dinner between friends was weird.

"We needed to talk."

Here it comes. I am about to get my "talking to." Before he could start the homily I blurted out, "She—"

"She started it," he interjected, his chiseled features slowly giving way to a smirk.

"No, she was on my property and I had the right to react the way I did." I had moved past "she started it" and right on to self-righteous indignation.

He nodded his head slowly but remained quiet. He was silent until the server brought our food. I pushed the dessert aside, took another drink from my glass, and then started to eat. Sebastian ignored his food. "Ethan feels that because of your friendship, you are being more resistant to his advice," he said.

Friendship? Whoever is responsible for the rumor mill is really bad at their job. Ethan and I weren't friends. We were two people bonded by our mutual oddities, forced to deal with each other in order to survive. He yelled, I yelled—it was our thing. He threatened, I rolled my eyes and moved on. We dealt with each other and continued to irritate each other. That wasn't the foundation for a friendship but the beginning of a cage match.

"Michaela can be difficult to deal with," he acknowledged, taking a bite from his steak.

Is that the euphemism we are using for crazy *and* insensate? "She isn't difficult to deal with. She is coddled and excused for behavior that would cause others to be punished for."

"She is the Mistress of the Northern Seethe," he reminded me in a low voice.

"And?"

How quickly the soft, warm gaze could switch to stone with just a blink. "That isn't an 'and'. That has meaning. We will not start a war with them over a crush."

"It's not a crush." But defining my obtuse relationship with Quell was always difficult.

"I don't care what it is, Sky, but it is a problem and it shouldn't be." Usually his deep baritone possessed a mesmerizing lilt that made my name sound musical, but not now.

Maybe it was the topic or the dessert but I couldn't eat any more and pushed the plate aside. When Sebastian became preoccupied by something behind me I didn't have to look. I knew what or rather who had distracted him. A brunette, two tables over with her friend. The sleek black dress she wore didn't leave anything to the imagination, and if your imagination failed you, her plunging neckline would kick start it. I glanced over, and she looked at Sebastian and smiled.

There wasn't any denying it, he was a very handsome man who wore the assurance of command as easily as he did the mint green button-down and dark brown slacks. I had become immune to him, or as immune as one could be; but the woman in black was just as enthralled as I was when I first met him. That diametric feeling of fear and attraction was something hard to ignore.

He excused himself to go to the bathroom, and I wasn't surprised when the lady in black excused herself from her friend and went to the bathroom, too. He better not leave me for Ms. Oh-is-my-cleavage-showing-in-my-absurdly-low-cut-dress.

It wouldn't be the first time. Steven had left me twice for some scantily clad woman at a bar. He often said he had a hard time controlling his primal urges no matter how hard he tried. It's funny how those primal urges never run the show when a single sexy grandma is near. It seems to only overtake them when a hot thing with questionable morals comes into view. When I'd pointed this out, he'd simply chuckled and said, "Well, they always turn me down politely, telling me that I remind them of their grandson."

Sebastian was gone for nearly ten minutes, and when he returned he was ready to end the dinner sooner rather than later.

"I thought you were going to ditch me."

He grinned.

Yeah, I get it, you're hot. There's no need to make a big deal out of it.

"Because your admirer seems to want to spend the rest of the night with you," I pointed out, looking over my shoulder at her, and as I suspected, she was still eyeing him.

His attention slipped in her direction, a lascivious smile stretching over his lips. "Well, what a dilemma I have. Should I stay and finish dinner with the smart-mouth, snarky brunette who gets in more trouble than she can handle or go with her?" he joked.

Alpha and comedian, he sure has a lot on his plate. "I'm going to guess smart-mouth, snarky brunette. Is that wrong?"

He laughed, a sound that quickly dissolved any feeling of apprehension I had.

"We're having dinner. Tonight my time is yours. She can wait."

Wow, should I be flattered that the Alpha of the most powerful pack in the country set aside a night just for me?

He leaned into the table, his eyes narrowed. "Has someone left you before?"

"No," I lied, refusing to admit that I had to catch a cab home.

His eyes narrowed further at the lie.

"I can take care of myself." Then I put my hand to my head in overacted gesticulation, like in the old movies when a woman was overtaken by a fainting spell. "I declare even with my delicate woman sensibilities I've managed to call a cab or Uber driver to help me find my way home."

He was frowning when I finished with my little performance. *Hard crowd.* I made my voice serious. "Sebastian, I can take care of myself. You all seem to forget that."

"That's not the point. It's a principle. You don't leave someone behind."

"Yeah, in battle. I think I'm okay around a bunch of inebriated people."

Sebastian had strangled me, locked me in a cage and a room, and often lied to me—or rather "got me to see the reality that he wanted me to see"—on many occasions, but I guess he would be damned if someone would leave me at a club. He was a very unique white knight; well maybe he was a gray knight. Depending on who was telling the story, he could very well be the black knight. I had gotten used to the blurred lines that surrounded Sebastian and the Midwest Pack.

Over the past few months Sebastian's protection of and interest in me had amped to a new level. I couldn't help but wonder, *Has he found out something he wasn't sharing?*

I leaned in and hit him with a very maternal tone. "For the record, a woman like that, who has little concern that you are already here with someone, is nothing but trouble. Be careful."

His eyes held a miscreant twinkle. "That is wonderful advice. I will consider it. Will you now take my advice?" He drained his glass, chewed the last bite of his steak, and then relaxed back into the chair. The stone cold gaze held mine. "Stop screwing with Michaela. Quell is hers. Period. If I need to make this easier for you, I will. You want to save Quell, walk away from him. Don't force my hand on this. If he continues to be a problem, then I will make sure he stops being one."

Unable to hide my irritation, I wrapped it around my words. "You mean *you* would dare to upset Michaela."

He responded with a stern silence. I realized the consequences of me killing Michaela in a fight and Sebastian getting rid of a vampire that had become a pack problem were two different things. I understood the politics, but it didn't make it any less frustrating.

"She'll be angry that I destroyed her little plaything, but I assure you it will occupy her mind for mere moments. Do what you need to—but end it with Quell."

It seemed like he was waiting for me to say something, but I didn't have a response.

I nibbled on my food—it had lost all flavor. I needed to talk and think about something else. "What are we going to do about Kelly?"

"Kelly?"

"I don't know if Gavin is overreacting. Maybe we should be concerned that she just disappeared. Is it really like her to do something like that?"

Dismay was something that I'd never seen on Sebastian's face and it looked odd now. "She's such a wild card, I don't know how to predict her behavior. If she left, it is understandable; she went through a lot."

Kelly wasn't really a wild card—I got her. Her emotions and sensitivity made her vulnerable to making decisions that the pack didn't like, and she seemed to always be at odds with Sebastian. I still didn't quite understand why a person who was wholly human chose to work for us, but I knew it had a lot to do with her curiosity about us and her adoration of Dr. Jeremy. She was ours to protect, and I felt like we were failing.

"I just think she would have said something to us, even if it was to tell us to screw off."

"You can't judge her actions by what she would have done before we nearly killed her."

Is that a smile? No, my bad. Tilting my head, I waited for it again. She did have that effect on a lot of people, her ebullience something that was appreciated more often than people would admit. Josh referred to her as a "pint-sized menace," and her tenacity was entertaining, especially when it was directed at someone else, more often Sebastian.

"If she did leave, she left some things behind that seem odd." I wasn't sure if telling him about the purse would make sense to him. It wasn't that it was a purse she wanted, but because it was given to her by Dr. Jeremy. "And it wouldn't hurt to look into her leaving, maybe even question Sable," I offered.

His brows rose. "Sable?"

I nodded my head. "She threatened to kill her. She thought that Gavin was spending too much time with her."

"Why is this the first time I am hearing about this?"

"It didn't seem relevant. I may be way off. Who among us hasn't been threatened by a vampire? He made Sable promise that she wouldn't hurt Kelly."

"A promise from a vampire not to do any harm, especially Sable, means nothing. He should have told me this," he snarled. Sebastian was worse than Ethan when it came to the need to have all information.

He pulled out his phone and pressed a number. "Demetrius, I need to speak with Sable," he said in a low voice into the speaker. Like most things it had too much of a command to it, and I knew it wouldn't be well received by Demetrius.

I could imagine the insolence on Demetrius's face. His silence stretched from seconds to close to a minute. It was so long that I thought he'd hung up. That wasn't below something he would do if he felt affronted by Sebastian. It wasn't until I heard the noise on the other end that I knew he was still considering the request for longer than he had to just to annoy Sebastian.

He finally spoke, his voice crisp and urbane, with an accent that I still hadn't placed over the years. "Very well, but I will need to speak with Skylar as well. She has been quite busy disrupting things in our Seethe and it needs to be addressed."

Dammit.

Sebastian glanced in my direction, considered it for a fraction of the time Demetrius had, and finally agreed.

There were many things I would have preferred to a meeting between Sebastian and Demetrius, two men who hated each other and make no attempt to hide it. Both had immense power and the type of will that could stop a truck, which they didn't mind asserting. The venomous glares, subtle threats, and displays of impudence ever present whenever they were in the same room—there wasn't a way to ignore it because you found yourself drowned by their animosity and power. It was hard to withstand and even harder to disregard.

Demetrius answered the door of Sable's home. His odd black opal eyes regarded me for a long time before he directed them toward Sebastian. Demetrius opened the door wider to let us in but seemed reluctant to offer us a formal invitation, his irritation apparent as he drew his lips into a tightly fixed line.

Each time I found myself in a vampire's home, which happened more than I wished, I was always impressed with the elegant design that was often more contemporary than I expected. There was always an anachronism oddly placed, but it added charm, a reminder that most of them had been alive for more than a century. Sable was young, changed when she was just nineteen, but had been a vampire for a little over twenty years. Her home was everything I'd once expected—walls painted a muted red, textured to look aged. Black curtains were pulled back to reveal floor-to-ceiling windows and a perfect view of the large trees that surrounded her home and obscured the moon. They were closer than what would be acceptable for most people. Her home was bare, except for a brick-colored sofa and matching ottoman and two black leather chairs. Everyone had some kitchen appliances, although they didn't need it; but Sable decided not to put up such pretenses and instead had left an empty space where they should have been.

She sat on the sofa and was genuinely disinterested, exanimate. She didn't acknowledge our presence until Gavin, whom I didn't know was behind us, moved farther into the house.

We really need to get him a bell to wear.

She approached us, her piercing gaze focused solely on Gavin. Each time I encountered her, it was hard to believe that she was the girl who made the headlines for weeks after she brutally murdered the family and friends of the assailants who had killed her family during a home invasion. She made the invaders watch while she did it, and then she executed them in front of neighbors and sat next to their dead bodies and waited for the police to show up.

A broken young woman who was made into a broken vampire. Wide-eyed and round-faced, she had soft, placid features that were a contrast to her personality and reputation. She walked slowly around us, and even Sebastian tensed, ready to engage if necessary. In silence she studied everyone, her tongue running over her fangs. Every once in a while she drew her lips back, exposing them like weapons. In her own little world, she refocused her attention back on Gavin and seemed to forget anyone other than him. She didn't hear Demetrius when he called her name and didn't respond until he said it again. His sharp hiss jerked her attention from Gavin to him.

Her face and eyes were blank, as though if they couldn't focus on Gavin she wouldn't bother to focus on anything. I still didn't understand her obsession with him. She considered him beautiful —that is the extent of what I knew of their odd, sordid dealings. She had started to take on the characteristics of her creator, Gabriella, another unconscionable vampire. Her midnight hair was bone-straight, wisped just above her shoulder, with pastel pink and lavender hair extensions underneath. I could see the disgust on Winter's face if she were here and she most certainly would have muttered what she always does, "They are weird for no damn reason." It was a comment she always spouted about Gabriella and her partner, Chase, who must have spent a great deal of time getting pierced, tattooed, and changing their hair in unique and eccentric ways.

"Yes?" It was a weak, distracted sound as she split her attention between him and Gavin. Like her creator, she had an odd affinity for feeding from were-animals, although they didn't offer any nutritional value.

She finally took up a position next to Demetrius. Forcing focus, she kept her eyes trained on him, attempting to give her undivided attention.

"Sebastian has some questions for you," he said.

With much effort, she looked at Sebastian.

"Have you seen Kelly?" Sebastian asked.

Slipping her gaze to Gavin for a second, she quickly returned it to Sebastian. "Your human pet?".

"Yes, the woman that works for us," he said.

"Is she missing?" she asked in a low, despondent voice.

"Yes, have you seen her? It's been brought to my attention that you threatened her. Did you hurt her?"

Sebastian finally garnered her attention. She tilted her head, the wilted deviant smile a reminder of her past as the psychotic woman who killed several people in cold blood, who was nothing more than a ball of unfettered violence.

"No, I didn't hurt your pet." She dismissed him with a roll of her eyes before returning to her seat on the sofa as though we had disappeared.

"Did you have anything to do with her being missing? Have you had contact with her since the last time you visited our house?" Sebastian asked.

She turned, barely. A hapless glare rested in our direction for a moment, her voice soft. "I don't allow others to do my work for me. If I wanted her dead, I would have done it. If I wanted to hurt her, that too is something I would have handled. I don't see the purpose of abducting if it isn't to kill." Once again, she had withdrawn from the conversation and focused on the television in front of her, which wasn't turned on.

"You have your answers, but if I hear anything, I will let you know," Demetrius said, ending the interrogation. One of the more favorable qualities about vampires is that they didn't lie. Their narcissism and egos gave them a sense of entitlement that makes them feel and act as if they are exempt from consequences for their actions. And they felt that everyone else should take that stance as well.

"Now may I ask my questions, Skylar?" My name rolled off his tongue in a velvet-soft seductive drawl. He wasn't asking permission; he never did, for anything. It was a simple courtesy that he offered.

"It is a pleasure seeing you again." He took hold of my hand, then he brought it to his face, a gentle, smooth movement as he inhaled, his nose barely touching my skin before his cool lips did. Demetrius was beauty and seduction, violence and sin, treachery and torture wrapped in a beautiful package. Everything about him was a warning and I didn't trust him past the front door just four feet away.

"I have a couple of questions for you, Skylar."

He was so close that all he had to do was just bend down and his lips would have easily touched mine.

"I have some questions of my own, do you mind if I ask them first?" I countered.

I appraised him for a long time, then looked down at his hand, now holding mine. Demetrius's attractiveness disguised his cruel proclivities. He was dangerous, and no amount of gentle reassurance and touching would ever make me forget it.

He inched closer, amused by my attention. His head tilted with a look of intrigue and curiosity, so I finally asked my question.

"Is this supposed to be seductive or creepy? I want to cast my vote as it being creepy. So. Very. Creepy. And on the perv scale of 1 through 10"—I looked down at my hand as he slowly and rhythmically brushed against it, a prelude to what I assumed was more unwanted fondling—"I'm going to give it a hard 9."

His movements were fluid and graceful as he released his grasp but his fingers trailed along the sides of my hand, slowly and steadily. He stepped back, his smile dwindling to a smirk as his eyes narrowed to study me with a new and odd interest. He looked at me, but directed his comment to Sebastian. "She's turned out to be more than any of us could have expected. Your protégée is quite something. It must be nice to have been given unformed clay that you can mold into what you want. I for one enjoy the challenge of a wild one that needs to be broken. It's invigorating."

"Okay. Am I the only one taking issue with this conversation? Anyone? 'Wild one'? 'Broken'?" I demanded, meeting everyone's gaze in the room.

Sebastian studied me for a few moments and then chuckled. "Unformed clay?" He chortled again at this. "I wasn't given unformed clay. Instead I was handed a fully molded statue, glazed with obstinacy, audaciousness, and the tenacity of a bull. I do believe whatever you are giving, whether it was a compliment or a thinly veiled insult, should be directed solely to Skylar; this is none of my doing but her own."

Really! Even after our nice dinner together? I guess Sebastian wasn't taking credit for the mess he considered me to be. There was truly an insult in his comment but the obvious look of respect belied it.

Sebastian turned his attention to Demetrius, who had a patent on smug arrogance that not even Ethan could wear with as much casual ease as he did. "Looking at the state of your Seethe and the people in it, *you* seem to be the one being broken. It's my understanding that Chris has left you. *Hmm.* That had to hurt," Sebastian said. They hated each other and most dealings involved poorly veiled insults and threats.

Chris is gone?

"Yes, Chris chose to leave, but I am aware of the consequences of choosing the women that I do."

Sable laughed. It still possessed the jovial sound and gentle cadence of a person who hadn't seen the violence and horror that she had. It was pure, and for a moment, I nearly forgot what she was.

Since Demetrius was involved with Michaela, I wasn't sure why choosing other women was an option. I just didn't understand their polyamorous relationship.

Eyeing Sebastian, Demetrius twisted his lips into a mirthless grin. "I do hope you find Kelly," he said. It was an underhanded slight. The pack prided themselves on keeping those they considered protected safe. If Kelly was indeed missing, this would be the second time they failed, and I knew it didn't sit well with Sebastian.

Demetrius seemed pleased with the response he lured from Sebastian—anger. I understood why he was so quick to assist: he considered Kelly a replacement for Chris.

His features relaxed. He smirked and maintained his hold on my hand. "Tell me, Skylar, do you plan to attack all the women in my life?" He stepped closer, and the threat in his eyes wasn't belied by the small smile that lingered on his lips. "I must warn you, if you break them, I expect you to replace them."

"I am sure they would be delighted to find out that you are outsourcing for their replacement if they can no longer perform their duties as concubine and/or Mistress," I snarked.

"There needs to be no more discussion of this. If you break them, you will replace them or maybe even take their place." He tilted his head and spoke softly. "I am curious, why aren't you and Michaela getting along?"

Well Demetrius, your partner and I aren't getting along because she is a self-indulgent psycho who doesn't care about anyone's feelings or happiness other than hers, but you already know that. It's probably the reason you chose her and are drawn to her. I wanted to say it, but instead I said this: "Michaela and I are fine." I moved closer to Sebastian. I didn't trust Demetrius and wasn't foolish enough to believe that his desire to please Michaela wouldn't trump all—if I was in the way of her happiness he'd be content to eliminate me. I knew that, and the charcoal crystal gaze that stared at me with intent supported my assumptions.

"I do not enjoy it when she is dissatisfied," he said.

"Yeah, I got the memo. The world needs to bend and reshape to make sure Michaela is happy," I said. "Because apparently her happiness is of the utmost importance to everyone and if we haven't taken notice, we should."

The obligatory smile stayed on his lips but his eyes hardened. "Quell is hers. It is important that you understand that."

"And I foolishly thought he was his own person."

He moved too fast and was in front of me before I could react. Sebastian quickly stepped between us, his eyes narrowed to slits, as he assumed a defensive stance. "It has been addressed. Skylar has no such control of Quell as Michaela has over him. She will not be held responsible for his actions or feelings," Sebastian touted, baring his teeth in the same manner that Demetrius had. Yes, Demetrius's could be used as weapons, but I was sure, if necessary, Sebastian would find a way to use his that way, too.

Sebastian placed his hand behind me and was guiding me out the door, with Gavin close behind, when Sable asked Gavin, "Do you miss her?"

"I notice she's gone." His tepid look matched his voice.

She steadied her gaze on him. "I hope she's dead.".

He stared at her for a long time, expressionless. "You and I are done."

She scowled and exploded from the sofa so quickly, she seemed to have taken flight. Fangs exposed like daggers, she lunged at Gavin. He grabbed her, quickly moving to the side, bundling her arms against her in a hold that immobilized her. He pressed his lips against her hair and spoke softly. Yelling and screaming, she thrashed against him, spewing curses and threats. I took mental note, because she was blasting some good ones. I wasn't sure what a "Fuck twat" was but it seemed as good an insult as any.

He loosened his grip, and she grabbed his arm and sank her teeth into him, gnawing at him out of anger. Gavin remained still, vaguely interested in what she was doing. Demetrius called her name several times but in her fit of rage, she ignored him. His eyes narrowed, his features hardened to stone and it looked like he was about to intervene, when Gavin spoke.

"She's fine. Let her get it out," he said softy. But she wasn't fine. She was an avalanche of uncontained emotions trying to inflict as much pain on Gavin as possible to abate the ones that she was feeling.

Finally, she sagged against him, resting her head against his chest. For a long moment he let her rest against him, then he brushed her hair away and kissed her tenderly on her temple and slipped out the door.

She dropped her head, sadness draping her like a blanket. When she looked at the open door, her eyes fluttered several times as though she was blinking back tears.

Dammit, I actually feel sorry for her. I need air.

We headed for the door, but before we could leave, Demetrius stopped Sebastian. "I am confident that you will use all your available resources to find Kelly. And I would like to be notified when she is found," he asserted with the confidence one would expect when giving a task to a personal assistant.

Sebastian's smile lacked humor. They did seem to gather a great deal of pleasure annoying each other and making attempts to display their dominance every chance they could. I agreed with Josh: they almost needed each other in a sick codependent way. "I want you to wait on the notification. Will you do that?" And with that he ushered us out the door.

Gavin was driving off by the time we got to Sebastian's car.

"Do we have a pack therapist?" I asked, opening the car door.

Sebastian's brows rose. "Yes, I can have him contact you."

"Me? I don't need a therapist, but you saw what just went on there. Gavin's not right. There is something wrong with him."

Sebastian shrugged. "He's fine. He handled her well."

Fine. Well. We definitely aren't using the same source for any of our words. "I don't think so. If we ever need any information from Sable, he's just ensured that we will never get any. I think she hates him."

With a shrug of indifference Sebastian opened the door. "What you saw in there wasn't hate. He probably just ensured that she will help us. She will do anything now to please him. To get him back. I doubt she will do anything to hurt Kelly, but now at least we know she will help." He shook his head before he ducked into the car. "The relationships you and Gavin have with *your* vampires are complex."

Our vampires. It was hard not to be offended by that. My relationship with Quell was so different from the complex thing that went on between Gavin and Sable. "Can I get a copy of the dysfunctional playbook you all are using? Because what Quell and I have and whatever is going on with Gavin and Sable is very different."

He frowned. "One day you will see it as we all do, there isn't a difference."

I didn't get in the car immediately, stopped in my tracks by the comparison. Was my relationship as warped and disturbing as Sable and Gavin's? Both Sable and Quell were two sides of a damaged coin, a human life cursed with death, pain, and sorrow only finding solace in vampirism.

Sebastian was studying me with interest. "Some things you can't fix. They are too damaged, necrotic, and will only infect the rest of the body. You don't keep that limb, you sever it from the body. You've taken him as part of you, and he is in fact dead flesh, and if you let him, he will destroy the body. You need to understand that I care more about saving the body, and eventually if you don't make the decision to sever it, I will."

I was so tired of the "necrotic tissue, gaping wound that can't be repaired" argument. Quell wasn't like that. And I was about to respond when Sebastian's focus moved from me to the jackal that was slowly backing into the woods. It disappeared before we could go after it.

Too many things went through my mind to rest at home when Sebastian dropped me off, so I got in my car and went for a drive. I'd like to say I was on autopilot and it was coincidental that I ended up at Quell's home, but I wasn't. It was intentional, because I wanted to see him. Ethan's warning haunted me. Michaela wasn't above hurting him to get back at me, and we had to work something out. Something had to give, but my motives were masked by selfishness and I wasn't proud of it. I needed succor. The type that, for some odd reason, Quell provided. He once said that I was his link to humanity and benevolence. I disagreed with that; at times I felt I was deficient in both. I felt my hold on kindness and altruism was slipping. He was darkness, void of something he claimed he lost in WWII. He didn't go into detail, but he said he had experienced moral fatigue and it was during that time he had betrayed humanity and become the monster he thought he was fighting. He felt there was a void where his humanness should have been, and the guilt had led him to Michaela and being changed into a vampire. He said she saved him because vampires aren't burdened by expectations of humanity and altruism. Most of them were self-indulgents who felt their pleasure and desire trumped all and took umbrage with anyone who dared to think differently.

I knew I needed to distance myself from Quell, but it wasn't as easy as Sebastian and Ethan wanted to believe. A barrage of curses came out, not even under my breath, but loud enough that if anyone was within a foot of my car, they would have heard them. Ethan's ostentatious car was parked behind a dark blue Subaru, and I was about to back out of the driveway and leave when he stepped out of the house. He was next to the car before I could start reversing.

His unctuous smile made me want to back away with him holding the door. But instead, I gave him a smile just as wide and even more insincere. I glared at his extended hand but took it after a few moments of contemplation. *Fine. I'll play your little game.*

"I'm so glad you are here." And then he gave me his trademark smirk.

Can I just go a week without seeing it?

"As if you could stay away." His hand slipped down my arm, and his fingers intertwined with mine. He tightened his grasp each time I tried to tug my hand away. "We asked you to stay away, which undoubtedly ensured that you would be over here as soon as you could," he said.

"I hadn't heard from him in a couple of days. I was just checking on him."

"Of course. After all, him managing to stay safe and alive the seventy years he had prior to meeting you was clearly a coincidence. And he can't possibly take care of himself."

We were in the house before I could respond, so instead we both fixed phony smiles and kept our snide remarks to ourselves.

"I thought I heard Sky outside," Ethan said.

Of course you heard me. You can hear changes in someone's heart rate, you freak, why the hell wouldn't you hear a car?

I kept my comment to myself and played nice. Even Quell was doing it, because he disliked Ethan as much as Ethan disliked him.

With all this fakery someone should get an award or something. We seemed to be putting on the performance for the blonde sitting next to Quell on the sofa.

"This is Fiona," Quell said, introducing the very attractive woman.

Perhaps I came in at the wrong time, or missed the tale that Quell must have told because she looked intrigued by him and whatever he had to say. A gentle curl nestled on the ends of her generous lips. I pulled my gaze from her to Quell, who had a smile on his face—a rare sighting and one I couldn't believe was being brought out by this stranger. My attention bounced between them as I attempted to ignore his gaze laid heavily on me.

I focused on her. Her voluminous hair was upswept, exposing her long languid neck that seem to be of great interest to Quell. Periodically, he would focus on her features, which mirrored his own striking good looks. His appearance was the reason Michaela was drawn to him. Often taking credit for his beauty in the way only a narcissist could, she took accolades for something that clearly belonged to his parents. Fiona's honey-colored eyes stared at me with interest, her full lips spread into a wide smile. Delicate features perfected her heart-shaped face and genteel appearance.

Dressed in a simple pair of blue slacks and a pale pink flounced shirt that did nothing to brighten her parchment skin, she looked comfortable next to Quell. Her and Quell's were the only authentic relaxed attitudes in the room. Quell's Tuscany-inspired home always made me feel like I was in the Italian countryside. The subtle variations of colors on the walls added a warmth that Fiona seemed to appreciate.

"Nice to meet you." I wanted to be polite but my skepticism radar with clicking at an alarming rate.

Ethan moved away from me and leaned against the counter, a gentle smile playing at his lips, as he put on a look of innocence.

"Fiona is a professor of Psychology at the community college nearby," he offered. Then he directed his attention to Quell. "That was what you studied as well, am I correct?"

My eyes narrowed and homed in on Ethan. *How does he know that?* I had just learned that information about Quell less than a month ago.

Quell nodded. "Yes, that was what I studied, and when I returned I continued on to get my Masters," he said softly, brushing over the time between studying psychology and eventually getting his advanced degree. The time in which he was convinced that he'd lost himself.

I often wondered how horrid were his acts that he could live among the vampires, whose acts at times were atrocious, and still feel justified in his beliefs about himself.

Fiona didn't get the hint that he was vague for a reason. "Returned? From Germany? Ethan told me that you were involved. What branch of the military?"

Ethan ignored my glare and focused on them.

I mumbled, "I guess we're telling everyone about us now."

He didn't respond; instead he watched them and how Quell responded.

He took a while to answer, and Fiona focused on him intently.

"Army. Ground," he forced out, the corded muscles of his neck, bulging as he pushed the words through clenched teeth. With a vacuous stare, he drifted off somewhere.

When Fiona looked in my direction, her smile disappeared as she sat up a little taller, scooting back a little farther in the chair as though she was trying to gain more distance between us. I tried to relax my face, widen my eyes, and straighten the curl in my snarl. And although I hadn't said it, she'd gotten the message loud and clear: *Stop it!*

Her gentle reassuring smile reemerged. "Freud, what do you think: genius or unjustly revered idiot? There have only been a couple of times I wished I were a man and they all were during a road trip when I couldn't find a restroom. Other than that, I'm pretty happy with what I have."

A melodious deep sound filled the room. It was a laugh—a real one. Not the ones Quell gave to mollify me when I made a joke he didn't quite understand. He eased into her touch as her hand gently caressed his.

Ethan's plastic grin evolved into something real, too: satisfaction. They quickly delved into deep conversation and lively debate over the theories of Freud, Bandura, Erickson, and other notable psychologists.

'His Smugness' seemed quite pleased with himself when they started to discuss the Milgram experiment. He took my arm and guided me out the door. "Sky and I are going to leave. And Quell, Fiona's the coach for the debate team, good luck," he said, before looking over his shoulder at her. I didn't know what it meant but I halted at the door and it took a little effort to ease me out.

The moment we were out, I was about to say something when he pressed his fingers to his mouth. "Save it. We don't need an audience." I was so angry that I'm sure I wouldn't have been able to speak low enough to keep Fiona from hearing, let alone Quell.

I yanked my arm away and walked quickly to my car with purpose, Ethan on my heels.

He sighed, deep and heavy, as he rolled his eyes and leaned against his car. "Okay, go ahead with it. This should be entertaining."

Too many thoughts, insults, and quips flooded my mind and I needed to organize them. His pomposity just made things worse. *Why the freaking smirk?*

He scowled. "Go on Sky, say your peace so I can go home, it's late," he said in a low drawl.

"If it's past your bedtime, then shouldn't you be at home instead of trying to pass off one of your half-night stands to Quell? How insulting it must be for her to have you give her away like a free sample with purchase."

His chuckle was dark and lacking of any humor. "I haven't been with her. If you have a problem with Fiona and her interaction with Quell, discuss it with Claudia. She's the one that considered them a good fit. She's the one that wanted me to introduce them."

Ethan's godmother was involved. *Dammit! Why do so many people feel the need to interject their unsolicited help in my life?* Months ago I found out that there was more to Claudia than just being a trader of overpriced art. She was linked to serious magic and connected to the otherworld. I hadn't quite figured out her role, and no one seemed to be open about volunteering the information.

"Funny, how did she find out about it? Did you run to mommy and tell her that I wasn't doing what you wanted me to do? Did I miss the tantrum?"

"Actually, I went to her to see if she wanted his remains. The fae find them valuable and she often gives it to them," he said. His eyes narrowed, deep gray rolling across them.

I sucked in a breath and looked at the face of Quell's would-be murderer. This was getting bad, fast. I'd dealt with Ethan enough to know when he was angry there wasn't any reasoning with him. I needed him to be able to grasp that I didn't need a babysitter or a guardian.

"You should hope that his interest in you is redirected to her," he said as he started for his car. The conversation was over. The decision was made and we'd passed the point of civil negotiation.

"You will not do anything to him, or—"

"Or what, Skylar? What exactly will you do? Yell? Not speak to me? Get into a little huff? Run off and hope none of the many people you've pissed off find you? Go ahead, tell me exactly what you plan to do!"

"Ethan," I said softly. Poking the angry wolf wasn't going to get me anywhere. "I swear, I have this. This is *my* problem and *I* will handle it."

"But you're not handling it! This is getting worse," he growled, stepping closer, his face just inches from mine. He looked away and sighed and took several slow breaths before he continued. "I can assure you I don't want to deal with this. Quell means nothing to me. I could go in there right now, kill him, and not give it a second thought. But he means something to you, so I'm trying to get this Michaela situation under control."

Michaela. I was so tired of everyone trying to accommodate a self-indulgent narcissistic psycho who derived pleasure from others' pain. It was frustrating.

Ethan regarded me for a long time. His hand rested on my side, and the silence extended for long enough that it was uncomfortable. He moved even closer, eyes narrowed as they fastened on me, the moue on his lips deepening. "Are you jealous of Fiona?"

"So she's supposed to be my replacement? It will not change anything between Quell and me, we are friends. That will not change."

"Answer the question," he commanded.

I'm not sure why it took so long to answer. But it did and the seconds quickly passed. Finally, I shook my head.

"I need to hear you say it."

I had the full intensity of his attention and now knew why he was so focused when he dealt with people: the very person who had a rather casual relationship with the truth, especially when it came to protecting the pack, their secrets, and his own, couldn't stand to be lied to. Yet, he never seemed to get the irony or hypocrisy in it.

"No."

His hand slipped from my waist as he stepped away.

"Am I telling the truth?"

"You want it to be the truth." He started for his car and wouldn't look at me.

"We're friends, I care about him. I want to keep him safe and I want to make sure he doesn't hurt or kill anyone when he feeds. Why is that wrong?"

The frown had become a fixture on his face and he slowly shook his head, but he wouldn't look at me. When he finally looked up, there was disgust. I remembered that look. It was the same one he gave me when he realized I had a *terait*, something seen in vampires when they were experiencing bloodlust. He gave me a similar revolted look after I'd fed Quell and saved his life. But not one time in the past did he look disappointed. Now he did. It was an unattractive shadow that lingered on his face.

He stopped abruptly. "Do you see it?"

I bent my head in a barely discernable nod, catching a glimpse of the jackal out of the corner of my eye.

"Is it the same one?"

Again, I gave a simple undetectable acknowledgment.

"How fast can you change?"

"Not as fast as you can."

He moved slowly, positioning himself to have quick access to his wolf. The benefit of Quell's home was it was in an open field, fallow land.

"In your car, you will cut him off from the back, okay?"

I was still holding my keys in hand when Ethan gave chase, sprinting toward the field. Seconds later, his shirt flew through the air and he burst into his wolf. The cloak of fur covered him as his body transformed midair, and when he hit the ground he was charging at the jackal in wolf form. I sped forward in my car, wheeling across the field, placing an obstacle too difficult for the jackal to negotiate. He had no choice but to face Ethan.

Lips drawn back, teeth exposed, they rounded each other looking for an opening. The jackal barked, Ethan howled, and they charged at each other. The jackal took to the air and before they could hit each other it disappeared.

What the hell?

One of the benefits of being a were-animal was that magic

didn't affect us in animal form. Ethan and I were the only were-animals I knew that possessed magic, something frowned upon by the Creed, the governing body of the witches. In the past, they ensured a were-animal that possessed magical ability didn't exist by committing infanticide. Ethan's mother took great care to make sure his abilities were never discovered. I didn't have such problems because most people didn't know I existed, and no one knew that my mother was a witch. I didn't know until a couple of years ago when I discovered the truth about my birth mother.

Ethan looked around for a moment before changing back. As he approached my car, I could feel the magic the moment I let down my window. It was strong and lingered in the air, but it was the smell that was the most disturbing. This was different than anything I had experienced. Josh's magic reminded me of the beach, the subtle scent of the ocean, sand, and hints of salt. Samuel's had hints of rosemary, but still the cleansing smell of the ocean was there. This was different, a putrid stink that burned my nose. Bad magic—wrong magic—deadly magic. I didn't like it.

Ethan walked across the field, naked. His torso a bundle of defined cords of muscles that wrapped around him like armor and contracted with each movement. He opened his trunk and slipped on a pair of boxers before closing it.

"I need to see Josh," he said, ducking into his car.

And he sped away, leaving me thinking less about the jackal and the wrong magic that accompanied it and more about why Ethan was trekking through the city in his underwear.

I chuckled, remembering what Joan, the Alpha of the Southern Pack and Steven's adoptive mom, had said: that most of the members of the pack would traipse through the city naked if it weren't illegal.

CHAPTER 5

*T*he insomnia made me irritable and when I reached for the phone, I knocked over the scabbard next to my bed. The sword was a gift from Winter, and it was definitely not on the list of things I'd suggested to anyone who'd asked what I wanted for my birthday. I wasn't nearly as excited about receiving it as Winter was about giving it to me a few months ago. A gift card would have been nice, cake even better, but instead she handed me a sword as though she had given me the gift to end all gifts. She presented it to me like she was giving me a red velvet cake, in a box filled with M&Ms, while handing me tickets to my favorite artist's concert. But that was just Winter, and her giving me a weapon was equivalent to telling me "I kind of like you, so don't die, okay?" And I took it, because there was no way I would actually hear her say it.

I no longer had my trusty nine iron but instead a sword, something that I changed last night. Michaela was vengeful just for the fun of it, and now she had a reason to attack me. Ethan was right, I wasn't underestimating her, and adding the disappearing jackal and strange magic, the sword comforted me. And so did the idea that if Michaela attacked me in my room, I would make sure it was the last time she was able to attack anyone again. Nothing lives very long without a head, and I can't accomplish that with a golf club.

"Yes," I said into the phone as I looked at the clock—7:20 a.m. I had to meet Winter at ten to spar. I had only been asleep for two hours and my voice was low and gruff despite my trying to clear it.

"Call Winter and let her know you won't be able to meet her, we have to see Logan, today."

No, we really don't. I'm giving that a hard pass.

Visiting a Tre'ase was probably the last thing on the list of things I wanted to do in life. No one really knew what they were: demon, witch gone terribly wrong, or immortal with benefits. Most speculated that they were demons. Whatever they were, they possessed a great deal of magic and were known for being tricksters that were dealt with only when it was absolutely necessary. No one wanted to be indebted to them or have them as an enemy. The latter is where I failed. Logan probably considered me an enemy. When the witches cursed me, I asked him to remove it, but in return he wanted me to give him Chris, Ethan's ex-girlfriend. I was supposed to be bound to her with a spell, which would have made her subservient to me and then I would be able to gift her to him. Desperation made me callous and convinced me that I could do it because she would have done it to me if the roles were reversed. But I couldn't. At the last minute I changed my mind, leaving him enraged. That wouldn't have bothered me too much, after all, he had been cursed as well and was restricted from leaving the territory around the house. Unfortunately, when we used the Clostra to remove my curse we lifted *all* curses. Because of me, the Tre'ase roamed unrestrained and unchecked.

I expected him to attack me, exact some kind of revenge, but I hadn't seen him since the night the curse was removed and I was content keeping it that way.

I sighed heavily into the phone. "Why?"

76

"Skylar, we need to find out what he knows about the Tre'ase that created Maya. It is irresponsible not to know who it is. You do remember what he said would happen to you if anything ever happened to that Tre'ase."

How could I not remember? I was eternally linked to a person that I didn't know. And if he died, so does the sprit shade, Maya, who was keeping me alive.

I knew why, but it didn't make the situation any better.

There was a long pause. "And Josh thinks he might be responsible for the jackal. No one else possesses magic strong enough to do it, and they are able to shift."

That made things worse because I knew what their true form looked like, and it was grotesque. I tried not to speculate about the amount of magic they must have to maintain their form, or to bind you with magic to an agreement, or to create spirit shades. The more I considered how powerful they were, the more nervous I became knowing I might have one as an enemy.

I rolled my eyes as I approached Ethan's black car, a different one. I'm sure if Steven were home he would be able to give me the specs on it, which I didn't want or care about.

"*Hmm*, I guess the saying is true, 'the difference between a man and a boy is the cost of their toys,'" I teased, dropping into the seat next to him.

His lips upticked into a smirk as his gaze lingered in my direction. "You and I both know that this car isn't the only difference between me and a boy."

The smirk remained, along with the silhouette of arrogance that he wore. His eyes stayed on me until he had backed out of my driveway and continued. Eventually he focused back on the road, stealing quick glances in my direction.

"Why did you bring that?" he asked.

It was hard to keep an illuminating globe hidden, and because of its size and odd shape, I couldn't just put it in any type of purse so I stored the Aufero in a large drawstring tote, which didn't do a lot to conceal it. It bulged out against me conspicuously, no matter how I positioned it.

"I brought it just in case."

"Josh said it was responding oddly and making it difficult for you to use the magic," Ethan said.

"It is, but if we are dealing with Logan, bad magic is better than no magic."

"Josh will be there," he offered.

I'd never insult Josh by saying he couldn't handle Logan, but no one knew the extent of his magic and we couldn't be too careful. It was still Logan: every little bit counted.

I slipped furtive glances at Ethan, who was concentrating on the road, his stern look lacking the emotions that usually simmered just under the surface. I wished we could have maintained a modicum of what we had in New York. It seemed like we had hit a milestone and were in a place where we could share freely with each other, all boundaries lowered, guards relaxed, and it was just two of us managing something civil. But I was a fool to think anything like that could exist between us. Ethan quickly erected the wall and ensconced himself in his bubble.

"Go ahead with it," he said.

"With what?"

"Your breathing increased, you're blinking less, and your heart rate has increased, short inconsistent bursts. This always happens when you are frustrated and have something you want to talk about. Talk."

I nodded my head slowly. "Okay. Well, I know this guy, let's call him E, and he has this really creepy and weird skill that freaks everyone out. He counts physiological responses. He's a total freak. And it doesn't help that his mercurial ways are off-putting and he's kind of a jackass, but doesn't seem to care. If he doesn't change his ways, I think he is going to die alone. What should I do?"

He chuckled. "Sky, ask your question."

"Have you heard from Fiona?" The moment I asked the question, I wished I hadn't.

"Yes."

"Is she okay?'

"We didn't talk long; she was still at Quell's when I spoke to her this morning," he replied, looking in my direction. He wanted a reaction. I wouldn't give him one. It had been days since Quell had fed, and I couldn't help but wonder if he had used her, but I wouldn't ask Ethan. I knew even if he had the information, he wouldn't give it to me freely.

"Good." It was the only thing I could say. There was plenty I wanted to say and many more questions I wanted to ask, all of which would have made that smug look of condescension reemerge. I would go visit Quell later.

I should have just asked my damn questions, because the haughty look was there when he regarded me for a few more moments, but he kept his comments to himself, which looked like a herculean effort.

"The information Chris gave us on the Tre'ases is useless, we can't find any of them. They've all moved."

"And their ability to change forms isn't going to make it easy to find them, either."

Ethan nodded slowly but didn't offer more. He never just let things go—he was a planner, constantly trying to figure out the next move if things failed.

It wasn't what was going through Ethan's mind, but I couldn't help but wonder who cursed the Tre'ase and why in order to keep them sequestered from the rest of the world. And what was an unchecked, uncursed Logan like?

We drove the rest of the way in silence. Josh and Sebastian were waiting for us when we drove up to the enclave, a section that separated Logan's home from the rest of the world. Large trees stretched overhead, filtering out the light and darkening the surrounding area. The pathway was cluttered by gravel and sidled by tall grass that was in desperate need of landscaping. I thought with everything that happened he would have moved away from the small, remote cottage tucked away and uninviting to the world. It was concerning that he hadn't. What were his ties to a place that was his prison?

We headed up the dark path, Ethan and Sebastian in front and Josh next to me I thought about how this could go very wrong. Contrary to what they believed, no one liked when the dynamic trio showed up at their house. They weren't standing behind the door doing their happy dance that the Midwest Pack's Alpha, Beta, and witch were coming for a visit, because nothing good ever came from it. That was an "oh crap" moment. But Logan was just a little different than anyone else. We walked up to the door, and he opened it before we could knock. I assumed it was Logan —he didn't look anything like he had when I first met him. The only things familiar were the odd lavender eyes, which were deep and entrancing. The runes that wrapped around his body and were used to magically bind you into an agreement were covered by a long button-down. His hair was longer and chestnut, different from the cropped dark brown waves that he had before. Wide, defined cheeks and sharp jawline were good choices. He was definitely very attractive. The ability to shift forms was definitely advantageous. I had seen his true form: large maw that protruded and was disproportionate to his face, horns, and a grotesque bestial appearance. This cloak of good looks was deceptive.

A casual smile remained on Logan's face as he rested against the kitchen counter. His home hadn't changed from the first time we visited. It was a mélange of modern and cottage-chic that was as dark and eclectic as his personality. Slowly his attention roved over each of us and then rested on Ethan. He pushed himself up from the counter, the spark of interest that captured him when he first met Ethan ignited. Ethan stilled as Logan approached, watching him as carefully as Logan watched him. He stood close, invading Ethan's personal space. The avid interest remained. His eyes narrowed, the peculiar markings were frenetic as they rolled over his arms. He panted, inching closer, reaching out to touch Ethan, a timid advance at first that became bolder. Ethan caught his arm at the wrist before he could put his hand on him.

"Step away from me," Ethan ordered. Logan was so enthralled he didn't immediately respond. "Now." Ethan's command rumbled deep in his chest. After long consideration Logan returned to his place against the kitchen counter.

Logan's attention grazed over Sebastian. He gave me a little more consideration, eyeing the canvas bag at my side. His head tilted, and he started toward me but changed his mind, choosing to direct attention to Josh, giving him a shallow smile of appreciation and curiosity that lingered for far too long. It was the same creepy boundary-less look he'd given Ethan.

If a person were drawn to magic then they would be in a state of euphoria around Josh. He was magic in its rawest and most potent form. It existed at his fingertips, strong and potentially catastrophic. I could see traces of the old Josh who viewed magic differently, as a casual tool at his disposal. The years had inured the old Josh and his magic. Were-animals had a symbiotic relationship with their beast. It remained dormant most times as we took advantage of the benefits it offered while in human form: speed, agility, heightened senses, and strength. Magic was the beast that shared Josh's body, and the relationship wasn't very symbiotic, it was possessive. I had a feeling Logan could see it and had an appreciation for it as it seemed that his magic had the same hold over him.

"Let me see what we have here." Another sweeping glance went over the room. "The Midwest Alpha, Beta, and their witch."

Logan shifted his gaze in my direction, eyes narrowed to thin slits, and then he frowned. "And my betrayer."

Ouch.

"I didn't betray you," I refuted.

The glower remained as he gave himself over to his ire, and although he was in human form, I could imagine his snout flaring with anger.

"To what do I owe this pleasure?" he asked, focusing on Sebastian once he had calmed.

"I need your help," Sebastian said.

Logan snorted. "I am sure Ethan has informed you that I am all out of favors for you. And now that I know your pack can't be trusted, I choose not to enter into any agreements you will not honor." Once again I was treated to another angry glare. "I definitely do not care to do business with you."

"We aren't going to bitch fight about how 'wronged' you feel by Skylar's alleged betrayal. It was a foolish agreement anyway. If you knew her, there isn't any way you thought for one second she was going to give you a person as a pet, so get over it."

Sebastian and Ethan must have attended the same seminar on negotiation and the finesse of the deal and left with the idea of winning friends and negotiations by telling people to "get over it." They didn't mind inviting people to do it at any given moment.

"We had an agreement and she reneged." The same anger that reflected on his face that day rekindled into something just as ugly. His glamour wavered, magic coming off him in jarring bursts.

Sebastian exhaled a slow breath and started to pace the area, measured, graceful steps that made him seem more predator than man. His toffee-colored eyes were now as cool as an arctic breeze. "You want to screw Chris, seduce her like anyone else. Don't pull us into your sick little perversions. Please don't think for one moment that I am naïve enough to believe you only wanted her for companionship, you sick bastard. The subject is moot. I am not giving you a fucking person. And I advise you, if you plan to try seducing her, this look—get rid of it. Looking like Ethan is not going to help you get in her bed any faster than the way you probably look without your little glamour."

Logan crossed his arms and looked over at the door, a subtle invitation for us to use it. "You know what I want, and if you're not going to give it to me there doesn't need to be any further discussion." Then he thought for a moment. "If not Chris, then Winter."

Sebastian sneered, rueful and hard. His whetted gaze fixed on Logan, who seemed uncomfortable, shifting and crushing himself into the corner of the counter as he attempted to distance himself from a very agitated wolf in human form. "Okay, let's get all this out of the way so there isn't any more of this foolishness. I am not giving you anyone, whether it be Chris or Winter. No. One. Period."

Sebastian paced the small area in front of Logan. "We can be mutually useful to each other. You seem to be enjoying your new freedom, which is only possible because of us. Do you think curses are just magically removed because you willed it? We did that. Just as easily as we removed it, we can restore it."

Just as easy? Are you kidding me? Sebastian must be the best poker player ever.

"Do you expect me to believe you had anything to do with the curse being removed?" Logan refuted as a frown distorted his appearance.

"We have the Clostra, so yes, we had everything to do with it."

Logan watched Sebastian with a level of fear and admiration. "How did you manage that?"

"We have two of them and access to the third if we need it."

We do? Now he was having a free-for-all with the truth.

"I think we can help each other," Sebastian said, but Logan still seemed disinterested in working with us. His lips twisted to the side, his gaze roving slowly over us until it finally remained planted on me.

"What do you want?" But he was finished with me and directed his question to Sebastian.

"Are you able to find out who created a particular spirit shade?"

"Yes."

"Good."

"And if I can do this for you, what do I get in return? Do you accept this as an obligation you must fulfill?"

He never gave it a rest. The odd inscriptions on his arms came alive, dark markings slinking about his arms, and his odd eyes pulsed as they constricted and widened. Josh frowned, like I did, probably feeling the wave of peculiar magic that overtook the room. I kept a steady eye on Ethan, who was unemotional, and if he felt the odd magic, he wasn't going to show it. After moments of feeling my attention on him, he relaxed into a simple smile. It was peculiar how easily Ethan slipped back into his role as a magicless were-animal. As if the last couple of weeks had never happened and I was a victim of an overactive imagination.

"No. If you can find it, you will remain as you are, free to roam the city, the world, without restrictions. If you don't—" Sebastian simply shrugged, allowing the threat to linger. A threat that I had no idea if he was going to be able to carry out if Logan refused. "So shall we do this now?"

Sebastian didn't seem bothered by the look Logan gave him and simply brushed it off and took a seat at the kitchen table, stretching his legs out in front of him and clasping his fingers behind his head. If looks could actually kill, Logan had destroyed Sebastian several times over in that moment.

"Give me a week. I am flattered by your confidence in me, but this isn't something I do often and it requires a few days to prepare."

"You have three days. I am quite confident you can make it

happen in that time frame. I trust that you will not betray us or try to leave without doing this. Am I correct in my assumptions?"

Logan rolled his eyes in my direction. "I enjoy my new life," he said.

Sebastian smiled, well, I am sure when he attempted to move his facial muscles it was supposed to be a smile, but it was an unsuccessful attempt and came off as a sneer.

"Are we done?" Logan asked.

Sebastian didn't answer immediately; he peered around the room and sighed before making his way through the house. Logan started to move but decided against it when both Ethan's and Josh's stances changed.

Sebastian stopped at a door, placed his ear closer to it. "Who's in here?" he asked Logan.

Irritation sparked and became a dense reminder that Logan wanted us gone. "That isn't any of your concern."

"Of course," he said before he opened the door. I heard him speaking to someone, and after a few minutes he guided a pleasant-looking woman dressed in just a shirt out. Logan's frown lines hadn't relaxed since Sebastian had gone toward the room.

"She's not here against her will," Logan said. But how could we be sure? Had he tricked her into it? A spell?

We waited for Josh, who had inched closer, his lips moving as he performed an incantation. Her static wide smile remained, her eyes glassy, her movement indolent and purposeful.

"Do you want to leave?" Josh asked her.

She shook her head slowly then looked over her shoulder at Logan. "I want to stay here, with him," she said softly.

I wasn't convinced, but everyone else had been. She was wholly human so it was doubtful that he had performed a *servus vinculum*—the spell he wanted to do with me and Chris so that I could gift her to him—but maybe he had.

As we walked out, I couldn't help but recall his words about pain being subjective and death being cleansing to the palate. I looked back in time to catch Logan's baleful glare as he closed the door behind us. It was the click of the lock that made me want to bust in and take the woman out and I wasn't really concerned if she came willingly. I would drag her out and tell her the handsome guy that had invited her to his house was in fact a horned creature.

I'd decided to do just that when we were a couple of feet from the house. I turned, but Ethan's hands pressed into my back, urging me forward.

"She wants to be there, you can't take her, Sky," he said.

"But—"

"But, nothing. The topic isn't up for discussion. You can't make her decisions for her. She wants to be with him. Period."

"She doesn't know what he is and I am sure that if she did, she would want to leave. I just need to talk to her."

"That is what you want to believe but it doesn't mean it is reality. You feed a vampire regularly, something most of us find reprehensible, but it is what you chose to do."

I stopped walking, his response stunning me into silence. It wasn't the same thing.

"Stop doing that!"

"Doing what?" I decided I really hated when his voice dropped low and he spoke in a soothing tone. He was being condescending and treating me like a child who needed to be placated into behaving.

"Just stop it." I picked up the pace and got in step with Josh, who was a couple of feet away. I considered questioning him again, asking him if he would go back to make sure the woman hadn't been enchanted or something, but Josh was good and if at any moment he suspected there was a spell keeping her there he would have been with me, hauling her out of there.

I smelled an odd fetor, before I saw the jackal just several feet from our car. The turbulent waves of magic that accompanied it stopped both Josh and me in our tracks. It barked, an unusually high sound for a jackal, and then belched magic that sent us back, stumbling to get our footing. Josh smashed into the car. Responding quickly to the assault, his hand gripped the air, seizing the jackal with magic and pulling it toward us. The jackal resisted, its paws gripping at the ground for stability.

Its howl whipped through the air and more animals emerged from the surroundings: two wolves, puma, coyote, lynx—I think, it was larger than I'd ever seen—and a snow leopard. Their movements were slow as they edged around us, forming a full circle. Sebastian's eyes narrowed, giving in to his predator, something worn so close to the surface at times he seemed more animal than man. His eyes locked with the leopard that was directly in front of him. His advance toward it was slow at first, becoming more powerful with each step, and with a sharp burst of movement, Sebastian shifted midair without breaking his stride. He careened into it, sending it back several feet. His powerful form overpowered the felidae, but not before its claws raked across his side.

There was a light rustle as the two wolves attacked, one from the left and the other from the right. Ethan had changed into his wolf form just moments after Sebastian, and when the wolf attacked from the right, Ethan waited. Just as its upper body was at Ethan's advantage, he thrust forward, his teeth capturing its throat. It wasn't moving by the time it slammed to the ground. I couldn't change fast enough to stop the puma that was just inches from me. Its claws raked at me, and I blocked it with the canvas bag. Another swipe and it ripped through the fabric, but I was able to grab the remains and get a close enough grip for leverage to use it as a weapon. It sprang at me and I punched the Aufero forward, into its face, stunning it and throwing it off balance. Before it could recover I landed a powerful side kick into his flank. It stumbled back, but it didn't put enough distance between us. When it charged me again, its claws caught my jeans, just enough to shear them and give me a superficial cut that drew a small amount of blood.

It was enough. Blood and fear ignited something rapacious in them. It edged their desire to have more: more blood, more fear, more violence. They devoured it as though it were food. I watched the puma, trying to anticipate its next move, aware that violence and blood was what it wanted. It would go for the kill. Staying close gave me the advantage. It didn't have the ability to advance or lunge at me. Because of the immunity that were-animals possessed against magic, the Aufero was useless except as a bludgeoning weapon. I heard light padding approaching from another direction, but I couldn't sacrifice the time it took to look. The puma reared back and lunged, a quick jolt of speed. I thrashed into it, slamming it on its back. Stronger in animal form than I was in human, I couldn't hold on to its paws long; if it were to strike me at this distance, the predator would get its wish —death.

At the high-pitched bark of the jackal, it stopped, easing back to the ground, placid. The fight was drawn out of it. But I didn't move immediately. Was this a trick? I sprang back with a quick hop, far enough to react if it changed its mind, and crouched into a defensive stance when it moved to roll to prone and then to stand. With a slow trot it left, and so did the wolf, coyote, lynx. When I looked around for the jackal, it was gone, too. The bodies of the wolf and snow leopard lay lifeless on the blood-sodden ground.

Josh's approach felt bizarre. He was recoiled magic, stepping cautiously back to the car. Strong magic, darker than anything that I had felt before, clouded the air. "What the hell was that?" he asked.

Magic had a fingerprint. If you were around anyone when they did it, then it could be detected in the future. I didn't know this magic, and based on the portentous energy that clung to the air and wrapped around us, I wasn't sure if I wanted to know it. A jackal that performed magic and somehow commanded a group of were-animals. I was with Josh on that. *What the fuck is going on?*

Sebastian was stepping into a pair of pants he'd pulled from his backseat. "The snow leopard was the Beta of the Ares pack. Anderson will want revenge for me killing his second-in-command." Sebastian cursed under his breath. He didn't mind confrontation—at times I think he enjoyed it—but I suspect he was considering the big picture. Why were the Ares involved? And what was their link to the magical jackal? Was this the beginning of a battle over territory or a potential hostile takeover?

Ethan and Sebastian looked at each other, the primordial tension still fastened to them. They always seemed resistant to settling back into human form and the tacit civility that accompanied it.

"What has emboldened them to do this?" Sebastian asked the question that needed to be answered. Did Anderson just wake up one day and decide he wanted to take over the Midwest, and why now?

"I don't know, but we need to pay him a visit." Josh got into Sebastian's car, and when Ethan handed me the keys to his car, I looked at them then stuffed them in my jeans and followed him to Sebastian's SUV.

Ethan stopped. "Be careful going home," he said.

It was worth a try.

As I sped down the street in Ethan's overpriced indulgence, it drove so smoothly that I was shocked to find that the speedometer was creeping past ninety-five. I expected to see flashing lights behind me. I would just tell the police the truth: I was preoccupied thinking about the perverted Tre'ase that we needed to help locate the Tre'ase that created Maya, because if someone finds them before we do and decides to kill them, they kill me. That's how the crazy host/spirit shade thing works. *And to make things worse, Mr. Officer, we removed a curse from me and we have no idea how badly it affected the otherworld. By removing the curse, we removed a ward that limited the depraved Tre'ase Logan from leaving his home. The dark magic that the jackal performed—yes, Officer, that is correct, a jackal used magic. Crazy, right? If that isn't dire enough, we have a pack that seems to be increasing and mobilizing and we don't know why. So Officer, I think I have earned the right to drive ninety miles an hour because life is a real clusterfuck and I needed to clear my head.* That should get me out of the ticket, or get me committed.

My intentions were to go home but instead I found myself pulling into the parking lot of my favorite art gallery. When I walked in, Claudia's eyes widened as she quickly walked toward me. Gently taking hold of my arm she said, "Oh dear, you're going to scare away my customers." She swiftly guided me out of the showroom toward her office.

Distracted, I hadn't noticed the splotches of blood on my jeans and my tattered shirt. Any other time I would have been embarrassed to visit her in my blue jeans and shirt. Bloodstained and disheveled definitely wasn't acceptable. Most of the time I made an effort to never wear jeans. She hated them, but was too polite to say so. Instead, in her soft voice enriched by her beautiful South African accent she would tout, "I do believe I was born in the wrong era. I would have fit in quite well in a society where women wore beautiful things." And if that wasn't enough of a gut punch, she would always lightly brush aside the hair that always managed to spill from my braid or ponytail.

As she guided me out of the showroom, I glanced at the art we passed, appreciating the wonderful and unique creations, fully aware that they had price tags to match. But Claudia had a way of convincing you that high four figures was never too much to pay for art. I've even watched as she persuaded people to pay even more for what I would have described as unfinished pottery work. I wasn't a virtuoso and didn't share the same appreciation that many people who visited the gallery had for art.

. . .

Always exquisitely outfitted, Claudia wore a pearl-colored pantsuit, accented by a blush camisole. A string of pearls draped around her neck. It was an outfit that only she could get away with wearing without coming off as pretentious. Gray was barely distinguishable in her ash blonde hair. Her refinement often over-shadowed her ageless beauty.

"I wasn't expecting you; but as always it is a pleasure," she said, urging me into her bathroom. "The tea will be ready when you return."

It was her polite way of telling me not to come out until I looked presentable for tea. I surveyed the bathroom before I made my way to the sink. Only Claudia would have a vanity and cheval mirror in an office bathroom. I took a look; it wasn't that bad. I fixed my ponytail, tucked in my shirt, and washed the grime off my hands and face as best as I could.

"That's better," she said when I came out, pressing her gloved hand against my cheek before giving me air kisses on each side of my face. As an augur her situation was made more difficult by her skills as an empath. I felt a special connection with her, even more so when I found out that she was a Moura, like me. Because she was Ethan and Josh's godmother, I felt there were boundaries that I needed to respect and made an effort to distance myself, but I couldn't quite commit to doing it.

Warmth was something she possessed in droves and she didn't mind sharing it. She comforted me. With everything that had transpired over the past few weeks, I realized that Claudia had turned out to be more than she seemed and a bigger player in the otherworld that she ever led anyone to believe. There was a small part of me that questioned how dangerous she was to command so much respect. When Kelly was injured and Sebastian couldn't get anyone to cooperate or assist, one call to Claudia started the sequence of events that led to us helping her. She was a powerful enigma who hid behind the disguise of a peddler of overpriced modern art and the promoter of the most avant-garde work in the city.

"I really need to talk" I said, taking a seat at the small table in front of the tea and biscuits she set out for me. I really wanted coffee, and these things that she gave me every time I had tea with her were an insult to cookies. But I knew if I dared to ask for anything else I would insult her refined sensibilities.

She glanced at her watch and smiled. "Well, of course, but my time is limited today."

That was a first. Her schedule, when it came to me, always seemed open. I assumed it was one of the benefits of owning her own business.

Like her gallery, her office was a large open space where her personality came alive in the design. Original art decorated the walls and nothing was more fitting than the traditional furnishings, complete with an antique writing table, vintage ivory letter opener, and pen with inkwell. On the far end of the room was a fainting couch.

She sat in the chair next to me, the warm inviting smile coaxing me to talk, but her eyes were clouded by distraction. She was present but her thoughts were somewhere else.

"I can come back," I offered.

"Of course not, don't be silly. I will make time for you. How are things, Skylar?"

Claudia's presence made me drop my guard and give more information than I should. She often listened, which made me talk more to fill the silence. I wasn't the only one she did this to. I've watched her employ the same tactic with Josh and Ethan, but it never worked with Ethan because he was just as comfortable with silence as she was. So conversation between them was like being at a tennis match or a golf tournament, complete silence as you waited for someone to serve or tee off.

"Why didn't you tell me you were a Moura?"

"As you should follow, it is something that you shouldn't

advertise. I don't see how it changes things between us or how it is information you needed to know," she said softly.

"It would have been good to know."

"Why?"

I didn't have a response. *Because I like to know things. Because I am hosting a Moura reunion and I need to know who to invite. Because.* That was all I had. "Just like you, I don't like to be in the dark."

"We are all in the dark about many things, and I do believe at times darkness is where you need to be to stay safe. The light is where you are most visible—a perfect target," she said, crossing her legs.

"I don't function that way."

She nodded, always agreeable, which made me believe that she was a person who would agree with you and still do whatever she wanted. "I apologize, I will remember that."

Yep, she's going to do whatever the hell she wants.

"Is there anything else you would like to talk about?"

My tried and true response was something that I heard a lot, and it was very fitting at this time—"What are you"—but I felt it was inappropriate when it came to Claudia. Her refined presence always demanded a certain level of propriety when speaking with her. As much as I wanted to just say, let's drop the pretenses and tell me everything you know, for some reason it felt as though I would be committing a horrible faux pas.

As she took furtive glances at her watch I realized I needed to prioritize. "Do you know Logan?"

She nodded. "I am aware of who and what he is."

"I don't trust him, but Sebastian wants to use him to find the Tre'ase who created Maya." I didn't bother explaining who Maya was because I had a strong suspicion that anything I brought up, she already knew about. She probably knew I was a Moura before I did. And I am pretty sure she knew about Maya's existence before anyone else. This woman was a vault of knowledge; I just had to ask the right questions. But what were the right questions?

"I don't question many things Sebastian chooses to do, he has earned that from me. Of the Tre'ase that I've come in contact with, he will be your best choice." She watched me carefully, and limited time didn't seem to be a problem any longer because the silence stretched into minutes. "I know whatever I say will not give you the confidence and comfort you need, but keeping you alive is something Sebastian wants to do. I don't want to deny your curiosity but I need you to trust me on this, he wants you alive. He needs you alive."

There was more to this. *He* needs *me alive? Why?*

"Why?"

She looked at her watch again, this time a more dramatic statement announcing the ending of the conversation. "Samuel will be here in a few minutes, and from my understanding he would like very much not to see you again. I am going to request that we continue this conversation at a later time," she said as she came to her feet.

What? Who? Huh. I wished that all stayed in my head, but it didn't. I blurted them out trying to make sense of the situation.

"You are meeting with Samuel? How did you find him? When did he agree with this? What is the meeting about, the Clostra?" I didn't have problems coming up with the appropriate questions at the moment. I had many more.

She smiled. "It is my understanding that he will meet with me, but it was confirmed through a third party."

"But Ethan and Josh said he went deep underground and couldn't be found."

"Yes, he did," she said as she walked me to the door, a subtle invitation for me to use it. "Ethan has many great qualities, but I do believe Theodore Roosevelt said it best, 'speak softly but carry a big stick.' Ethan has the latter down but it is the former he has difficulty with."

It's okay Claudia, you can say he is a mordant, domineering jackass. That is how I describe him and often to Josh and to

Ethan's face. But instead I simply smiled and lingered at the door.

"Skylar, I will discuss my meeting with Samuel with you later," she said. And that was all I needed to hear.

～

Damn. Damn. And I tossed in a couple of fucks as I drove up to find Sable sitting on my car. It wasn't even three o'clock—how in hell was she out in the day? She didn't have the tell-tale gray coloring they got when they fed from fae in order to walk in the day. No, she was her typical parchment color. Even with her looking me straight in the face, I considered scooting down in the seat. I just couldn't and didn't want to be bothered.

Her approach to Ethan's car was slow. Maybe she thought this was as big of a deal as I did. I took in a deep breath and got out and she flanked at my side. I tried not to be nervous, but she was erratic and a lot of crazy in a small package, which made her even scarier. Her large eyes stayed on me as she sidled in next to me and fell in step as I headed to the door.

"What's wrong, Sable?"

"He won't take any of my calls and when I go to his home he will not let me in. He has a ward, I can't get in his house now."

Gavin and Sable were a couple made in boundary-less stalker heaven. Neither one seemed to adhere to the expectations of privacy or limits, and a person's personal space and autonomy seemed like a mere suggestion to them.

"Give him time, he's concerned about Kelly," I offered, and I hoped that was enough of a consolation because I didn't have anything more to offer.

"So?"

I sighed as I rested my head against the door, wanting her to leave before I considered opening it. Turning to her, I had to ask, "Do you have anything to do with her being missing?"

She shook her head. "But I think I know what happened to her," she admitted.

"What?"

"I think she was taken. The same men that were watching three other women's homes were watching hers, and those women haven't returned home."

That just gave me more questions than answers. Did she just watch random homes? And if she did, why?

I mumbled a couple more curses under my breath and then opened the door, whispering the words to break the ward that prevented vampires and all the other things from entering. But it was especially for vampires because unlike everyone else, my home didn't have a natural immunity that prevented them from entering since I was connected to vampires due to my odd birth— or rather my unique death.

Without being invited, the minute I dropped the ward, she walked in and took a seat on the sofa.

Go ahead, make yourself at home.

"So there were men watching Kelly; why is this the first time we've heard about it?"

"Because I don't care who watches her. I promised Gavin I wouldn't touch her. So I just hoped they would kill her. I didn't want to break my promise to him."

I winced at her words. "You know you don't have to tell me everything that comes to your mind," I offered. I'm sure on some days vampire's honesty was refreshing; their tenet that they could do whatever they pleased with impunity was deeply rooted in their narcissism.

The dark marbles watched me with interest. "You will tell him I'm trying to help, won't you?"

I shook my head. "No. If we find her and she is unharmed, if it is because of you then I will tell him. And I will also let him know that you knew that someone was watching her and didn't care enough about her safety to warn him or any of us. I don't think he will be pleased with that at all."

The obsession she had with Gavin was dysfunction on steroids but I might as well use it to my advantage to help Kelly, if in fact she was missing.

For the first time Sable showed an emotion that wasn't lust for Gavin, anger at Gavin, or indifference to everyone else: she looked sad. The onyx eyes glistened with unshed tears. I looked away. *Don't feel sympathy for her. Don't.* I scolded myself but it was easier said than done.

"Can you locate the men, again?".

"I can take you to the last house where I saw them."

When I pulled up to Winter's two-story French Provincial home, with its steep roof and formal style, I still thought it was just a little too posh for her personality. The inside definitely didn't match. Winter was minimalist right down to the sparse decor of her home. Her living room had just a sofa and chairs. The storage ottoman was just a leather armory. One of the four bedrooms was made into a makeshift sparring room, and her guest room consisted of a bed only. If by any chance you were under the delusions that she wanted guests for any extended period, the bare room would confirm the opposite. And the basement reminded me of a prepper's bunker.

She was already standing outside, a knife holstered at each side of her waist, a sword in her hand, and a gun in her shoulder holster. Her long charcoal-colored hair was pulled back and pinned atop her head, drawing attention to her exotic features: high cheekbones, narrow-edged nose, and full lips complimented by her sun-kissed complexion. Winter was beautiful but she preferred it to be ignored by everyone. I looked around for neighbors. Like most were-animals, her house was a distance from the nearest home, nearly fifty yards away.

"Oh are we doing a hostile takeover of gang territory?" I joked as she approached the car.

Sable laughed loudly, an odd high-pitched sound.

She was twenty shades of crazy but at least she got my sense of humor.

Winter didn't take her eyes off of Sable and kept her hand placed casually over one of the knives at her waist. I wished I could have assured her that Sable was harmless, but I wasn't so sure about that. She was unpredictable with a violent past, and there wasn't anything innocuous about her. When Sable offered the front seat to Winter, she declined, opting for the back, and they kept a careful eye on each other the entire drive.

Sable jumped out of the car before it came to a full stop, looking around the area, her search becoming more frantic as time passed. "They were here," she said.

I surveyed the area, but the home looked empty and there weren't any cars parked on the side of the street. "Do you smell that?" Winter asked.

Inhaling the air, it hit me—fumes—oil, and an acrid medicinal smell. Something seemed off about the place and before I could acknowledge it, both Winter and Sable had made their way into the house. The setup was similar to Kelly's. Everything looked tidy, as though the person was gone on vacation. Winter studied the pictures on the wall, looked through the mail, and then searched throughout the home.

I went through the rest of the small home, looking for anything suspicious, but the only thing I gathered was "single woman." If she had a boyfriend or a man in her life, she wasn't allowing him to keep his things in her home.

"Have you spoken with Gavin?" Winter asked.

"Not since the other day when he suspected that Kelly might be missing." Winter was silent for a long time, considering the situation. She inhaled a slow breath and then exhaled, shaking her head. She spoke but it seemed that she was speaking to herself. "They are only taking women," she mumbled.

Worry spread across Winter's face as she started to chew on her bottom lip.

"What do you think is going on?" I asked.

She shrugged. "You all have been getting this jackal with the ability to use magic and now women are missing." I followed her out of the house to the car, Sable was nowhere to be found. I didn't bother to look for her. I was sure she was investigating Kelly's whereabouts. I wish she would have done it because it's the right thing to do, as opposed to trying to make things right with Gavin. But despite her motives, I was glad to have her skills. As a teenager, she tracked down the people who killed her family when the police department had failed, so I felt more confident knowing she was assisting.

Winter leaned against the car, stroking the handle of her knife as though she was trying to console it for not being used. She had an affinity for violence that I would never understand.

"The vampires are no longer restricted by the daylight," she acknowledged once we were in the car.

The weight of guilt settled in my chest, and I couldn't ignore it. "I know."

Aware of her gaze on me, I glanced in her direction. Her face was strained with uneasiness. "Do we know if staking them through the heart still works? What about holy water?"

Unfortunately, Steven had prevented me from finding out whether staking someone actually worked, and holy water just hurt like hell, it didn't kill them. But if you let them tell the story, it didn't work at all.

I wanted to fill the silence with idle chat but I had too much on my mind. Was the jackal, who could use magic, a result of us using the Clostra? We had unleashed dark magic, different from anything I had experienced. The Tre'ase were free and I could only imagine the problems they were causing.

"I didn't change last night," she said in a tight voice. "We had an eclipse and I wasn't forced into change." Winter was a rarity, a were-snake, and only forced into her animal form during an eclipse.

There was a full moon at the end of the month, so I would find out if it affected the canidae, and next month Mercury would rise again and we could determine if the felidae were affected as well. We didn't have any ursidae and equidae in the pack so when transit of Saturn occurred we'd have no idea of how they would respond. I think there were a few in the Eastern Pack.

Each day was a new discovery of how we had changed the otherworld. I needed to find out what the jackal was. I was considering going back to Logan's, the last place it was encountered. It wasn't a stretch in logic to think there was a link between Logan and it. After all, if he could make a spirit shade, what else could he do?

"Sky!" Winter yelled then grabbed my steering wheel and jerked it to the side, keeping me from slamming into the man who had run into the road. Dressed in shorts and bloodstained shirt, he stopped, looking panic-stricken. His odd amber eyes resembled that of a wolf. Typically, were-animals' eyes sparked the color of our animals, often when angered or in fearful situations as if it were awakened. He was human with wolf eyes. His eyes widened and then constricted before he shot past the car.

Winter jumped out and ran after him, calling after him to stop. Winter was fast, but he was faster, darting through the trees in a panic, looking over his shoulder at her. I drove up and then bolted out of the car to cut him off at the path. I ran through the thicket, over the uneven terrain, finding it hard to get my footing. The man-animal didn't have any problems—he ran through the area at speeds that pushed Winter and me. We had gone deep in the woods, and I had cornered him from the back. She had him in the front, and the crowd of trees on each side of him would make it difficult to negotiate without getting caught.

Panting, he looked between us, his eyes glowing with a predator's ire. He looked scared enough to be erratic. He obviously felt trapped and would do anything to get away. "Hi." Winter finally spoke in a low, calming voice. He couldn't focus. His head kept scanning the area, his body tensed and ready to strike at any moment. I wondered how long had he had been out here. His clothing was dirty, his blond hair and haggard short beard dingy from dirt. His skin was pale and hadn't been exposed to the sun in some time.

"What's your name?" Winter continued, lightly and soothingly.

He relaxed but wouldn't look her directly in the face, something she needed. She needed him to look her in the eyes, so that she could charm him. He turned to look at me, and I smiled.

"I'm Skylar. You can call me Sky," I said, my voice matching Winter's. Inching a little closer, I asked gently, "Are you lost? We can help you."

He kept saying our names over and over as if they held some importance, and when he finally spoke his voice was deep and hoarse as though he hadn't used it in some time. "Sebastian, do you know him?"

"Yes, we know him. We can take you to him," Winter said, taking small cautious steps toward him. Fear had made him unpredictable. The wrong move and we didn't know if he would attack or run. His wild eyes kept scanning the area, ears perked at the slightest sound, and he was so withdrawn, he was coiled mass on the brink of explosion.

"Did someone tell you to find him?" I asked.

He responded with a shaky nod and then his head shot up at the sound of approaching steps, and the panic returned. He darted out past Winter, knocking her to the ground, and ran. I took off after him, but couldn't get close enough to stop him. He changed direction from the sounds I heard in the distance: a car, male voices, the pounding of footsteps. His speed increased and he darted around the trees as heading toward the street. By the time I got there, Winter was waiting by the car, scanning the area.

"What the hell was that?" I asked between gasps of breath.

She shook her head. The smell of car fuel wafted through the air, along with a sage and pine mixture that people used to mask their scent. It worked well if you were hiding from a shapeshifter —it was an irritant and made tracing a scent impossible.

"I think someone grabbed him," Winter said, kneeling over the tire marks near me.

"We need to go to Abigail's," Winter suggested as we got in the car. When the discussion of weird hybrids is ever in question, the elves are usually people of interest. In Elysian I was introduced to unique hybrid animals that didn't exist in the regular world, including their mishaps, which were hidden away in the heavily warded dark forest.

Winter was noticeably tense as we pulled into the driveway of the two-story home. The Doric pillars that encircled the porch gave it a palatial feel with a hint of pretense that embodied Winter's ex-girlfriend's persona. Abigail's father once ruled the elves, and due to their antiquated and misogynistic rules, she would never hold such honors, but she didn't let a little thing like that stop her. She manipulated her way into power through her brother, who had declined the nomination for the position because he considered it only a result of his people's love for his father, who had ruled for over seventy years. But when he was poisoned and nearly killed, he assumed it was a political move to ensure that he would never accept the position. He wasn't aware that his sister was behind it. For the pack's silence about it Abigail and Sebastian colluded to incite a civil war against the *Makellos*, who were the self-indoctrinated elven elite, in order to force the elves to be under one rule— her brother's. Sebastian and Abigail had formed an alliance, and her brother was none the wiser. He only knew that the pack had saved his life and his sister was at his side, appalled that someone would dare attack her brother for political gain.

The underhanded dealing, colluding, and manipulation were done to protect Ethan, who should have been killed based on a covenant made by everyone to contain *Dunkell*, dark elves.

Abigail greeted Winter with a smile, and when she stepped forward to hug her, Winter recoiled, frowned, and stepped back. The vertical slits that I hadn't seen in sometime flickered.

Abigail's smile melted as she moved back several feet. Their appearances were complete opposites: she was as pale as Winter was dark. An abundance of long platinum hair, usually in a French braid, was loose and draped over her shoulder. Abigail's frame was very similar to Winter's tall, sleek body, but her features mirrored her brother's in a bizarre way. They were far too similar to be fraternal twins. Abigail and Gideon both possessed distinctive and androgynous features of narrow face, sharp defined cheeks and jawline, thin aquiline nose, and pale lashes that veiled violet eyes.

"We saw something quite odd today, and I believe Liam may be responsible," Winter said, taking a seat on the sofa. Abigail started to join her but was deterred with a sharp look. She stepped back, opting for the armchair across from her.

"And what was that?" Her smile was genteel and warm and may have worked on anyone other than Winter, who wasn't able to forgive her for using her as a pawn as Abigail executed her scheme to get her brother into power as the new leader of the elves.

"We saw a man today who looked like an animal in a human body. His eyes were that of an animal, although he was human form. He was definitely not a were-animal. Is Liam experimenting with humans?"

Abigail was a skilled liar and a gifted performer. The presentation she put on when her brother was found nearly dead was worthy of an award. I wouldn't trust whatever came out of her mouth even if her tongue was notarized and she swore on a stack of holy books. I believed Winter felt the same way. She stilled, watching Abigail closely, paying attention to her. Sebastian and Ethan were masters of studying the physiological changes to detect a lie. Gavin was nearly as good but the rest of them had to work a little harder at it and I was still a novice.

Winter looked in Abigail's direction but refused to give her the courtesy of any emotions. Abigail's lips pulled into a thin line, and she looked at Winter. Winter looked through her. Winter ascribed to the belief that there wasn't a thin line between love and hate, but there was one between love and indifference. Feeling nothing for a person was worse than hate in Winter's mind.

Parting her lips to speak, Abigail quickly closed them instead. Taking a moment, she considered her words, and when she finally spoke, her voice was soft and entreating. "Winter, I didn't enjoy deceiving you."

Winter's empty gaze peered through her, and when she spoke, her intonation was as devoid of emotions as her look. "Whether or not you enjoyed it isn't what bothers me, it's the fact that you did it. I thought *we* were better than that." Winter leaned forward, studying her. "Do you think Liam has anything to do with it?"

"Is Liam capable of doing something so cruel? Of course, and probably worse; but he knows it would not be tolerated and violates our laws. If it were ever discovered that he was doing such things, he and anyone involved would be severely punished. With everything that has transpired recently we would have discovered it, if it were going on."

Winter and I gave her our undivided attention. "The ward fell two weeks ago in Elysian and your pack and the elves helped Liam contain everything. Sebastian and your pack have been very helpful with cleaning up Liam's mess. It was very kind of him to help; it was only fitting that Liam forgave him of the debt he had incurred to help Kelly." Sebastian wasn't busy cleaning up Liam's mess—he was cleaning up ours and had his debt forgiven in the process.

I sucked in a sharp breath. We removed the curse and apparently shattered wards as well. My chest was so tight that breathing was becoming a problem. And the chorus of the clusterfuck song played over and over in my head because that was exactly what this was.

"Was everything that escaped recovered?" I asked. If not, the strange man we saw today might not be the only thing running rampant in the city. What would be the reaction of someone who saw an okapi/horse hybrid, like the one I rode when I was there? Or worse, something that was kept hidden in the dark forest? One of the creatures paralyzed Kelly, and it took another bloodsucking creature from there to repair her. Sebastian left the dark forest with talon-like claw marks on his back.

"Yes," Abigail said, barely turning her head in my direction, keeping her focus on Winter. Her entreating eyes and delicate features belied the power-thirsty ice princess who kept a handle on politics and the strings that controlled her brother, as well as her skills of manipulating the weather as an elemental elf

Abigail's eyebrows furrowed. "Sebastian didn't tell you?" She chuckled. "Of course he hasn't." She sighed and then rolled her eyes. "I forgot, I've been ordered to stay away from you."

At Winter's silence, Abigail continued, amused. "He seems to believe his control extends further than the pack. Perhaps he felt one way of ensuring that was to make sure we are never around each other. Your pack has been very busy cleaning up Liam's mess."

"Are the wards up?" I asked.

"Yes, the ones to Elysian and to the dark forest are in place and I hope they hold this time. My brother and the others have taken notice. This is a problem, something that I am sure would not have happened if my brother were in control of the *Makellos*." I held my tongue and didn't tell her it would have.

Winter was the first one to stand, declining Abigail's invitation to stay longer. She hadn't looked at Abigail for most of the visit, and it bothered Abigail. We had more things to worry about than Abigail's hurt feelings. I couldn't help but wonder when we would find ourselves faced with a taloned creature that had escaped from the dark forest and was wreaking havoc on the city.

It was close to eleven at night and I had given up on the idea that I would hear from Ethan or Sebastian regarding the information Abigail gave us today. My mind kept revisiting everything that went on earlier and the things that had occurred since we removed the curse. The ward was back up in the dark forest, that was good. I really didn't care if Elysian was exposed; it would serve those snobs right if people just starting visiting it like it was the new local weekend resort. It was a beautiful place that they had created just for them. Their egos wouldn't take the idea that mere humans were enjoying their things. They didn't want elves that were half human or any part human near it. Elysian was to be enjoyed by those considered pure and untainted by what they considered the weakest, humans.

The jackal that was able to perform magic, the *manimal*, unrestricted Tre'ase, and vampires that were no longer inhibited by sunlight were on the list of the new things that had occurred in the past two weeks. I conceded. Claudia was right, we should have the Clostra. We needed to fix this, and without all three books, I wasn't sure how we would.

Steven was in his room. Any other time I would have been there with him or he would have been in here but he spent most of the time packing. Stay away from Quell. That was all I needed to do and my life would get easier. It was hard letting go of him: as much as I believed I was there to help him, he was there to help me. David kept me anchored to humanity, and Quell helped me stay firmly in the middle, away from a darker side that seemed to be at every corner.

Steven's moving out seemed to be going faster than his arrival. When he moved in, it was a molasses-slow transition. He slowly moved his things in, infiltrating my space day by day until I realized more of his things were in my home than his, and before I knew it I had a housemate. At first I minded it, but it didn't take long for me to like having him here.

Sitting up in my bed, I scanned my laptop. Gibberish jumped off the pages. I had been distracted, and the assessment that I was working on for my job reflected it. It wasn't my best work and would probably shatter the fragile existence of said job. With a deadline in forty-eight hours I didn't have the luxury of procrastination. I deleted the pages and started typing trying to put together a coherent evaluation of the private practice that I had assessed a couple of days ago.

I heard the thunderous sound of a door breaking open—I assumed my front door—and then the window in my room shattered, spraying glass. Several fragments became imbedded into my arm as I attempted to protect my eyes. I tossed my laptop aside and leapt for the sword. A man swung through the window, his gun aimed at me. I lunged to the side as bullets whizzed past me. I was at an awkward angle when I swung the sword but was able to thrust with enough force to sever the arm. Blood spurted as it dropped in front of me. Howling in pain, the man lunged at me; a side toss got him out the way in time for me to grab the arm of the other man as his elbow jutted into my face and he jerked the sword out of my hand. Grasping his arm, I pulled it into extension and jabbed my fist into the joint, breaking it. He stumbled back, and I thrusted the palm of my hand into his nose, swiped his leg, and kicked the gun he dropped out of his reach.

I doubt I would get any answers, but before I could question them, I responded to the sound of wood splintering, drywall smashing, and brutal fighting coming from the other room. Sword in hand I ran, moving around the pools of blood on the floor. The crashing sound magnified, and when I got to the living room there was a man on the ground, his throat open, a butcher knife tossed at his feet. Another man's head was turned at an odd angle, motionless, a few feet from Steven. He had a third man in a chokehold. The seconds crawled by and eventually the man lay withered at Steven's feet.

Steven stood and whipped around in my direction, feral as gold rolled over his eyes, lips drawn back, a vicious growl vibrating in his chest. Calming him down wasn't an option, I needed him fight ready. We waited for more, and after several minutes, standing in defensive stances prepared to fight, it seemed like that was it. Five men sent to my home, but we weren't sure if it was for both of us or one in particular.

Three out of the five men who attempted to ambush us were alive. The man whose arm I severed wasn't any use, drifting in and out of consciousness. The man with the broken arm had been secured with belts and ropes and sat against the wall refusing to talk to us. The guy Steven had rendered unconscious was bound, too, but tight-lipped.

"Who sent you?" Steven asked after checking them for any identifying information. Nothing.

The man whose arm I broke seemed to be the leader, and if the other ones looked like they were prepared to speak, one glare from him and they reconsidered.

"Who fucking sent you?" Steven demanded. He slammed the man's head into the wall.

Steven's breathing still hadn't returned to normal. Ragged growl-like sounds escaped with each expiration. Now more beast than man, I expected him to shift into his coyote, but he didn't. Gently touching his arm, I covered his hand, forcing myself to calm hoping it would affect him. If he killed them, we wouldn't find out anything and he looked like he was just moments from doing just that. By the time he was calm enough to interrogate them again, Sebastian walked in.

Broken Arm's stern, defiant look faltered at the sight of Sebastian. Steven could be ferocious, having a limited but symbiotic relationship with his animal that allowed remnants of his humanity to peek through. There was a glimpse of hope that he was capable of clemency—even mercy. Sebastian's bestial ways shrouded his humanity nearly into obscurity, giving you the impression that interaction would never be anything other than primal, stripped to its very essence. He possessed no mercy to give, and it showed profoundly on his face.

He walked closer, grabbing the knife off the floor, with the look of annoyance and anger expected from anyone who was awakened from his bed at one in the morning. He inched closer to Broken Arm and then knelt down to eye level with him, his glare hard enough to cut diamonds. Sebastian held the knife casually at his side, but I knew not to underestimate his lethalness with any sharp object. I'd seen him at work with a sword—skills and speed that would rival a machine's.

Sebastian's voice was so soft it could have induced a tranquil calm. But Broken Arm wasn't comforted by it. Perhaps he had dealt with people enough to know there was always a calm before the storm and he was preparing himself for Sebastian's wrath. Like a gentle snow, before you are hit by a blizzard that you may not survive.

He looked over at the guy whose arm was severed and looked stricken by a new fear.

Sebastian was gentler than I expected, but I guess he didn't need to yell or sound angry while holding a knife that was positioned in a manner to cause damage at whim.

"There were five, now you have three. I am prepared to allow all three to walk out of here—I am also prepared *not* to. Who sent you?"

The man's lips tightened for a mere second; he looked at the knife in Sebastian's hand then made an effort to hold his gaze. A hapless endeavor, because most people couldn't hold it—most people didn't want to.

"I don't know who actually paid us. We had an intermediary."

"Who was that?"

Broken Arm inhaled a ragged breath as his eyes roved over the room at his fallen partners, the blood-soaked carpet, and back to Sebastian's stone-set face that hadn't faltered once since he had positioned himself in front of him. The cognac-colored eyes could switch from warm and gentle to hard and cold in just a blink.

"Sean," he said.

Sean was the new hunter of choice since Chris had been changed. She had been the go-to person for anything needed because she was the best. Upon her transition, Sean and Ann emerged as her replacements and together didn't seem as good or effective as Chris. Sean was the worst; his combination of arrogance and incompetence made him more of a danger than a help in the otherworld. We'd met him last year when we were looking for other Tre'ases in the area. He didn't know who Ethan was. How did he expect to function without knowing the chain of command of the largest pack in the world and not being able to identify them?

"What were your orders?" Sebastian asked.

"I'm not sure what you are asking." I could hear his heartbeat from across the room.

"Was it just to kill her? Did they want proof of death? Did they want the body?"

"Dead and proof," he said evasively.

The bile crept up, catching my breath. *Proof. What suffices as "proof of murder"? An arm? Leg? Head?*

Feeling the blood drain from my face, I started to feel lightheaded. I rested against the counter.

"You have five minutes. Take your men and get out." The man

scrambled to his feet, taking the armless man with him. The other guy was still groggy and staggered out behind them.

Once they were gone Steven asked, "Why not send Chris? She usually handles jobs like this and quite efficiently. Why deal with them? Do you think it was a warning?"

"No, it wasn't a warning. Chris wouldn't have taken that job," Sebastian said casually.

"Really? Why not?" I figured the money wasn't enough. Chris made it very clear that for the right price, she could be bought. But whatever she was charging had to be less than hiring a five-man team.

"Ethan feels confident that she won't hurt you no matter what is offered." He shrugged.

I couldn't help but be flattered because no one had been given such honors, even Ethan and he was her ex. And a vampire who was a sharpshooter as an ally was one of the few things in my life that I was very happy about. I gained a friend in Chris but made an enemy in Logan. Worth it.

"You can't stay here. Pack a bag."

"Where am I going?"

"With me."

"I can go to Winter's," I offered. I'd experienced Sebastian's brand of protection more than once, and it always involved me being locked in. I just couldn't deal with his level of security.

Sebastian's lips pressed into a stern line, and my small smile wasn't going to make them relax. He studied me for a few moments, which became a long stretch of silence. With a roll of his eyes, he dismissed me as you would a petulant child.

I pressed the issue. "If it is about my safety, her home is as safe as an armory." It was dangerous if you weren't welcomed and not lacking for weapons of any sort. Looking for a sword? Check the closet. A gun? Pick a drawer and the odds were in your favor you would find one. Need a knife? Pick a cabinet drawer or oddly placed console and you will find one in it. And if you were short on time, just move any table, sofa, or ottoman aside and you'd find something that could hurt, mutilate, or kill someone.

"I didn't give you that option. Now go pack."

I looked in Steven's direction. He was still leaning against the wall, the dark cast of his features making him look hard, overshadowing his cherub looks. "He's not safe here, either," I said to Sebastian and then directed my attention back to Steven.

"Don't worry about me, I am leaving, too. I'll stay at my new place."

I didn't know how long I would be gone and when I got back, Steven may have moved all his things out and be officially gone. I convinced myself that the bile that crept up was from the smell of blood, fear, and death, but it wasn't. When I returned, Steven would be gone and it bothered me. For days, I had convinced myself that it wasn't going to happen and we would work it out at the last moment. I clung to the hope that at the last minute, this fight, like the rest of them would end with him flicking my ear and then a quick side hug. It was as good as a heartfelt apology— but it hadn't happened. This was it. No apologies. He was leaving.

I walked into the bedroom, the severed arm was a reminder of the violence that had just taken place—my violence. Packing didn't take long because I never unpacked my "running away" bag. Running was no longer something I thought about anymore, but as with today, my life was complicated. I didn't have the luxury of sleeping in my bed, in my home and consider myself safe. People came through windows and crashed through doors for a single purpose—to kill me.

I grabbed the large overnight bag and threw in a few more clothes, blinking back tears.

"I was unfair," Steven said from behind me.

I shrugged, finding it difficult to face him without displaying maudlin emotions that neither one of us needed. I just glanced up in his direction and continued putting things in the bag. Things I wouldn't use, but I needed to busy myself with something. "We're fine," I lied.

He was closer. "You're not fine. I don't like what is going on with you and Quell. It's just another situation that could put you in danger."

"You think this is Michaela's doing?" I said, turning.

"Nah. She wouldn't give anyone else the pleasure of killing you. That is a reward she'd want for herself. Go with Sebastian, and when this is over, we'll discuss our living arrangements."

That was total BS. It was a perfectly worded noncommittal—a pack favorite. He wasn't staying, but this wasn't the time to say it. It was his poor attempt to soften the situation. I tried to smile. I'm sure in some circles it may have been okay. The muscles on my face seemed tight with too much tension to do something as banal as smile. I just nodded continuously until he had disappeared back through the door.

CHAPTER 6

*S*ebastian drove into the private parking lot and quickly got out, grabbing my bag. I had to nearly run to catch up. "Where are we? I thought I was going to the pack's house."

"This is one," he said as his fingers skipped over the buttons of his phone, sending a text message.

This was very different from the massive house in the middle of nowhere, surrounded by enough greenery that its existence was hidden. It doubled as a wildlife conservation area where we could run in our animal forms without the risk of being seen by a neighbor—the closest home was nearly five miles away. It was off the beaten path; you didn't stumble upon the house without knowing exactly where you were going.

As the elevator eased up the floors, Sebastian finally relaxed against the wall. I could feel the intensity of his attention on me, his presence, the anger and tension that had enclosed him like a wall. Periodically he checked his messages.

"Who gave you the sword?" he asked, still looking down at his phone.

"Winter."

"Are you proficient with it?"

Who wasn't proficient? You grab it, swing, and hit something soft. Even if you hit something hard, that person was having a bad day. A bad bloody day.

He glanced up from his phone, waiting patiently for an answer.

"What do you mean?"

"How would you fare against me?"

"I would die, like probably anyone else. That's hardly a fair question." It wasn't. Two years ago Demetrius and Sebastian had a sword fight and it was as violent as it was beautiful. If one didn't know any better, they would have thought it was choreographed. They moved through the air, lithe and graceful, swords in both hands moving with a smooth rhythm as though just extensions of their limbs. The clank of the swords had become a constant beat of violence and a determination to kill the other. It was another testimonial of Sebastian's skills and why he held his position as the Alpha of the Midwest Pack and the Elite of all the packs in the country.

"Then I will have to teach you, so that you can."

"Can what, beat you?" I scoffed at the absurdity of it. "Okay, and I'll show you how to use a golf club—I'm a pro."

He gave me a side look and then smirked.

"There's more skill to it than you think and you'll realize that the moment I whack the hell out of you," I said.

He must have really thought my day was bad because he tried to laugh, but it was choked and forced. But those muscles probably never got used. After his pitiful attempt at a laugh, he was back to Sebastian Super Alpha, Mr. No Smiles, King of I'll Kick Your Ass. "Let's stick with that sword. You might not be able to beat me, but at least you'll be skilled enough to make me work for it."

Work for it? After seeing Sebastian fight with a sword the only way I was going to make him work for it was if I had a couple of people with me. It was a generous offer, but my mind was working overtime for an excuse to decline. Winter was a tyrant of an instructor but at least she would make a joke, crack a smile, let me rest on the ground if I started to hit it too many times. I couldn't imagine any of that would happen with Sebastian. How many times had I seen him smile? It was definitely in the single digits, and his jokes usually were at my expense. Maybe I could convince him to let Winter train me, she was skilled as well. Maybe not as proficient, but she was definitely a fierce fighter with a sword and knife. Shooting furtive glances, I was just about to suggest it.

"No. I will instruct you," he said before I could get the words out of my mouth.

You can join Ethan at the freak table.

"Am I really that easy to read?"

"You might as well hold up a sign," he said as the elevator opened and he stepped out and unlocked the only apartment on the floor.

I looked around the large penthouse and decided without a doubt that this was where I was going to stay forever. Floor to ceiling windows surrounded half of the room and provided a great view of the city, a small corner with a built-in desk to our left, large kitchen with stainless steel appliances to the right. The hardwood floors didn't look like they'd ever seen traffic and I felt bad walking on them with my dirty shoes that I was sure had traces of blood on them. I inhaled the air; unlike the pack's retreat this place had never had blood spilled in it. It was too clean for anything to have occurred here. But like the retreat's, the three sofas were large and sturdy. The only other thing in the open space was an oversized coffee table placed on a rug with geometric shapes that complemented the eggshell-colored walls. There weren't any pictures or art on the wall. It was plain, but nice—very nice.

"How long have you had this place?"

"It's not mine, it's the pack's. No one knows about it. I don't want you at the retreat until I find out who was behind this." He glanced in my direction. "You looked like you were about to be sick earlier. You needed some space from everyone. You'll be safe here."

I shrugged and tried to smile, as I recalled the image of the man's severed arm. "I get that way when I dismember a body. It's one of my quirks. That damn conscience is a horrible son of a bitch."

"He tried to kill you—anything that happens after that is warranted."

I had to look at him. The sincerity of his words, the coolness of his demeanor, were testaments of his beliefs in what he said. If you attack them, whatever happens is justified. Mercy wasn't an option. On a primal level instinctively I got it, but trivializing violence and the potential loss of life was just difficult despite the inciting incident. Just when I felt comfortable around him, considered him "just another guy," he ripped away that naïveté with the subtly of a bull rampaging through the streets.

Walking farther into the room, I looked around again. It was breathtaking. I felt out of place in my bloodstained clothes. Although I knew it was just my imagination, the smells of violence and sweat seemed to linger on me. Fresh air was exactly what I needed, and I couldn't believe the place didn't have a balcony.

"This isn't much of a hideaway or safe house."

"Really? You don't feel safe here? How is someone going to get up here? How can they get to you?" he asked with a smirk, the keys to the elevator still in his hands.

"The window."

He chuckled. "You think that someone is going to scale the building and then throw something through double-paned glass? And then what? The place has a ward; no one can just *travel* in here. On the off chance that someone does find you here, point out the vulnerable spots? There aren't any. Where can they get to you? The highest point on the buildings surrounding us still doesn't give access to this apartment."

Calling this place an apartment was being very generous with the usage. I've lived in an apartment before, and this wasn't an apartment. Even *luxury condo* seemed too simplistic of a description.

I had stopped thinking about vulnerable spots and focused on the fact that the pack had a lot of businesses, and they worked hard to keep a steady flow of income. Everyone gave 12 percent of their income, but I knew what I contributed and there wasn't any way anyone with that amount of money was going to purchase an *apartment* in the city that took up the entire top floor and had its own private entrance.

As the silence persisted, I stared out the large window, aware of the glances Sebastian shot in my direction. "You'll only be here a couple of days. We need to place another ward and to change your windows to something that can't be broken. I want to change your doors as well and make a few other modifications."

"Cool, my own fort." The changes were needed, but it still bothered me. I didn't want Sebastian and his extreme paranoia to be the decorators of my home. I didn't want it to become like Winter's. Yes, it was nice and quite beautiful, but the well-made furniture was sturdy enough to be placed against the door to barricade it. A storage ottoman had weapons on top of the blankets stored in it. Expensive knickknacks were sharp or glass that could be easily broken to be used as weapon. Large floor vases placed strategically around the room were too decorative for their purpose, which was to hold the gilded scabbards poking out of them. Her home was like all their homes and lacked warmth. Instead, there was a sterile feel like a hospital ward, or better yet, a prison.

Walking around the room, I studied it in great detail, taking in the books on the shelves, clearly there for decoration only, the expensive appliances and furniture. I couldn't help but ask, "What exactly do we do?"

"Well, you try to be witty but it's seen as snarky 70 percent of the time, and the rest of the time you manage to get yourself into situations that require a lot more manpower and money to fix than the ones that anyone else in this pack gets into."

Forget being the Alpha, you need your own comedy special. You are hilarious!

"Yeah, I know what *I* do, and your response was neither needed or appreciated," I said in a saccharine voice, shooting him a grin when he scowled at my response. "But what does the Midwest Pack do for money? Seriously? How do we afford to charter planes, have safe houses, and have a staff of people that work just for us?"

"We don't sell body parts on the black market, no human trafficking, nor do we work in blackmail or whatever other things are going through your head. I think too much television has given you a very active imagination."

"Nope, books. The wild things I read, TV can't even begin to compare."

Sebastian regarded me for a long time but I had no idea what he was thinking—I never did. The indecipherable look remained his mask. When he finally spoke, his tone was soft and gentle. "When I took over the pack there were things that needed to change. Safety was my priority and I never wanted to be compromised by money or the lack of it. Nor did I want us to be reduced to being muscle for hire for others. So I changed things. As creative as your imagination is, and I don't want to begin to delve in the type of ideas that goes through it, your concerns are unwarranted."

His smiled faded, and he had the same look they all gave when they had grown tired of interaction. They were not a social bunch. He gave me a passing look. "The shower is that way."

I guess the conversation was over, but I didn't move—I'm not sure why. Then his brow raised. Just like Ethan, nothing was just a mere suggestion but rather a command expected to be followed. Sadly, the expectations extended further than just in the pack. He turned away and went to the desk, ending all hope of more conversation.

A rainfall showerhead is something I never thought I needed, but as I stood under it and the refreshing warm rain washed away the blood and grime it quickly made it onto my list of must-haves. But that was the only thing that it wiped clean. The memories were there, haunting. Who wanted me dead? And what type of depraved person needed proof of it? I had to agree with Steven, it wasn't Michaela. She would never deprive herself of such macabre fun. The act of violence that ended with the loss of life was a pleasure she would never give to another person. Violence was the prelude to her masterpiece—death. She enjoyed it far too much.

Who wanted me dead? I was starting to think the list of people who wanted me alive might be shorter.

When I came out of the shower, Ethan was propped on his elbows on the bed, dressed in a pair of jeans and a relaxed t-shirt that hugged the muscles of his chest and stomach. Hair mussed, the similarities between him and Josh were very apparent. Securing the towel around me tighter, I ran my hand through my hair, wishing I had spent a little more time detangling it.

He eased off the bed and approached me with slow careful steps as though he was moving toward a deer or a timid creature he was afraid would scurry away.

"Where is Sebastian?" I asked.

"Gone."

"It's just us?"

He stroked my hair, his fingers running along the length of it and then lingering playfully along my jaw.

Move. I should move. And I had every intention of doing so, but I couldn't.

He smiled, and it reminded me of his wolf: sly and devious. "Why, is that a problem?" he asked.

Yep. But instead I shook my head. "No, it's fine."

He nodded. "Good."

I took a step back, opening up space between us, and he moved closer, eliminating it. *"Como você está?" How are you?*

"Fine."

"Diga-me o que aconteceu." Tell me what happened.

"I already told Sebastian." Each time was like reliving it again. I'd already been through it once, twice when retelling it to Sebastian. I'm sure the third time wasn't going to be a charm.

"Now tell *me*. You might remember things a little clearer." He slipped his arm around my waist. *"Por favor." Please.*

I started off in Portuguese but the word finding was getting difficult. Within minutes I was speaking in English and switching back and forth, but he seemed to be able to follow.

"Sebastian was right, it was a very amateurish attempt," he said.

"Since I haven't had a lot of people try to assassinate me, I'm going to take your word for it."

He chuckled, and whatever space I managed to steal between us, he grabbed back. Light, tenuous fingers moved over my shoulder before brushing strands of hair from my face. I couldn't deny the pleasure of his touch, the warmth that enveloped me, the gentle prick of electricity that slinked over me when he was this close, nuzzling his nose against the crook of my neck. I wanted to say something, to do something, but instead I stood there aware of Ethan and the intensity that surrounded him. The warmth of him shrouded me.

He kissed me lightly, his supple lips gently pressed against mine, entreating a response, and as always—I responded. My attraction to him was instant as a commanding finger entwined in my hair pulling me closer, his breath warm and light against my lips. Experienced fingers pressed against my side, gentle, seductive, awakening feelings that existed between us on a carnal level. We were pleasure, hedonistic and beguiling. It was what I needed, and freely I gave into him. The day became a haze and everything seemed to consist of just me and Ethan.

I wanted him. Craved him. Needed him. Lusted for him.

But logic was a horrible overlord that controlled my actions when it came to Ethan, and reality hit me hard. I remembered the last time—the way he had touched me. His sinuous, sexy movements and the heaviness of his body against mine that left me entranced and craving him. I had been here before, lusting for him, willingly giving into him, wanting more, and he left me doing just that—wanting more. He left me feeling dejected and embarrassed, and days later he was so casual about telling me not to make things awkward. Awkward. We were awkward and so wrong for each other. I couldn't have a replay of that. I refused to.

Pulling away, I attempted to slide to the side, but his arms were planted next to me, limiting movement.

"What's the matter?" he whispered against my cheek.

"I need to get dressed."

"Okay, then get dressed."

I shifted my gaze to the door, a subtle hint for him to use it. I really just needed a minute. A minute without him to control the urges that he kindled in me. Was he doing this on purpose? Was this a game for him?

He smirked and tossed a look in the direction of the door. "I think we are past that." Ethan was as intoxicating and as habit forming as any drug. It was so easy to be seduced by him and the sexuality that existed on a primal level.

I nudged past his arm and then sidestepped to put more distance between us.

"I don't want to play your games. I am not some toy you get to play with whenever the mood strikes you," I said, responding to his amused smirk. "You said not to make things awkward between us, but you're the one who keeps making it that way."

As he took several steps back, his tongue grazed across his lips moistening them. He seemed so relaxed and tranquil. I guess there is some truth to the saying that there is a fine line between love and hate, because there was one between passion and dispassion; the ambivalence had me one moment considering kissing him and the next wondering how bad it would hurt my hand to punch his sharp jaw.

Arrogance sheathed his face; a whisper of amusement played at his lips and eventually draped over his face. Josh often joked that almost every woman Ethan had dated had either destroyed something of his or accosted him and I was starting to see why. His arrogance taunted, and it just seemed like assaulting him was the right thing to do. "Tell me, what game am I playing with you and what type of *toy* are you?"

"The type that isn't going to deal with your BS. That night"—I had to look away from his gaze, the intensity of it making it hard to hold as his lips beveled into a grin as my face flushed. I could feel the red burning along my cheeks and jawline—"when we were together it didn't end the way, um ... the way I expected. The way it should have, and you left without any explanation."

The amusement faded and he considered me for what felt like eternity. "I thought I was doing the right thing," he admitted softly.

"What's wrong with you? Are you really this narcissistic?" *Why am I asking questions I already know the answer to?* "How is seducing me and then leaving me without anything happening 'the right thing'?"

His sharp assessment of me continued before he asked, "When is the last time you got laid?"

"What?"

"When was the last time you made love? Got laid? Screwed? Banged? Did the horizontal tango? Fucked? Use whatever euphemism you want but the question remains: when is the last time you've done it?"

Rendered silent, I stared at him for a moment. If I was prepared to sleep with him, I should be okay admitting that I hadn't done it with anyone before; but instead I wanted to tell him it was none of his business.

"Exactly." His gaze rested on me. "Sky, I'm not a teenager and the idea of being a woman's first does nothing for me. I don't need the ego boost or have something to prove by doing that. Honestly, I don't want to be the star of your fond recounts of your first time. It was the right thing to do because for me it would have probably been just a one-night thing and for you, it would have been more."

His hubris had no end. I pulled the towel tighter around me, feeling the heat on my cheeks and aware that they were probably an awful ruddy color. Hadn't I learned my lessons with him? "You're an ass."

He nodded slowly. *"Eu sei." I know.*

He moved to the wall to my left, near the door I wanted him to use earlier, and rested casually against it, his thumbs looped in the pockets of his jeans. He exhaled a long breath and when he spoke his voice was softer, I could barely hear him. "I've cheated on almost every woman I have ever dated. I have no interest in monogamy. When I get bored, it's over. Tears don't bother me nor do they change my decision when I decide to leave. The list of women who I have left broken is long, and they are hurt. They even break my things, call me every combination with *fucker* or variations of *asshole*; but eventually they get over it." He shrugged his indifference and then ran his hand through his hair. "You would be added to the list, and you're different, I don't think you —" His words clipped to a short pause. "I'm a real SOB, and I'm okay with it and I'm probably not going to change."

I didn't know if I should be appalled or impressed with his self-assessment. Was he trying to warn me off him? I was speechless. How do you respond to something like that? I racked my brain for a good retort but came up short. Did I say, "Sorry you're an ass, better luck with your next life?" or look for a pill that could fix narcissistic jackass, SOB syndrome? *There has to be a pill for that, right?*

"Can you think of anything else about tonight's attack?"

Just like that the conversation about *us* was over. Or rather over as far as Ethan was concerned. The elephant in the room just smirked at our inanity and I didn't blame him. He was a self-proclaimed SOB, end of story.

It took me a long time to answer. I considered going back to the us conversation, but why bother? What more did I have to say?

I shook my head and thought that would be the cue for him to leave. But he didn't. Instead we stood there, looking at each other, paralyzed by the discourse that was the essence of what we were. It didn't matter how many times I looked over at the door, he ignored it. Instead, his gunmetal gaze fixed on me. I fidgeted under the intensity of it. His lips relaxed slightly as though he was going to speak.

"I love this place," said Josh's voice outside of the door. "I brought food and everything on the list, just as you commanded, sir."

Josh and Ethan's strange dynamics were always good for entertainment. One being a powerful witch and the other the Beta of the strongest pack in the country often made their interaction difficult. They were a pack of two; Ethan had taken on the role as Alpha, and Josh was reluctant to accept it. Strong personalities, insolence, and stubbornness often meant their conflicts were never easily resolved amicably.

He slid past his brother and stood between us. He looked at him and then me. Always sagacious, he took a moment to study us and frowned. "You should check and make sure I got everything you wanted. The rest of the bags are on the counter," he said.

Ethan's arms crossed over his chest and he remained leaning against the doorframe. "I trust you."

"That's a first." Josh replied. "You've always felt the need to check my work. Why don't you do it now." And with a light nod, Ethan was given a magical incentive, a gentle push toward the door. When he didn't take the hint to leave, Josh gave him another push, hard enough to get him out the door. With a flick of Josh's finger, it closed in front of Ethan. A quick whirl of his second finger, and the lock engaged. *I can't say it enough—it's good to be a witch.*

He smirked as he stepped closer to me, as we both waited for a thrashing at the door. Surprisingly, we were met with silence.

"Hi," he said, doing what he did best—ignoring social protocols of personal space. He kissed me lightly on the cheek. "So, you've been upgraded to gold card membership I hear. You know each time someone tries to arrange a hit on you, there's a little bump in your pack-cred." He grinned. "My brother's at triple platinum status, I think."

"Steven's moving out," I blurted.

"What?" I figured he had to be just as confused by the statement as I was. I didn't want to talk about people trying to kill me, or how much we had changed and probably ruined the other-world, or the complicated problems that existed between Quell, Michaela, and me. Ignoring them didn't make them go away. They were still there even after I spoke. The problems loomed and were ever present.

He nodded slowly, demonstrating a level of understanding of the situation—that was a quality about him that I adored. He walked over to the bed and plopped on it. "Why?"

I went into the bathroom, keeping the door open so he could hear me tell him everything that had occurred over the past few days while I dressed. When I came out in a Hello Kitty t-shirt with matching shorts, he stopped focusing on my story and laughed. "You're so sexy I don't know if I can keep my hands off you."

Giving him a once-over, I glowered at his blue Oscar the Grouch t-shirt and trademark dark jeans. "Really, you're in no position to talk."

Crawling onto the bed, I laid back next to him. "I've made a mess of things and I don't know how to fix it," I admitted.

His hand covered mine, thumb stroking the side of my hand. "It's not a mess, just give Steven time."

Someone wanted me dead. Sebastian considered the job at my house amateurish. I assume it was to send a message. "Hey Skylar, I want you dead." At this point, who didn't? Logan wasn't a fan; I am pretty sure Michaela and Marcia wouldn't lose sleep if they found out I had been killed; and Samuel, the witch with an agenda to rid the world of magic, might not want me dead but he wasn't in the Skylar fan club.

"Sebastian doesn't think Michaela would be involved with something like this. She wouldn't hire out" I said.

"I have to agree. Michaela wouldn't do such a thing. This is someone who wanted to keep their hands clean."

"Logan?"

"Maybe," he said without confidence, and I could understand where he was coming from. How would it benefit Logan if I were killed? He didn't know I was the only one who could read the Clostra, and he had to know that if they suspected it was him, they would reverse the curse and he would be imprisoned again.

"Marcia?"

A sigh rumbled his lips, and when he closed his eyes I knew the answer before he said it. "Yeah, more than likely."

He rolled over to look at me. "I wouldn't put it past her, especially now that you are linked to the Aufero. You die and so does the connection." He stretched as he came to his feet. "We can look into it more tomorrow"—he looked at his watch—"later today."

It was nearly three o'clock in the morning, and I needed sleep and Josh looked like he did, too.

"It's okay if you stay in here." I didn't have to say anything more. He kicked off his shoes, slipped off his shirt and tossed it on the dresser, and slid out of his pants and was under the covers before I could even consider retracting my offer. He was asleep not long after. Sleep was something that I didn't find as easily. I had a powerful witch next to me, a vicious wolf in the other room, and was on the top floor of a massive building and I still didn't feel at peace enough to fall asleep easily.

The next morning, we were awakened by a banging on the door. Josh rolled over to face me, draping his arm over me. The knocking persisted, and Josh mumbled into the covers, "What?"

"Get up," Ethan commanded from the other side of the door before turning the knob. "Unlock the door."

"What time is it?" Josh grumbled.

"Eight thirty."

"Are you kidding me? Go away and come back in four hours."

"Get your ass up now."

"No, I had to work last night and I'm tired," Josh groused, and he gathered his pillow and began readjusting it.

Seriously, are we still calling what he does working? I realized that because of Josh, we had one of the most popular clubs in the city. However, calling what Josh did "work" was definitely taking creative license with the definition. Drinking with the city's "it" girls, socialites, and people famous for being famous; throwing back shots with the local talent; and hanging out in the VIP section with professional athletes was hardly what I called work, but as the manager that's what he did and the pack paid him for it. In fact, they paid him quite well.

Ethan pounded on the door again. "Josh I'm not playing with you, get up!"

The door creaked as Ethan pressed against it. It was only a matter of time before he broke the locks. I went to the door and cracked it. "We'll be out in a few minutes."

Ethan could barely focus on me as he tried his best to peek through the small slit.

"Why do you guys irritate each other so much?" I asked after I closed the door and headed to the bathroom. Josh laughed, but still rolled back over and was back asleep by the time I had showered and dressed.

The moment I entered the kitchen Ethan fixed me with a hard stare, his jaw clenched so tightly he could turn coal into diamonds. "Did you sleep well last night?" he asked.

"As good as could be expected," I said, moving toward the plate of food. Ethan was a lot of things but a bad cook wasn't one of them. I filled my plate with French toast, egg, steak and grabbed a yogurt from the refrigerator. "And you?"

Ethan shifted closer to me. The turbulence of his emotions filled the space between us and his predacious gaze remained planted on me. We stayed like that too long, a repeat of yesterday. He chewed on his words but refused to let them out and finally he turned and started out of the room. "Nothing is going on between me and Josh," I said.

His shoulders relaxed and by the time he had turned to face me, the tension in his jaw had eased some. "I'm not a teenager," I said, softly repeating his words from yesterday while looking over in his direction. Despite everything, there was still that hint of arrogance, and I just wanted to strip it away. I walked over to him and met his gaze with the same intensity. "Since you're not one, shouldn't you stop acting like one?"

The scowl was so firmly etched on his face that he had to work at relaxing it when Josh walked into the kitchen—dressed similarly to Ethan in a pair of boxers and nothing else. Neither one had bothered to comb their hair, the mussed bedhead didn't take away from their appearance at all. Standing in the kitchen half-naked seemed like just another morning to them. For a brief moment, I couldn't help but imagine what it was like for their mother, trying to wrangle two boys who clearly had an aversion to clothes into them every day. Something they carried into adulthood.

Returning to the food, I added some fruit to my plate and took a seat. "I didn't know breakfast was so formal."

Ethan and Sebastian both thought that Marcia was the likely culprit to have hired Sean and his crew, and like Sean she had disappeared, which made her guilt seem even more apparent. But while Sebastian and Ethan considered her disappearance evidence of her being dormant I didn't hold such belief. I had a feeling she was plotting something bigger, more extravagant, and that made me nervous. As we drove to my home, I tried not to display the nervousness that I felt with each passing moment. Sitting next to Ethan I was reminded of it as the steady beat of his fingers against the steering wheel kept time with my heartbeat, which was racing. Since her hired help failed, I doubted she would outsource next time. I wasn't safe. Even Josh's strongest ward wouldn't be a match for the five powerful witches of the Creed. Marcia was violent. She had derived great pleasure in gutting Ethan with shards of glass just to get me to give her the Aufero, and I'm sure she would do even worse to me.

"We can go back to the condo," Ethan suggested as we neared my house, and I was grateful for the offer.

I nodded, and he turned around and started back toward it.

Josh hadn't said a lot the entire trip, sitting in the backseat preoccupied by whatever was on his phone. He shuddered, his face becoming flushed, beads of perspiration forming along his brow. The turgid muscles of his neck protruded as his eyes eclipsed to night. He tensed again, closed his eyes, and whispered, evoking a spell. "Someone's trying to break the ward at the retreat—" Before he could finish Ethan's phone rang.

Sebastian's rushed voice was on the other line telling him that he needed to get to the pack's retreat home because it was under attack.

Neither Ethan nor Josh asked by whom. They assumed it was the Ares Pack in retaliation but I suspected it was Samuel. He had been gone for too long. It was only a matter of time before he attempted to get the third Clostra again. A fanatic with an agenda like him wouldn't go away quietly. A world without magic was such a heavily held tenet, he would not rest until he had done everything he could to make it a reality.

I expected it to be a full onslaught attack but I wasn't prepared for the number of were-animals that surrounded the house. Dismembered parts and lifeless bodies scattered over the open space, some so battered I barely recognized the faces and others I didn't know because they were part of the other pack. The ground was tinted red and sodden with blood. How did Samuel get them to come over to his side? How did a man offering to divest them of the ability to change into their animal forms convince them to fight for him?

While I focused on the fighting outside, Ethan watched his brother with concern. Josh winced, beads of sweat pooled at his temple, his eyes shifting to that darkness as he did when he used stronger magic. "He's breaking the blood ward."

It was the strongest ward a witch could do and because it required them to be actively connected to it at all times, they were rarely done. He'd placed one on the pack's retreat once we had the

Clostra in our possession. And now Samuel was trying to get to them.

Ethan jumped out of the car, Josh close behind him. I scanned the area but didn't see Samuel. We couldn't let him get to them.

Nearly thirty members of the pack were trying to hold off a small army of were-animals. Steven, Gavin, and Dr. Jeremy were in animal form along with the others. Steven stood over the body of a disemboweled lynx and was baring his bloodstained teeth at an approaching wolf. The vicious massive tiger that showed no signs of being our pack's mild-mannered physician took off after a retreating leopard that had realized it had lost the battle. Gavin coalesced with his panther whether in human or animal form; it was always present, making his transition to savage animal seamless. His black coat was sodden with blood, the bodies of several animals lying at his feet. Winter held her sword steady, prepared to engage as a small pack of wolves and a man started to approach the house.

Another man, who I hadn't seen before, approached Sebastian who was still in human form. The man's stocky build easily emulated that of an animal, I suspected he was a feline. His agile, graceful movements were quick and sharp and Sebastian watched his approach carefully. Within moments, it was a run as he charged at our Alpha. Sebastian lunged at him, and they hit the ground with a powerful impact.

A quick jab into his throat left the man gasping for air, and tears streamed down his face. A sharp thrust into his nose and his face became stained with the blood streaming from it. Unable to breathe or see, he wasn't able to respond when Sebastian tossed him to the ground, then grabbed him, a hand on his head and chin. I looked away—seeing someone's neck get broken is something you only need to experience once. I turned in time to dodge a hyena that lunged at me, hammering a front kick into his torso hard enough to send him back a few feet. He started for me again, and I shot another side kick into his jaw. I couldn't let him near me, or he would be able to use his best weapons: his claws and his teeth.

He was about to charge at me again when a sharp pop barked through the commotion. I looked over in time to see a bullet slice through Sebastian. The impact sent him back; another shot went through his chest and he collapsed to the ground. Winter tried to get to him as she slashed her sword chaotically through air, cutting through anything in her path. Ethan also started toward Sebastian but another were-animal lunged at him and they crashed to the ground. Seconds later that animal lay on the ground, its head twisted at an odd angle away from its body. The attacks continued, preventing us from getting to Sebastian. The car door was still open so I jumped into it to check the glove compartment for a weapon while trying to keep the hyena away. As I kicked at its face, it clenched my ankle in its mouth but the positioning put it at a disadvantage and its grip faltered enough for me to yank it loose while hammering my fist into the side of its skull. Its withdrawal allowed me enough time to search the glove compartment. I knew there had to be a weapon of some kind in it. A hunter's knife nearly fell out when I opened it. I had just grabbed it when the hyena jumped into the car, his teeth clamping down on my arm as he attempted to drag me out. I shoved the knife into his gut and twisted. It snarled and whimpered and I only had to twist a few more times before it released my arm. I lunged at it again, and forced it back until it gave up and took to the woods.

Scanning the area, I could see Winter heading toward Sebastian. Another shot whirled past her; it missed her but hit its intended target—Sebastian. He had stopped moving.

Winter's scream rang out through the commotion, a bloodcurdling sorrowful wail. Although I knew things weren't slowing down, it seemed like they did. Another shot punched through the ground barely missing his head. We all tried to get to Sebastian. Josh got to him first, his body covering his, and a protective field stretched out and covered them both. Sebastian was dead weight, solid muscle, and Josh struggled to lift him and position him in a way to move with him. Seconds later they were gone, a pool of blood left in his place. The animals retreated, running to get away. I wanted the shooter.

I ran in the direction from which the shots came. It was level, so the shooter wouldn't be in a tree. I didn't have to look long or hard. The piercing gaze stared at me from the woods, and a satisfied smile swept over his face as he turned and ran. Clenching the knife, I gave chase, following him into the thick bosk that was once our haven but now had been turned on us, camouflaging our enemies and cloaking them from sight. He darted around the trees, swiftly changing direction once in the middle of the thicket. It was too late when I realized I wasn't chasing him; he was leading me somewhere. To someone.

The jackal stood between two large oaks. That odd aura of magic drifted off it, its eyes different than I remembered, and as it slowly padded toward me, it shed his animal form with the ease of a person taking off a shirt. The odd platinum hair was the same as before, the distinctive amethyst eyes fixed on me in a hard stare. And I would never forget the ominous smile that vowed torture and death if his demands weren't met. Ethos.

I held the knife closer as he approached, ready to defend myself when he attacked. He was going to attack. I was sure of that. After all, I had stabbed him in the neck and left him for dead, and now Ethos was back.

We stood in silence just inches from each other; his relaxed appearance didn't match the stern gaze. He opened his hand; a sword appeared and he held it casually at his side. "Derrick, please stay, I may need you to hold something for me if Ms. Brooks chooses to become unnecessarily violent."

The violence was necessary. He may have just been responsible for killing Sebastian or at the very least had a big hand in it happening. Derrick didn't understand, but I did. Once I was dead he would need another body to host Maya.

"Ms. Brooks, are we going to be civilized so that I can allow Derrick to leave?" he asked in a low, polite voice. I forgot he was a courteous psycho—the worst kind. Polite enough to ask if it was okay for him to kill you now or if you wanted to wait to enjoy the moment a bit longer. He was that kind of cruel.

I hesitated and dropped the hand with the knife to my side, making sure to keep a distance between us. His sword disappeared, which most would have considered a good thing, but as easy as it disappeared for him, he could make my knife disappear, too. Without the Aufero, I was magicless and needed to be near it to use it. Josh and I had estimated that I had a range of about fifty to sixty feet to have access to its magic.

"My little amphora, we meet again. You've been quite busy since we last met, haven't you?"

"You seem to have been, too. After all, the not being dead part surely had to be rather time consuming," I said with a forced smile.

He chuckled. "That glorious sense of humor. How often has it nearly gotten you killed?"

"I lost count."

"*Hmm.* Well, this will be the only warning you get from me. I don't care to hear it. The next one will cost you dearly."

I guess I won't be cutting the tension with a joke this time around. "What do you want?"

"My desires haven't changed. Now that I've seen what has become of the Midwest Pack, I see they are in need of guidance more than ever."

It took everything in me to keep my eyes from rolling at the absurdity of his desires. Ethos wanted to be the "Lord of the Other-world." His words, not mine. Because the vampires and the pack were the most powerful, he wanted to acquire their allegiance first and force the others to concede to him. He failed, and it ended in an epic battle with me stabbing him in the neck and him trying to suffocate me with his magic. Ethan told me that Ethos was Maya's brother. It seemed like he was trying to reunite with his sister.

Taking several large steps, he was just arm's reach away from me, and I gripped the knife tighter.

"You are just full of surprises. I thought I had you when Marcia and I cursed you. I thought you'd be desperate enough that you would accept my help when I came to you. And once again, my little amphora rose to the occasion. How clever you have proven to be." There was an amused expectant look on his face. Did he expect me to be flattered that a narcissistic psycho was blandishing me?

Damn. It had been him in the cloak, hidden as he helped Marcia place a death curse on me. I should have known she would gladly accept his help. Drawn to power, she would ally herself with anyone who possessed magic that she could use. It all made sense now. Her ability to hide the Aufero with dark magic, her ability to perform dark curses that most witches couldn't. How long had she been aligned with him? How long had he been the puppet master pulling the strings behind everything? Had he given her the Aufero in return for her alliance?

"So Marcia has been your little business partner all this time. Then you aren't as wise as I thought, because I assure you the moment she sees a weakness that she can exploit, she will."

"You mean like stabbing me in the neck? Well, I've survived that. I am sure I can survive anything she doles out," he said, dismissing me. "Ethan, your lover, is the next in line as Alpha. As his partner, you will be able to influence him more than Sebastian. Hopefully Sebastian will not survive, and you and Ethan will understand the gift I have presented to you."

He was like a cat presenting a dead mouse to me. In the cat's mind, he had given the ultimate gift, a grand sacrifice, but in my eyes, it was just that—a dead gross rodent in front of me that I didn't want or ask for.

"You do realize there are other places to get your information than Wikipedia, right?"

The bark of a tree bit into my skin and I groaned as my head smashed against the trunk. Ethos had me by the throat, my knife now in his hand. Warm blood trickled from the cut the knife left. I slowed my breath, closing my eyes, warding off the sudden influx of dark magic that had swept over the area. Ethos's magic always felt wrong. It was a dark eruption of energy that overtook and destroyed everything in its path— a subversive wave that could never be controlled. I'd been foolish enough to try, and it never behaved as it should.

"We will have no more of that. Do you understand me?" he whispered.

Silence, extended and cold.

I studied him. The ability to assess a heartrate, changing breathing patterns, and eye blinks was a skill I hadn't mastered and probably wouldn't, but the nuances of expressions was something I was good at. There was a desperate resolve to him, urgency and even panic behind all of his blustering. As angry as he was, he would be just that—pissed off. But he wouldn't act on it. I'm not sure why, and at the moment I didn't care.

Gingerly taking hold of his hand, I moved the knife away from my throat and pushed him back. For whatever reason, he needed me alive or he would have killed me and used Derrick, someone who would have been more acquiescing.

I slowly backed away, watching his reaction as his eyes narrowed into small slits, the coolness of his ire drifting over them as the grip on the knife tightened.

"I'm leaving," I said.

When I turned a diaphanous wall closed around us. "Why don't you stay."

I pressed with force against the wall, but it gave and rebounded with equal force. It wouldn't give. Concentrating, I allowed the magic of my wolf to flow, accepting the pain as my joints slacked, preparing to contort and accommodate my new form. My skin tingled and pricked, the familiar tightness crawled over my body, tugging at my skin as I prepared to transform. It hurt like hell as tension against my bones increased, preparing to break some and stretch others as I transformed. The fur punched through my skin, making me grind my teeth to keep from yelling out. And then my heart lurched in my chest, as it stopped for that fraction of a second as the transition started. That small moment when the breath and heart stopped had always before convinced me it was the wolf trying to kill me. Sometimes I still felt like it. The symbiotic relationship I was supposed to have with my animal half, at times like this, seemed to be missing.

In wolf form I lunged at Ethos, he vanished, the wall disappeared, and I darted through the thick forest taking a circuitous route, only cogently aware of the magic in the air that breezed over me ineffectively while I was in wolf form. But a well-placed ward would stop me, or another magical wall. *Please have the ward down*, I thought as my paws pounded against the ground and I started for the pack's retreat. Would Ethos follow me there and risk having to go up against Josh and several angry were-animals? My howl held the necessary urgency and distress I felt, hoping someone heard it and could disarm the ward, because if not Ethos would catch me. He didn't want me dead but he definitely didn't want me near the pack.

I nearly skidded into the house, slipping on the pool of blood at the entrance and tumbling over Josh's foot. He closed the door. After giving me a quick once-over for injuries, he moved away, trying to get out of the way as people moved quickly throughout the room. Urgent voices went back and forth. I needed to concentrate to make them out.

"Get Ethan in here," Dr. Jeremy's voice rang over the chaos.

"How is he?" Winter asked, her words choppy and barely

discernable through the sobs.

"Get Gavin, too," Dr. Jeremy ordered.

"Winter, you have to move aside," Josh said softly. I didn't see him until he stepped closer, gently guiding her out of the way. His hand glided around her wrist. Eventually she pulled away and walked past me, her features distorted by her frown, stains from tears marked her skin. The weight of today hung heavy on her usual smooth, graceful movements now lumbered and fatigued. I whined a mournful sound. *Is he dead?*

There was too much commotion, Jeremy was still barking out orders, people were moving about, speaking with urgency, and I hadn't heard anyone say he was dead. Surely there would be more mourning if he was.

Josh said something but I couldn't make it out. I needed to change—deciphering conversations were harder in animal form. I followed Winter and Josh up the stairs and went into a room and changed. I found a t-shirt that was too big and a pair of sweatpants that fit okay.

The room that Josh and Winter went into was slightly ajar. I peeked in and found Josh with Winter's face buried into his neck. He was hugging her with one hand and gently stroking her hair with the other.

"Leave," he mouthed. My heart started to beat too fast, surely they could hear it. The hope I held on to that Sebastian was going to survive vanished. Winter must have felt the hopelessness, too. "Now," he mouthed again. I stepped back and the door closed in front of me. Leaning back against the wall I closed my eyes.

I convinced myself not to go down to the infirmary because I would have just been in the way. I was scared. It was so easy to think that were-animals were indestructible and easier to view Sebastian that way. Each time I tried to force myself to go downstairs, I came up with a million reasons not to. Instead, I laid on the floor in the room I thought was closest to the infirmary and listened to the noise. Lots of it, and I appreciated every minute of it. It meant things were happening. Sebastian was still alive, and Dr. Jeremy was fighting to keep it that way. It was silence that I dreaded: it meant the fighting had stopped, the battle had been lost.

The gruff sound of Dr. Jeremy barking orders, the machines that were just murmurs and swooshes from so far away, the urgent padding of the feet below were all welcome sounds.

Ethos's magic still lingered around me, dark, ominous, and powerful. Like the smell after a smoke-filled run, it fused to my hair and clothes, a constant reminder of his presence in my life. *He's alive. Dammit.* The most powerful purveyor of dark magic, who wanted to use me to control the otherworld, was alive.

The door opened and a blanket of different magic spread over the room, familiar but just as powerful. Despite being a little off, I welcomed the cool ocean breeze that defined Josh's magic. It was what I needed and the closer it came, the more comfort I felt. I opened my eyes to meet his, and at first curiosity blanched his appearance as he looked at me on the floor and then over to the empty bed next to me. He simply shrugged and lowered himself down and laid next to me. His hand covered mine, and I wasn't sure who was comforting who at this point, as he fiddled with a loose strand of my hair, his fingers coiling and uncoiling around it.

A sharp, ragged breath accompanied my words. "Ethos was behind the attack."

Josh noticeably tensed next to me, I'm sure remembering his last encounter with him. "That explains a lot. They took it all, the Clostra and *finis* book." *Finis* was the book that held the Gem of Levage after Josh used magic to contain it.

The tension on my hair was getting harder. It wasn't a nervous tug, I felt like he was ripping the strands out of my scalp. "Ouch."

Threads of my hair slipped out of his hand as he unraveled it from around his fingers and released it. "I'm sorry. I knew someone powerful had to be behind this, the magic was too strong. I have blood wards around the retreat and they shattered them as though they were nothing more than a simple ward made by an amateur." He came to his feet and started pacing. "I hope Samuel still has the third one."

Me, too, or we're done. Ethos had his eyes set on controlling the otherworld and I doubt he had any restrictions limiting what he was willing to do to get it, including threatening to divest us of our ability to shift.

"If he can't read them, they are useless," I said. "But the were-animals, how in the hell did he convince them to get involved?"

"The Ares have been staying low for a while, but Sebastian suspected they would eventually be trouble. Anderson, their Alpha, gave us the impression he wanted to head more than a small pack. The thirst for more was there. He was just waiting for the opportunity. What's better than aligning yourself with magic and power like Ethos's? Ethos probably promised him this pack or something just as enticing," Josh offered with a frown.

"It seems like Ethos is creating alliances with everyone." I told him everything that happened in the woods, including his attempt to get rid of Sebastian as a gift to me in order to allow my "lover" Ethan to take the position.

"Lover? Ethan?" His brow furrowed.

Yeah, focus on that part, not all the other horrific things I just told you. "I wonder if Anderson knows. Maybe he does and feels that being the Beta of everyone is still better," I offered.

He nodded absently. His thoughts were probably where mine were, on Ethos. He would be coming for me even more aggressively. I was his endgame, the key to his success, and he had an army of were-animals and a group of powerful witches as allies. The more I thought about it the sicker I got.

Josh's features were tight and withdrawn, desolation weighing down his movements, and he simply rested against the wall. Ethos wasn't the only thing on his mind. "How is she?" I finally asked.

Something changed—a torrent of magic was expelled, like a vacuum, suctioning out the oxygen in the room and replacing it with powerful layers of magic. I suspect this is what it felt like standing just inches from a tornado, bracing yourself to be yanked into the massive wind and hurled with force throughout the world without direction. Josh was magic. His emotions so entwined with it that he wasn't able to separate the two. I liked that he was stronger, but sometimes I wanted Josh, old Josh. The Josh I knew before secrets were revealed and he treated magic like a hobby and being near him and his magic was always comforting. His magic might not be dark but there was something different with it. I didn't feel the need to possess it because I felt I would never be able to completely control it, and like Ethos's magic I felt like it was easier to lose control of it and become subservient and be used as a vessel to do its bidding.

"I don't know," he said with a sigh. "I'm sorry I made you leave, but I couldn't let you see her like that," he said softly. "I couldn't do that to her."

Winter might have a lot of emotions but she seemed to be okay with expressing anger and disdain more than anything else. Affection and concern were something she displayed sparingly. It was shocking to see her respond like that. Was it just the loyalty that she had for the pack?

Josh turned and studied me for a moment, in that way that made me question whether or not he could read thoughts. I was convinced that he and Ethan could communicate with each other in nonverbal ways. But Josh was always more perceptive than most people and tuned to the subtle nuances of emotions. Talking to him never felt invasive; even strangers seemed to consider him a friend.

"I'm worried about her," he admitted. "If he doesn't recover ..." His voice trailed off and sat next to me. When I sat up, he slipped his hand under mine and linked our fingers. "He means a lot to her. She will never admit it, but he does. If it weren't for Sebastian, Winter would have been killed as a child." The placid blue eyes displayed the same worry that I felt. It wasn't just Winter who was taking it hard. "I'm assuming she never told you the story of how she came to live here in the states?"

I shook my head.

He released my hand, came to his feet and started to move slowly throughout the room. "I only know the story passed down from member to member. Ethan wasn't the Beta then and Sebastian had only been the Alpha for just a year or two, I think." He stopped pacing, considering his words very carefully. "There aren't a lot were-snakes. Some like to guesstimate that there are about fifty. Winter is the only one I know personally. An anomaly that some people consider a curse." He frowned, running nervous fingers through his hair.

I waited patiently for him to continue, but whatever he was thinking about seemed to irritate him. The frown became a fixture on his face, deepening with each passing moment. A hard, coarse wave of magic shot through the room. It scraped across my skin; the smell of his old magic was still there, and little remnants of "old Josh" magic still lingered long after the assault of its stronger companion. Josh—our Josh—my Josh—was still there.

"When she changed into a snake at four, her parents freaked out, especially since neither one was a were-animal." He made a face and stopped moving. "I will keep my speculations to myself because they don't put Winter's mom in a favorable light. But I find it odd that Winter doesn't have any of her dad's features. Needless to say they tried to find an answer to why their child was turning into a snake. A shaman directed them to their city's pack." Josh inhaled and took a moment to exhale before he continued. "They accepted Winter into their pack, or so Winter's mom thought. But they didn't: their intentions were to "fix her" because turning into a snake was an abomination or the result of a curse. After a long pause, "They considered Winter someone they had to save the city from. You turn into a wolf every full moon, no one has problem with that. Change into an oversized house cat when Mercury rises, and it's no big deal; but I guess turning into a snake during a lunar eclipse is the line in the sand. That's the thing that is just too weird to exist," he said with annoyed sarcasm. "The pack used all their resources to try to get rid of her curse and to rid the city of the dreaded 'snake-girl.' From my understanding, she had been to every witch, shaman, and magical being they could find to try to rid her of her curse. The Alpha decided if they couldn't 'fix' her then they would have to get rid of her." His face was red, jaw set as he clenched his teeth so hard that there was no way that it wasn't painful.

He started pacing again, but it didn't help. He was still flushed, his hand brushing away the hair that used to being there—he must not be used to the new shorter cut. He went to his "tell," biting on his nail bed. I waited for him to continue. "Winter's mother found out their plans and I'm not sure how she did it, but she got in contact with Sebastian and within twenty-four hours he had returned from Egypt to the States with her and her family."

"That pack just gave Winter to him?" I inquired, surprised. It was hard to imagine an Alpha anywhere, that was as obstinate and dogmatic as Sebastian, allowing someone to overrule his decision.

"Probably would have been better if they did, but of course they didn't. Sebastian had to challenge the Alpha and take over the pack. He wasn't the Elite then, but it really wouldn't have mattered. That status doesn't extend past the United States. But the rules of a challenge are standard everywhere. That day he challenged and won the position of Alpha. Of course the Beta challenged him and lost. The challenges continued until he had won against their five ranking pack members, and then Winter and her family were brought here. So she is alive because he pretty much demolished a pack to save her."

Sebastian was the king of jerks and definitely enjoyed wearing that crown, but he had a code that he lived by. Most of the time he seemed to be the only one privy to the boundaries and rules that made them, but this explained Winter's blind loyalty to the pack—to Sebastian.

Josh had taken a position near the door and I had a feeling he was itching to go check on Winter. "She's the only were-snake we know of."

"Joan said there were more," I said.

The smile didn't quite fully emerge; it was a polite response. "Ask her to introduce you to one. No one has ever seen another were-snake. There are rumors, but not one of them have been confirmed. I think it's something we've perpetuated because Winter isn't the type who enjoys the "special snowflake" title. She needed to think she wasn't the only one, but based on what I've seen, she is."

Winter has it right, it's never a good thing to be a special little snowflake. In the human world, you were adored and received accolades for being unique. In the otherworld, it could get you on the short list for being put down like a disease-ridden animal.

But knowing that Winter might be the only were-snake made her ability to control her animal half even more impressive. How did she learn so much about herself? "She didn't have anyone to help her with learning to shift?"

He shook his head. "Everything she's learned she did by trial and error. Even learning how to shift intentionally. She's one of the few who can't be assisted into animal form."

I could still hear noise coming from downstairs, and found comfort in it, but Josh didn't seem to feel the same way. He went back to biting the bed of his nail.

CHAPTER 7

I was a half an hour behind Josh before going downstairs. I didn't need to see the commotion. Each time I started downstairs I envisioned the grass, sodden with Sebastian's blood, and the pools of it that met me at the entrance. Death and blood—I had seen so much of it, I figured at some point I would become immune to it. I was still waiting for that to happen.

Preparing for the worst still hadn't worked. Seeing Sebastian lying on the bed stilled, on machines, tubes connected to him, was harder than I expected. Ethan lay in the bed next to Sebastian in wolf form, identical marks on his body and blood staining around the open wounds. Gavin, also in animal form, was across the room propped on his paws. I'm sure his position hid similar wounds on his chest. It was something they'd done before, when I first encountered them and Steven was badly injured. The stronger members of the pack were able to absorb some of the injury, which in theory was fine and you saved the life of the one most severely injured, but then you had more injured pack members. I felt its magic and how it worked but I'm not capable of doing it. I assumed that Sebastian had only involved me because I needed it. Steven was dying and I felt helpless, and at that moment I felt like I *needed* to help—to make a difference.

Winter and Steven wouldn't be there. As a were-animal changed and not born, Steven couldn't have helped, and Winter couldn't because she was a lesser-species. They both would have had a harder time healing.

"Is he going to be okay?" I finally asked Dr. Jeremy, who was sitting in his desk chair across the room. Acculturated to violence and near-death injuries, he usually handled crises and emergencies with the expertise and fortitude necessary to deal with such situations—usually with Kelly at his side. But she wasn't around, and he seemed to be feeling the effects of her absence.

His shoulders dropped with his sigh as he looked over the room at the depleted bodies and our Alpha, who didn't look like he was going to make it. "I don't know. They weren't regular bullets. His body was injected with silver upon impact. I think I flushed it all out, but if I didn't, then he will heal slower, respond to things as though he is wholly human. I won't know much more for a couple of hours."

That was about all I got from Dr. Jeremy before he began to go into medical terminology, giving complex explanation of his injuries. He was too kind to tell someone he didn't want to be bothered, so he slipped into MD mode, giving information that a layman wouldn't understand and eventually would give up on attempting. Kelly ordinarily was there to translate, and times like this I missed her even more. She was the emotion that no one would show, often found in the corner or giving a litany over someone.

I went to Gavin first and softly said his name as I brushed his silken coat, black with an undertone of midnight blue, which made him one of the most beautiful animals in the pack. Lethargically he lifted his head, the marble eyes dull as he worked to keep them open. He leaned into me, and I started to stroke him until his massive head bumped me away, then a swipe of his paw nudged me even farther. *That's right. Stay true to yourself. Sick or well, you're always a caustic tool.*

Josh sat in a chair next to his brother, his hands resting on the paw closest to him. Ethan's eyes were open but he looked as though he was using all his strength to do so. Learning my lesson from Gavin, I simply said hi and started to walk away, when a claw caught the edge of my shirt and gave it a light tug. I sidled in close to him and moved slightly on the bed. Did he want me up there? His massive body took up most of it, so I sat sideways at the top. He dragged his body up a few inches and laid his head in my lap.

I didn't think I could doze off in such an uncomfortable position, but I had and was awakened by Ethan, who was showered, dressed, and looked nowhere near as worn as the wolf that was in my lap a few hours ago. But he was plagued by the same troubled eyes. Gavin, too, was up and dressed, and as usual he'd splayed in a corner where he seemed to become nothing but a shadow against it.

Not creepy at all. Nope, totally normal. Gavin, you want to try to be more menacing and weird?

Sebastian was no longer in the room. "Where is Sebastian?"

"We moved him to another room." The machines he was attached to were still in the infirmary: that was a good sign, so I didn't understand why Ethan looked so bleak.

"He's better?"

"It's been twenty-four hours so we took him off. His wishes."

Twenty-four hours? How long had I slept?

He fished a set of keys out of his pocket and handed them to me. "You have to leave. Your home has a blood ward and everything was changed early yesterday. It should be safe, but if you want to go back to the condo, I understand," he said in a stolid voice. He barely made eye contact.

Something was off. When I saw Steven and Winter walk past the door down the hall I had a strange feeling. Ethan wasn't looking at me, but past me, speaking in that same tone they switched to with things that involved pack rules and laws. *What happens after twenty-four hours?* My heart raced, my thoughts murky and chaotic as I tried to think back to the classes. I tried to remember the rules. What happens when the Alpha can no longer lead? What was the procedure? Could he just leave? Did he face a challenge? *Dammit, I wish I had listened instead of secretively watching videos and people doing stupid stunts on YouTube. I should have been listening to the boring history, the rules.* They took him off the machines—were there some type of DNR rules? My head started to pound and I kept waiting for Ethan to look at me, but instead all I got was a stoic expression and no eye contact.

They called it "relieving," another soft word for *euthanasia.* Did he have a choice? Was this his choice? Did he feel that if he could no longer lead the pack he would rather be dead? *Everything about our rules, codes, and dogmas is stupid.* We weren't animals, we weren't soldiers. We were humans first. *Ignore the fucking rules!*

Ignore Sebastian's requests!

I thought the words were only in my head until one look at Ethan, and I realized I had shouted them at him.

The words were suspended in the air. I had said them. All the disdain and anger I had for the pack, for the rules, for this day had spilled out in an uncontrolled rant.

Ethan looked at me, silently taking in my words, his face blank. I expected anger, censure, and a fervent rebuttal about how the rules kept us strong and were needed for our survival. But all I got was silence. They were the rules, and he would abide by them until his death, simply because they were pack rules. Other things he ignored with discretion, but the packs rules were sacred and he wouldn't.

"I don't want to leave," I finally said. The rules weren't sacred to me—I couldn't care less about them.

"It's not about your wants, Sky. I am tired, don't make me force you out."

I started to cross my arms, a passive act of defiance, when another person passed the door. I knew very little about him, but I knew that Steven was sure that he wanted his position as fifth. Was this the changing of the guard? Were they so callous as to "relieve" Sebastian and then start promoting people? We were being attacked and I realized things had to be handled quickly, but it just made me angry and I was about to voice it when I looked at Ethan and stopped.

I thought I'd see anger at my defiance, but it wasn't there; instead, a hint of grief that must have been too great because he didn't seem like he could hide it. The day had taken as much from me as it had from him. I could fight, defy, and scream like a banshee and at the end it, Ethan would go by the rule—Pack Rules.

I dropped my arms and then my head. "Okay."

He lifted my chin until my eyes met his and then he kissed me gently on the lips. Controlled and empty and very unlike Ethan. As though everything he had to offer had been drained from him.

My intentions were to go back to the condo, but I ended up at Quell's. He studied me carefully as I followed him to his stairs in silence. He frowned, tracing the small line that Ethos had left on my neck when he pressed the knife to it. The cut was barely noticeable and tomorrow it would be gone, but the way Quell looked made me think that it looked worse than I remembered.

"Why would they let someone do this to you?" His cool fingers still moved along the ridges of a small cut that he was treating like a gaping wound in need of urgent medical help.

"Why did you let this happen to me? They had just as much

control over this happening to me as you did. It's not even a large cut, it was done to make a statement. I took care of it."

His brow furrowed. "If you took care of it, why do you look like that?"

"Like what?"

"Sad," he said, putting his hands over mine. His dark eyes rested on me with such gentleness it was hard to hold it together. But I did. If I started talking about it, I wouldn't stop and would be in a state that wouldn't have helped me.

I detected the light hint of primrose in the air, on the sofa. It seemed to be everywhere. Fiona.

"Do you like her?" I asked.

He nodded. I'm glad he nodded, because based on his expression he seemed indifferent. I rested back against the sofa, giving his home a once-over. On the kitchen island was a clean plate and glass. I wondered if they were the only ones he had or if Fiona had brought her own to leave. The glazed orange stoneware plate went well with the decor of the kitchen so I imagined they were already there.

There were other traces of Fiona in his life. Draped across the chair in the living room was a sweater, and a blanket was folded in the corner. I didn't remember it being there before. How many days had it been? Three? Five?

"Have you fed from her?" I knew she spent the night the first time she came over but I wasn't sure what else happened. If he liked her, she would be safe.

Midnight eyes narrowed and held my gaze. His hand linked with mine, and when he closed his eyes, I started to worry. *What happened?*

"And?"

"And, nothing," he said softly.

I needed more. "Is she okay?"

"Yes."

Covering the hand that rested over mine, I asked, "Will you tell me about it?"

"She's not you," he finally admitted after moments of silence. His movements were so quick, his transition from being next to me on the sofa to being on the other side of the room, his body resting against the wall, arms crossed over his chest, was nearly instantaneous. "She's not you," he said again.

His eyes remained closed as he pressed his head firmly against the wall.

My hands washed over my face several times: I wasn't sure how to handle this. "I need you to talk to me. You said you liked her—what's wrong?"

"It's easy with you. I know when to stop. I care about stopping. With her the only thing that keeps me from"—he stopped and finally looked at me—"is that you gave her to me. She's your gift to me and I don't want to damage her."

Despite what Quell had become to me, first and foremost he was a vampire. They held the belief that humans were items, things to be used for pleasure and food and they gifted them to one another in the same manner. Their garden, the people who lived in their home, served as dine-in dinner, nothing more than sources of food and sometimes sex. Fiona was just food, a commodity.

"She's *not* my gift to you." *That did not taste good coming out.* I tried not to fixate on discussing a woman like she was a shirt I was loaning. "The other day was my first time meeting her. But I liked you two together."

It was selfish, I know; but if he could feed from her without killing her and she was okay with him doing so, it was a good situation for us all. It made my life less complicated, it made others safe, and it got Michaela off my back.

"Ethan said that you wanted us to meet." *Dammit, Ethan.*

The relationship between me and Quell was based on honesty and mutual acceptance of our imperfections, and I refused to allow Ethan and his deception for the good of all to change that. "In Ethan's misguided way he is trying to help. Fiona makes things safer for me," I admitted.

There wasn't a need to go into detail about what happened between Michaela and me because I was sure he knew. He nodded slowly, but his attention remained on the wall behind me. His face relaxed into solemn acceptance and sadness.

"Quell, are you happy?" Of all the questions I had swirling around in my head, none of them meant anything if he wasn't happy. As he considered the question, I realized that he probably never thought about it. Vampirism had been an escape, but did he enjoy it? Demetrius seemed to love it and if he didn't, he was one hell of an actor. I could almost imagine that he did a happy dance with jazz hands each time he thought about his life. And Michaela was having a jovial time making everyone's life hell just for sport. Each day was just another to one up the cruelty of the day before. Quell didn't seem to find the same joy as they did in the immortal life. He was just going through the motions.

He spoke so softly I could barely hear him. "Happiness isn't something I strive for or feel that I deserve," he confessed.

"Then what *do* you strive for?"

"To be content. I am content when I am with you, and I wish I could explain why but I am, and I don't want to lose you."

"You'll never lose me. We are friends and will always be. But what's the point of this, if you aren't happy?" It came out wrong, it seemed like I was telling him to off himself if he wasn't happy. "Whatever makes you happy, you need to do it, because *just existing* is silly."

I waited, expecting him to tell me what made him happy and ignoring the dark things that popped into my mind. *He killed five women in a span of three days, please don't let him say that made him happy.* And when he was in the military during WWII he did unspeakable things that made him feel less worthy of being considered human, but he never said he disliked doing it. What if those were the things that made him happy and I just pushed him into it? *Quell, say something.*

I nearly jumped when he settled in next to me before I could start another sentence. I didn't think I would ever get used to the deftness and speed of their movements. "I'm happy when I'm here." He pressed his fingers to my temple.

That's even worse. I used to try not to think about anything because I knew he could read my thoughts, but the more comfortable I was with him, the less I cared about shielding him from getting a front-row seat to the viewing of *Hot Mess—The Sky Brooks Story.*

"That's it?" I smiled. "Fine, if a stroll into crazy town is all you need to be happy, I am here for you."

His hand rested against my neck, his fingers gliding gently against the pulse of it. He ran his tongue over his lips, the familiar hunger present. The same kind that led to him nearly killing me before he had awakened. Thirst. His desire came to life with a roar. He might have liked my entertaining thoughts, but I had a feeling he enjoyed the blood even more. All the signs were there for me to get the hell out of there—he looked dangerous. But it was Quell, and our peculiar bond transcended my fear, his primal and unbridled desire. I stilled as he moved closer and nestled his face in the curve of my neck. His words hummed against my skin as he spoke.

"May I?"

"Yes."

I winced when his fangs pierced my skin, but he was gentle, taking slow draws as he laced his fingers through my hair bringing me closer to him. The numbness took over quickly and the pain subsided and I relaxed into him and the familiarity of it. And I opened my mind, allowing him to read my thoughts, my frustrations and fears. I think after the feeding he would be cured of the desire to be in my head. He'd stopped for some time but his face remained cradled near my neck. His tongue laved gently over the opening, cool and soothing as he closed the punctures. His lips brushed against my cheek as he spoke. "What can I do?"

"Nothing," I said, coming to my feet. Nothing truer had ever been spoken. Absolutely nothing. I had let him in but there wasn't anything he could do about it, and even if he could I doubt I would have let him. This was my problem, my mess, and it was time for me to clean it up. I took ownership—this was my battle to win.

The dark mist of his magic welcomed me before I could get to the door that he'd left slightly open. The malodor of Ethos's magic seemed wrong and was a reminder that it came from a dark place. Nothing good could come from it, and I began to appreciate that Ethan had taken it from me. During my last battle with Ethos, I wasn't sure whether it was to kill me or to use his magic as a way to track me, but he forced so much into me, I thought I was going to die. Josh was able to remove it, but like any magic, it was hard not to be seduced by it—to long for the ability to have it easily accessible. I kept some of it, deceiving Josh into believing he had removed it all. Magic was power the ultimate weapon, and I wanted some of it. I didn't care that it was a way for him to track me or use it against me.

Having access to magic so strong can easily change people. It made me wonder if Ethos was really a mad man, or if he, too, had become a servant of diablerie and no more a master of his volition than a puppet. But I didn't believe that: my newly found in-depth contemplation about Ethos was nothing more than me procrastinating. I didn't want to talk with Ethos and be forced to listen to elaborate plans to conquer the otherworld.

The dust from the shattered ward loomed in the air and I expected nothing else. With the ward broken, Ethos could just *travel* into my house and I assumed that he had.

He sat on the sofa with a cup of coffee in hand as one would when you break in someone's home. *Isn't that what you do, break in and then fix yourself a warm beverage?*

His odd eyes gleamed with ominous amusement as I walked in.

"Would you like a piece of cake? Biscotti? Or perhaps a cookie to go with your coffee?" I asked mordantly.

Missing the sardonic cadence in my voice, he smiled graciously, and with a humble nod declined the offer. He just didn't get me.

He tipped his cup to me, took a long draw, and then sat it on the side table. "You left before we could finish our conversation."

"Sorry, I thought me leaving was as good as telling you to go to hell. Okay, well if that isn't enough why don't I tell you now. Go. To. Hell."

"My amphora, I do enjoy your obstinacy. My victory will be all the sweeter when you concede," he said. "Please, have a seat."

"I prefer to stand."

He relaxed back on the sofa and took another sip from the cup, settling in to quiet insolence. We sat in silence for nearly three minutes deadlocked into a blatant game of defiance.

"What do you want?" I finally asked.

He extended his arm toward the loveseat across from him, inviting me to sit down. I hesitated until his brows raised and eyes narrowed. It wasn't so much of an invitation as a demand.

"My amphora, it is really time for you to make a decision."

"About what, how I plan to kill you?"

He eyed me with mild indifference that only made me angrier. Chris and Winter had the right idea, have weapons stashed in every possible place. I hadn't gone to the extremes they had, but it brought me comfort that I had a knife under the loveseat and sofa in my living room, and all I had to do was just push the loveseat back to gain access. There was another under the sofa that Ethos was sitting on. And a 9mm under the cushion on the far right of the loveseat. I couldn't shoot a house from ten feet away but I was close enough to him that I doubt I would miss. The problem—he could travel, and he was faster than Josh. I would have to move quicker.

In a smooth sweeping wave, he came to his feet and was behind me. I took some slow breaths. I knew he wouldn't kill me and that was the only thing I could find solace in. But it was like I was standing in front of a loaded gun held by an unstable person: did I truly trust that he wouldn't pull the trigger? I jumped when he rested his hands on either side of my shoulder.

"You have put me in a very awkward position and forced me to end a very good relationship with Marcia. Why couldn't you have just left it alone and allowed her to have the Aufero? She would have been happy—and I would have made you happy. Instead you nearly killed her to get it back. I wished I could have been there, I'm sure it would have been quite entertaining." As quickly and smoothly as he had found a position behind me, he was back on the sofa, relaxed.

"No worries, you'll be present for your death," I said.

With an annoyed sigh he sat back, ignoring the threat. He looked against the wall, where I had left the Aufero, still in the ripped canvas bag, exposed. "You all behave as though you shouldn't be left to your own devices. Always scrambling for positions of power that can be so easily snatched away. I gave her the little toy and she gave me her alliance, only to have control over the witches and to be left in peace. But you messed that up. What will I do with you?"

"Let's come to a compromise, okay?" I suggested.

The contrite smile was a blemish on his odd face.

"You're a kick-ass magical thingy, have you considered Vegas? Maybe you can get a job as a magician or an illusionist. You'll make a crap load of money, and talk about being adored—you will have legions of fan girls and fan boys. They will worship you and adore you. And if that isn't enough, think about the money you'll

make. Not only will you have magic groupies but more women"—
I paused to give him an assessing look—"or men, who cares? I just
want you to be happy."

There was a long pregnant silence.

"Or?" he finally asked.

"Or what?"

"You said a compromise. What's the other option?" he asked,
frowning.

"*Hmm*. I got nothing. So either you do that or I kill you." The
ice in my voice made me shiver.

He laughed, a deep boisterous sound that reverberated
through the room, just as intense and overpowering as his magic.
"You're cute."

"I always get *cute*. Never *hot* or *sexy*. Is it the nose?" I tapped the
tip of it. "It's too nubby, isn't it?"

The smile vanished, his eyes narrowed to slits, and he blazed
with anger. "I strongly advise you to take me more seriously," he
growled.

"And I advise you to take *me* seriously. If your way of getting
me to concede is to kill everyone I care about, then what the fuck
do I have to live for? So the way I see it, I kill you or die trying and
guess who I take with me? Your little prized possession. You have
your option, if not Vegas, New York is nice, too."

I finally took a seat on the loveseat with the knife underneath.
I would end this now. "So you tell me, what will I do with you?"

The irritation marred his odd features as he took long
sweeping looks around the room. "She's getting stronger," he said.
"It's only a matter of time before she is the pilot and you're just a
bystander. I am giving you the chance that she will not."

"Well if that were true, wouldn't you just wait until she is?
Then the two of you can wreak as much damage as you like
without restriction. Do you really think I am that stupid, or are
you so arrogant you think I will believe your lies because you
want me to?"

He held on to the haughtiness, his lips pressed into a tight moue. "To the contrary, I wish you were unintelligent—it would make things much easier. You are pushing my tolerance to the limit but I will break you, amphora."

And that was what bothered me so much. Chris told me that an amphora was just a vessel, neither good nor bad, a tool to be used. I started to think of all the things I could do, and I wondered whether or not there was any good in me at all. I could read the Clostra, a book with powerful and draconian spells that had the ability to wipe magic from the world. I could feed vampires—something were-animals couldn't do. Manipulating and changing magic from dark to natural and vice versa was something even the most skilled witch was unable to pull off. And I was a Moura responsible for guarding a protected object and mine had the ability to divest people of their magic. Marcia was able to use it, but under my control it was far more dangerous. What good was there in my abilities? And now this psycho wanted to use me to control the otherworld. I swallowed hard and thought about the knife next to my feet.

Kill Ethos—again—and this all goes away. I could go back to my somewhat normal life, or what had become *my* normal.

I was about to push the loveseat back, when the Aufero manifested in his hand. It was still the odd orange and black color and it stretched to its brinks, controlled by him. He assessed it, seemingly introducing himself to it, getting a feel for the magic it held, its strengths and weaknesses, considering the magic that changed it into something just as dark as that he possessed.

His lips curled into a mirthless smile; as his brows came together, and the Aufero twirled effortlessly just above his face. "More of your friends can die. You decide how many, because you will not win this," he promised. "You'll give me your decision tomorrow or—"

It was over.

There was so much truth to what he said. More people would

die. This would not end until he was dead or everyone I cared about was.

I pushed the loveseat back, grabbed the knife, and lunged at him in one swift move. The knife didn't connect. He moved too fast, dropping the Aufero, which rolled a couple of feet away. He snapped into position and pushed me forward, and I gained enough leverage to spin, shoving the knife into his side and grabbing hold of him to keep him from disappearing again. I ripped it out and lunged forward again, aiming for his neck. He moved enough to protect the carotid, and I jabbed into the large muscles of his neck, blood spurted onto my shirt, and he hissed out in pain. I held him, concentrating as the protective field formed around us; as the dark bubble ensorcelled us, the myriad of magic, most of it different, chaotic, and uncontrolled, rebounded against it. The oxygen became thin, and my lungs grappled for enough to keep me conscious. I had to hold out. Enveloped in a sort of gas chamber, I needed to stay conscious just seconds longer than Ethos. I could see his struggle for oxygen, the strain in his face as he willed his heart to beat a little faster, the panic when he realized it wouldn't. The field shuddered as he attempted to break it. His magic pounded relentlessly against it, and each time it clamored into me like a fist. I had to hold it.

His eyes glowed with anger, a powerful burst of magic demolished the field, and he waved his hand, slamming me into the wall on the other side of the room. He barely held on to his human form: it wavered, his anger heightened, and I didn't think preserving my life was important to him anymore. I concentrated, trying to remember everything Josh had taught me over the years. But I didn't have use of his magic, just the Aufero, and it was magic gone terribly wrong. It didn't matter, because good magic, bad magic, obscure magic, I didn't care which one it was, I needed it to kill Ethos.

The same anger that had taken me over with Michaela had

reasserted itself, and instead of fear, he showed appreciation. Would he appreciate how many ways I wanted to make him dead?

"I do believe Steven will be next, the coyote, right?"

Magic shot through me like an explosion, sending Ethos into the wall, drywall crumbling behind him.

Countering with just as much force he slammed me into the wall where he left me pinned, immobile. Magic was like a live wire inside me ready to be released, and the more I remained restricted the more it clamored to be free. It coursed through me in a way that was unfamiliar—yet, familiar. I could taste it, smell, see the various colors of its existence as it painted the air. It felt strange—I felt strange.

"Ah, there she is," Ethos said, closing in on me.

He was right—there was a "she," because I didn't feel like me. The anger didn't feel like mine. The control of the magic had exceeded my ability and wasn't mine.

The curiosity that covered his face quickly slipped into intrigue. "Maya," he said softly. "Wake up. It's time."

Something stirred in me. He felt it, too. A smile licked at the corners of his lips. An insatiable thirst for power drenched his being, I felt it. Longing for a time when people like him ruled and everyone else were just servants were my desire and memories. She possessed that greed, and it felt odd—dangerous. Living far too long in a docile body, one that only managed magic but never truly controlled it, she wanted control and it punched through my chest.

He spoke gently in a language I didn't recognize. His mesmeric gaze pinned me and I couldn't manage to pull away from it. But it felt like he was trying to usher her forward in a hostile takeover of my body. He seduced out complacency and her desire for power and reverence for a moment became mine. The thirst was there waiting to be quenched.

Damn.

I looked away, stumbling back as I snatched control again. My vision was different, viewing the world from a different position. A position where Ethos sat, where he viewed we would be. I tried to temper it. For so long I had been in control, and now Maya was trying to claw her way out.

Damn!

The harsh reality dawned that for so long I just didn't have the control that I needed. I existed because of a host I knew nothing about, Ethos wanted me to control the otherworld and saw me as nothing but a means to an end, Sebastian was dying if he wasn't dead already, and probably more would die if I didn't comply with Ethos. There weren't many other things to describe what went on in my head except my life was a clusterfuck and I didn't have any more care to give. This wasn't a life, living in fear, knowing that my friends would be assassinated because this ass had delusions of grandeur and a narcissistic need to be revered like a god.

I was so far into I-don't-give-a care land that I was dangerous. And it was the source of what drove me. I didn't care if I hurt him, didn't care if the only thing standing at the end of this fight was the frame of the house. I didn't care if I drained the Aufero and shattered it into bite-size pieces of bad magic. Vengeance was the driver and I was so happy to be along for the ride.

Ripping from the wall it felt like I lunged through a glass window, the shard of broken magic stabbing into me. Panting, I needed to be close enough to use the Aufero's magic, within ten feet usually worked. I pulled it to me and twirled my finger, binding Ethos's arms at his side. I wasn't sure if this would stop him. More skilled magic wielders didn't need to use their hands to focus the magic, but it made it easier.

Forming the protective field around us, I held it as he used magic to thrust against it, trying to break it. Short gasps escaped from him as he attempted to find what little oxygen existed in the space. He slid to the ground, but I held it, my mind drifting from the lack of oxygen, my heart struggling to take that needed beat. I had to keep it up just a little longer. I clawed at the life that was slowly being pulled from me. Just one more minute, I could do it. *Ethos, stop moving.*

I kept it up. He flinched—magic punched me harder than I could ever imagine, and the field shattered, decimated to the point not even its existence lingered in the air as it usually did. He panted, his sharp gaze holding mine. I clenched the knife harder, ready to engage, when a wolf exploded through the door, and his claws embedded in Ethos's back, his teeth fixed on his shoulder. Ethos howled in pain, moving wildly as he attempted to throw Ethan off of him. When Ethan's grip loosened, Ethos disappeared, leaving a trail of his blood.

Grabbing a towel from the kitchen, I wiped up some of it, and then put it in a sealed bag to preserve it. His blood had helped locate him before, maybe we could use it again. I plopped on the sofa next to Ethan, who sprawled out next to me. When he melted into his human form I pulled the throw off the sofa and tossed it over him. He allowed it to fall from him as he sat up, baring everything I tried to cover.

There is nothing wrong with a little modesty, Ethan.

"That was a hell of a fight," he said.

"Not really, I failed. I needed more time." My failure made me feel like I might as well have been the one who shot Sebastian. Guilt was one of those emotions that lived in a place of irrational thoughts. It dragged you through your other emotions and tossed you about so aggressively that feeling it, even for minutes, left me exhausted and feeling pangs of remorse.

"You can't blame yourself. You did what you could."

"Did Josh tell you everything?" I asked. With all the commotion, he was the only person I had told about my altercation with Ethos and the shooter.

He nodded. "Everything, including that you went after the shooter with a knife." He shook his head and scrubbed his hand over the light stubble that had grown over the past few days.

His lips rested somewhere between an annoyed smile and a smirk. "So you literally took a knife to a gunfight," he exhaled, shaking his head. I slid my hand under the sofa until I felt the metal handle of the knife, pulled it out, looked at a target—a pillow that had been displaced through everything—and threw the knife, hard. It wedged into the pillow.

"I know how to use a knife. Can't shoot the side of a house from ten feet away but I can use a knife." Although a nine iron was my weapon of choice. People would laugh at it until they were whacked with it one good time and then laughter would stop. Add a little power to the swing and you will definitely get their attention. Swords are good, too, and I don't care what anyone says, they require minimal skill. Just swing one and you'll hit something that will make someone hurt. But you can't really walk around the house with a sword strapped to your back in a city; a knife can be easily concealed.

Ethan considered me for a long time. And I could tell what he was thinking. I had changed. But I couldn't tell how he felt about it. Sometimes I hated it, and longed for the person who was oblivious of such violence, darkness, magic, and all the odd things that existed in this world.

I could feel his gaze on me but I couldn't meet his eyes. Instead I looked down at my blood-covered hands and blood-washed shirt. "I still haven't gotten used to other people's blood on me," I admitted. I had times where I woke up in the woods with rabbit or deer blood, and I didn't like it, but I suspect no one really gets used to other's blood on them.

He nodded slowly, quietly concerned as he sat in silence. He looked down at my shirt again, the dent in my wall, and back at me. Tracing along my jawline, his finger ran its course and then rested along my neck. The side of my neck that was probably still discolored from Quell feeding from me. "You went to see Quell first?"

I didn't respond. He already knew the answer, and I could sense the shift in his mood.

"How is Sebastian?" I asked, finding his gaze more difficult to hold. The rolls of deep gray that moved along his eyes were more subdued but still present. He dropped his hands from my neck.

"He's breathing on his own, Dr. Jeremy seems hopeful. You didn't answer my question."

And that was not by accident. Don't wanna.

I wasn't sure why Ethan needed people to admit to things. He waited patiently for me to give an answer, and I was sure if it had taken me an hour to do so, he would have been there sitting next to me in silence.

"Yes."

"Okay. You should get the blood off." He stood, extending his hand, and when I took it he led me to the bathroom and remained distant and silent as he turned on the water in the shower, holding eye contact with me the whole time. With clinical detachment, he helped slide my shirt off and then slipped off my pants.

Say something!

Maybe the silence was better. My fight with Ethos and how he seemed to be trying to awaken Maya kept racing through my mind. I wanted to make sense of it before I started discussing it with others. I had taken back control, but I wondered if that would always be the case.

He bundled up the soiled clothes and left, still in silence, looking back at me once more before he left the bathroom.

I stood under the shower until the water ran clear, hoping to cleanse my mind enough to think of a plan. It gnawed at me—how did Ethos get the Aufero in the first place? My thoughts were interrupted when the shower door slid open and Ethan stepped in and sidled in next to me. The water drummed against our skin, the fragrance of my strawberry body wash wafted through the steam-filled air, a far better scent than blood. He still hadn't said anything. As the water kept splashing, blurring my vision, his fingers grazed over my neck where Quell had fed from earlier. Warm lips melded over the spot as he licked at the tender area. Gently his lips moved to my jaw until they reached my mouth. He kissed me, soft and commanding. His languid fingers glided along my shoulders, my breast, down my stomach until they had reached the intimate spot between my legs. I gasped; his kiss became more forceful. Ethan wore his emotions too close to the surface and always had an air of turbulence that seemed to be waiting to expunged. The power of his touch commanded my body and I relaxed into him.

The water cascaded over us as he pressed me into the wall. His experienced sensual hands roved over my body, gliding over the curves of it, until he reached the intimate place between my thighs. His lips captured my gasp as his fingers slipped inside of me coaxing, a feeling of pure eroticism. I dug my fingers into the thick cords of muscle on his back as he nipped my lips before tasting them again. His heavy body rested against me. I clung to him even tighter, hungry for more, my fingers entwined in his hair pulling him, unable to sate the need to feel him closer to me. When he tried to move back I hugged him tighter, afraid that we would lose the moment. Afraid that I would lose him. All the issues between us and the problems of the day dissolved. I needed it, even if it were just for the moment and a pseudo minute of peace. I'd take it.

Guiding me out of the shower, he stayed close. His lips barely left mine as he made a feeble attempt to wipe off some of the water with a towel he grabbed off the rack. The warmth of his body and touch as he lifted me made the cool air that brushed against my damp skin barely noticeable. I curled my legs around his waist even tighter feeling the heat that connected us at my core. My lips remained pressed against his and refused to part even as laid me on the bed. With reluctance, he pulled away, his lips leaving trails of warmth as they slowly crept down my body, kissing every part of me until I was panting, unable to catch my breath.

His muscular body, draped over me and nestled between my legs as I ran my hand along his back. Ethan pressed into me. I gasped at the pain, my fingers digging into his back. Closing my eyes, I succumbed to the unfamiliar pain and tried to relax. He rocked his hips into mine gently; I sucked in another sharp breath as he eased my legs wider to accommodate him. And he waited, his warm breath beating against my lips, his liquid silver gaze holding mine, waiting for me to get used to him inside of me.

"Você está bem?" Are you okay?

I didn't answer immediately because I wasn't. When I finally nodded, he made gentle, firm pushes until he broached the restriction. I bit into my lip, breaking skin. I felt him, all of him inside me. My nails burrowed deeper into the sinewy muscles of his back. Ethan remained still allowing me to get used to the turgid invasion.

Then he moved slowly in me, languid gentle movements, and his hips hit a gentle rhythm that managed to bring me intense pleasure and a new discomfort so blended that I couldn't distinguish the two. The pleasure quickly overshadowed everything and I wanted more. More pleasure, more carnal bliss, more him.

His muscular body draped over me and nestled between my legs as I ran my hand along his side. He was gentle as his hips moved against me, intimately joining us. I attempted to hold his gaze but eventually closed my eyes, unable to ignore the intensity of his passionate unfettered sexuality that existed even through the gentleness.

"Olhe para mim," Look at me, he whispered, watching me attentively. My eyes lifted to meet his. I unfurled at the fervency of his movements, his fingers grazing over my body while his lips brushed over me. I couldn't watch him anymore. No longer in command of my body, I felt as though he had taken it over. I

closed my eyes, and we began to move in a fevered rhythm as he elicited more from me than I thought I was capable of giving. I clawed at him as ecstasy overtook me, pulling him closer as he moved deeper inside me. He kissed me harder as his movements escalated, pulling me deeper into pleasure. I hung on to him tighter hoping the feeling would never end. We reached a point of heated euphoria that elicited utter ecstasy and gentle moans from us both. His lips caressed the pulse of my neck as we remained connected. He kissed me lightly, his weight covering mine, and my grip loosened slightly but I couldn't completely release my hold on him. He kissed me again, resting against me until my body finally relaxed.

After a few minutes he moved off me, nudged me to my side, and cradled me to him. I shifted back farther—he still seemed too far away. He was like a blanket, covering me, and I relaxed in a deep slumber.

CHAPTER 8

$\mathcal{O}$nce again, I rolled over after a night with Ethan to an empty bed. *Son of a bitch.* His scent drifted throughout the room and I was reminded of the night before. Why did I expect more? I shouldn't have had any delusions about who he was—his reputation spoke for itself. But I still called him a few choice words as I pulled the covers around me tighter. They smelled like him, too.

But hunger pangs kept me from sleeping. When I went to the kitchen I found the front door was slightly ajar. I peeked out and saw Ethan going through the trunk of his car, a towel barely concealing him.

"Are you serious?" I barked from the door.

He grinned. "Good morning."

"Get in the house!" I looked around what was about to be become a busy street in a few minutes. Clothes in hand, he walked toward the house but not before David drove by, smiling as his car came to a slow crawl. *Perfect. I know what the topic of our next meeting will be. He'll want details about my night with "sour face."*

As he returned to the house, the taut muscles of his chest, abs, and legs contracted and relaxed with each step. The pronounced ridges just below his stomach barely kept the towel on. "If that thing falls off, the neighbors will have you arrested," I said.

He gave me that self-assured smirk and kissed me on the cheek. "I think I'll be okay."

"Why, because you're an attorney or because you don't think anyone will call the police on you?"

He leaned down kissed me again and said, "Both."

I still had a hard time believing he was an attorney, laws just seemed optional to him.

I found Ethan in front of the dented wall after we had showered and dressed. "You did this?" he asked, looking over at me.

I nodded, standing next to him. The Aufero was in the corner, still pulsing the odd color that had become the norm, but the magic that drifted off it was stronger and more beseeching. As though it had a mind of its own, its aversion to Ethan remained. When he came near it, the beat quickened, and a diaphanous field protected it from being touched by him.

Ethan pressed his hand against the field, slowly moving along it, like Josh did when he was looking for a weakness in mine. "Tell me everything that happened yesterday with Ethos."

I retold it, Ethan stopping me often to ask for more detail. "I know you didn't know that language, but can you repeat it?"

Closing my eyes, I tried to replay each moment of the encounter in my head, the way the magic felt, the way I felt, the sound of Ethos's voice, the smell that lingered in the air, everything. And then I mumbled the words Ethos said, trying to get Maya to respond.

He kept repeating them over and over to himself.

"How many languages do you know?"

"I speak four, well five now." He grinned. I wondered how long it took for him to learn Portuguese, especially since he spoke it well. It reminded me of my family, when I visited them last year. It would have been nice to have family to speak it with, but they had to ruin things by trying to kill me.

"I knew Anderson was going to be trouble the moment I met him. I can't believe he is okay with working with Ethos" Ethan said, sneering.

"He was promised the position of Beta of the were-animal pack, definitely an improvement, being the leader of two hundred to being second-in-command of thousands."

"Whoever is the Alpha couldn't turn his back for a second without having Anderson's knife shoved into it. He will only be the Beta temporarily before he does everything to claw himself to the Alpha position," Ethan said. He frowned and then asked, "And the shooter? Who was it?"

"Ethos called him Derrick."

After a long pause, Ethan identified him as the fourth in the Ares pack, and another wolf. He took out his phone, and I could feel the anger coming off him. Ethan's emotions were very hard to ignore, a turbulent wave that overtook the room, singeing anything nearby. I touched his hand. "Who are you calling?"

"Anderson."

Ethan wasn't very diplomatic. His skills of negotiation were often reduced to telling the person his expectation of compliance, with a poorly veiled threat for good measures. This situation was bad; I thought poking the Alpha would only make it worse.

"I think you should wait."

"Wait on what, Sky?"

"How will speaking with him change anything? He has an agenda, and you aren't going to coerce him to change. He sees Ethos as a means to an end and that is where we should direct our attention."

"Ethos wouldn't have been able to do any of that alone. Without them, how would it have ended yesterday?"

He had a point. Were-animals' immunity to magic in animal form made them hard to be overtaken by mages, fae, and witches.

And most of fae, mages and witches weren't skilled enough fighters to be able to win. That was our advantage and when we needed magic, we had Josh and me. But there was more to it— Ethan had subdued his anger about Sebastian long enough, and he wanted revenge. The anger that sparked in his eyes made it more evident.

"Have you heard anything from Dr. Jeremy?" I asked.

He barely moved his head in a nod.

"And?"

"Nothing has changed since last night."

I studied Ethan but didn't get much from it, his stoicism didn't reveal whether he thought Sebastian would survive. What would happen if he didn't? Part of me wanted to hang on to the bliss of ignorance but I needed to know. "What happens if he survives but isn't the same?"

"Hopefully, he will step down."

"And if he doesn't?" Sebastian couldn't function as anything else. Being the Alpha came as natural to him as breathing. Would he step down?

"Skylar, you know what happens if he doesn't," he said, his eyes holding mine.

"Will he accept a challenge of submission?"

"You know where Sebastian and I stand on that. It hasn't changed. If we can't handle our position and someone feels strongly enough to challenge—" He didn't finish the sentence, not because he didn't want to, but because I was barely holding it together. I blinked back the tears that were threatening to fall.

"You don't have to do anything. It's our rules, we made them and we can break them," I said. "If you don't feel he is fit to lead, do what you are supposed to do, support him. That's your job. No one has to fight, no one has to die."

He listened in silence, his determined presence just frustrating me more. "I won't let you do it."

"Sky." The sharp edge to his tone didn't faze me one bit.

"No! I don't want to hear anything you have to say. Promise me you will not challenge him, no matter what. Promise."

"No," he said softly. "If Sebastian isn't able to continue as Alpha, I will only challenge if he doesn't step down."

"No. No you will not. You have to promise me you won't." He kept calling my name, but I refused to hear anything other than his promise to me. When he attempted to take my arm I jerked it back. "You have to promise me, Ethan."

His voice softened, and I hated that I hadn't been able to brush away the tear that had managed to escape. "No. I'm not going to do that. Things are the way they are. I don't like all aspects of it, but they are our rules and nothing you say to me is going to change them. If you need to cry—go ahead, let it out. You need to scream—do that, too, but it will not change anything."

He reached for me again, and I tried pulling my arm away but he held on tighter, drawing me closer to him. He rested his forehead against mine and cradled my face. "This situation is black and white. I know you want it to be a gray area, but there isn't," Ethan said in a low voice.

I yanked away from him—he would not ease me into this or charm me into thinking this was okay. I wasn't going to accept this as anything more than what it was—murder. "Is that what you want to call it to make it easier to accept? So you just plan to 'black and white' the situation? Call it what it is, you two will fight until one of you murders the other," I snapped.

Ethan didn't possess a great deal of patience and his taut frown showed that I had reached the end of his. "You want to be a child about this, go ahead, Sky." The coarse words were forced out through a tight jaw and clenched teeth. "A pack is only as strong as their Alpha. You've enjoyed the luxury of being part of one that most will not consider screwing with. You've never been a woman in a pack that others consider weak, because then you would understand that need for a strong pack. I don't want to kill anyone in my pack, but if they feel the need to challenge me, they see a weakness in me; and if they see it, so will others outside the pack. If you need this to feel better then fine, get upset with me and we can fight about it all night, but after today we will not have this discussion again because it will not change anything."

Tension filled the silence as we stood in the middle of a destroyed room, with stains of blood from a man who had orchestrated the attempted murder of our Alpha, glaring at each other. Okay, I was the only one glaring; Ethan had said what he needed, and I was fuming because I hadn't changed anything. When someone knocked at the door, I didn't care to answer it. I figured it was David, and I didn't want to talk or be subjected to his questioning that would quickly devolve into him interrogating us like he was an investigative journalist.

I wasn't in a good place to deal with it.

The knocking persisted, and Ethan made his way across the room to answer it. I hadn't moved from my position of staring at the empty space where he once stood with my arms crossed over my chest. I only looked at the door when Ethan exhaled an irritated sigh and opened it, leaving barely enough room for Quell to get through. It didn't escape me that he didn't seem surprised that Quell was out in the daytime without turning that odd gray color that happened when vampires went outside in daylight.

Quell stared at me for a long time, too long. It started to feel uncomfortable having his onyx eyes studying me for such an extended time. Then they swept over to the stains of blood on the floor, the cracked wall, the jumbled furniture that we hadn't gotten around to rearranging. Next he regarded Ethan until Ethan's eyes narrowed on him.

"What?"

"You failed and let her get hurt," Quell said, his voice as dark and cold as his eyes.

I really don't need this.

Ethan quickly closed the distance between him and Quell; I had to run to get between them. I felt like I was trying to move a parked car as I pushed into their chests trying to separate them. "You go over there and you over there," I said pointing to opposite sides of the room.

Why in the hell did I think that was going to work? Neither one of them budged: instead they locked their eyes on each other. "Fine, I'll leave and you two can have at it. I don't have time for this," I said, starting for the door.

Quell was the first to move, slowly backing several feet away but nowhere near where I wanted him. Ethan remained in the same spot. *Stubborn bastard.*

After long drifts of silence, Ethan was the first to speak. "Are things with Fi going well?"

Quell nodded slightly.

"Then why the hell are you here?"

"I was worried about her, and rightfully so—you've proven to be inept at keeping her safe."

Yep, this day is going from bad to worse.

"Quell, I'm fine. It isn't anyone's job but mine to keep me safe." And if I said it a million times, with a bullhorn, had it skywritten, it wouldn't have mattered to Quell. The pack, in his opinion, was to keep me safe. If I got a splinter, he would attribute it to their negligence. He wouldn't be happy until I was placed in a nice little bubble where I could only be viewed, never touched.

Quell stepped closer, his nose flaring as he noticeably inhaled and then slowly looked me over; then he directed his attention to Ethan. The brackets of Quell's frown deepened. If he were a were-animal his eyes would have been flooded with the color of his animal. But he was a vampire and glints of more black smothered any remnants of light that his eyes might have managed to possess.

There was a noticeable change in his mood as his attention went between the two of us, and a knowing look of disgust fell over his face.

The heat of my embarrassment ran along my cheeks and neck.

Hell woman, if you are okay with doing it you damn well need to be okay with people knowing about it.

The subtle disdain Quell had for Ethan quickly upgraded to hate as he dragged his glare away from him.

Ethan wasn't making the situation any better. He looked like he was ready to show Quell how effective he could be at protecting me, mainly from Quell. I wasn't going to fix this, no matter how I tried.

"What's the matter?" I asked Quell. There was something wrong: he was pulled so tight it was only a matter of time before he rebounded in a fury of violence. He wasn't usually like this. I wasn't going to fix Ethan, either, unless I found a time machine and went back to the moment when he decided that being an indomitable stubborn jackass was his life choice.

Quell spoke, his tone nearly a whisper. "I didn't want you to leave last night, but I couldn't stop you from doing so." He took my hand and ignored Ethan's low rumble. I wished I could have said his bark was bigger than his bite. "Fiona," he continued, his expression vacant as he looked in Ethan's direction, "came by and I couldn't leave to check on you. I just needed to know you were okay." His attention returned to Ethan. "You have someone watching the house now, but where were they before, when she was attacked?"

"Quell." I gave his hand a little squeeze in an attempt to redirect him. Keen attention was focused on him and I wasn't sure if I liked my position in between. "No one attacked me." *Well, that's sort of, kind of, a smidge of the truth.* This was escalating to a wildfire that I would not be able to contain if I didn't stop it right now. "Don't hold anyone other than me responsible for my safety. Okay?"

When I squeezed his hand again, he opened his and linked it with mine.

I hesitated before I turned, and when I did, I found Ethan

peering out the window of the kitchen. "They aren't part of our pack," he said.

Ethan headed out the door with me close behind. Four were-animals were off to the side, cloaked by the wealth of thick trees that surrounded my home providing the privacy I wanted. Noticing our presence, Anderson, flanked by another man and Derrick, stepped closer to the house until he was just a couple of feet away.

He was as tall as he was broad, powerful-looking. His dark hair was scalp short, and caramel-colored skin was offset by cognac eyes that possessed a dark, ominous glint. His features were broad, including his lips and mouth and a striking jawline that was a good target for a punch if only to wipe off his smirk.

"The one on the right is Derrick, the shooter," I whispered to Ethan.

Ethan and Anderson locked gazes and I knew this wasn't going to end well. Surveying the area, I remembered that we were still trying to keep our existence quiet and a bloodbath in the middle of the suburbs wasn't going to help with keeping our presence unknown. Rage pulsed off Ethan like a current; the air became hostility riddled and I knew it was a matter of time before this devolved into something so violent it couldn't be contained. I pressed my hands against Ethan's back and said softly, "This isn't the time."

"Oh sweetheart, this is the time. He no longer wants you as the Alpha—your protection is gone," Anderson said to Ethan as the three men advanced closer. Four animals slowly padded closer, feral eyes glowing, teeth drawn back, and just a few feet away, they paused.

This couldn't happen now. It was close to nine in the morning; the streets were quiet but at any time a neighbor could drive by. The last things I needed them to see were were-animals in my front yard trying to destroy one another.

Ethan exhaled the tension, but his shoulders still couldn't

relax, jaw clenched tighter than before, and his hand balled into a fist at his side. He knew this wasn't the right time and we would risk being exposed.

"You all have grown soft. More concerned about your cars, your businesses, and the appearance of strength that you no longer have," Anderson continued.

Diplomacy wasn't something Ethan possessed much of and he was having trouble with it now. He'd forced a relaxed position, but the gunmetal still drowned out the blue in his eyes. He struggled to ease his tightly drawn lips. A rare display of diplomacy. Ethan sucked in a deep breath. "She is right; this isn't the time. You want to challenge me, accepted."

"Waiting, a coward's approach," Anderson said. Then a salacious smile overtook his face as he looked at me. "And the things I plan to do to you when he's gone." He licked his lips.

"Why wait." Striking my hands through the air, I threw them to the ground and leapt from the stairs and had one hand around his throat, the other over his heart. It was horrible magic, dark and lethal, and I absorbed everything the Aufero had to offer. The magic flowed into me, curdled with darkness; the vile smell lifted and presented to me as natural and pure as Josh's magic. It felt as much a part of me as my skin, as necessary as breathing, moving with the ease of my limbs. I owned the magic as my own, no longer something I used—I had become it.

His heart dragged to a slow beat. Sharp ragged breaths seeped out between his lips. His face was fear-stricken as I slowly pulled the beats from his heart and right before he drifted out of consciousness, giving into the darkness of a body that didn't provide enough oxygen to survive and a heart that wouldn't pump enough for survival, I stopped. Allowing the body to recover, and then I did it again.

I found pleasure in torturing him, watching the wistful look on his face when he thought there was a reprieve and he would survive, only to have his body forced into a state of struggling to survive. My face just inches from his, I watched the struggle, inhaled the fragrance of fear, and enjoyed every moment of the power I had over whether he would live or die.

His eyes bulged under my control, and a small voice inside me pled for his life. I ignored it. This power lust wasn't mine. The adoration for the torture and pain of someone else wasn't mine. The magic that I was wielding with a vengeful skill wasn't mine. I was barely aware of Ethan on the side, keeping the other two men at bay while I tortured this man to death, in a cruel manipulation of his body. I was barely aware of Quell, who was off at a distance fighting off three were-animals that were trying to stop me from murdering their Alpha. I wanted him to beg for a life that I planned to take anyway. I had every intention of doing it to Derrick, too, and I hadn't decided what I would do to the third man.

Stop! The voice was louder, but I ignored it. Soon it would be drowned out.

The voice that pled for his life tried to temper the magic, suppress the lust, fight off the desire for power. I ripped my hand from his throat and pulled myself to standing, taking several steps back. Ethos was right: Maya wasn't dormant anymore. She was awake, and I was a fool to let her stay. She played me, showing compassion and understanding as she ushered me into a life she wanted me to have. A life that she had every intention of taking over. A pack that she would infiltrate, magic that she would harvest and use in the way she saw fit. I was screwed.

Everything was a blur as I looked at the world through a haze of betrayal and suppressed magic. I could hear Ethan and Quell calling my name. They were close. I looked around the yard, and everyone was gone except the three of us. Ethan's hand covered mine and I pulled away. "Don't touch me."

I started to walk away when his hand snaked around my waist, hugging me to him. He spoke into my hair in a low soothing voice. "You're fine. You are."

Ethan was wrong. I wasn't okay; and no matter how many times it came from him, we both knew it wasn't true. I rested against him, my heart racing. He wrapped his arms around me tighter; slow exhalation wasn't working for me. I simply rested against Ethan and eventually mine mirrored his; slow and steady.

I don't recall the last time I had said anything since I tried to kill Anderson. I had just a vague memory of Quell's concerned face in front of me talking to Ethan about something I couldn't force myself to care about. When Ethan told me that Sebastian was awake, I cared enough to follow him to the car but the words just weren't there. The entire trip to the retreat, Ethan focused on me more than on the road, his hand resting over mine.

"I want her out of me," I finally said as we pulled into the driveway of the retreat, which was full of cars.

"Okay."

"Don't just say it. Please, I want you to do something about it." I tasked him with the impossible and it was unfair. And Ethan would never let me know that. But desperation had made me devoid of logic. I only seemed vaguely aware that if Maya and I were linked by a shared life force, I couldn't live without her; but what was slowly happening wasn't something I could live with, either. Maybe I was better off dead.

I had gotten used to the feel of the warmth of Ethan's hand next to mine and when he released it when we got out of the car and kept his distance from me as we started toward the house, I didn't know what to think. I expected him to take it again or at the very least close the distance that he kept between us. When I stopped walking a few feet from the house he released an exasperated breath. "What is it, Sky?"

I chewed on my bottom lip and shook my head. I didn't have anything to say. For all I knew, last night was just sex for Ethan; after all it wasn't his first time. This could very well have been just a one-night stand for him and nothing more. I felt foolish to expect it to be something more. It seemed like more, but what did I know?

Sebastian sat on a bed surrounded by vibrant blue-colored walls that were decorated with wildlife art. Steven was in the corner sitting in a sleek modern chair watching television. He looked like he'd been there for a while. The recovery rooms looked nothing like what I'd seen in hospitals.

Sebastian's alluring amber eyes shone with the same strength and assurance as they always had, his satin mocha skin as vibrant as before. He was shirtless, and there wasn't any evidence that silver-infused bullets had punctured through the muscle that covered his body. He was our Alpha, and he seemed as good as new. But I kept studying Ethan as he looked at Sebastian.

"How do you feel?" Ethan asked.

He shrugged and stood: he didn't move the same. The lithe predacious movement had been lost to something more lumbering and purposeful. "I may need a couple of days, but I understand," he said.

What exactly does he understand? Dammit, they're talking about this challenge foolishness again. "No," I said.

"Sky," Ethan said through gritted teeth.

He could grit them until they were ground to nubs, I didn't care. They weren't going to do this. I wouldn't let it happen. "No."

They had both dismissed me. I was white noise to them—they had been reduced to predators assessing the weakness of the other. Examining whether or not one was more capable than the other to lead. And every second, every moment of it made me despise the pack and them for being nothing more than primal beasts.

I waited for them to speak, and in the silence I heard my heart beating and violence that had become a significant part of my life echoing in my ears, overtaking my thoughts, and I couldn't stand it anymore. I started to leave. I didn't need to be there while they decided which one of them was going to die. I'd reached the door when Ethan said, "I feel very comfortable with you as my Alpha."

It wasn't until I exhaled that I realized I'd been holding my breath. A weight that I didn't know was even there seemed to be lifted. Winter nearly knocked me over when she entered the room. She stood several feet away from Sebastian, her eyes wide, arms fixed at her side as though she didn't know what to do with them. *What took her so long to get here?* I suspected she was afraid of what she might see. Like me she couldn't bear to see him as a fragment of his former self, bloodied and wounded as he was the other day.

His lips kinked up into a smirk. "Hi."

She swallowed but didn't say anything for a long time. Instead she just looked at him, her eyes glistening under the harsh lights, and she made several efforts to speak but was unable to find the words. Sebastian approached her, a relaxed reassuring smile brightening his features. He touched her shoulders, and she let a light sob escape. "I'd like to be alone," he said as he looked over the room. Winter started to back away. "No, you stay."

As the door closed behind us I got a glimpse of him drawing Winter to him.

Two days later, and the incident with Anderson wasn't any less vivid in my thoughts. The feelings overtook me, the intoxicating feeling of power and the immense control I had over magic that for weeks Josh and I couldn't manage to control. It wasn't that I had more control than I had before; it was the diablerie. I didn't care that it was dark and wrong. In fact, I welcomed it as a way to wreak more havoc.

Josh was less focused on me than he was on Ethan, who was sitting next to me, perusing the book in front of him. Josh watched him with a suspicious glint, his gaze narrowing on his brother. Ethan pushed the book away and crossed his arms over his chest. "I think getting rid of Ethos is what we need to focus on rather than getting rid of Maya. She was fine until a couple of months ago. It's likely his resurfacing has awakened something in her. Get rid of him and things may go back to the way they were."

"And if it doesn't?" I asked.

"Then we worry about it then. Ethos is the immediate threat, and Claudia hasn't been able to meet with Samuel. For all we know Ethos has all three books."

Josh listened but his attention wavered between me and Ethan, jumping back and forth between us.

"Find out how we can draw Ethos out of hiding," Ethan commanded, coming to his feet and leaving. Unless he could put the books in a chokehold he wasn't really interested in them. I was surprised he lasted the two hours he had.

The empty space where Ethan had stood still commanded a great deal of Josh's attention, and when he looked in my direction, he forced a smile.

"Come with me." He scooped up the Aufero and grabbed me by the wrist. I hated being near it, and I damn sure wasn't interested in anything Josh was considering. I followed him downstairs to what had become our "practice room." Set up like the sparring room, the walls were padded as we had crashed into them one too many times causing damage. The open space allowed us freedom to practice without the threat of injury.

I took up a place in the middle of the room, still considering how the Aufero responded to Josh as opposed to how it did to his brother. It protected itself from Ethan, as though it sensed danger.

Josh's light assuring smile always made me feel emboldened, as though magic was simple. Just an extension of my natural movements to be directed and controlled with the same ease I did my arms. And as usual, I held his gaze as the knife slid across the palm of his hands and we connected as the spell that would bind us fell from his lips. Surrounded by the coarse, draconian magic of the Aufero, his was a welcome feeling. Despite being darker than it was when I first met him, there was still something soothing about it. There was still a hint of "old Josh" in the magic. Perhaps he was suppressing it because he knew I needed to feel his familiar magic. It felt cleansing as it spiraled through me, the gentle but powerful breeze that rekindling my love for magic. It wasn't ominous, deadly, and harsh. Josh moved closer and I was enveloped by the comfort of the first magic I had ever experienced. "Now use it," he said.

A protective field billowed around us, its diaphanous covering shimmering a light lilac. The air inside wasn't toxic, we could breathe. Taking my free hand, I placed it on his chest. Nothing. I smiled. Slowly I dropped the field. With a whirl of my fingers a towel danced across the room. Josh's keys performed a clunky bounce as I sent them across the room. I had relaxed into the magic.

Josh took several steps from me. His keys soared toward me, and with a twist of my hands they went in a different direction. Flicks of my finger nudged him back. I pushed a little harder, too hard. He slammed back into the padded wall, his head bouncing a little against it. "It's still a head, padding or not, it doesn't like to be slammed against things," he teased. I released him from the wall. The stress and worry over the past two days seemed nonexistent.

"Make a field," he instructed. This was how we assessed how weak the magic that I borrowed from him was getting. I barely created a shimmer. I needed more. Before he connected again he brought the Aufero close, and I sucked in a ragged breath. I closed my eyes, feeling his familiar and comforting touch as his fingers interlinked with mine, hands pressed palm to palm.

"Again," he told me. The tranquil soothing covering of his magic washed over me. Snaking around my body, I pulled from the magic in Aufero, it crept alongside Josh's magic mirroring its movements making every effort to overshadow it. Josh's fingers gripped tighter around mine; as the space became stifled he gasped.

Making more choking noises, he managed to speak. "Skylar, you need to change it."

Yeah, better said than done. Concentrating, I could feel the beads of perspiration forming along my brow. Josh's breath beat lightly against my lips, and I felt my control of his magic waver. He was no longer assisting me. Dark magic crept along the side of his magic, wrapping around it. I forced it to mirror Josh's magic, entwining with it so that they were indistinguishable from each other. The air cleared, and the smell of fresh linen, jasmine, earthy spice, and a hint of the metallic odor of blood inundated the shell that formed around us.

Josh released my hand but stayed close enough that his lips brushed mine as he spoke. "See, I knew you could do it."

Well, at least one of us thinks I could. There was a happy dance promised to celebrate this moment but I was too tired to give the much-needed enthusiasm it called for. I didn't tell him that there was a part of me that liked the magic a little too much, a part that thirsted for the darker side, but the feelings didn't matter—they were just that. I controlled the end results, and that's all that mattered. At the moment, next to Josh, with dark necro-magic interlaced with natural magic, I had learned to control it without giving into the lust I had just two days ago. My eyes had been closed the whole time and when I opened them, the first thing I saw was Ethan leaning against the wall.

The pretty colors of the protective field exploded into the air, fragments of it drifting for just a moment.

"I got this Ethan, you can go," Josh said as his focus remained on me. I started to step back, but he placed his hand around my waist. "No," he whispered. "We need to finish."

"It's okay with me if he stays."

"He's a distraction."

"For who, you or Sky?" Ethan's hard voice asked from his position from across the room.

Josh wasn't looking at me anymore but was focused on the wall behind me, his face drawn into a tight glower. "Both," he finally said.

Ethan hesitated, looking at the Aufero, whose previous smoky orange coloring was a little lighter and more translucent.

In silence Ethan went upstairs.

Five long grueling hours later, I lay on the ground next to Josh, my hair damp with sweat, my head pounding, and my mind fatigued from controlling all the thoughts that invaded it, even the one that briefly considered how wonderful it would be to have access to his magic at all times. So I laid next to Josh, so close our arms were touching, holding back the confession that for a few seconds, I had considered taking his magic. Nothing like telling the person that helped you, "Hey for a brief moment, I thought about stealing your magic. My bad."

When he sat up, I did, too. I was ready to go home, eat, shower and—

"How long have you been screwing Ethan?"

Yeah and that. I planned on doing that—a lot—when I got home.

I blinked several times. Not because it was on my list of things I planned on doing when I got home, but because it surprised me again that they didn't just talk to each other. Life would be so much easier if they did.

The deep, inquiring cerulean eyes waited for an answer. An answer that seemed to be stuck in the pit of my chest. Why did admitting it feel like a betrayal? If admitting it to someone was so hard, should I really be doing it?

"I don't want to talk about my personal life, Josh—it's weird."

"So, recently," he said, coming to his feet. He was halfway up the stairs when he turned to me. "Whatever happens between you two, don't let things change between us, okay?"

I nodded, reading the meaning between his veiled words. Ethan's reputation was something I was aware of. I like to think I was going into whatever existed between us with my eyes wide open. But it didn't mean I couldn't be knocked on my butt, even if I prepared for the worst. I would just see it coming, be a little more expecting when it did, but still totally unable to deal with it.

From behind, I watched as Josh passed his brother. Their eyes fixed on each other in the way they often did, when words were never exchanged but I was sure some form of communication took place. They both denied they could communicate other than verbally with each other, but I was still finding that hard to believe. One look between them seemed to have more information than most people could express in a minutes-long exchange.

CHAPTER 9

The decorative pillow was pinned against the wall, a small vase moved slowly around me, and I held the protective field around me and Ethan while he pressed against my jaw, then his tongue licked at the pulse of my neck. "Will you stop?" I snapped.

After we left the retreat, we ate and I showered but not until after I convinced Ethan bathing wasn't a group project and we didn't get around to having sex. Josh was in my head and I just couldn't do it.

The feeling of having total control of dark magic was exhilarating, and subduing the taste for power and violence that had overtaken me so often in the past few days left me feeling weak. I didn't like that. I still wanted Maya out of me, because she had shown who she was, and being in a protective state, trying to make sure I could control her and keep her from taking over wasn't how I wanted to live.

He kissed me, and his fingers slipped under my shirt, rolling languidly over my skin. A light touch that made my skin tingle even moments after fingers left the spot. "You have to be able to perform with distractions," he teased.

"If this is the distraction they employ, then I'm pretty sure things are just going to get weird fast," I said, keeping the objects levitating around me.

He touched my hand. "Drop it." Ethan stepped back, the field separating as he slid out from it. My eyes narrowed with curiosity. *Okay, that's different.*

He simply returned a crooked grin, standing outside the field watching. Slowly the field slipped away, the objects around me eased to the ground, and the Aufero pulsed at its same rhythmic beat.

Closing the distance between us Ethan said, "Very good,"

"Very good? Did you see that? I just made magic my bitch."

"That you did," he said in a low rumble, the warmth of his words breezing against my lips before his pressed against mine.

He drew me closer to him, pulling me into the kiss, and for a few minutes I forgot about Josh's words; but it didn't take long for them to reassert themselves.

I pulled back, taking several steps away, and when there was adequate distance between us, I asked, "What is going on between us?"

The deep gunmetal eyes held mine with lascivious intent and the little lilt of his smile seem to mock me. "It was just a kiss, Sky."

Nothing was "just" with Ethan. Displays of affection were a salacious prelude to more. A simple hand hold led to me pressed against the wall, with us clawing at each other's clothes like we were in heat. I'd seen the carnal side of him that enjoyed violence, but I now experienced that side of him that approached sex in the same manner. Unfettered, primal lust coursed through him. His sexuality was raw and carnal, and being with him was absolutely sinful. Each time we were together it was as beseeching and overwhelming as our first kiss. His sensuality was every part of my body, a masculinity that inundated my senses. He had quickly become a craving, an addiction, a necessity. *This is bad.... So bad!*

"No, it's not just a kiss. What happens next?" I looked away from the miscreant smile.

"Whatever you want to happen."

There was a long silence and I waited for the words to come. For me to spout out that I wanted things to go back to the way they were. But I couldn't even let that lie pass. The words just didn't come out, and any that came to my mind weren't what I wanted to say.

"What happens when you get tired of me?" I asked.

There weren't any truer words. He was the king of one-night stands and fleeting relationships and the only lengthy one he'd ever had was so dysfunctional people had bets on who would kill who first.

He smiled. "What happens when *I* get tired of *you?* How about when *you* get tired of *me?*

I didn't answer his question because I wasn't the one with the questionable past. "Don't play games with me. Answer the question."

"It's not very hard. We move on" was the simple response he gave me.

I didn't want to talk about it anymore. Why did I make this more than what it was—sex. Pleasure. Fun.

When he stepped closer, I kept moving back, trying to keep the distance between us, but quickly ran out of space, my back pressed firmly against the wall. Tracing his fingers down my arm, he waited until I lifted my eyes to meet his. "Where is this coming from?"

I shrugged, but it wasn't enough of an answer. "I just don't want to be a throwaway." *I wish I was cooler than this.* "Someone you quickly lose interest in."

His voice like velvet spoke into my cheek, warm kisses melted against my skin. "How could I lose interest in you?"

It was a line that I willingly accepted. And I let myself fall into returning his kiss.

. . .

I was wide awake lying next to Ethan; my overactive mind had decided that sleep wasn't necessary and pondered over everything. Maya, Moura, dark magic, Logan's information about the Faeries, and even Ethan. Logan's avid curiosity with Ethan hadn't diminished despite us removing the elven magic. And Ethan's effortless movement from the protective field weighed on me.

"What is it Sky?" Ethan said in the pillow before rolling over to look at me, watching me through slits in his eyes.

I shook my head. "Nothing."

"Seventy-seven heartrate and your respiration is twelve, you want to try again?"

"No, I just want to know why you are such a freak."

He chuckled and sat up. "What's wrong?"

"Why did Logan react to you the way he did?"

He shrugged. "Who knows why Logan does any of the things he does. I'm not going to waste time trying to figure it out." But the nagging feeling persisted. Something was off. Ethan never just skated around an issue, he performed a full-on dance ensemble around it.

"You just walk out of the protective field as though it wasn't there," I offered, my curiosity at full bloom.

"Sky, you were using magic all day, it was a weak field. Anyone could have broken it. But it will get better with practice."

It took a while for me to take my eyes off him, waiting for something to falter to confirm my suspicions. The more I found out about Ethan, the more there seemed to be to discover. His mother was a witch, and he possessed magic that he rarely used but I believed was stronger than he let on. "Okay." My suspicion permeated the words.

He leaned forward to kiss me but I didn't respond, keeping my lips pressed firmly together. *Distractions. Distractions. Distractions.*

MCKENZIE HUNTER

This was now his new sleight of hand and I wasn't having any of it.

"I keep thinking about what Logan said about the Faeries," I said. "What if Maya was one? That would explain so much. It would definitely explain why they resorted to infanticide to get rid of her. If she is, how horrible were the Fairies that people would resort to such things?"

A lot of the things that happened in the otherworld as an effort to prevent future problems were cruel by most standards. Its denizens often "contained" situations, which meant they killed off many for the pure agenda of keeping the world safe. But were you really ever safe in a world with vampires who devoured blood to survive and had moral compasses that seemed to be perpetually broken? Or elves who lived in the shadows, hidden from the world by glamours, and spent most of their time genetically engineering creatures that if released could cause the type of havoc that could destroy this world and the real world? Or their lesser counterparts who could control weather and agriculture? Fae who could control the mind, force the truth with a kiss? Or were-animals who shifted into creatures larger than the animal counterpart found in nature, who accepted fights of dominance as pack culture? Witches, despite their objections, were just as much a part of this world as anyone else. Magic and the depth of their control to cast curses that could kill, to form barriers that protected them from most things. How did the people in this world decide what addition to this ominous and bizarre place was too much for it to handle?

Ethan ran his hands through his hair and heaved a ragged breath. "If my research is correct, I think the best choice was to kill them before they could reach their full potential." I knew what he was eluding to—and it made me sick.

"No, that is never an option."

His lips dipped into a frown. "Sky, the Faeries were not good

192

people. And because of how powerful they were they couldn't be destroyed, so what other options did they have?"

I didn't know what options they had, but I hated the very idea that someone thought it was okay to kill a child because it *might* grow up to be something horrible.

Ethan rolled out of bed and started for the door.

"Where are you going?"

"I need to get something out of my car."

"You're going out there like that? Clothes please."

He looked out the window—it was still dark outside. Then he glanced over at the clock on the nightstand. "I doubt there's anyone outside. I'm used to my home."

The estate which Ethan called a home did provide a lot of privacy. There were only six homes in the subdivision and they were so far apart I doubt he ever saw his neighbors, I'm pretty sure he was pleased with that.

"Well, I have neighbors, and I doubt they want to see your naked ass and junk while having their morning coffee."

They were probably used to it. After multiple discussions with Steven, he finally at least started wearing pants. The neighbors didn't seem to mind. In fact, most of my neighbors happened to make too much of everything and used that as a reason to come over and share their various dishes with us. Free food. The pang of Steven's absence hit me again. Sometime over the past couple of days he had removed more of his things. I wasn't sure if he was saving me the pain of an uncomfortable departure or he didn't want to deal with my maudlin display of emotions that I wouldn't be able to control once he actually left. I pushed the thoughts aside.

He sighed, frowning as he grabbed his underwear and slipped them on as he headed out the door.

It's just clothes.

He returned with a book that he dropped on my lap. As I read through the pages, I was met with recounts of enslavement, torture, destruction, and exceptionally cruel displays of power. They were cruel, and the more I read, the less the idea of "containing" people seemed abhorrent. Many of the Faeries were eventually killed, but not without the loss of thousands in order to kill a few. Limited in their ability to procreate, they started to do so with humans, but doing that left them the less powerful progeny that we called fae. Logan described Faeries as godlike, and as I read on, I realized he wasn't far off. They fought hard to retain their status, finding that witches produced a stronger offspring.

I don't believe in infanticide. I don't believe in infanticide. I repeated that mantra over and over in my head despite reading how they forced were-animals into animal form and treated them as such. The anxiety of my new discovery wound tight in my stomach as I came across the names Ravyn, Emmalesse, Leonel, and Ethosial. Considered the strongest of the Faeries because of their ability to manipulate magic, shapeshift, perform necro-magic equivalent to that of dark elves, and transfer magic similar to what I was able to do with Josh. I stared at the names as my fingers went numb and my hand became cool and clammy. Was Ethos a descendant of the Faerie himself? If a knife in the throat didn't kill him and enclosing him in an oxygen-deprived protective field barely stopped him, he might actually be. How old were they? I could only imagine the extent of his magic. Emma's story of losing her child, Maya: was it really as tragic as I believed? Emma—was it coincidently similar to Emmalesse? Who was she?

"How long have you had this information?" I asked.

"Not long."

"And you didn't tell me about it? You can't continue keeping information like this and then just springing it on me," I snapped. I wanted to be upset and angry with someone. It was the only emotion that was easily at my disposal. The others had retreated, leaving me feeling empty. I kept looking at the names, the familiarity and how unusual they were. I just didn't believe in coincidences anymore after witnessing collusion, secret alliances, worlds hidden by glamours, creatures created by the manipulation of magic, lives captured into shades, and natural elements controlled by the wiggle of a hand. I didn't have the luxury of believing that things were coincidences, because they never were. Was Emma a grieving mother or participant in making sure that Faeries continued to exist, maintaining their hold on the otherworld, living as gods, and expecting reverence? As the mother of such a powerful being she would hold a place of power by association.

I'd read enough but I forced myself to continue, hoping someone had written a how-to on killing them, but there wasn't any such luck. Pages and pages of their talents, when they could have simply written, "They can do everything—the end."

Startled, I quickly grabbed the phone as soon as it vibrated and played David's ringtone. I answered, expecting his typical greeting of calling me a feline or a pastry. Instead, his voice was shaky and raspy. "Skylar, I need you here, now." Then he hung up.

I wasn't sure what to expect when I got to his house, but I was prepared for anything. I didn't care about the peculiar look Ethan gave me when I grabbed a hunter's knife and the Aufero and headed out the door with him in tow—thankfully fully dressed.

"What's the matter?" I asked the moment David answered the door. In response, he moved aside, and curled up against the wall was a man covered by a blood-speckled sheet. David pulled back the covers, exposing a half-naked man, hair punctured through his sallow skin. I knelt in front of him, and he attempted to speak but could only get out a pained "k" or "ca." I tried to make it out but couldn't.

"Don't try to talk. I'm going to help you." I sounded a lot more confident than I felt because I didn't know how to help him. His eyes resembled the odd ones of the man I nearly ran over. Was he a mutated were-animal, and if so, what the hell happened? David plopped in the chair next to us and looked relieved that I had a handle on things.

"Where's Trent?" Ethan asked.

Even David looked surprised by the question, probably because Ethan had never met him.

"I had to give him something. When the guy started growing hair he freaked out. He's sleeping right now."

"I need to take off the rest of your clothes, okay?" I said to the injured man. I used my knife to remove the rest of his clothes and then placed my hand on his sweaty warm skin trying to force a change. I wasn't sure what he was going to change to. My experience with helping someone change was novice at best, but since I'd helped Ethan, I felt confident I could do it. Closing my eyes, I felt the tingles of the change that happened in my body, the prickle of my skin as the hairs prepared to force their way through. The tension on my joints as they prepared to be stretched and contorted to accommodate a new form. My heart slowed and I could feel my vital organs starting to perform at accelerated levels, preparing for what my body would endure.

The man squirmed under my touch, but eventually he relaxed against the floor. His eyes widened, and a frown made its way across his face distorting his appearance. Sweat started to pool and roll down his face. He appeared to be waiting for me to make the pain disappear—something I wasn't sure I could do. Time stretched, and nothing happened. The same obscure hairs remained, and his eyes had the odd appearance of an animal's stuck in a human's body. In the background I could hear Ethan on the phone with Dr. Jeremy and Josh. Once he hung up with them he took up a position next to me. Moving my hand, he continued trying to force a change. The man's back rounded, the crunching of his bones breaking and reassembling filling the air. David looked like he was about to lose whatever he had eaten in the past week as he retched behind us. It would have been rude to suggest that he take whatever he had given Trent, but he needed something.

I went to the kitchen to get him something. At first I considered ginger ale, but hell, he was about to see a man transition to an animal and our transition wasn't pretty and fluid. It was going to be ugly and gross. Instead, I brought back vodka, but I didn't bother with a mixer or a glass that I knew wouldn't be used. As soon as I handed it to him, he threw back the bottle, and gulped down most of it before he stopped and wiped his mouth with the back of his hand. This disheveled, flustered mess wasn't David, and I felt like crap that he was going through this.

I guided him to the sofa, and he took another look at the corner to get a view of the man that was a wolf from the waist down. The cracking continued, along with the screech-like sound of ligaments being stretched beyond their physiological tensile ability. The panic of knowing the heart was about to stop for a few moments sent Strange Eyes into a panic.

"You didn't look like that when you changed."

I didn't want to lie to David, our friendship was better than that. "It gets better each time. He's different and I don't know what his deal is, but when I know something I'll tell you, okay?"

He nodded. And then he frowned. "Oh kitten, I hate that my cupcake has to go through that every month."

Look at that a twofer, feline and a pastry in one sentence.

Another look at Strange Eyes and then David took another hard hit from the bottle. By the time the man had fully transitioned David had excused himself to the bathroom, bottle of liquid courage in hand. His tenuous grip on bravery had snapped, and I would have followed him, but I had a feeling he really wanted to be alone.

Dr. Jeremy, Josh, Sebastian, and Winter had filed into the room when David returned, having somehow gathered his composure.

A smile eased across his lips as he greeted everyone as though an exhausted Ethan wasn't propped against the wall with a fully formed wolf that was barely breathing lying next to him. But he was so obviously drunk off his ass, something like that just wouldn't seem so bothersome. He nearly ignored everyone and went to Winter, whom he had seen numerous times at my house but had never been officially introduced to.

"The dark swan, how beautiful you truly are in person." Sober David was going to regret that statement. I needed to get him out of here before he started espousing all his little nicknames he had for people. Winter's didn't make a lot of sense, either. He said it was because she was beautiful, graceful, and pleasing to look at, but her resting bitch face made her seem dark and menacing.

The glare she gave him only served to prove my point. Her eye thing freaked him the hell out—amber slits flashing in her dark pupils. It freaked me out the first time I saw it and pretty much every other time she did it. But not David. It seemed to add to her mystique and he appeared to be even more intrigued by her. I could imagine him doing something totally inappropriate with her, like treating her face like putty and trying to push a smile on it.

I formed a tight gird around his arm and guided him to the kitchen to get water and whatever I could to help get him sober— or the nicknames he thought were clever and cute weren't going to make him a friend of the pack.

From his kitchen I could see everything while I kept handing him water, and he sat on a stool. After a few minutes he seemed better and chomped down the sandwich I quickly assembled. I didn't blame him—this was a lot to handle, and since I'd only changed once with him and most of it happened with me behind a tree, this was the first time he'd actually seen a change, and it was a horribly grotesque one. I made a promise to allow him to see someone else change, preferably Gavin. His change was absolutely striking, pure fluidity and as graceful as the panther he became.

"Is he okay to question?" Sebastian asked, entering the kitchen.

David, who had lowered his face onto the counter resting it on his hands, rose up and immediately started to stare at Sebastian. It was the same look that most people had when they first met him: diametrical chaos. He was the living embodiment of a beautiful monster. An alluring predator that incited the desire to have him and the need to run and cower. Just forty-eight hours after nearly dying he still possessed it like a second layer of skin.

David straightened. "I'm fine." His self-assurance was fake, and if I could see it, I know Sebastian could as well.

His deep baritone voice was genteel as he addressed David. "Can you tell me what happened?"

"I was getting ready for work." David worked in public relations. Most of the time he worked from home but went to the office once a week. He was always so stylishly dressed I never knew if it was the day he went to the office or not.

He looked around the kitchen; I was sure he was ready to take another drink of liquid courage. I slid a cup of water over to him. He took a sip and continued. "I heard a light knocking. He looked injured so I opened the door. I was about to call the police when I got a look at his legs, that's when I called Skylar."

Sebastian shot a glance in my direction and then back at David. "Did he say anything?"

"Just partial words, 'kil'l'... kela' maybe. I couldn't make out any of it."

"Could it have been Kelly?" Sebastian asked.

"Maybe."

Sebastian thanked him and quickly made his way back to the living room. Reluctantly, I left David and followed Sebastian, who was going through the man's discarded clothing searching through the pockets of his pants where he found a license. Kelly's license.

"She didn't leave, she was taken," he said and then swore under his breath. I couldn't help but feel sorry for Sebastian. At every given moment he was playing three-dimensional chess with the otherworld, and just when he was about to call "checkmate" everything gets knocked over and he has to start over and he's given a hell of a hand to play with: Your Beta is a dark elf. Kelly, your employee, becomes injured by a creature from the dark forest. You fix her, and now she is missing. You have to placate a psychotic and troublesome Seethe's Mistress to prevent a war with the vampires. Someone calls you to tell you they are about to kill a child because of an antiquated belief and you have to fly across the world and decimate a pack to save her. I couldn't believe he would challenge anyone to keep his position. I'd offer pie to anyone who would take it.

Sebastian was about to speak when Dr. Jeremy started yelling for assistance. Strange Eyes was convulsing on the ground. The short spastic movements came to an abrupt stop, and Dr. Jeremy checked him and immediately started CPR. Winter took over while he searched through his bag and gave him a shot directly to the heart. Things had to be bad—my mother was a pathologist and I'd seen this done so many times on television shows that I thought it was a viable option, and she'd simply rolled her eyes and said, "Now if only they would show the doctor going through his malpractice case, this story would be more realistic." It was a procedure done in emergencies only. Like now, when a recently changed were-animal, and I'm not sure if we could categorize him as that, went into cardiac arrest.

He didn't move. We waited. Nothing. Dr. Jeremy's hands ran through his hair, ruffling the silver mass that already looked like he had just gotten out of his bed to get here. I could tell Dr. Jeremy didn't lose patients often. His typically relaxed demeanor was constricted, and the gentle lines that gave his regal features character made him look weathered and aged. "I want to take him back to the retreat to study him," he said.

Sebastian turned to David, who had made his way out of the kitchen with the horrible timing of seeing the were-animal die.

He blanched and looked like he was going to be sick. They took the wolf to the car through the garage; since it had been hours, we were well into the day and I was sure the neighbors were out.

After Dr. Jeremy left with the body, I was nervous when Sebastian came back in to talk to David. "He won't say anything," I assured him.

"I know. But I still need to talk to him."

"About what?"

His eyes narrowed to small slits. Sebastian hated to be questioned, and his firm handling of his job confirmed he wasn't very often.

"He's scared and you're kind of "—*Raging box of scary*—"intense and I think he's been through enough."

Sebastian considered it for a few minutes and then me for even longer. "Give him my number and have him call me. He needs to call me, Skylar, okay?" As he walked away, he shot back over his shoulder, "I will see you tomorrow at five for training."

No you won't. "P.M., right?"

He simply laughed.

David was better when I went back to see him a couple hours later to the point that he made a joke about Sebastian wanting him to have his number. Trent was a different situation all together. His flair for the dramatic made things worse, and when I changed into my wolf form, he started day drinking—hard. A bottle of wine later he wasn't any better, just drunk and very inquisitive.

"You all turn into animals?" he drawled out as he took another long gulp from his fourth or fifth drink. It might have been ten since he kept filling up the oversized glass that looked like a bowl with a stem.

I nodded. "Except for Quell."

His mouth twisted as he tried to remember which one was Quell.

"The broody one," I offered.

"What is he?"

"Vampire."

He was alcohol-numb enough to just laugh. "Eh, why not."

"Josh is a witch." Trent was calm and relaxed at this point. I could have told him I was Spider-Man on Monday, Wednesday, and Friday and moonlighted as Wonder Woman the other days and he would have been okay with it. But that intrigued him.

"He can do magic?"

I nodded.

"Your life is so freaking interesting."

I laughed but it wasn't jovial, lacking any humor at all. It was a manic chortle. My life wasn't interesting; it was fucking scary. David and Trent stared at me wide-eyed and concerned. Day drinking didn't seem like such a bad idea, and when I asked for a glass of wine, David brought me one and sat the bottle down next to me. I told them everything: my strange birth, the real reason for the fight with Michaela, Ethos and his goal to control the otherworld and use me to do it. They got the rundown on Maya and how I felt like she was taking over, and even the assassination attempt.

At some point I just started rambling, and they didn't seem to mind but struggled to keep up with all the information.

"Do most were-animals die?" David asked as troubled eyes stared back at me. He was handling things remarkably well, but I suspected he was wondering if I ran the chance of dying each time I changed.

"I don't know many changed were-animals, most of us are born were-animals. I'm not sure what that thing was. He was different."

David looked down at his hand. The extended silence was welcomed although uncomfortable. I had just bombarded them with a lot of information and was starting to feel a little guilty for making them my therapist and sounding board, and irreparably changing their world. "Could Ethos have made that thing? If he's able to shift into a jackal could he make someone else change into something else?"

That was the question. If Ethos was Ethosial or a descendant, then there wasn't any telling what he could do. Last year he used *genums,* small shapeshifting animals that everyone thought was extinct, and forced them to shift into massive creatures strong enough to attack and kill vampires and were-animals. At this point, I couldn't put anything past his capabilities.

"What about those books, do you think they help you figure out the animal or at least stop Ethos?" David asked.

I shrugged. Since we hadn't translated all of them I didn't know, but it would definitely explain why he wanted them. But everyone wanted them. Samuel wanted them to rid the world of magic; I had no idea why Ethos wanted them. Was it leverage over the vampires and the were-animals to force them into subjugation for fear of being killed or losing their ability to shift?

I didn't want to talk about it anymore. I wanted to day drink and slip into a nice alcohol-induced calm or nap, I didn't really care which one. David had eased over to the chair I was sitting in and had placed his hand on my back. I didn't need sympathy, I just needed to vent. I felt like everyone in this world was just fine with the violence, the constant discoveries of new and horrible things that occupied it, and had become immune to how petrifying and exhausting it could be. It was my life now, I got it. But every once in a while I wanted that "it's not fair" moment and sulk over the brevity of my somewhat, kind of, normal life. I was going to take that moment.

"Can we stop talking about this stuff for a little while?" I asked playing with the rim of my glass.

Trent gave an enthusiastic yes. He was dealing with it, but we were on the same page and wanted to drink until the world made sense, or at least drink until we forgot it was just screwed up.

"Okay, all the other stuff is off the table, but you have to tell me about Sour Face. How hot is that guy?"

"Ethan?"

"Of course, the intense one who must have been born without smile muscles," David joked. "He's the new guy, Steven's gone?"

I moaned. That was something I left out of my vent session. Probably because I was still holding on to hopes that he wouldn't leave, but I hadn't seen him since Sebastian was shot, and we hadn't even talked, either. We exchanged a few texts but that was it.

Trent and David were waiting for me to talk, and it was then I had an appreciation for Quell being able to read my mind and Winter not giving a damn about my personal life. I'm sure if I called Winter and told her that I was sleeping with Ethan she would just say something along the lines of "Why are you telling me? Do you want me to give you a cookie or an award or something?" I didn't get a lot of girl talk from Winter, and I didn't realize how much I actually liked that.

With David and Trent, our conversations usually revolved around them. They were great men, but they didn't mind talking about themselves a lot. I'd settled into that friendship well because their lives brought normalcy to mine. David worked in public relations, and a bad day for him was a client writing something stupid on social media and he had to do damage control. Trent was an event planner, and although someone making a mistake with decorations or bringing the wrong mic, in his mind, was equivalent to the country going to war or a hostage crisis that required federal action. Their mishaps in life were minor.

David filled my glass, which was half-full. I'd been too busy venting to drink it. After taking a long drink, I was ready to take part in the frivolity of their life and love every moment of it and maybe talk about Sour Face, too.

"Okay, you have your wine, now talk," David ordered. He wasn't going to let this go.

"I can't, it violates my 'I don't want to talk about this world rule,'" I teased, taking another sip.

"You aren't going to get off that easy." Trent was on the edge of his seat waiting for me to talk. *Really? I miss Winter.*

It was odd, telling them about the ominous and perilous other-world wasn't a problem. The dam broke and the information came out easily. Talking about whatever was going on with Ethan and me was harder than I expected. The second glass of wine made it a little easier, and I thought I could satisfy their curiosity with a condensed version of everything that happened, but Trent turned into an investigative reporter and asked so many questions that before long they knew everything from the first time he kissed me, the night he jilted me and I woke up alone, his assertion that he didn't want to be my first, to ultimately his becoming my first.

I kept looking back at them and the satisfied look on their faces and felt like I had drifted out to the intensity of the other-world into young adult land. I didn't think I could take Trent saying, "That's hawt" again. Because they had the same look on their faces that I get when I have red velvet cake. Ethan's and my story wasn't red velvet cake good. It was riddled with conflict, doubt, and his mercurial behavior that I didn't think I would ever understand.

"I would like to invoke my statement again: your life is so interesting," David said as he headed for the kitchen. He returned with another bottle of wine, white this time, cheese, chocolate mini cupcakes, and grapes. The decision was made, I was moving in with Trent and David.

My reprieve was short-lived. Before I could try the chocolate cupcakes someone knocked at the door. David answered it, and Ethan and Josh came in. Ethan had my phone in his hand.

When the brothers stood next to each other, I couldn't help

but notice the resemblance. Both of them were very handsome with strong jawlines and defined features, but Josh's eyes were clear and oceanic blue, Ethan's were dimmed by the gray coloring of his animal that was always lurking. Josh held his intensity but it was there, magic so strong that even humans who might not be able to feel it or sense it felt the pulsing of something different coming off him. Ethan, from the lithe predacious movements to his keen look, touted his power like a flashing banner.

"How did you get my phone?" I asked.

"You left it at your house." That only raised more questions than it answered.

"Okay, just for fun, do you want to tell me how you got in my house?"

His look was similar to the one Gavin gave me when I asked whether or not Kelly knew he had a key to her house. The look that attempted to make me feel absurd for even asking a question. After all, why wouldn't they have a key? *Of course, it's not invasive and borderline stalker-y to have a key made without me knowing or breaking in for the hell of it.* The lilt of Ethan's smirk just made the situation worse, because he didn't seem to care about the invasion of privacy. The anger was there but good manners prevented me from reacting the way I wanted to. I wanted to go ballistic, to respond in a manner that could be used during a promo of the *The Real Housewives of Whatever*.

Before I could react, he handed me the phone and said, "Steven let me in." And then he looked at the empty bottles of wine on the table and then back at me and grinned. Stepping closer to me he lifted my chin until my eyes met his. He might have blocked out the other people in the room but I was very aware of everyone there.

He leaned down, his lips brushing against my ear as he asked, "How many have you had?"

I didn't know. I stopped counting after two and since their wineglasses were Big Gulp size, it was double what I had anyway.

In my peripheral vision I saw David laugh, open his hand and flash five fingers, and then pick up a bowl-like glass. "Of these."

Snitch.

Aware that Ethan's close proximity and my leaning into him made Josh uncomfortable, I stepped back.

I looked past Ethan to Josh. "Why are you here? Is something wrong?"

"I tried to find Ethos using the blood you collected and I couldn't." Trent's light umber eyes sparked with interest, his full attention fixed on Josh. But he possessed the same look that most people did when they realized that Josh was one of the most powerful witches in the country, avid interest with a tinge of doubt. Trent took in Josh's disheveled hair, tapestry of exotic body art that wrapped around his exposed arms, small studs in his ear, and wrinkled blue t-shirt that read ALWAYS BE YOURSELF, UNLESS YOU CAN BE BATMAN. THEN ALWAYS BE BATMAN in bright orange letters. Even David had that look as he gave Josh a once-over. That same look was on my face when I first met him. The *Really?* look. Josh's appearance often caused most, to their peril to underestimate him.

Josh smiled, his typical swoon-worthy wayward grin that seemed to make Trent and David not care one way or the other.

"Did you find out anything about the man?" David asked.

"Dr. Jeremy is still working on it. His bloodwork is different than ours. He's definitely not one of ours," Ethan said.

"Is this Liam's and the elves' handiwork?"

Ethan sighed, and I wasn't sure when he had moved and closed the distance between us but his hand was placed casually around my waist, and I became increasingly aware of it and his touch. I didn't like it, this feeling of vulnerability for a man whose reputation came with a warning sign. Again I attempted to step back; with a smirk, his finger slipped into the loop of my jeans securing my position.

"He says they didn't have anything to do with it, but we spoke to him on the phone so I had no way of knowing if he was telling the truth."

Responding to the confused look on David's face, he added, "Everyone has physiological changes when they lie. Most of us can detect them."

David seemed like he was information-weary and numbed by the summation of new knowledge about the otherworld. His lips pulled into a tight line, and I could hear the quick pacing of his heart rate. For the first time he was showing signs of being uncomfortable around us. I understood we were obtrusive.

"I don't do it. Not intentionally. Sometimes if it's really noticeable I can, but I wouldn't do that to you all." I'd worked hard to improve my perception of these changes, and with David and Trent I would work hard to ignore them.

"I don't detect their elven magic on the were-animal. There's something else weird about it and I can't quite put my finger on it," Josh said, his gaze slipping over in the direction of his brother's hand.

Magic's peculiar fingerprint was helpful, but if you had never encountered it, then it makes it hard to place it. After Kelly was bitten by a *Tod Schlaf* or *sleeper* we were given a sample of magic from the Makellos, the self-entitled elite elves. And thanks to Gideon using magic around the pack's house to impress Kelly, Josh knew what his magic felt like.

My day of blissful normalcy was over the moment Josh and Ethan had arrived, and it was back to my real life. When Josh suggested we try finding Ethos using my magic, I was back to the otherworld. There just wasn't a middle ground.

When we started to leave, Trent was on our heels like a kid ready to see a magic show. I tried to let him down easy, I didn't think it would be safe. I didn't know he could be so obstinate, and no matter what I said, I couldn't deter him. A flash of platinum eyes and a sneer from Ethan and he reluctantly stopped in his tracks.

Josh seemed to be feeling as sympathetic as I was to Trent, who looked crestfallen, his disappointment trailing up his face and settling on his features hard. Before we got out the door, Josh turned, twirled his fingers, and a glass lifted off the table. With the other hand he lifted the bottle of wine, tilted it to fill the glass, and slowly lowered them both back on to the table. Both Trent's and David's mouths were slightly open—they were dumbfounded and far more impressed with him than seeing me turn into a wolf. He could add them to the list of fans.

Josh and I stood in the middle of the room. I was a little tired after changing to wolf form a couple of times to try to burn off some of the alcohol. Josh as usual had invaded my space, so close that if he leaned in just an inch or so more our lips would have touched. Smirking, he looked at Ethan, who was leaning against the wall. I didn't like having an audience when I did magic with Josh. Magic was our own special world: I experienced it on different levels that I had learned to appreciate. The wispy aura as it surrounded me, the unique and comforting feel of the breeze of natural magic. It was more powerful now, but it was still Josh's and it was familiar. I didn't have to manipulate it and controlled it with less effort. There wasn't a caliginous cloak that lingered hours after the magic was performed.

"I hear you've mastered using the Aufero."

"Well, if master means no one died, Maya didn't take over, and the house was still standing after I used it, then yes, I am the grand master."

He laughed, moving and smothering out the few inches I had managed to put between us. "Then you'll take the lead and I'll help."

What? Was he day drinking, too?

"You have access to dark magic. I think if we are tracking Ethos, you are going to be stronger." Then he explained what I

209

needed to do. He made everything about magic seem easy, emboldening me. I always felt like I could do anything until I tried it and things went terribly wrong. But I had this, I'd made a safe protective field, I've moved objects with magic and even managed to do a spell with Ethan to remove the elven magic from him. I could do this.

He laid out the stained towel we'd used to clean up Ethos's blood. With the Aufero close I said the invocation. Midway through the invocation, magic took on a life of its own, flowing through me with little effort. The glow of the Aufero lit the room, a cyclone of magic engulfed us, the blood pulled off the towel, and directions were scribbled on my carpet. It was a good thing Ethan had the presence of mind to start writing them down, because seconds later they had disappeared. Then the blood vanished from the towel, not even a stain of it remained on it. This wasn't anything like other locating spells I'd experienced—no 3D map occurred, no sparks of light that fell over an existing map.

Ethan looked at the directions again—it was about an hour away—and then he grabbed his keys. Josh wasn't too far behind.

Seriously, we're really going to a location with coordinates given to us in blood?

The answer was a resounding yes, as we got into Ethan's AMG and sped down the road. I was still reeling from the dramatic change of events from day drinking with my neighbors to following blood directions to a remote location. With the Aufero in hand, I found some comfort knowing that Josh was with us, although he didn't seem to feel the same. The last time he fought with Ethos, he lost—badly. It was that loss and the one against Samuel that created the Josh we now had. Paying very little attention to his brother's erratic driving, Josh concentrated on something else. His features hardened, and it was the first time I'd noticed the change in his eyes: they were midnight blue, just a shade lighter than the dark coloring they turned when he used stronger magic. I'm not sure if he was doing it on purpose, but turbulent gusts of magic came off him.

Ethan must have sensed it, too, because I caught him looking back at Josh several times. The navigation system said that the time to our destination was an hour and ten minutes, but we did it in forty-two. If it could be called a destination—it looked more like a forest, dense large, verdant, extending out for miles crowding the area and obscuring everything. If there was a house in there, it was well hidden by the trees.

"This can't be right," I said, as Ethan stopped the car after looking for an opening that would lead us into the forest and driving for nearly five minutes with no luck.

"Of course it is. You don't discover this by accident. It's a perfect place," he said, getting out. Josh and I followed him as he walked around the periphery to find a small pathway, barely noticeable. The farther we walked the thicker the forest became and the more difficult the circuitous trail was to negotiate. But we were close: if I'd failed to smell the noxious odor of Ethos's magic that wafted through the air, the fingerprint of its existence and use tainted the air too much to be missed. We no longer needed to follow the trail because the strong presence of magic led us to a small wood survivalist home that blended well with the massive amount of bark that surrounded it.

Ethan took off his clothes and changed into his wolf before we advanced through the door. From a few feet away, Josh punched the door in, blasting it with a wave of magic before we stepped in. His magic clung to the air along with Ethos's and another familiar magic. Its fingerprint lingered and before I could place it, I spotted the familiar grungy blond male sprawled out on the floor facedown. Specks of blood surrounded him along with shattered plaster from the wall. He was barely breathing. Samuel.

Running to him, I turned him over and checked his pulse. It was weak but there. Josh walked past me and started to search the house with Ethan at his side. I tried to wake Samuel but he was out, his breathing becoming increasingly irregular. Magical fights were worse than cage brawls—you might not be able to physically slam a man into wall, but with magic you could crush him into one with the flick of a finger. Samuel looked like he had been pummeled against every wall in the small house. I could only imagine it was because he wouldn't give up the third Clostra.

When Ethan returned from searching the other rooms with Josh he was in human form and had been clothed by Josh. "The Clostra isn't here," he said in a level tone.

Although he would never show it, Josh's biting on his nail bed was the telltale sign, his nervous tick that things were bad. *Really bad.* Ethos had all three books.

Ethan asked for Josh's phone and called the East's Alpha. After telling him everything, he asked him to put extra eyes on Senna, my cousin and the only other person we knew who could read them.

Both Ethan and Josh headed for the door.

"Ethan, will you help me with him?"

He stopped midstride and turned. "Help you do what?"

"Get him to the car. He's just dead weight and you're stronger than I am."

Ethan stood in silence, the indeterminable look on his face quickly turning to stone, and cool indifference displayed on his face. "No, we're leaving him."

He spun on his heels and continued out the door. I gathered Samuel and started carrying him. I had the benefit of being stronger than a woman my size, but carrying someone who had me by at least thirty pounds of mostly dense muscle was still difficult. I hauled him along the uneven terrain far behind Ethan and Josh because I needed to stop frequently to reposition him. Unsure of how much damage there was, I tried to handle him gently. A quarter of the way to the car, Ethan stopped.

"Are you serious with this?" he snapped.

"I'm not leaving him unconscious in the middle of nowhere so he can die."

When he approached, his jaw was clenched painfully tight, his eyes blazed with irritation and anger, and his emotions were so turbulent I felt like I had just been hit by a windstorm.

"If he had all three books, you know exactly what he would do to us. Or have you forgotten his goals? He doesn't want magic to exist. He doesn't want us to exist."

Samuel had an agenda and was rigid about his beliefs. Magic shouldn't exist and he was ready to sacrifice everything to make sure that it didn't. He was misguided, but I couldn't leave him there. "Sebastian once choked me; Winter was president, vice president, and co-founder of the "let's kill Sky club"; and you've told me you didn't like me and have threatened me on multiple occasions—people change, things change. You don't dislike me now—"

"Don't be so sure about that part," he grumbled as he took Samuel from me and slung him over a shoulder and started toward the car at such speed I started jogging to keep up.

"You're jostling him too much. Be care—"

He spun around and looked at me. I hadn't seen the snarl in so long I forgot how freaking scary Ethan could be, and the growl just cemented it. "That's enough, Skylar."

Biting back my words took a lot of effort and I bit down on my tongue hard suppressing them. My glare matched his but I was fighting with too many people—I just couldn't add Ethan to the list.

About a half an hour from the retreat house where Dr. Jeremy was going to examine Samuel, he woke up. His deep amber eyes were clouded with confusion. He looked at Josh, then Ethan, but his attention stayed fixed on me. "I don't have the book anymore."

"We know," I said. "Do you remember what happened?"

"Three of your kind"—disdain hit almost every word—"and a witch ambushed me."

"That wasn't a witch. It was Ethos."

"That's not possible," he said, shaking his head. "Not at all. I watched him die."

"Let me guess, someone stabbed him in the neck or something equally as fatal," I offered.

"I shot him. I shot him after he killed my best friend."

"How long ago was this?"

"Five years ago."

I didn't need any more proof than that. The only documented supernatural that was that hard to kill was the Faerie. This was the second time someone thought Ethos was dead and was wrong. Then I considered the strange language he spoke to me when he was trying to awaken Maya.

"What do you know about Faeries?" I asked Samuel.

He still didn't look as I remembered. His hair was dirty blond and long, in need of a haircut and something to tame waves to soften the casual mercenary look. He didn't have on fatigues, but his khaki military cargo pants came pretty close and the blood-stained t-shirt completed the uniform. Just like the first time I met him, he had a faint smell of cigarette smoke.

His eyes were slowly regaining their vibrancy and intensity. The slight shift in his nose and the dried blood over his top lip made me think it was broken, but he didn't behave like it bothered him. Either he had a high tolerance for pain or his nose had been broken so many times he'd learned to deal with it. The gashes on his arm would need stitches.

"They are extinct. There are rumors that a few remain as spirit shades, but I believe those are just tales that keep people wishful of the opportunity to be a host and have omnipotent power."

"Then why did you try to kill Ethos?"

"He killed my friend. Like most foolish level fives he wanted more power, more strength, and the name Ethos was passed around like an urban legend. He would let you borrow his magic. Magic so strong you would be close to a level one. But Ethos's magic is different. The rumors of him being a demon-witch hybrid must be true. My friend called me, and when he changed his mind after making a blood contract with him, Ethos killed him. I was too late."

I looked over at Josh, wanting to correct Samuel's misinformation. I had a feeling that Josh did, too, but we needed to keep the information secret, especially since we didn't know what side Samuel was on. I didn't want to leave Samuel and possibly have him die, but I still didn't trust him to do what was in our best interest.

True to his nature, as soon as he was in a position to get away from us, he did. Once we were close to the city, he asked to be let out of the car. I tried to convince him to let Dr. Jeremy look at him. I was sure he had a concussion, and as he hobbled out of the car, I figured there was something wrong with his leg. But he and Ethan had spent most of the ride establishing that they didn't like each other. Whether I helped him or not, until I was on Team Samuel I was just as much the enemy as anyone.

It was Josh who took the diplomatic position and said, "We want the Clostra back just as much as you do. Our agendas may be different but we have a common goal, to possess the Clostra. I am a lot more comfortable with you having it than Ethos."

Standing away from the car, as though he feared we would force him back in or something. He looked at Josh with casual regard, and then his gaze moved over to Ethan, but it was me to whom he seemed to devote a great deal of his attention. "You could have stopped this," he said softly. "When magic is involved people will always fight for more of it, to subjugate and control. It was in your control to stop this, so whatever happens, know that you could have stopped it."

I wished I could dispute what he said. What would the world be without magic? What if we hadn't just stopped at removing my curse, but removed magic? Logan wouldn't have the power to perform magical bonds, and the witches would be neutered and divested of magic but so would Josh. We would no longer be able to change into our animal form. I still didn't think that was a bad thing, but what if Ethan and Sebastian were telling the truth? What if "laying the beast to rest" actually killed us? There wasn't a do-over in that situation. And I would have had to sacrifice Quell to do it. I couldn't do it to him or my pack. Being a were-animal and the life that came with it I accepted, but begrudgingly at best. I couldn't fool myself enough to believe that if I could do a spell to remove the were-animal, Maya, and magic, I would.

"Yeah, I get that. I wouldn't change a thing. I don't claim to know what is best for other people. You are welcome to your belief that *all* magic in *all* people is bad, but you don't have the right to take it from others. And as altruistic as you believe your motives are, they aren't. You want to kill a group of people for your belief. How are you any better than the people and the magic you claim to hate?"

He listened, and the fatigue of the day, or perhaps the pain he had to be having with a broken nose and possibly a sprained or broken ankle, softened his hard, stringent features.

"Your blissful naiveté may be appealing to others, but I find it very dangerous. I find *you* very dangerous. The vampire is nothing more than an abomination, and you and your kind are a vile mockery of magic. Animals that present themselves as human are just as abhorrent as the dead presenting themselves to the world as men."

I see the gloves are off. Fine.

I got out of the car despite Ethan's objection. Just a few inches from Samuel, I held his amber eyes. My voice was harder than I wanted but I was struggling with anger that was ready to explode. "I could have left you back there and you could have died. I didn't.

Yet as we stand here trying to help, your response is to tell me I am abhorrent and vile—can you remind me, who's the real monster between the two of us? This fantasy world of lollipops, rainbows, and all babies dressed up like an Anne Geddes photo is just that—a fantasy. I get it, you want to believe that the people who live in this world are assholes because of the magic. Maybe that's the reason you are using to justify you being one, too. 'Like alcohol, the magic made me do it.' You forget that there are vampires who have friends and loved ones who aren't vampires. You kill them and you kill someone those people loved. How are you better?"

I sighed, but I could tell I wasn't getting through to him. "The people who are evil with magic will be evil without it. They will just find other ways to achieve their goals. I'm not as naïve as you choose to believe I am. I know I'm not going to change your mind, but you are strong and we may need you. However you feel about magic, if Ethos and Marcia get their way, you will be a servant to one of them, and I don't think you will like that."

His hand raked through his wavy mass of hair and he looked away and focused on something to the right of me. "I shouldn't have insulted you," he said coolly. It wasn't much of an apology but it was the closest thing I was going to get from him.

"I can't go back to my place. When I've found a place, I will contact Sebastian. I will help you with this, but Skylar, my views still stand."

"We can find a place for you to stay for a while, if you need it." I didn't have to look back, I could feel Ethan's eyes narrowed on me, the achingly tightly clenched jaw, and the ire.

"No. I'm fine." He limped away; his tenacity and dislike of us overrode any pain or adversity he was facing. He would sleep on the side of the road or walk a mile on a broken ankle rather than take succor from us.

I could give him a bulleted presentation noting the flaws in his beliefs and logic and he would look at them, thank me for the donuts, and go on his merry way ready to create his magicless world of nice people who weren't afflicted by the terrible magic that made them evil once. *Nonsense.*

I wasn't back to the car a good minute before Ethan turned to me and said, through clenched teeth, "We aren't going to keep taking in your strays. Stop trying to save the world. It's not your job...." And he went on and on.

I was kind of listening. Who am I kidding, I wasn't listening. *The scary wolf is yelling at me again. Yada, yada, yadda, growl, more caustic words and ranting. Look at me, I'm Ethan.... I'm scary, growl.* And he really was. But after being in a state of extreme panic and fear for so long, those had become my norm. He couldn't get to me and as he went on and on about me getting out of the car and possibly putting myself in danger and not leaving Samuel where we found him, I considered tweaking his nose and saying "boop" while I did it. But I was only 30 percent confident that he wouldn't bite the finger and maybe take the tip off.

His rant lasted only for a few minutes, but it felt like it was hours. I never possessed the cutesy charm that allowed some people to get away with so much, but I tried it with Ethan. I gave him a cute simper and said in a gentle cloying tone, "Okay."

Neither worked—he didn't believe me any more than I believed I could change Samuel.

CHAPTER 10

*W*hen someone knocked at my door close to midnight, I expected it to be Quell. Vampires were often out now in the daytime, but Quell preferred the darkness. It was where he felt he belonged. I looked at the peephole expecting to see his vacant marble eyes but instead was staring at the back of Michaela's long anthracite hair that almost blended in with the darkness. After the day I had, I wasn't considering letting her in.

Just as I turned, ready to go back to bed, she said, "I have something for you."

"Mail it to me," I said through the door.

Her knocking was more persistent this time. When I looked out the peephole, she was facing the door with a lifeless body draped over her arms—Fiona. But I couldn't tell if she was dead or just unconscious.

I jerked the door open and Michaela took a step forward and winced, Josh's ward stopping her from entering.

"She is prettier than I expected," she said, her tone low as she took a long lingering look at the body draped over her arms. "We need to talk."

I looked down at Fiona; her head lolled to the side, her face pale, dried blood crusted around the puncture wounds on her neck. I hesitated but had to ask. "Did Quell do that?"

"Of course not, she's your gift to him. I did it."

I looked away. I just couldn't tonight. There wasn't any way I could control my temper. It was doubtful that if I let her in she would be walking out. I would try to kill her, and we didn't need to have a war with the vampires on our hands. "We have nothing to say."

"Of course we do, and if you don't let me in, your little friend from across the way will be the next body I bring by."

I grabbed a stake out of the drawer on the table against the wall and stuck it in the back of my leggings. I disarmed the ward and stepped aside to let her in.

Even carrying a body, her movements were svelte and graceful. Once in the middle of the room, she let Fiona drop to the ground as though she were refuse and not a person. I tried to look at the lifeless figure lying in the middle of the floor. My fingers clenched at my side and fixed at my hip. I counted backward hoping that would help. It didn't.

When she took a seat in the oversized chair across from me the only thing I could think of was the knife tucked under it. Her long legs casually crossed, her opal eyes focused on me with disdainful interest. Long languid fingers twisted around one another as she clung to the uncomfortable silence between us. I tried hard not to focus on the dead body in the middle of my living room, but with each passing moment it became more difficult.

"Skylar, please have a seat," she invited, waving her hand toward the chair in front of her."

I stood taller, keeping my position near the door.

"He's trying to replace us," she said. I dismissed the hint of sorrow that hinged on her words. She didn't deserve my sympathy and I refused to give it. But the solemn look continued. "I made him."

"And you've been making him pay ever since," I growled through clenched teeth, making a poor attempt to subdue my anger.

Her eyes narrowed, but she forced the demure smile that had become her mask and weapon. It belied her misdeeds and made her seem sweet, vulnerable, and dare I say—kind. But she was a monster in designer clothing.

"I am getting tired of people taking things that belong to me." Her gaze slipped in Fiona's direction. "First Quell took you from me, and now you are trying to take him from me. I guess in a warped way, it is fitting," she said lazily, sinking back into the sofa, closing her eyes for a second, pulled into her thoughts which I was sure were all types of crazy and dysfunction. With a heavy sigh she continued. "I take those that I consider mine serious."

"You considered me yours?"

"Of course."

"Then come and claim me." I really wanted her to try. No one was present to stop me. It would be just the two of us, and I wanted Michaela dead so much that it made the bones in my face hurt from clenching my teeth. Since our first meeting, Michaela had so-called claimed me. Like many of her created, she gathered an odd pleasure from feeding from were-animals, although, except for me, we weren't able to sustain them. I believed it had everything to do with dominance and the sick pleasure she gathered from subjugating someone perceived as powerful.

The smiled wavered for just a moment and then faded; seconds later she was just inches from my face. "Your little show the other day has given you confidence that you don't really deserve." Her movements where smooth and dramatic as she made her way back to the chair. A delightfully menacing look fell over her appearance and she smiled, baring fangs. "Please sit, we need to talk."

She waited patiently; the silence didn't affect her, but it made me nervous. Taking a seat made me feel like she had won something. I didn't want her to win, but if I didn't sit we would spend the rest of the night in silence glaring at each other from across the room. After a few more moments of quiet defiance, I took a seat in the chair across from her. After more silence I met her gaze. It wasn't cold at all; in fact, she looked dejected. "I saved him, he is mine," she whispered. "He was a broken man when I met him. Haunted by his past, unable to forgive himself for it. A beautiful broken man with endless potential. He asked me to change him but I declined. He wasn't ready." She smiled at the memory of Quell that predated my birth. "He hanged himself, and if it weren't for me, he would have died."

"He was trying to escape from the demons you want to unleash." I wasn't sure why she was here trying to have a civil conversation with me since there wasn't any civility between us. I am sure she wanted me dead as much as I wanted her to revert. "What do you want from me?"

Giving me just a hint of a glance, she returned to preoccupying herself with looking around the room. "His demons haunt him because he allowed them to. He held his humanity to a standard that no one else did. No one cared about the torture or the murders he committed. It was war and was accepted—to some, expected. The rules were different. I've done worse and will never allow the triviality of so-called human morality to stop me. And even once I changed him and he became one of us, where things are different, he clings to the memories and guilt of betraying humanity. How can he be so foolish? We are exempt from it, yet he holds to it." Her chest heaved in a long sigh allowing her disappointment with him to drape over her.

I really hated her. "No. The rules aren't different or the expectation for all of you to adhere to them. There is still a modicum of humanity expected from the vampires, but you just chose to ignore them. The loss of your human life doesn't exempt you from humane behavior, that is a belief about yourself that only you and your Seethe hold. You want Quell to become as morally bankrupt as you? I can't help you with that because I refuse to let him become what you are."

In a flash of movement, she was lying across the chair, her legs dangling over the arm, her head resting on the other, her silky hair splayed over the side. "I've created hundreds, but only loved a select few. I love Quell and at one time he loved me, too. I was his savior and he adored me. I don't have that anymore because of you. The relationship between Quell and me isn't the same."

"Well that's a shame. Now you will be forced to just sleep with Demetrius. Can you imagine that? Forced to only be with your mate. What will people think?" I said, rolling my eyes at her. The polyamorous relationship that she and Demetrius had was beyond my understanding.

"Skylar, I miss the way Quell and I were before." Her gentle voice was mesmeric, entreating sympathy that wasn't warranted or deserved. "I'm unhappy."

Michaela had taken narcissism, egomania, and self-importance and melded it together to create something that was uniquely hers. How big was her ego and thoughts of herself that she felt that everyone should be concerned about her happiness?

"Are you? Again, that's a shame. Sadly, I can't tell you how little I care about you being happy. In fact, I might be happiest knowing you are miserable. Was daddy mean to you? Still don't care. Did mommy not love you enough and now you crave it like a drug? Guess what? I still don't care. If Quell doesn't love you anymore or adore you the same, good. You never deserved it anyway. Are we done now?"

"Shut up! Just shut up!" She was upon me so fast I didn't have time to act. Fiery dark eyes were full of hate. "I don't know what he sees in you. We were all intrigued by the Midwest Pack's new little pup, but like all toy bitches the yappy little barks just get fucking annoying. You will not take him from me, do you under-stand? You fix this! I don't care how you do it—but you will do this for me. I will not be replaced!"

She headed for the door but stopped, her voice a cool drift as she turned to face me "We both care about him, but if he isn't mine, he will not be yours, either, and I will see to that. His death will be your burden to bear."

The words had barely left her lips before my hands closed around her throat and I slammed her into the wall. In one swift move, I plunged the stake into her heart. Her eyes widened, her mouth lax as I let her fall to the floor. Since she had just recently fed from Fiona her reversion happened slowly.

I crouched over her. "Good. Now I have your attention. Let's discuss my terms. You will allow him to have the Hidacus, he needs it. No more playing with him, he doesn't deserve it. Any issues you have with me, you address with me. He's not yours, he's not mine. This ownership crap is ridiculous. Do we have a deal?"

Her eyes were screwed closed, and the necrosis that crept up her leg made it hard for her to concentrate on my words. I inched closer. "I need an answer. You really don't understand the week I'm having so you don't realize you are just a blip in the crap salad that is now my life." Giving her body a sweeping glance, I leaned into her. "From the looks of it, you only have a few minutes to make this decision." I sat back on my heels and waited for a response as she struggled on the floor. The vampires were a lot of things, but they were bound by their word. It wasn't anything magical from my understanding but another part of vampire code. That and the narcissism that led them to always tell the truth were in a distorted way attributes.

"Yes."

"I need to hear it." And through clenched teeth she agreed to it.

I grabbed the knife off the sink and held it to my wrist, preparing to open it up to feed her, but stopped. I wanted her dead. Every part of me wanted to say to hell with it and just let the reversion happen and do the otherworld a huge favor. But most of all, I wished I could blame my actions on Maya. I wanted to say that a dark force was guiding my actions, but they weren't. My tolerance had been tried to the very end. My well of forgiveness was bone dry, and the ability to deal with the cruelty of others without retaliating had withered to within a fraction of nonexistence. Michaela of all people didn't deserve anything from me. The seconds became minutes and I sat against the kitchen counter, knife in hand, with the ability to save her and unable to do so.

Thoughts of Quell kept coming to mind. Although she didn't deserve it, he had a pervasive dedication to her that I would never understand. He wouldn't care that she threatened his life because she had saved him, and he believed his life was as much hers as it was his and she had the right to do with it as she pleased.

I moved closer to the body with a vile delight, which should have brought me shame, as I watched reversion slowly take over the greater part of it. In that moment I tried to find the very humanity she considered herself excluded from in me, to force me into saving her. But there wasn't anything there. I was going to let her die. Each time I thought about Quell, I tossed the thought away. When he inevitably started to look for her, would I let him and not say anything? Would I tell him the truth and hope he would forgive me?

This secret would go with me to my grave. Everyone was better off with her gone. And no matter how reprehensible this was—I just didn't give a damn. I was going to let her die.

"Please don't let me die," she finally said. It shouldn't have gripped me the way it did, but it did. But not enough to help. Several more minutes passed, and I waited for her to die. She would be dead soon.

Dammit!

I couldn't!

Slicing the knife across my wrist, I held it to her lips. Her hands had started to go through reversion and she couldn't use them and I fed her until she was whole but weak.

But the worst thing about the situation was that I was saving her life because her death would hurt Quell. He was the only one keeping her alive. Whether she accepted it or not, she was alive because of him. He saved her.

I opened the door for her. The lissome way she moved was gone, her movements disjointed and laborious. I'd like to think the final look she gave me before she walked out the door was gratitude, but I knew it wasn't. We were firmly seated in a place of mutual disdain and hate, and I was cool being in that place with her.

As soon as she left, I called Josh. "I have a dead body in my house."

"I'll be there in a few." The pack and their allies had a lot of flaws—a lot—but crisis of conscience wasn't one of them. I call and tell them I have a dead body, they send someone to clean it up, not a lot of questions asked. Preferably our witch, who cleans it up without evidence that a body existed. I tell them a skeleton is peeking out of the closet, heaven and earth get moved to stuff the bones back in there. A secret needs to be hidden, believe me they will collude with whomever to keep it just that. A few years ago this would have made me sick; now I understood some of it was necessary to remain safe in this world. It was a necessary evil.

It wasn't surprising that Josh showed up with Ethan, who greeted me with a half-smile that didn't make its way to any part of his face. Taking a whiff of the air he then focused on the pool of blood near the door. "Michaela was here."

Crossing my arms over my chest, I looked at the blood, too. There was more than I thought. I nodded. "I staked her."

Expressionless, he nodded and became a fixture against the wall as he waited for Josh to clear out Fiona's body. I wasn't getting anything from the brothers. Josh had also adopted a stoic persona. A kaleidoscope of colors covered Fiona as her body disappeared from existence in a blanket of magic. No matter how pleasing of a spectacle it was as magic swaddled the body, it would always seem like a cruel way to end a life, glamorizing a tragic end.

I hated Michaela.

When he was done, Josh asked, "Are you okay?"

I shrugged; there wasn't much more to offer. No, I wasn't okay with Fiona being dead. I had to be okay with us making the body disappear.

"I'll be fine; I just need to get some sleep." It was inching toward three A.M. and I was supposed to meet Sebastian in the morning.

After Josh left, Ethan stayed behind, still pressed against the wall in silence that extended so long, I started to fidget. He pushed up from the wall and took a seat on the sofa. "Let's talk," he said softly.

It took a while for me to make a decision to do so. I didn't want a lecture, and there was nothing he could say to me that I hadn't said to myself a thousand times over. He couldn't shame me about my feelings or actions toward Michaela because it didn't bother me that I wanted her dead. And he couldn't smooth this over and tell me it was going to be okay because everything that had happened over the past couple of days had proven otherwise. I had no idea what we needed to talk about.

"Please," he added as I continued to contemplate the request.

I nodded slowly and approached the chair but before I could take a seat he pulled me onto his lap. The defiant part of me just did not want affection because I felt it was a smoke screen, a prelude to conversations I didn't want to have. I assume he sensed my reluctance because he said, "I just want to talk, okay?"

Curling up on his lap, I cradled my face in his neck and listened to the slow, steady beat of his heart.

"Tell me what happened?" he asked. He was more relaxed than I expected, but I could feel the clench in his jaw against my face and the corded muscles in his neck.

I told him everything, unfiltered and uncensored, and I even told him the only reason I stopped. And for a long time he didn't say anything. His chest heaved in slow, measured movements as he stroked my arm while he listened. After a pause, he kissed me several times lightly on my forehead.

"Are you in love with Quell?"

The answer should have been an emphatic "no," but I hesitated. I didn't love Quell any more than he loved me. Our relationship was complex and even I couldn't describe the unique nuances of it. I saved his life, but it wasn't altruistic in intent; it was selfish. I couldn't live with myself knowing that he died, even though death was what he would've preferred. I forced him to live in a world where he found no comfort. So no, I didn't love Quell, but the feelings I had for him were probably just as strong as being in love with him. I didn't know how to explain that.

I pulled away and looked up at Ethan, trying to read the expression on his face. As usual it was indiscernible as he waited for an answer. I didn't want to answer because part of me wanted to say yes, because saying no felt like a lie.

Ethan was patient and when I attempted to distract him by kissing him, he turned away. Shaking his head, he said, "I need an answer, Sky."

"No, I don't think I'm in love with him" was my honest assessment. I didn't offer much more because I didn't know how to answer it. Maybe he would have understood if I tried to explain—Ethan dwelled in the gray areas, and that truly fit the complexity of my relationship with Quell. But it was Quell, a vampire; I doubted he would try to understand.

Ethan nodded slowly

"But I hate Michaela and it is because of Quell. I hate the way she treats him. She was cruel to him for no other reason than she could be. She wants him to be a monster like her."

The rigid muscles of Ethan's chest tightened and his lips dipped into a frown as he suppressed his own words. He considered Quell a monster as much as he considered the other vampires. The were-animals or the vampires never considered the hypocrisy of their beliefs. The vampires considered us animals although their deeds were far more savage than a beast's. And the were-animals considered vampires soulless fiends—I'd seen some of the things we'd done, knew our history and what has been done to keep the pack safe—we weren't saints.

I relaxed back against Ethan, cuddled in his arms in silence for what was nearly five minutes before he spoke, "Skylar, things are a mess."

It was obvious he wasn't just talking about the Michaela situation or Fiona. The last couple of days *had* been a mess, and it didn't seem like there was going to be a light at the end of the tunnel. Ethos had the books, and I was pretty sure we could agree that Maya was a Faerie that we had underestimated. There was a weird *manimal* or some odd-animal hybrid that we couldn't figure out. Kelly was missing and probably connected to the manimal thing. We were still doing damage control from the curse we removed. Ethos wanted to take over the otherworld, and the Ares were acting as his henchmen. And if I had actually gone through with killing Michaela, we could have added a war with the vampires to that list.

Ethan wore his emotions so close to the surface I usually knew what he was feeling, but tonight he was different. Was this desolation? I couldn't take it from Ethan or Sebastian, because they always seemed to have a trick up their sleeve, a plan for the worst-case scenario. Was every possible avenue exhausted and they really didn't know how to fix it?

"Has Dr. Jeremy found out anything about the were-animal?"

"Yeah," he sighed, and when he tightened his hold on me, there was a part of me that just didn't want to know. There weren't bunnies and rainbows at the end of that tunnel. "There was a synthetic virus in his system, similar to the one that's found in us."

Yep, no bunnies or rainbows there.

"Someone's trying to make were-animals?"

"Seems that way, but Jeremy thinks that whoever is responsible doesn't want them to change, just take on the other characteristics of were-animals. That's why his change was so difficult and he didn't survive it."

It wasn't the elves then because their genetic manipulation involved magic.

And Kelly might be going through the same thing. "We have to find Kelly," I said.

"Gavin's on it. He won't be any good to us now." That was the strength and weakness of Gavin. He targeted a single mission. When he set his sights on something, he had tunnel vision and nothing else mattered. He was good at what he did, which was only a problem when you were the target.

Ethan was comfortable with silence: we could stay there for hours and not speak another word and he would be okay. I was fighting the urge to turn on the TV or hum or something just to distract.

"Let's go to bed," I suggested. I don't think either one of us was going to sleep and it wasn't going to be because of amorous activities.

Things were a mess.

My attention kept moving between Ethan and Josh, both of whom had fallen into an annoying silence. Ethan at the wheel, his long fingers drumming against the steering wheel but not to the quiescent beats of the low music on the radio, but to what they usually did, the beat of my heart. It was fascinating and amusing at first, but I just found it hauntingly freaky at the moment. The double beats and then the slow downbeats as I attempted to calm down were echoed into the beats against the steering wheel.

He responded to my glower with a grin. "Stop that," I said.

A smirk replaced the grin but the beats continued. I rolled my eyes and turned to face Josh. "Why do you think this is a good idea?"

"Samuel made me think about it. If we are able to *call* Ethos like his friend was then we have the advantage."

"How is that going to help us get the Clostra back? You think he's just carrying them around in a satchel or something?"

"Getting them back is secondary. Ethos is the primary threat. We've found the Clostra before. We can do it again."

I wanted Ethos dead as much as the others did. Once he was, life got a lot simpler. I understood that, it's the calling thing that didn't sit well with me. When things seem too easy, there was always a price to pay. Nothing about magic was easy, especially strong magic.

As we pulled into the driveway of the familiar town home in an eclectic bohemian part of the city, the other obstacle presented itself. Not quite twelve and the area was buzzing with people. Just like the last time, I felt out of place in my simple t-shirt that wasn't worn ironically or paying homage to *The Big Bang Theory*, *Star Wars*, some superhero franchise. Three men had passed us as we headed to London's home; I suspected they were having a beard-growing contest, their features obscured by thick hair covering their faces.

We needed London's help. Although Josh was a level one and she was a three, her skills outshined his. What she lacked in power, she made up for with her ability to manipulate her magic in a manner that Josh couldn't. It was during their fight over this that I found out that Josh decided he wanted to graduate from the school of hard knocks and learn by trial and error instead of finishing magic school. It wasn't until he had been magically dominated that he recognized his limitations. He *was* magic, it was intricately entwined into his existence and he treated it as such. It moved with the same ease and control as his body, and there was a natural grace to it. But London controlled magic like a conductor of an orchestra, taking instruments and melodies that shouldn't be combined and merging them effortlessly. I could watch her perform spells with the same allure and fascination as I would a Cirque du Soleil show.

Last year Josh used their friendship to ask for a favor and got her involved with Ethos—something she adamantly wanted to avoid. London liked her world of anonymity—only Josh and the pack were truly aware of her talents—and she was happy to live the rest of her life that way. The crux of the problem was that London wanted nothing to do with the were-animals and the tumultuous problems that came with the otherworld. Her only connection to it being Josh, who had pulled her into it one time too many. That is what ended their friendship. She went as far as to block his number and after a couple of phone calls from Ethan, his number made its way on the blocked number list, too.

I didn't understand why they thought showing up at her house unannounced was a plan at all. It was a plan all right, as ridiculous as mine to find a fat-free, low carb, tasty red velvet cake.

Josh was reluctant to get out of the car; he looked at her house and exhaled a ragged breath. "She's not speaking to me because we involved her that last time." He hid his anger most of the ride; in fact, I thought he was okay with it until we were actually there. The pain of their fractured friendship was displayed on his face.

In a gentle lilt Ethan said, "We don't have a lot of options. You said we need to do it right the first time or Ethos will get suspicious. If you aren't confident in your ability to do it, we have to get someone who can. Okay?"

Josh sagged into his sigh, shaking his head slowly in quiet resolve.

"She'll be fine. It'll be fine," Ethan said. Neither Josh nor I believed that, no matter how confidently Ethan said it. And the confidence dwindled even more as we approached her small town house. London was a tiny ball of obstinacy and stubbornness and if she decided she wasn't going to help, then she wasn't going to help.

Ethan knocked on London's door and stood center of the peephole, and we waited, the seconds becoming longer and longer. Ethan knocked again, harder. Her VW Beetle was in the driveway, so she was home, and if we suspected she wasn't, we all saw her peek out the window.

"London," Ethan called out.

After a few more moments the door swung open and a pixie with pastel rainbow-colored hair that haloed in waves around her face stared out. Sweeping a strand of it from her face she exposed the identical tattoo that she and Josh had. Like Josh, her body was a canvas for art and although she didn't have as many as Josh, I counted five visible tattoos and speculated that her loose-fitting shirt and jeans were hiding more. She attempted a stern, baleful look and I am sure it would have worked if she were anyone else. I was the shortest of the three of us and at five eight, I had her by at least seven inches, and her full bowed lips and cherubic features weren't doing her any favors if her goal was to look menacing.

"What do you want me involved in this time that will likely get me killed?" she asked, her face set in a scowl that wouldn't relax.

"We just need you to show Josh how to do a spell," Ethan offered, stepping into the house.

Josh stayed behind, attempting to shrink into the wall as he leaned into it and watched. She stepped past Ethan and stood directly in front of Josh. Both of them radiating their brand of magic, that inundated the room, Josh's stronger than she remembered, or at least the change on her face seemed to indicate she noticed it, too. Her face relaxed and she stepped closer.

"What's wrong?" she asked, her tone more forgiving than when we'd first walked in. "Have a seat," she said pointing to the sofa. The tension between them vanished and Josh seemed like himself again.

I sat in the chair, Ethan on the arm, and Josh sat next to London on the sofa. He quickly moved, closing the distance between them when she sat at the other end. Josh told her everything. Ethan, guardian of the secrets, didn't look like he had a problem, and really at this point, the door had blown open and the pack's skeletons were on the floor for all to see. It was damage control.

"A Moura and a dark elf sitting in my living room. *Hmm, you all really know how to make life interesting. What do you want me to do?*" she asked, the hostility that was present at the beginning of the visit gone.

"Pala was a servant of Ethos; how did she contact him?" London winced at the mention of her good friend who had gotten involved with dark magic and borrowed it from Ethos. She lost her life when he decided he no longer wanted to share because it had weakened him too much.

"She called him." Then she said something that I assumed was Latin, but my rudimentary understanding of the language made it difficult to translate. I wasn't the only one confused. Ethan and Josh both knew Latin well, but they looked at her as though she had switched to an archaic language that they couldn't quite make out.

Her tone was as wry as her smile. "It's a very old spell and although it isn't against our rules . . ." She let her words trail off. It wasn't exactly an acceptable practice, either. Spells that lay in the gray area were just as dangerous as the forbidden ones.

"If you do this spell, how do you call him specifically? Without blood or a direct link to him, how do you know he will respond?" I asked.

"For lack of a better way of explaining, it is like putting an ad on Craigslist and then you wait." she said.

"And just wait for some random power to show up?"

She nodded.

Oh. Absolutely nothing can go wrong with a Craigslist power request. Nope, nothing at all. Okay, when do I start listing all the things that could go wrong with this?

"That's how Pala became indentured to him. It was too late for me to stop her when I found out," she said weakly.

"What if he doesn't show up?"

"That's the risk of doing this. You open your home, and you need to be versed on the powers that show. Because if you aren't, you have no idea what you are getting yourself into."

"Have Tre'ase answered?" I asked.

"I am sure they have. I only know about the spell, I've never done it," London admitted.

So we were going to do a spell that neither Josh nor London had done before. Put out a magical ad and hope that Ethos was the one to answer. There were so many things wrong with that scenario I didn't know where to begin.

Desperation had left us with very few choices so I knew we were going to do it. But I wanted to make sure we gave it a fighting chance at survival. "I have some of his blood." It was just a fraction of what we had collected after our fight and what wasn't used when we sourced his magic.

"How old?" London asked.

"Five days."

"We can try to source it, but it's old, and may not be as strong."

"We've done that already." I went on to explain what happened, including the fact that Ethos had the Clostra. Her frown deepened and mingled a little with the horror that was starting to take over her mood. She looked at the door a couple of times, and I wondered if she contemplated asking us to leave. She had a look as though we had just opened the doors of destruction.

"You need to find him," she said. Looking down at her fidgeting hand, I recognized that look: it was the one that said we couldn't give her any more bad news, and my heart ached at the fact that we had only hit the surface.

But I opted to wait. Let them try to source it. The sealed bag with Ethos's blood had been in the car, and I was glad I grabbed it just in case although it sickened me. *This is my life, driving around with a towel with someone else's blood on it. Eww.*

Ethan and I stood to the side as Josh and London attempted to *source* the magic. Josh performing magic had an impressive beauty, but it was eclipsed by London's mastery. Her skills made it seem effortless in execution and a wondrous event. Introducing technology to her magic, her dainty fingers danced across the keyboard, and a map flashed on the wall. The wrangled magic was pulled under her control, flicks of light bounced throughout the room, the map glowed a pastel rainbow. She looked over at Josh, whose mouth had opened as he watched her with the same wonder as a child at a circus. She winked at him and continued. The map flickered, different parts had addresses raised from it like a 3D movie, numbers popped out at us, and then everything went black; the map disappeared and so did everything on her computer. She cursed under her breath. "He's not Master of dark magic for nothing," she said.

"Let me try," Josh offered, standing next to her, but he had a hard time taking his eyes off her. They seemed to have rekindled their friendship and it looked like Josh wanted to move on to the benefits part of it, too. I got it, watching her with magic was so alluring it was captivating.

Josh's presentation didn't match London's. We didn't get the flashy lights, rainbows, and waves of numbers coming out at us in 3D but we did experience that tsunami of magic that took over the room. Cascading over it to present us with a map; a house emerged from it, barely readable cross streets, and a blurred address. It flickered, and Josh's eyes narrowed and became drenched in black as he used stronger magic to enhance the information and prevent it from disappearing again. This time it was London who stared in appreciation. The information stayed up for just seconds longer, but disappeared just as it had with London before all of it was displayed.

Ethan didn't look in my direction as he slipped closer to his brother and discreetly placed his hands against Josh's.

"Try again." Josh studied his brother with suspicion. Josh tried it again and his magic took on something that vaguely resembled his own. The room cooled to the point my fingers became numb, and I felt the air had been wrenched from me. London relaxed into the wall, her hand went immediately to her chest, and I could see her struggling as I did for air. Ethan and Josh became ensorcelled into a spiral of light that yanked at the map, pulling the information we needed. It held a little longer than before but the images were too dark to decipher. The information blinked erratically until it went blank and everything faded to dark, including the room.

Half an hour later we had lights but no information. "He doesn't want to be found again," London said, dropping into the seat next to Josh, so close she was nearly in his lap. As Josh rested his hands on her upper thigh, I was sure the "benefits" part of their friendship wasn't too far away.

"Should we try summoning him?" I asked.

"There will be an even larger chance that he might not answer. He's probably suspicious. But"—she dropped her gaze to her hands—"if I do it, I think he will answer."

Neither Josh nor Ethan asked for more information.

Really?

"Why?"

She took a long time to answer and chose her words carefully as she spoke "I wasn't that different from Pala. Everyone always wants to be stronger, have more power, have access to magic that is forbidden. I considered borrowing from him, but when I met him something didn't seem right. Pala didn't seem like the same person since she had gotten involved with him, and something was so off about him."

"You're sure it was him?" I asked.

She nodded. "Weird blond hair, odd purplish eyes?"

I'm not sure why he stuck with that, it wasn't particularly attractive but it was a step up from his regular form. If London thought that he looked odd as a human, she didn't want to see his other form.

I nodded.

"Yeah, then we met."

A couple of hours later, we were out in the middle of a fallow field nearly an hour from London's town house. She didn't want to do the spell at her home and I didn't blame her. This had chaos written all over it. It was the longest of shots and I had a feeling he wouldn't answer; after all, he'd killed all his servants before to retrieve the magic that he'd loaned them. He craved power more than reverence but it seemed that both of them were his weaknesses.

A few feet from us were Sebastian, Ethan, and Winter, the only ones in human form while a pack of twenty were-animals stayed behind them. Winter stood next to me, sword in hand, knife at her waist, two guns holstered along her side. She looked like she was ready to take on a small army alone, like there wasn't a small pack of were-animals and two powerful witches with us. Granted, London's Rainbow Brite hair wasn't exactly screaming "menace of the Midwest" and neither was Josh's disheveled coif and *Star Wars* t-shirt.

Sebastian, Ethan, and I stood back as Josh and London prepared the area, pouring a brownish substance that smelled oddly like sulfur and something metal. Then they stood with their hands linked reading the spell off her phone. I had become accustomed to the way magic affected the environment, the shift in the air, the way it swept over the area stifling it. But there was beauty in it as well; this spell shared none of those qualities. It was peaceful, unique, a quiet formed around us; small beats of magic's existence lingered, displaying none of the qualities that dark or natural magic possessed.

This should have been reassuring, but it wasn't. Quiet always meant there was a roaring storm just waiting to happen, and as expected it did. The change was sudden. Magic didn't just push us back, it slammed into us, sending Ethan, Sebastian, and me several feet as Ethos manifested. His attention fixed on London, the smile he gave her happened seconds before he wrapped his hand around her throat and wrenched her into the air. "This little witch stole from me."

She had. The *capsa* she gave us that possessed small amounts of his magic had allowed us to weaken him and ultimately kill him— or so we thought. Now, I feel like it had just pissed him off and he sat in waiting for a time to exact his revenge.

Her fist pounded into his arms trying to release his grip as she struggled to breathe. Her lips moved fervently as she invoked a spell, her hand covering his arms; a small flame roiled over his arm, the smell of burning flesh filled the air but he didn't release his hold. With a half turn, he chanted a few words and a small gust of wind brushed past us, blowing out the fire. London's cheeks were a ruddy color and her eyes started to bulge under the increased pressure he put on her throat.

Josh's arms extended and a force pushed through the air: it should have leveled Ethos and brought him to his knees, but it didn't. Instead a protective field enclosed him and his hold remained on London. The continued assaults to his arm slowed and the gasps for air became more shallow.

Josh's eyes were as dark as night as the field shattered and wrapped around them both, a powerful teal magical force pushing Ethos back several feet and snatching London from his hold. Josh kept it coming like jabs—they knocked at him and slammed him back farther and farther. Sparks came off Josh's fingers as they moved in a semicircle and a band formed over Ethos. For the first time the Master of dark magic looked distressed. The casual arrogance that often veiled his looks and the human face that he wore dropped, so that the charcoal creature with the odd orange eyes emerged, the forked tail jutted out and attempted to stab Josh.

Ethan and Sebastian, who had changed into wolf form, approached Ethos in slow deliberate steps, one on the right the other on the left. Ethan lunged first, claws and fangs exposed, ready to rip into Ethos. The screeching sound that came from Ethos was unbearable. Josh winced, shaking as he attempted to hold the binding. The sound continued sharp, shrill, and loud. We would all be deaf after this. The magical band shattered, Ethos's tail plunged into Josh and he collapsed to his knees, blood pooling around his abdomen once Ethos pulled out the fork. The tail lashed out at London, who moved in time to keep from being impaled but was nicked.

Sebastian jumped on Ethos and clawed his way up his back. Ethos violently bucked trying to shake him off, his tail twisting up and piercing Sebastian through his flank. He held for a while before being tossed off.

Ethos charged at me, heavy lumbered steps, the orange eyes widening with anger, his tail positioned to strike anyone who neared him. I turned and ran, trying to change into wolf form before he could get to me. The last thing I wanted was for him to get close enough to *travel* with me. I wasn't sure how far someone with his power could take me and I wasn't about to find out. The tingling started, I could feel the hairs pricking at my skin, the warmth that envelops me before my body fully gives into the transformation, but it didn't happen fast enough. The thick tail slinked around my abdomen and yanked me back, slamming me into his chest. I grabbed the knife tucked away in my ankle sheath and jammed it into his tail; the bloodcurdling scream filled the air, but he looked disgusted more than angry.

As if he made the decision reluctantly, something had changed in his appearance, his eyes. Preservation of my life was no longer the objective. The tail darted out at me with force. I flipped back and it barely missed me, but the wind from the force of the movement unbalanced me. Just as I got my footing, he grabbed my foot, slamming me to the ground and dragging me over. I contorted my body the best that I could to get at the knife, but the tail stayed rigid and out of reach. He tossed me next to London. His hands, or what were supposed to be hands but were webbed with phalanges longer than any hands should be, then pulled the knife from his tail, and he started to speak. The horribly shaped maw moved in an oddly disjointed manner as it forced out words. A spell. The same spell that Josh and my family had used to exorcise Maya out of me. He was going to use London as the new host.

I wasn't sure if London knew what was going on or just wanted to get away from him, but she started to move, and his massive foot came down heavily on her leg. I heard the bones snap under the pressure. She wailed, her body spasming from the pain.

Sebastian and Ethan, both with coats matted with blood, charged at Ethos. Gavin's body jolted into his lower half and Ethos crashed to the ground, his body flinched and stuttered as he attempted to *travel*, blinks of him disappearing only to be gone for mere seconds. A wave of familiar magic blanketed the air as Josh rolled to his side, his eyes the color of coal, one arm stretched out toward Ethos, the other bloodstained and around his wound. The grimaces on both Ethos's and Josh's faces intensified. Ethos sent the same bloodcurdling sound shrieking through the air, sharp and more intense than nails against a chalkboard. Like the rest of us, Josh had to cover his ears, and the moment he did, Ethos vanished.

Within seconds Josh was at London's side. Her eyes were screwed tightly together, ragged breaths escaped through clenched teeth, and her body seemed to have withered with the pain. For a few seconds she kept panting, hard, and eventually that slowed. Long deep breaths, and when she spoke it was in short bursts of words. "Broken ... it's broken."

Everyone had changed back to human form, and Ethan knelt down next to Josh, who was ignoring his wound and the blood that was still spurting from it, his attention solely directed toward London. When Ethan tried to move him away, he lightly pushed him back. Steven moved past everyone and then positioned himself next to her. Maybe it was the sincere, cute and innocent appearance, the very thing that caused people to consider him the unassuming predator, was the very quality that soothed people. His tone was low, gentle as he informed London about his plans. He was going to lift her and went on to tell her how she needed to place her hands to support her thigh to decrease the amount of pain she felt. And by the time he had went over everything, including telling her they were going to take her to the pack's house to have Dr. Jeremy look at her, she had calmed to the point her breathing was normal, the tears had stopped, and her heart rate had decreased by half.

Crap! I was counting heartbeats.

My injuries were minor compared to everyone else's and I didn't want any attention on me, not only because it was practical but also because I felt so guilty I could hardly stand to be around anyone, but I didn't know where to go. If I dared to go home, I had a feeling Ethos would be sitting on my couch, with a cup of coffee, wanting to talk. And it didn't bring me any comfort to know that he no longer cared if I died. This was a game changer. He wanted me dead and only wanted Maya.

As usual, I found myself back in my room in the pack's house. The shower helped and definitely made me look better than I felt. With the blood gone, my injuries looked better. They were just a few scuffs and bruises but I felt battered. Things had changed— Ethos didn't care if I died. That was the only weapon I'd had. It had offered some protection and now it had been stripped away. What would he be like now that the restraints were off?

If I closed the door, it made the room soundproof. After a few minutes I reopened it. I needed the noise: when things went silent it meant they were bad. Josh's voice floated upstairs, caring more about London and her fracture than the gash in his stomach. I heard Ethan's voice demanding Josh lie down and Josh telling him where to go and what compromising position he could take to get there.

Josh and Ethan were always competing for who could be the most stubborn and dogmatic. I always assumed that Ethan would win hands down, but it was a draw. Josh was just more covert with his obstinacy. Ethan let you know you weren't going to win with him. Josh played with you for fun, a devious charming smile on his face as he gave you the impression you had a chance in hell of winning, but you didn't.

I jumped when Steven's hand touched my shoulder. *Dammit, bells for everyone!* No one should be that silent when they walk—it was just creepy.

I could still hear Ethan and Josh going back and forth when I shook my head.

"If nothing else, they are entertaining," he said, leaning against the wall to face me. He had showered, too, but only had on a pair of jeans. His damp waves were a mess on his head and looked more ginger than usual.

"Are you okay?"

He moved closer. But I wasn't okay about a lot of things, including this being the first time we'd spoken since he moved out. He slid down to the floor and patted the space next to him. When I took a seat next to him, he extended his arm and opened his hands. I placed my hands in his and linked our fingers and we both rested into the wall.

"How bad are you beating yourself up?"

"My ears still hurt," I said, trying to take the attention off me.

When people were hurt because of me, I felt guilty. That wasn't going to change, and I doubt I would be okay if it did.

He rested his head against mine. "So, is beating yourself up about this helping in any way?" he asked, infusing his words with a little humor. He didn't have to, the Southern drawl just seemed to make me smile whenever I heard it.

"Can't help it."

We sat for a long while in comfortable silence, which I had to break to tell him that Ethos tried to drive Maya out of me and into London.

"He's getting desperate and angry." Steven seemed a little too enthusiastic and relieved by that. Nothing about that sentence was cause for relief. It just made things seem more scary and bleak.

"You sound like that's a good thing."

"It's not a bad thing. People act erratic when they are angry and desperate. It can work to our advantage. He's going to come after you, and we will be ready."

How do they seem so confident about things like this?

But I needed that confidence because it lifted the cloud of doubt that had surfaced, and even if it was just blustering it worked. The weight of the world seemed just a little lighter.

"You moved out without even saying good-bye," I whispered. Saying it out loud was like ripping the bandage off the wound.

"Things were chaotic and I didn't have a lot of choices."

"You had a choice, you could have stayed." My voice cracked, no matter how I willed it not to, and the ache returned just as strong as the night he announced it.

He moved, slipping his hand away from mine and positioning himself directly in front of me. He went to brush my face in the manner we had accepted as *our* apology. I didn't want an apology, I wanted him living with me.

He sighed, his face serious and tinted with frustration as he rested back on his heels with his arms crossed over his chest. "You know I would never do anything to hurt you, but I will if it is to protect you. You've made it clear that Quell is part of your life no matter how dangerous it makes things for you. Don't ask me to sit idly by and do nothing about it, because I can't. Living with you made it impossible for me to ignore it. So either way you're going to be hurt, but at least this way Quell lives." He made an attempt at a smile that just flickered away. He left without saying another word.

My life had become a series of compromises. I accept that certain things had to happen to make things easier and to survive. I hated violence, but I had to learn how to fight to survive. I was reluctant to accept my wolf but we lived as one—she was my best defense against magic and I needed her to survive. Was Quell going to be something else I had to compromise in my life? My relationship with Steven had become a casualty of my relationship with Quell. I washed my hands over my face and started to feel the small ache of a migraine coming on. I knew the answer; I just didn't want to accept it.

Ethan was standing outside the clinic, leaning against the wall with a painfully deep scowl fixed on his face.

"Josh?" I asked.

"Of course, because apparently being a witch is equivalent to holding a medical license."

I was about to ask why he was out there, but I was sure Dr. Jeremy felt like he had to separate them. I was going to stick to my feelings about the brothers when I first met them. They loved each other more than any siblings could, but whether they liked each other was questionable. They really knew how to get under each other's skin.

Just before I slipped into the room Ethan informed me that he would be staying with me for a while. I was used to him spending nights with me, but I knew now he was going to put on his crazy

245

hat. Things were going to get overbearing and suffocating. I was about to experience his and Sebastian's brand of protection, a nice place between stalker and obsessive-compulsive wacko. Any other time, I might have bucked against it and dug my heels in, but things had changed. Ethos no longer wanted me at his side; he was okay with killing me and forcing Maya to be hosted by someone else. I didn't mind Ethan being with me.

"Should I stay here?"

He tensed. The corded muscles of his arms felt like bricks under my head. His heart rate was steady, but tense lines formed on his face. He didn't need to say it: I knew what he was thinking. The pack's retreat wasn't as safe as it used to be. I knew it was only a matter of time before it would be abandoned. Apparently it was something they did often. When I first encountered it, I couldn't help but feel like I was in a fortress. The ward that protected it had never been broken and kept anyone uninvited out, it was an anonymous location, and you felt safe. It had been broken and the Clostra taken, our Alpha was nearly killed, and the anonymity no longer existed.

Did it really matter where I stayed? No place was safe when dealing with someone as powerful as Ethos. Wards were nothing, just small annoyances, and after today, I realized he was more than just a purveyor of dark magic or an incarnation of what was in me.

I'm not sure if Ethan could see my distress or sense my worry but he leaned forward and kissed me lightly on my forehead. And I stayed close, remembering what happened at London's.

"Your skills with magic seem to be improving," I said, lifting my eyes to study him. There always seemed to be an air of mystery to Ethan, his secrets unfolding but never giving a true picture of what he was. I moved closer to him, and something in him clenched—he was holding back something.

"Do I know everything about you, Ethan?"

His lips kinked into a crooked playful grin. "Of course not, that could take forever." I realized he was talking about his personal life. He didn't have to tell me about that, I knew more than I cared to.

"Not about that. About magic. I feel like there is more," I said coolly, easing into my accusations. His magic wiped out all the lights. There was magic that ensorcelled all were-animals, I was aware of it, nothing like that of witches, fae, or elves. But it was subtle and nothing to be alarmed about. Ethan's was always different but it had never bothered me before; most of the time the subtle nuances of it could easily be ignored. But with each thing I found out about him, I wondered if it should be.

"You know everything that is needed to be known." His balmy response quickly ended the conversation. He started for the clinic. I stopped him and walked him back a couple of feet.

"I need to check on Josh," he said pushing his way past me.

"Don't hide things from me, because I always find out."

Amusement made it all the way to his steel gray eyes. "Of course you do. I need to go check on Josh."

I continued to block his advance. "I know, but don't be *you* when you go in there," I said with a grin.

The smug smirk barely curved his lips. "Who exactly should I be?"

"Someone who can be reasoned with. A person who believes that others' opinions have merit and his way isn't the only way."

Ethan spoke five languages that I knew of and apparently I wasn't speaking any of them, because he looked at me as though I asked him to perform an acrobatic routine while singing the Peanut Butter and Jelly song.

I sighed. "Don't fight with your brother, please."

Josh was in one of the beds, propped on his arms, looking at the stitches on his stomach. There were a lot, and I'm sure Dr. Jeremy could make sure there wouldn't be any scars, but Josh was going to use it as an excuse to get more body art. His arms and most of his chest were covered with ink. Steven was sitting in a chair next to London, who was on the bed trying, unsuccessfully, to lift the casted leg without the use of her arms.

"How are you?" Ethan asked.

"I want to go home," she said firmly, her usual gentle features hardened by the glower.

Josh winced as he came to his feet, pressing into his stomach as he made his way toward her.

"London," he said. She wouldn't turn her head to look him and when he was just inches from her, she gave him a magical shove that pushed him back a couple of feet.

Yeah, we get to deal with an agitated witch.

But there was more than just agitation, there was fear. She'd worked so hard to be removed from this world and on so many occasions Josh pulled her into it.

"I want to go home." Her eyes narrowed, her lips set, and for the first time her angelic features looked hard, menacing.

Her angry glare rested on Ethan. "Now."

London that's not going to work. Is this your first time meeting him?

She jumped off the bed and would have tumbled to the floor if Steven hadn't caught her. Scooping her into his arms he held her; she buried her face into his shirt, lightly sobbing. Steven pulled her in closer to him. "Just let her go home. Can't Jeremy check on her there?"

Ethan looked at Josh, whose focus remained on Steven and London until he looked away. His sullen mood shrouded his appearance and he barely lifted his eyes to meet Ethan's. Guilt was something else. It made a bad situation seem almost unbearable, and getting London hurt was as bad as things could get for him at this point. Ethan regarded his brother before nodding, agreeing.

We pulled up to London's home and she hopped out as soon as the car came to a complete stop. Her crutches were too large because not one of the three pharmacies that we went to had some that could accommodate her petite stature. Josh got out of the car right after her and attempted to offer help that she quickly refused. Hopping up her stairs became too hard, and it didn't take long before she tossed the crutches aside and went up the stairs scooting on her butt, using her arms and good leg.

When she finally got to the top step he sat next to her, but she refused to look at him. He lifted her chin until her eyes met his and leaned into her as he spoke. She seemed only casually interested in what he had to say. As he continued I couldn't hear the conversation but reading their body language, seeing his grief and her determination to hold on to her misplaced anger, I knew they were going to be there for a while. I started people watching because it was in that moment I fully understood the depths of their friendship and how much he didn't want it to end.

Josh was a hard person to begrudge. His expressive eyes were as enchanting as any spell he could perform and his confident but approachable personality made staying mad at him more work than most people were willing to put in. Only Ethan had the level of fortitude, and Josh just seemed to like to irritate him for fun. Whether she conceded to forgiving him because she quickly realized he wasn't leaving until things between them were okay or she actually wanted to, by the time I looked back at them the anger had crumbled away from her cherubic face and she let him take her hands.

Sebastian was still talking, and I really tried to listen, but how long could a person talk about swords and blades? The answer was twenty-five minutes. He had been talking about swords for twenty-five minutes. A discussion about swords should start and end with "pick it up and swing." The end.

Yesterday, both Ethan and Josh stayed at my place, and I still couldn't sleep because I was expecting Ethos to just show up.

Everyone seemed confident that he wouldn't. I wasn't sure what about the situation gave them that confidence. Yes, Ethos was injured, but a being that didn't die from being stabbed in the neck probably didn't need a lot of healing time and there was no telling what type of magic he possessed to help him heal faster. I just didn't sleep, and when Ethan reminded me I was scheduled to train with Sebastian, it made sleeping even harder. Training with Sebastian. There were so many things wrong with that—especially the *training* and *Sebastian* parts.

At six o'clock I'd returned to the retreat, and Sebastian was waiting with several swords laid out. We hadn't practiced because he was yammering on about the various swords. *Hey, Mr. Alpha, give me the one that can cut through a body part—I'm pretty sure that would be all of them, let's get to training.*

Then he asked, "Which one do you think is best for you?" with a smirk, and I was pretty sure he knew every thought that went on in my head.

I stepped closer to the katana. "I would prefer to use this one. It's lighter and can cut off a hand or arm. Similar to the sabre Winter gave me." I pointed to the straight thin one, the rapier. "Don't want to use that one because stabbing him didn't work the first time, no need to try it again."

He continued to listen to me and the amused smirk remained but was brandished with intrigue.

Then I picked up the claymore. "His skin is so thick and scaly that if he's not in human form, this is the only thing that will behead him. Nothing can live without a head."

I really hope nothing live without a head. But Ethos was full of surprises, and I wouldn't be too bewildered if he picked the damn thing up and walked away.

Sebastian had the most melodious deep laugh; it was heard so seldom that it was enchanting. "And each time I looked at you, I could have sworn you weren't listening."

"Me?" I gasped dramatically. "I listen to everything you say."

"*Hmm*, that must be something new you're trying." He picked up the katana and moved, whirling around in a coordinated dance of silver. As it crossed midline, cords of thick muscle contracted and relaxed under his t-shirt. He controlled the blade with the same ease as his own body, just a sharp extension of his smooth, graceful movements. I forced myself to listen as he went through the stances and the best way to hold it to gain an advantage.

After five hours of training, I was pretty sick of having a sword in my hand, but apparently I wasn't leaving until Sebastian was metaphorically dead. He walked toward me, his blade moving in fluid and continuous figure-eight movements in front of him, a predacious elegance that pretty much screamed that death was coming. His light smile didn't belie the fear of seeing him come at me with a blade.

I lunged; he parried then moved to my side and thrust an elbow into my ribs. Pain seared through me. I pivoted to strike and thought it would come close enough to get my so-called kill, but he blocked it. He grinned then swiped my leg. Collapsing to the ground, I kept the sword extended in order to defend myself. An impressed brow raised as I parried each strike. Spinning on my butt, I blocked and returned enough strikes to move to my knee. When he struck again, I blocked it and quickly jabbed into his solar plexus and thrust the side of my fist into his knee, hitting hard enough for him to feel and know that if it were at full force it would have brought him down, like he did with me. I felt the pain, but not enough to be seriously injured. He dropped to the ground, and I brought the blade to his throat.

He grinned.

"Did you let me win?"

"It was a good sequence; it would have worked with anyone."

But not him. If I weren't so tired I would have wanted a rematch.

Coming to his feet, he placed the sword aside. "See you tomorrow, same time."

"I slayed you. How about eight?"

He chuckled as he went up the stairs, passing Ethan, who had been seated there for I don't know how long. "You defended your-self well. Six o'clock, Skylar."

"I kind of kicked Sebastian's ass," I joked. My body ached and tomorrow I was doubtful I could go another round, while Sebastian looked as though he could go several more. Violence and fighting seemed to energize him, a pure adrenaline rush. Would they ever admit that violence was their drug of choice, an addiction that made them higher than any drug?

Ethan was silent as he approached me with a hint of a smile. His lips brushed against my cheek. "You did very well." And then his lips covered mine, warmth pricked at my skin as his fingers dug into my side, walking me back into the wall. His kisses came harder, rough breaths beat against my lips. He tugged at my shirt, yanking it off, and then tossed it aside. Attentive lips coasted over my neck, my chest, down my stomach, leaving warm trails as his tongue licked at my skin until he had reached the edge of my pants, and then he pulled them off. He quickly discarded his. My legs curled around him as he lifted me.

I was distracted, aware that we were downstairs in the gym, in the open. Anyone could come down and see us. I reminded him of it, but he couldn't care less. I tried not to be pulled under the wave of raw sexuality that commanded his every move. "Someone can—"

His lips covered mine, kissing me harder, as the weight of his body draped over me and he pushed into me—hard. The wall bit into my sore back as he thrusted me into it. Warm fingers dug into my thighs and I tightened my legs around him and wove my fingers in his hair, I pulled him to me, the need to be as close as possible to him increasing. His intensity commanded the moment as his ragged breath beat harshly against my lips. I clung to him even tighter as he drew a moan of pleasure that exceeded the one before and then a deep growl that reverberated in his chest as we reached the height of our carnal pleasure.

He kept my legs secured around him as he rested against me kissing me lightly several times.

"Should I be freaked out that kicking Sebastian's ass turns you on? Because I need to tell you this is all kinds of strange. And a little twisted."

His fingers swept lightly against my lips and then he kissed me again. "Winter has trained you well."

Violence wasn't just their drug of choice, I'm pretty sure it was their aphrodisiac, too.

CHAPTER 11

*I*t had been three days since the incident with Ethos, and I couldn't blame Josh for getting restless sleeping in my guest room. He only left my side to visit London, who had been saddled with Gavin and Steven. It was hard hiding my surprise when he said that London had grown fond of Gavin. She disliked being pulled into the otherworld but didn't have a problem with the ominous guy who moved in silence and nearly disappeared and when you least expected—*Bam*, he's in front of you. *That's the thing she's okay with?*

Josh had gone to bed, and Ethan lay next to me as I kept going through the book he'd shown me about the Faeries. I wished I could put it down—other than recounting the horror at the height of the population there wasn't more information. I pieced things together operating mostly on speculation and assumptions. Emma was a witch, there wasn't anything to disprove it, but it didn't seem like she was as much the grieving mother as she was, like most of the witches, in collusion to help repopulate a dying race. I will never accept infanticide but understood why that was used as an option to keep Faeries out of power again. So many people died to kill them.

I had conceded that this just wasn't a coincidence. Maya and Ethos were the same, from the same ilk as he put it. He'd become known as the purveyor of dark magic, but to him it was just magic, it wasn't dark and insidious.

Josh's sharp groan alerted us before the crashing of the shattered magic that covered the area like a dense shawl could. We jumped up, Josh was standing near the front door. A blood ward when shattered has the same effect on the witch who created it. He was linked to it metaphysically, and he could control it, make it stronger if someone tried to break it. The ward was broken, and the door blasted open. A wolf lunged at Josh, pinning him to the ground, and before Ethan or I could clear our way to him we were hauled back by powerful force. Ethos walked in, wearing his human shell, his odd violet eyes sparking like fire. I struggled to rip myself from the wall but his magic was strong.

He went into my room and returned with the Aufero in hand. It attempted to form a field around itself, but Ethos's hand waved over it, dissolving that into a diaphanous sheet of destroyed magic that coated the air. I dug deep inside, pulling in the magic from it, trying to draw in the connection and force it to me. I released myself from the wall and summoned the magic to me. I thrust him into the wall with force and then tossed him to the ground. Anger washed over his face. He smashed his hands into the ground, and fire blazed around me full circle.

"That's for you," Ethos said.

Panic made it harder to think. I needed a spell, something, but before it could close in too much it disappeared. The burns on the rug were all that remained. And it had done its job—distracting me.

His lips moved quickly and he said the incantation over the Aufero. It regurgitated black fog that formed a thin stream and wrapped around Ethan. He gasped a deep breath. I could hear his heart pounding at an erratic rate, and his face flushed red, his breathing shallow pants as he slumped over. Released from his magical binding, he lay on the floor struggling to take deeper breaths. They came slower, matching his heart rate. Too slow to be functional—to live. It dragged until it was nothing more than a periodic thump accompanied by shallow slow breaths. When his eyes rolled back and he stilled, I screamed curses at Ethos.

He smiled with pure deviance and malice. "You made your choice."

Ethan hadn't moved in several minutes. Not a breath, not a beat. I blinked back the tears I would never give Ethos the satisfaction of seeing. As he watched me with warped pleasure, I vowed I would kill him.

As though he had read my thought—but I was sure the anger and thirst for vengeance covered my face—he headed out the door with the Aufero in hand, the were-animals close behind, one of them leaving a trail of blood, injured by Josh. Josh had quickly come to my side, kneeling next to his brother saying a series of invocations that didn't work.

Ethos stopped to glance over his shoulder at me, frowned, and turned around. Josh had taken a stance, ready to engage. Ethos simply rolled his eyes in disinterest. "If you want him to live, you will step back."

Josh wasn't able and I didn't blame him. He couldn't be trusted.

Ethos stepped closer to Ethan and blew over the Aufero. It crystalized to an odd color of red and started to pump. And Ethan took a breath, his heart beating slowly at first, a gentle beat, but the moment he saw Ethos it pounded harder.

"He will be as he should have been," Ethos said. And then he vanished with the Aufero.

"So he has them all?" Winter asked. It was the first time she'd said anything since she arrived at the house and she, Sebastian, Steven and Gavin were told everything about Ethan and the Aufero.

Most of their attention was divided between Ethan and the burned carpet. I expected anger and a stout sense of betrayal but they all seemed to understand.

"Yeah," I said, leaving out the part about the Vitae, leaving it up to Sebastian to tell them. As much as I hated it, I'd promised Ethan I wouldn't tell Josh, and I would keep my promise.

"If he destroys the Aufero, then Ethan will stay like this?" Steven asked. It was something I had asked myself over and over. Josh and I had discussed it and he seemed as desolate about another outcome as I did. If there were options, I really hoped they would explore them instead of going straight to "containing" the situation—murder.

The long uncomfortable silence persisted, but I could sense the worry from people extended further than Ethan. As far as they knew, Ethos had all the protected objects. What were his plans with them?

Dr. Jeremy kept checking Ethan, trying to ensure us he was okay, but he'd been asleep for over an hour. Although his vitals were all normal he hadn't woken up. At the two-hour mark, Josh still hadn't moved from his brother's side. I was slowly moving to panic mode when he came to. He didn't look like himself, and the tension that surrounded him made it apparent that he didn't need to know.

"Don't," he said when I moved closer but kept several inches between us. It took a lot of willpower not to touch him although I knew I shouldn't. The distant expression remained and he barely held contact. This wasn't Ethan.

He was okay, or as okay as he was going to be as a *Dunkell*, dark elf.

"I'm fine," Ethan snapped after Josh had inquired several times. It probably didn't help with everyone there, and Dr. Jeremy was the one to suggest that everyone leave. Josh was reluctant to leave and settled on just leaving the bedroom.

Ethan's frustration had created armor around him; he was

guarded. When I moved to touch him, he rolled to his feet and moved to the other side of the room.

"You were able to control it before," I reminded him.

"I know, it'll take time."

"Come with me," I said softly. When I extended my hand it took him a moment to take it. He moved closer, and it took even longer before he leaned forward and kissed me lightly. But it wasn't the same, he was off. He just wasn't Ethan. Although it frustrated me, he was usually unrestricted in all his emotions and at times his words. I wasn't fond of that part of him, but it was undeniably Ethan.

The symbiotic relationship he had with his wolf made his emotions raw, carnal, and unfettered. He was his emotions, and a simple kiss was like being swept into a wave. Now he was so subdued that he was unrecognizable. He followed me out to the backyard and I immediately took off my clothes and stood naked, trying hard not to wrap my arms around myself.

He grinned. "Not so modest, are you?"

"Yeah, it is still odd standing outside naked for the world to see all my lady parts."

He looked around at the thick crowded bosk that stretched for several feet, extended leaves masking the sky. Ethan stripped quickly, changed effortlessly into his wolf, and rushed into the woods.

I changed and went after him, just steps behind as he took off, weaving past the trees enjoying a freedom that he must have felt he'd lost in human form. Ethan's wolf was massive, nearly double my size, and keeping up with him was getting harder and I fell behind. When he noticed I was no longer behind him, he quickly turned around and was next to me. He nudged me with his nose and then buried his face in my neck, and I enjoyed the moment until he licked me. I hated that and he knew it. Playfully he tried it again, and when I bared my teeth, he grinned.

He rested his face against my neck before dropping down and

resting on his paws. I followed, nestling in next to him. It was comfortable—we were comfortable.

Sebastian, Ethan, Josh, Winter, and I were in Sebastian's SUV, with Gavin and Steven following close behind us. I was trying to hold on to my diplomacy, but anger was boiling in me and I bit down on my tongue until it was in a pain-induced numbness.

"Why are we going? There isn't anything forcing us to go. Just because Marcia calls some kind of conclave doesn't mean we have to accept."

This was politics and I knew it. Every sect of the otherworld was invited, and I wasn't naïve enough to think there wasn't some malevolent intent behind it. Ethan was now a dark elf and a conclave was coincidentally called.

"Skylar." Sebastian's tone was soft but firm. "We need to go. If it goes well, we have an opportunity to end the covenant. If we don't go, it would be an insult and slight to all involved and make us look guilty."

"We are guilty!" We had been driving for nearly forty minutes; I knew we would be there soon and I really wanted to talk them out of it. "We violated it. So why the hell are we going?"

I was being petulant, but this was going to end badly. We were walking into the lion's den to admit it, with indignation as though we had a sliver of hope to cling to. The covenant was simple: dark elf means death sentence. And we knew about Ethan and kept it hidden. As we pulled into a driveway, I became more desperate.

My debate was lost on Sebastian, so I turned to Ethan and said, "You don't have to go. *We* don't have to go."

He inhaled a breath and sagged into the exhale. "What do you think will happen if we don't, Sky?" he questioned.

What was the alternative if we didn't? I knew it must have

been worse because we were going into a situation that I couldn't see ending well.

The conclave was held at a large single-story stone building located on a grassy plain isolated from anything for miles. There were only a few windows and they were blacked out. Before Sebastian could ring the doorbell of the steel door, the only decorative thing about the nondescript building, the door opened and I saw the tortoiseshell-framed glasses before him. Bernard. The haughty man that Claudia had help us find a cure for Kelly's paralysis.

As he stepped back to let us in his lips pulled into a straight line, his hazel eyes heavy with disdain. Although he didn't say it, I knew he was calling us "the cursed," which was what he considered were-animals.

I still didn't know his title or job—maybe lackey. The same stern look steeled his appearance and periodically he pushed up the glasses on his face as we followed him past the entry to a narrow hallway. He stopped us before we could pass the second open door and was immediately flanked by two large men.

"We will need your weapons," the largest of the two said to Sebastian.

"We don't have any."

"Do you mind if we check?"

Sebastian pulled back his lips in a tight smile that looked more threatening than anything and then he nodded. Once the guard had checked everyone, he stepped back. Both men kept a careful eye on Sebastian and Ethan, and based on the looks on their faces, they had concluded that they could be trouble if things got out of hand.

As we walked into the room, Josh was stopped by Bernard, and the other large guy advanced with two large iridium manacles.

"You will have to wear these," Bernard told him.

Josh paused before he extended his arms. His eyes narrowed as his gaze landed on Marcia and the rest of the Creed, who were seated across the room behind a large ornate table, the only lavish thing in the whole plain building. If they were trying to hide it, they had failed miserably at disguising the sobering look of fear that shadowed their faces as they regarded him. He wasn't Josh, a powerful witch with mediocre skills, anymore. He was a menace to them and everything from their glare and the stiffening of their posture indicated it.

Marcia lifted her arms to show that she, too, had manacles on. Well, at least the field was leveled. This was just a meeting, there wouldn't be any violence. Yet, I didn't feel overly confident about that.

I guess I was the only one who didn't expect the pat down because my knives were the only things confiscated. When I attempted to advance the two large bodyguards stopped my approach. "You'll need to wear cuffs as well."

Good grief, does the pinky swear mean nothing to people anymore? It took me a minute to present my arms because I thought it was stupid. I could only use magic if borrowed or the Aufero was near: I hadn't borrowed any, and Ethos had taken the Aufero.

"We will only ask once," Marcia said. *The next time it will be done* by force was implied. They clamped the bracelets around my arms and then I followed behind the rest of them. Runes were scrolled across the wall, a spell that inhibited us from changing to our animal halves.

A haughty Marcia was surrounded by four other powerful witches who had willingly relinquished full power and authority to her. Her hair was still short and blond but it was pushed away from her face, drawing attention to deep-set eyes that were framed by small lines. Her thin lips never formed anything other than a stringent line, and her sharp broad cheeks made her delicate features look harsh, or maybe it was the glare that remained fixed on us as we took a space up close and center. To her left were Demetrius and Michaela. His supple lips were fixed into an amused smile and his hand was over Michaela's as it rested on the table. Her boredom had quickly made her look in a quiescent state.

To the right were Gideon and Abigail. Their appearance always struck me as odd. They were supposed to be fraternal twins, but except for their gender they were weirdly similar. Her hair was a long mane of platinum waves; his was short. The winged cheeks made him look too feminine and her too androgynous. Their bowed lips gave them a gentle appearance, and wide pale lavender eyes made it hard to describe as anything other than peculiar. They were both thin. He had a thing for Kelly, and Abigail was Winter's ex-lover. To the left of them was Liam, the ruler of the *Makellos*, the self-proclaimed elven elite. The two guards with him were dressed in the same military attire they had worn when we visited Elysian. His eyes were going to cross if he looked down his nose any further at us.

There was silence for a long time. "Should we get started with this witch hunt?" Sebastian said.

"We are still waiting for the Fae. They must not be excluded in this matter," Marcia stated.

When Claudia, Ethan and Josh's godmother, walked in, Marcia's eyes narrowed as she watched her approach the table. Marcia kept a focused eye on her as she removed the beige pashmina that matched her ocher-colored suit. Her beige high heels clicked across the floor, making her entrance grander than I think she would have liked.

"I apologize for my tardiness, but I wasn't going to miss out on a sale of one of my favorite artist's work for this contrived nonsense," she said, walking in Demetrius's direction. He pulled out a seat and helped her into it.

"I am not sure why you are here, you were not invited," Marcia said.

Claudia pulled a small envelope from her purse and handed it to Demetrius, who took it to Marcia.

Marcia made a grand presentation of pulling it from the envelope and slowly reading. "You are not a fae, I am not sure why they would send you as their representative," she said through gritted teeth.

"I have no home, therefore I belong to all and none," Claudia replied. "The fae have welcomed me as their own. It was your request that all sects be represented. They chose me to do that. You have no business questioning anything further than that. The fae are being represented." Claudia slowly looked around the room. "It appears all are represented, shall we continue?"

"There is no way your presence here is appropriate. You are biased and won't be able to accept all evidence against the men you have a maternal relationship with," Marcia hissed.

"You have no business here, either. You will not be able to take the same evidence and assess it without bias because you have already labeled them as your enemy. If I have no business here then neither do you," she said firmly, holding Marcia's gaze. "If you would like, we can waste more time and hold it to a vote. But the vote will be for us both. Either we both leave or we both stay. If I am to recuse myself, then so should you."

Marcia's eyes drifted over the faces of those sitting at the table, I assumed quietly assessing their standing with the pack and Claudia. She looked down at the letter again and frowned, I suspected looking for a loophole. In the time I'd known Claudia, I'd come to doubt she would ever allow a loophole to exist unless it was to her advantage.

The long drawn-out silence persisted until Marcia conceded to the fact that Claudia wasn't leaving. She had a problem with Claudia being there; I had a problem with Mason, the some-what leader of the elves. A feckless leader whose vote was as worthless as the paper it was written on. The position hadn't officially been given to Gideon, that would happen in two months, but upon his acceptance of the nomination it was tacitly accepted that the position was his. Gideon's presence was a constant reminder that he was not the leader anymore. If they could impeach him now and open the office to Gideon they would. I considered saying something but tucked away the disagreement if I needed it later.

When Marcia stood she commanded the room in a manner that made it apparent why the other witches had relinquished their authority to her. Her confidence and poise commanded a level of veneration that was awe-inspiring. She spoke with confidence and captivation. "We all agreed that due to the nature and the danger that the dark elves posed to us, regretfully they had to be contained."

I hated that word. It was such a diminutive word for such a vile act. *Contained*, the lovely word they chose for *assassination* or worse, *genocide*. I understood why they did it, but it didn't make the act any less abhorrent and to pretend otherwise was just infuriating.

Everyone nodded. She continued, "The covenant wasn't entered into lightly, but it was something we all agreed to uphold for our safety and of those not in this world. It was necessary to prevent exposure, but unfortunately Sebastian and his pack feel that they are exempt from any of our rules and reneged on the very covenant he agreed to." She stopped and slowly looked over the room. Her voice dropped, low and grave. "Even if we chose not to protect ourselves, shouldn't we protect being exposed?"

Demetrius leaned back in his chair, obviously unimpressed with Marcia's entreaty. I assumed that he felt that at any given moment he could be on the other side of this meeting. After all, his Seethe often found themselves doing damage control when a new vampire allowed his lust to overtake him, or one of the pretty psychotics that Michaela had created was unable to be controlled adequately. Michaela looked equally apathetic, finding more interest in her black cherry-painted nails. With a hazy ominous smile, her attention moved around the room, resting on various faces. Josh seemed to garner a great deal. When he noticed and looked in her direction, her smiled flourished into something lascivious.

Josh jerked eyes from hers and quickly returned them to Marcia, who was walking the small section of the room in front of us, casually tossing baleful looks in our direction, disdain escalating in slow beats. Her tone still grave, she continued, "Am I the only one concerned with what Sebastian is doing? He has a witch whom he has formed an alliance with that supersedes our control. He is strong and I assure you has the potential to be dangerous. He no longer follows our rules but adheres to theirs. His final slight against us is Ethan"—she looked at him—"the descendant of a dark elf, one who recently died. One that they kept hidden, and now..."

I didn't know we kept her hidden. But it was his grandmother, and of course he wouldn't kill her and I am sure Sebastian had his hand in the situation at all times. Sebastian's jaw clenched tight and his hands remained balled at his side. Amber rolled over his eyes, and if looks could have killed, Marcia would have been a dead woman.

"Is there a point you plan to get to or will we be treated to more of your show? I can do without the community theatre, get on with it," Claudia snapped. Rarely giving into emotions, she was usually placid. The room tensed. Why was everyone afraid that Claudia was angry? Who the hell was this woman skillfully hiding behind the disguise of an art peddler?

"Marcia, if you have a point. Will you please make it?" Her voice returned to its usual gentleness, emanating the same warmth she used with her patrons as she helped them part with obscene amounts of money for a painting or sculpture in her gallery.

"Of course you will take this lightly, after all, you consider them perfect, entitled, and impervious to our rules," Marcia said.

"No, not at all. But I see this for what it is, a witch hunt. Lay your torch and spear down and let's focus on what is real. Don't make this seem more detrimental than it is. Has Ethan hurt anyone?"

Oh, that's not the question you want to ask. Come on, Claudia, I thought you were on our side.

"As a dark elf. Do you know of anyone who has been injured or killed by him?" Claudia added.

"Well, of course not. You and I both know that they are quite capable of covering it up if it were to occur."

"Then if that is the case, why are we here? Your argument is that they broke the covenant and are at risk of exposing us. If they are in fact covering it up adequately, why are we here?"

Marcia flushed, losing the calmness that had colored her demeanor and mood. "Because they are dangerous, rule-less monsters incapable of being civil. Do you know why there isn't any evidence? They removed it from him!" she shouted.

Demetrius finally seemed to speak up as the debate became heated. "Wait. If they are capable of removing such things, I must agree with Claudia on this, why are we concerned?"

Even Sebastian was taken aback by Demetrius's defense of us. His face had slackened, mouth slightly open, before he found his composure once again.

"Honestly Marcia, this is a waste of time. They keep to themselves and whether it is out of their delusion of self-importance or they know their kind are the only ones that can tolerate them, either way, it is no concern to me. If Ethan is a danger, it will only be to them. Let them have at it. If he kills them ... so? And if they can control it—then even better for them. This brings forth another issue, how are they doing it? If they can do it, I am confident they should be given the responsibility to do so. Perhaps it will keep them busy enough to stay out of others' affairs."

Nicely done Demetrius. Always nice to be on the receiving end of your backhanded compliments and poorly veiled insults.

"Why don't you tell them why you are or rather were able to

control Ethan's ability," Marcia urged Sebastian in a smooth voice and took a seat.

Sebastian's expression was hard to read. The stern look faded into a smile as his eyes locked with Marcia's. He quietly accepted her challenge. "Recently we came in possession of the Aufero. Before it was being hidden, unused. Our research had shown that we could use it to stop more containment." His voice became tepid and smooth. "Marcia, you of all people know I share your desire to maintain our anonymity to the humans. But we don't share the same belief about killing Ethan. As you so assiduously pointed out, I had it under control."

Sebastian was doing what he did best, the thing that Ethan and he were very skilled at, which was giving just enough information to color the situation the way they needed. I wasn't happy about it, but I suspect it was a good idea not to tell everyone that I was a Moura. I am not sure why but he seemed to want to guard that information, and so did Marcia. But I was equally sure her reasons were quite different.

The moue spread over her entire face to her eyes, making them narrow. Her heart was beating faster, anger had turned her peach color ruddy, and I could feel that magic pooling over her, as the need for violence heightened.

"Yes, recently the pack has acquired a lot of things, including your little special wolf. She is quite the peculiar thing, isn't she? A wolf, with the *terait* and the ability to perform magic." She looked around the room. "You all know this, right? She is wrong, very wrong. From her recent arrival on the scene and the outbreak of chaos that soon followed."

She had everyone's attention. Each person except for Claudia had shifted forward in their seats and was paying close attention to me. "I know you all see her as a little oddity—the pack's problem. But Demetrius, were you not going to use her in a ritual to remove the curse that binds your people? It wasn't able to be used on any other were-animal but her. Is anyone curious as to why? Is that bothersome to anyone?"

We watched as concern swept over the room. While we were watching the front door making sure it was secure, she crept in through the back. This didn't have anything to do with Ethan, it was about me. We were being handed false flags and Ethan was just a casualty of the situation.

"Those of you who can sense magic, the variations and changes, have you noticed the change? Tre'ase, once controlled by the curses that limit their ability to wreak havoc on this world and restricted only to interact with those who seek them out, are no longer under such restrictions. Am I the only one who has noticed? Perhaps Liam can elaborate on the changes he's experienced over the past few months."

This was going downhill fast. The freight train was out of control and I didn't know how to stop it. What happened if they decided the weird oddity ends today? The six of us against them. Could we make it out?

"Are you saying that we need to be concerned about Skylar? She seems harmless enough, but I could be wrong," Michaela's saccharine voice asked before she turned to me, and I knew her question had malicious intent. She was planting the seed of doubt. She was trying to add fuel to the fire by just being an innocent observer allowing others to speculate while she stood back and watched a small flame become a forest fire.

Everyone was considering the changes over the past year. Was it coincidence that they occurred when I entered the scene? Was I dangerous to them or just the pack? If so, would the danger eventually affect them? Did Sebastian really care about protecting them? All those questions showed on their faces, the tension in their posture, the cool drift that came over their stares. Abigail whispered something to Gideon.

"It seems as though we have gotten off the topic here," Gideon said. "You brought us here to discuss a covenant that had been broken by Sebastian; now we somehow have moved on to his new little acquisition."

Seriously, stop it. Acquisition as though I was a pawn, someone's property, a thing that one put on display as a prize possession. I bet Sebastian didn't consider me a prize possession, not with all the peculiar things that came with me.

Gideon continued, "Let's discuss Ethan." Then he directed his attention to him. "How long have you been like this?"

"Initially seven days, then we found a way to get rid of the ability. Unfortunately, it has returned." If anyone expected anything less cryptic they didn't know Ethan at all, and they would probably be given something just as ambiguous from Sebastian.

"That's not really answering the question, and since your life is on the line here, it will be to your advantage to give us more." Mason spoke up. Abigail rolled her eyes dismissively, and I was still trying to figure out which one of them would cast the vote as the elves' representative. Mason was ornamental. There wasn't going to be an election in two months but rather an induction, because no other nominations were made once Gideon accepted.

Gideon casually looked at Mason and then disregarded him. He might not have initially wanted the position but he had slipped into the role quite nicely.

Before Gideon could continue, Marcia interjected, "We would like to know how you purged yourself of the ability. After all, we had tried for years, the elves have tried and the fae as well. Yet, the were-animals with access to a mediocre witch were able to." Marcia's cold glare shot in Josh's direction.

Mediocre my ass. People don't hate mediocre—they hate power. A couple of months ago Josh demonstrated that his skills and power now exceeded hers, and she wasn't very happy about it.

The dissonance continued as they waited for Ethan to respond. Ethan considered the question in silence for a long time, his gaze easing over each person, and he worked to squelch the disdain that worked over his features. He didn't like to be questioned: as someone who felt the need to only answer to Sebastian his contempt for the situation was apparent.

He chewed on his lips, I am sure biting back a caustic response, carefully choosing his words and making sure to only give enough information to diffuse the situation. He looked to Sebastian, and the nod he gave him was so slight, easily unnoticed.

Ethan smiled. "Skylar, our new acquisition as you put it, is a Moura Encantada. Most of you know what they are—if you don't, she is responsible for guarding a protected object. She is the protector of the Aufero, which she had in her possession until yesterday. It was stolen from us and the spell reversed by Ethos. Before she had it in her possession, it was in Marcia's. It is odd that she used it to punish the witches but not once decided to use it to help the elves from having to kill their own. That was our intention. We were fortunate to be able to practice on me, to perfect it. The reason Skylar didn't have it in her possession before was because it was being hidden by dark magic. Now, I guess we should all consider how it was hidden by dark magic, by a witch."

Well, that's that. When the pack decides to yank open the door to expose the skeletons they make sure they take other people with them. The best person—Marcia.

All eyes went to Marcia, and her face flushed, the mesh of lines around her eyes narrowed and focused on Ethan and Sebastian.

Sebastian added, "If you all can't see this, Marcia's motives aren't as pure as she would like us to believe. Last year, Demetrius's Seethe and my pack were attacked by Ethos. His sole purpose was to control us, and the rest of you were expected to fall in line as a result of it. Now let's think about what has occurred recently. Marcia had the Aufero, with the potential of removing the magic that makes dark elves lethal to us—she didn't. Instead, she kept it hidden with the use of dark magic. Ethos has taken the Aufero from us and restored Ethan to the way he was, and now, we are here. My pack and I are depicted as having this

Machiavellian plan. I ask you, who is the one whose behavior seems unscrupulous?"

"My actions aren't in question here, it is their pack's, and I hope you aren't swayed. It would have been a bigger disservice to give false hope," Marcia said, her face still flushed as she was left wondering how quickly the tides had turned on her.

"But you didn't even do that, did you?" Abigail asserted. "You didn't give an ounce of hope. Instead you kept this information to yourself."

Marcia looked at Abigail but barely acknowledged that she spoke, as though she was decoration for her brother. Gideon's lips tightened. "My sister asked a question, and when she does, you treat it as though it is coming from me or Mason."

It was apparent that Mason didn't agree with this and I didn't try to sort out their complicated situation.

The focus remained on Marcia, as they watched her, waiting for an answer. "I follow the rules. Adherence to the covenant has always been my utmost importance, not falsehoods and the hope of something that may never manifest. You all are being swept up in the little smoke screen that Sebastian and his group of rule breakers are putting before you. I am not the one who needs to be discussed, they are. We have a dark elf living among us, one who will not and cannot be controlled. What do we do? Do you trust Sebastian to handle the matter? Perhaps he will handle him in the same manner as he handles his new little acquisition."

Their stratagem had caused Marcia's plan to fall apart at the seams. It took the sting out of them calling me an "acquisition."

How quickly everyone's attention went back to Ethan, then to me, hopping back and forth with a look of curiosity and derision.

Sebastian's lips pursed slightly as he regarded Marcia with the full intensity of a predator's gaze. "That's doubtful, but maybe we should stop considering how I will treat Skylar and consider what you are willing to do to get your hands on the Aufero again. After all, you went as far as to have someone try to kill her, just so you could get it back. But was it motivated by your desire to make sure we no longer needed to contain the dark elves or your desire to have more control over the witches?"

If I could hear the quickening of her breath and the change in her breathing pattern, I knew Sebastian could, too. Until that moment, all we could do was assume; now she had just confirmed our suspicion. Marcia couldn't be trusted, she had betrayed her alliance with Ethos and attempted to have me killed, just so she could get her hands on the Aufero again. She might be allied with Ethos, but they definitely didn't have the same plans for me.

Abigail leaned over to Gideon and they went back and forth for a few minutes. And then he spoke. "I guess in this situation, we must consider him the responsibility of the elves, and if it was controlled before, I believe in good faith that Sebastian will handle it again."

Sebastian smiled and nodded his appreciation.

"I disagree," Liam stated. "I have very little confidence in Sebastian or his ability to control the situation. Gideon, you are now showing exactly the essential differences in how you will rule, as a fool."

Gideon simply smiled, allowing the insult to roll off him. Why not? I was sure when he was fully in position as the leader Liam would not have a voice in decisions anymore. Sebastian and Abigail had more or less ensured that a civil war would take place, and Sebastian seemed confident that Gideon would be the victor; Sebastian will probably have some hand in making sure it does. I tried to be okay with these things, it was a matter of survival. My ethics kept tugging at me, telling all the back-alley dealings, collusion, and silent alliances were wrong.

"This has gone on long enough. Frankly I am bored. You brought us here for a reason, Marcia, and I assume it was to vote on what will be done about this situation," Sebastian said.

Dammit. What happens once they vote? Do we get a vote?

I kept staring at Sebastian. *Come on, of all times this is the time you should be the jerk I know you are capable of being. Launch your threats. Tell them that if they touch Ethan they are all going to die. Come on, Sebastian!*

Bernard and his guards stepped out, I guessed to escort us out while they decided. Sebastian dismissed them with a look. "We aren't going anywhere. Any decision I make I stand behind it. I will not do it behind someone's back. If I decide you are going to die at my hands, I have no problem telling you to your face. I expect the same from you."

Liam stood. "I will not be threatened by the likes of you."

"It's not a threat."

Sounded like a threat to me.

"Simply, you are asking them to kill Ethan because of what he is. Yes, we have a covenant that I supported only because the dark elven magic wasn't controlled, and it couldn't be helped. And if this was the case here, I would have supported it as well. But it isn't. It was controlled; Ethan hasn't killed anyone accidentally. So you want him killed, we have every right to know who wants it," Sebastian said.

"Everyone wants Ethan dead," Demetrius offered lazily, still relaxed back in the chair, his interest in this meeting slipping with every moment. "The question remains should he die because of what he is? Stay, I have no problem with either of you knowing my vote or how I feel."

"You all are welcome to stay; I don't care, either. Understand that it is a collective decision. Any retaliation against any of us based on this decision is a retaliation on all of us and it will be treated as such," Gideon added, but I'm not sure why because I was sure how he was voting.

Sebastian gave a noncommittal nod.

Marcia spoke first. "I think the covenant should be enforced."

No surprise there.

"I disagree," Gideon responded.

One to one.

Marcia rolled her eyes before anyone could look at Claudia for her vote. "Do we need to ask?" she scoffed.

"It would be nice if you did, but you know the answer."

Two to one, our favor.

"I support Marcia. By allowing Sebastian to circumvent this you are condoning his rogue behavior. At some point we must stand against this man who feels that the only rules he must abide by are the ones he chooses. When chaos ensues as a result of this, I want those who do not side with us to know you are to blame." Liam's arrogance laced his words.

Demetrius's disinterest in the situation continued and I feared that he would go about making the decision with just as much interest. But he didn't; he studied Ethan for a long time. The mocking kink in his lips touted the power he had in hand. He hated Ethan. I looked around the room and tried to determine if we could make it out. Then what happened if we did?

"I think Ethan should die, and I am very happy to be the one to do it." The mocking smirk continued. "But it will not be this way. Sebastian is a son of bitch and his pack of animals are an annoyance at best, but one thing I am confident of is his commitment to not exposing us and his silly beliefs and rules. If he didn't think it was within his control, he would do whatever he could to make it so. He found a way to do it before and I am sure will again."

That's a color red I haven't seen on anything but a radish.

Marcia was so angry she was trembling. No, she wasn't just angry, I expected her to go down the line trying to bitch slap sense into anyone who voted against her. A few controlled breaths and she had found a semblance of control, although the bleak shadow of her discontent lingered long after she ushered the simple smile on her face. The room settled into an atmosphere of speculation and disdain had covered us as each person questioned everyone else's decision. Swaddled in it, everyone came out just a little more soiled than before. I watched with contentment as the arrogance of victory diminished on Marcia's face. Anger flashed unfiltered and nearly uncontrolled.

"The decision has been made. It should be respected but those who advocated for the demise of the covenant, understand that is essentially what you have done. Now we need to hold someone accountable for controlling the situation. I think it should be the elves, the Seethe, fae, and the Midwest Pack. I've washed my hands of this situation."

Look at that, a good old-fashioned tantrum.

"I am not accepting that responsibility," Demetrius scoffed.

"Then you are changing your vote?" Marcia asked hopefully.

Demetrius frowned, considering the question for a long time, his gaze cruising over Gideon, Sebastian, and then Claudia. "Fine, as long as they know I don't plan an active role in this because I can't express how much I *don't* care."

Vampires were affected by dark elves: it sent them into reversion, but if they were fed before it was complete, they were whole again. No one else had that advantage. You were dead, the heart stopped.

Gideon, Claudia, and Sebastian agreed without hesitation. Liam sat in silence doing what he did best, looking down his nose at everyone. He thought little of were-animals, he thought little about any elves that weren't Makellos, and with the disdainful look he cast in Demetrius's direction, it was pretty safe to assume his feelings about him, too. The only people who seemed to garner a level of respect from him were Claudia and Marcia, the latter of whom I was sure he had established some type of alliance with.

"Are we done here?" Sebastian asked.

Marcia could barely answer the question through her anger. "Yes."

Michaela and Demetrius were the first to leave and everyone else quickly followed behind. We were soon left with the Creed, who were not happy with the turn of events.

As we headed out the door Marcia stood. "Josh," she said in a low rough voice still angered by her loss. "Stay, we need to talk."

Barely giving her request consideration, Josh flicked his eyes in her direction and stopped in front of Bernard to have the manacles taken off his wrist. As he continued toward the door Marcia slammed her hands on the desk, sending a thunderous sound throughout the room.

"Josh! We need to talk now!" she demanded.

He only hesitated for a moment and turned to face them. Fishing in his pocket he took out a small oddly shaped medallion and tossed it in the middle of the floor. "There is nothing more for us to say, I am done."

I thought she had reached the height of her anger, but whatever he had tossed insulted her more than anything Sebastian and Ethan had done at the meeting. His eyes rested on each one of them, casting his anger in their direction, before leaving.

When the doors closed behind us we could hear the dead bolt lock. Sebastian scanned the area. It was dark and the cleared path that surrounded us made it easy to see everything around us. It was clear, but there was definitely a presence there: I felt like we were being watched. The caustic smell of Ethos's magic was dense as it coated the air. *Come out, come out wherever you are.*

"He's here," Josh said, looking around.

Of course he is. Waiting for the room to turn against me so that he could swoop in and claim me. I was scared of Ethos, a new feeling for me. I had been able to cling to the fact that he wanted me alive, and that wasn't the case anymore. I wouldn't be his ally as he took over the otherworld, I denied him too many times, and I was just a shell that held his prize possession—Maya.

We advanced toward the car but Ethos stayed hidden. Just a few feet from the car we were confronted by a pack of were-animals. Anderson, the Alpha, remained in human form at a distance, watching as the pack approached us. A large man approached Sebastian; he slowly started to shift mid-run and was in cougar form before he was less than a foot away. It didn't give Sebastian enough time to change and the large felidae slammed into him. He soared back, crashing into the SUV with a thud. He recovered quickly before the cougar could advance again. When it charged at him again, Sebastian slammed his fist into the feline's throat, and it dropped to ground gurgling. Sebastian slipped behind the animal and twisted the head until the neck snapped. The cougar lay still, body slumped against the ground. Before the coyote that had been stalking near Sebastian could approach, Sebastian was able to change into his wolf and collided into him mid-lunge.

A hyena's jaws were clamped about Steven's arm, and I ran over, jamming my knife into its side. It quickly released its hold. I kicked hard into its side until ribs cracked. It snapped at me, its teeth tearing over my skin drawing blood, but it wasn't able to get a good hold. It started for me again, lunging. I positioned myself to move but before I could Gavin, in panther form, crashed into him. His claws ripped across its stomach before doing the same to its throat.

Josh was a couple of feet away surrounded by several were-animals attempting to get past the protective field that surrounded him. A coyote beat its head against it several times, a lynx clawed at it, and an oversized dingo kept thrashing its body into it, doing more harm to itself than the field. Knife in hand I started to approach, going for the coyote, who was closest to me. Then a wave of magic surfed over me, and I fell face-first into the ground. Josh's field shattered, the last thing I saw before I was yanked up and pulled into what felt like a cyclone of magic. I heard my name in the distance before it all ended. Silence.

CHAPTER 12

*T*he nausea hit fast, and the bile crept up but I couldn't give into it. *Traveling* was still the worst way to get anywhere, and I didn't know how anyone could ever get used to it. The moment my feet were planted firmly on the ground I slipped the knife out of sight—I didn't need him to take my only weapon—and then spun, punching Ethos in the mouth. He stumbled back, red staining his lips and his eyes blazing. With a quick whip of his fingers I went back several feet. He sucked in his lips, tasting blood as he glared at me. Anger licked at the features of the odd form he'd chosen. His coloring was too pale, and the blush of his rage made him look ruddy.

I looked around the large space; stone walls surrounded me. The few circular windows were too small for me to fit through. I was in a blockhouse of some sort. I tried to find comfort in the fact that I wasn't underground. To escape all I had to do was get past the only exit I saw, which was directly behind Ethos—no problem.

The smell of dirt and something pungent filled the air along with magic, odd magic—dark magic. There was something different about it that I couldn't figure out. A mixture of magic that went wrong. To my right on a table in the corner were the Clostra, the Gem of Levage, and a copper-looking object made of a series of interlocking circles, which I assumed was the Fatifer. He had four of the five protected objects, and I'm sure he was working on finding the fifth. The one that Claudia had. I kept glancing around the room looking for the Aufero, I knew it had to be close.

I couldn't ignore the bloodstains on the leather bindings of one of the books of the Clostra. What did he try to do with it? Whose blood was it?

"You could have made it easier on yourself. It didn't have to end this way," he said. He seemed almost apologetic. The odd violet eyes shone like crystals, contempt and sympathy an odd combination.

"How should it have ended, Ethosial?"

He smiled in appreciation. "I go by Ethos now." Fear rolled over my stomach, but I didn't know why. We knew he was powerful and had been around for hundreds of years, the strongest link to dark magic, so I shouldn't have been surprised.

I took several steps back and he laughed. Looking around the room he frowned. "Why are you moving away? There isn't any place for you to go."

"Where are the others?"

"Others? I know of no others but you and rumors."

Being under his intense gaze was starting to make me uncomfortable.

"I want it the way it used to be. That was a life, people revered us for no other reason than that we existed. I didn't have to share power with them, to earn their adulations. The world is different." He stopped and gave me a once-over. "Even your kind is different, human-like. Before you were beasts we used for nothing more than entertainment or punishment of others. The vampires, what has become of them? The looks of angels, when before they were monsters barely able to stand upright. Gross creatures that commanded the night and preyed on the weak for food." The world he described sounded horrible, but he spoke of it with wistfulness and a tinge of sorrow. He missed a world that I could barely stomach hearing about.

Yes, the devil always wanted sympathy. Wah, people don't worship me. Wah, I don't get to rule people with an iron fist. Wah, I may be the only horrible one of us left. Wah, the vampires aren't ugly monsters that terrorized the night. Give me a break.

"Are you sure we are the only ones?" I asked.

He smiled at the use of the word *we*.

"I've spent decades chasing rumors," he admitted. He stepped closer to me, and I jerked back when his finger trailed up my cheek. "That's what I have you for, my sweet amphora. If they exist, we will find them. If they don't, we will make things as close to the way it was as possible. We will control again."

I jerked away. "No. You don't have me. I won't help you. This will not end well for you," I said, boasting a level of bravado I shouldn't have.

He smiled, his teeth stained from the blood spilled when I punched him. He winced a little. Really—the big bad Ethos found a busted lip painful? If the situation wasn't so dire I would have found it funny.

He gnashed his teeth and shrugged. "Very well, I no longer have use for you, my little amphora. You had more value when I thought you were the only one."

The footsteps were soft at first but quick, more than one. Rushed voices came closer and then Marcia came through the door, behind her three of the other members of the Creed carrying a limp body. As soon as they were over the threshold they nearly tossed the body on the ground.

"Don't you hurt her."

Dark curly waves covered her face; with her head turned to the side, I couldn't see the face, but I had a sense of familiarity. Ethos knelt down, gently repositioning her, brushing the hair from her face. Even unconscious she still had the same scowl of youthful defiance as she had the first time we met. Senna, my cousin, and the only other person I knew who could use the Clostra.

Damn. Things just got really bad.

As if he read my mind, Ethos gave a smile that displayed self-assurance and defiance. A big fat "I told you so."

"She's no more fragile than that one," Marcia said, her eyes trailing in my direction where they stayed.

Ethos's eyes lifted in my direction and there was a hint of sorrow. "She is, she will be less durable, human," he said.

Marcia made an irritated sound. "These affections you have developed for her are absolutely ridiculous. You realize she isn't anything to you, just a shell that hosted Maya, not her. It's misdirected affection for someone who isn't your kind. It is foolish. Were-animals are susceptible to fragilities that you don't see in humans. If my silver blade cut into her, how do you think she would respond?"

I wanted so badly to tell her nothing more than what would happen to her. A side effect of hosting Maya, and perhaps being changed as a vampire in vitro made me an anomaly. Silver didn't affect me. But that lack of information gave me an advantage. It's not like I was enthusiastic about the possibility of being stabbed, but I would heal fast even if the knife stayed embedded in me.

"You've been trying to use any excuse possible to keep her," she accused.

"And you've been using every tactic not to," he snapped. The odd violet color was barely visible through the slits of his eyes. "You tried to have her killed—that wasn't our agreement. Your impatience almost ruined everything. Do you know what would have happened to Maya without a host near? Of course you didn't, you just had your sights on one thing." Anger changed his appearance and he went into a defensive stance. Maybe I didn't need to run, if I stayed long enough the arguing might become more combative and then they would destroy each other.

Marcia pursed her lips together. "At least I would have gotten something done," she said through clenched teeth.

I wanted the fighting to continue: it was serving as a good distraction for them and for me to escape. The idea was quickly killed as Marcia's features softened, her eyes gentle and unassuming, her voice having a light timbre that made her seem kind, maternal. "My actions were selfish and impulsive. Know that it will not happen again."

Yeah, right.

"You've bonded with a body that you are convinced is Maya—a descendant. Sky is nothing more than a shell, deserving of no more consideration than you give that one. Senna is a better choice. As long as Skylar has the Midwest Pack, she will not subjugate herself to you. They have given her a sense of false security." Once again she looked in my direction, dismissing me with an upturned nose.

I wouldn't betray the pack—the alliance made me strong—and I wasn't likely to give in to Ethos. But would Senna possess the same veracity and ability to deny him? Was my family, if they were even still alive, enough to protect her, to give her the fortitude and confidence to refuse Ethos?

I glanced again at my cousin, still on the ground. They were going to remove Maya from me and I wasn't going to live through it. I didn't have a lot of options. To my right was Marcia and the other witches. Even if I had the Aufero, how would I fare against three other witches and Ethos? I was good with a knife, but not good enough to fight my way out against the three of them. My only option was to try to change. As long as I was in wolf form, they couldn't use magic against me. I didn't want to leave Senna but there wasn't any way to get her out in animal form. I inched into position, knowing everything had to be done quickly. I still wasn't able to change as fast as I needed to, but if I made it past the door and got enough distance I could change. I prepared myself for the pain of shredding through clothes. That always made things harder. I bolted, slamming into the witch standing in front of the exit. They had waited too long and she had put down her guard. I grabbed the arm that reached out to stop me, giving it a sharp powerful thrust that broke it. I could hear the high-pitched scream as I shifted into my wolf.

My paws pounded hard into the ground as I ran as fast as I could, trying to take in my surroundings. I kept a steady pace until a tiger smacked into me with so much force I tumbled across the grass, rolling onto my back. It burned. I spun around to see Anderson, two other wolves and a lynx at his side. I moved back several feet, surrounded by them, looking for an opening. The only thing I had was speed, and if I could get enough distance I would be okay. I lunged, they all started to jump toward me, and then I did a quick spin in the opposite direction. The coarse grass bit into my paws; as I made it to the side of the road the gravel cut into them. I could hear the pounding of paws behind me. I hoped there were just twelve, but the sounds mingled together, forming a thunderous rumble. I thought I would be safe in the street, a car had to be coming, but it was dark, not a car in sight, not even the sound of one approaching.

The good and bad about the Midwest was the abundance of farmhouses spread so far about by acres of fertile land. A porch light about a mile away breached the darkness and I ran toward it hoping that someone was home. I'm not sure how they would respond to a bruised naked woman at their door but I needed to try. Just a couple of feet from the home, I was about to stop and change back to human form when a body crashed into me and fangs sank into my side. I howled as another claw slashed my side and another swiped across my face. Blood dampened my face and blurred my vision; I tried to stand but my hind leg went limp under me.

Teeth gripped my leg and dragged me back slowly into the woods. I opened my eyes: two wolves were at my side, I guess Anderson was the one pulling me back to the blockhouse. I snapped at one of the wolves, taking a chunk out of his leg. He growled in pain and bit me, and more pain seared through me. My head grazed over the ground as Anderson roughly pulled me toward the house. Blood blurred my vision but I heard that familiar growl—Ethan.

The sound of crunching bones filled the air. I could only see shadows, but they moved around me. The pain was starting to feel unbearable and I had to keep fighting to remain conscious. I closed my eyes for a second, needing to rest. "Skylar." The voice was familiar but I couldn't place it. He said my name again, and when the person attempted to move me, I groaned, batting with my hand to try and protect myself from more pain. "Skylar, It's me Sam." I tried to open my eyes, but blood distorted my vision. "I need you to move, there's a lot of fighting going on and you're going to get hurt."

I rolled over to my stomach, the pain from the slashes on my stomach and back aching, and when I pushed up to my legs, I collapsed.

Samuel grunted as he lifted me and pulled me over to the side. I smelled blood and heard bones crunching. The chilling sound of a high-pitched wail was cut short and the shadow of something moved past me. I tried to make it out—it looked like part of an animal's body.

There was a large crash, and pellets of stone hit me. Josh's magic was strong and it overtook the air, bursts of it, and when large chunks of debris rained over me I dragged myself farther away from the house using my front legs. I was starting to get light-headed from the loss of blood. More debris splattered around, and when I tried to move again, the world started to swim around me and darkness hit.

· · ·

"Skylar." Steven's voice was gentle against my ear. I attempted to open my eyes, but they were swollen shut; and I was still in animal form. I craned my neck to look around. I was in the infirmary but my body ached just as much as it had before. Steven gently stroked the fur running along my back. "You've been out for a while."

I growled a response and tried to change but everything hurt and even holding my head up was a struggle. How much blood had I lost? How long was I out?

Firm light hands ran along my side, a feather touch, I could barely feel it. "Skylar, sweetie," said Sebastian. That had to be bad. Sebastian didn't use maudlin terms of endearment. *Sweetie, honey, sugar, baby*, those weren't words I had ever heard him use. The panic came on fast. I tried to move my legs, and they moved—I think. Then I tried to turn and bile crept up my throat as I tried to ignore the pain. How badly was I injured?

"Skylar." Sebastian's voice was soft and kind and guided me into a gentle reverie. "Lay here and take gentle breaths, okay? We need to change her back into human form."

"I tried, she's stuck," Steven offered.

"You have to be more dominant to force a change." Sebastian's tone was soft, but he was too calm, which only heightened my fear about my injuries. "It's not an insult against you; I think we keep underestimating her dominance."

Ethan was next to my ear, his voice so soft, I could barely hear it. "We are going to force a change. It will hurt and there really isn't anything we can do right now to ease it, okay? I'm sorry."

I couldn't concentrate on his words, just everyone's mood. How bad were the injuries that both Sebastian and Ethan had been reduced to this? What did I look like that my mere appearance left such a morose look on Winter's face?

Sebastian's hand laid over my front legs, firmer this time, and I felt the tinges of the change. My body elongating and reforming, my heart stopping just for a moment, the tension on my ligaments stretching to the limit only to rebound and reconfigure as I molded back into human form. But all that didn't matter because my back and chest were on fire, like someone had dropped acid on me. The pain ripped at me, and I felt like I was physically being flipped inside out. I screamed at the top of my lungs, but still that didn't relieve the agony and then I was whole—human—but the pain compounded. I couldn't see anything; my eyes were nearly swollen shut. I ran my fingers over my stomach, this was more than just blood. I felt something that didn't feel like skin but all the things that skin covered. I am sure my back looked a lot like my front where a claw had dug in and dragged across it. Each breath hurt so badly that I was forced to take small, shallow ones.

"Close your eyes, Skylar." I was trying so hard to force them open. Ethan held my hand. I think it was Ethan, it felt like his touch, but something was off. It was missing his emotions. He was forcing himself into an odd calm just to hold my hand. Unlike the turbulent intensity of who he was, this felt like the touch of a stranger.

I tried to sit up. The pain cut through me like a knife and I dropped back on the bed. "Don't," Dr. Jeremy advised, and then seconds later I felt a sharp prick in my arm and a haze overtook me, followed within seconds by darkness.

When I awoke, I felt odd. My body was so used to a high amount of pain that it felt strange not to feel it.

"Slowly," Steven instructed, moving from the chair next to me to help me. There were so many bandages on me, I felt like I should have been in a horror flick as an old-school mummy. I started to pull off the ones on my stomach when Steven's hand covered mine to stop me.

"Don't look at it yet," he ordered, his appearance dull against the vibrant green eyes that were wide and lively looking despite the bags under them.

"When is the last time you've slept?" I asked.

"I've been here two days since Dr. Jeremy sedated you."

"Then why do I still have injuries?" That was one of the perks of being a were-animal, we take a licking and keep on ticking, and if we don't it's just a day or so and we're back to it. *Okay, maybe bullets left us a little more damaged, but all I have are claw and bite injuries.*

"They're healed, but he wants to make sure you don't have scars. The scars were pretty bad yesterday."

When I picked at the edges of the bandages on my abdomen, he grabbed my hand.

"I just need a quick glance."

"No you don't."

"If I can tolerate looking at your sword wound and Sebastian's bullet wound, and the damage done to Winter last year, I am sure I can handle it."

"Fine. *I* can't handle seeing them again. Please don't take the bandages off." His gentle eyes entreated, and I couldn't help but obey.

I didn't touch the bandages. It wasn't until Steven sat back in his chair that I noticed that Samuel was leaning against the wall.

"Hi," he said. "How's your leg?"

Good question. I scooted to the edge of the mattress and then slowly moved to my feet. They seemed relieved when I bore my own weight. Samuel looked like he had seen better days—his hand was bandaged, there was a small scratch on his cheek, and he had a cane resting next to him.

"Is he dead?" Everyone knew exactly who I meant. Ethos.

"No," Josh said while walking in. He didn't look as bad as Samuel. He had just a bandage on his hand but he'd obviously had a battle that didn't go his way. "He was gone by the time we got there, but we have the protected objects."

"Even the Aufero?"

Josh grinned. "Especially the Aufero. Marcia didn't give it up without a fight."

A fight that he must have won and he seemed to be very about it. "Is she …"

"I wish."

Based on the grimace on Samuel's face he seemed to share the same sentiments.

"What about Anderson?" I was sure he was dead, along with the were-animals that were with him.

Steven made a noise.

"What?"

"After Ethan saw what they did to you—" He stopped and made a face. Steven had a high tolerance for violence so it had to be pretty bad. "Marcia and one other witch got away; the others weren't so lucky."

I couldn't say I was unhappy about it, but we were responsible for killing two members of the Creed—how would that play out? After being on so many ends of the political spectrum of the politics of the otherworld, I was aware that things like that had consequences. Things always had consequences.

I hesitated, thinking about the building crumbling next to me and my cousin in there unconscious and unable to protect herself. "What about Senna, is she okay?"

"She's upstairs, and I doubt she wants to see you any more than us. She locked herself in the room and is doing a great impression of an overwrought teenager," Josh said.

"Well she's not much older than one," I reminded them. "Why haven't you all taken her home?"

"We need to keep her safe until we find Ethos. If not, he's going to try to get to her again." Josh's wry smile showed he was sympathetic to what she was going through. She was probably scared after being taken from her home, and the were-animals weren't known for their hospitality.

"Ethan, Gavin, Sebastian, and Winter are cleaning up the situation with the Ares," Steven said, his voice tense as he sagged back into the chair. "Ethan and Sebastian don't want any more packs in the area. They helped with all the attacks, and Ethan and Sebastian think that Ethos wouldn't have gotten this far if it weren't for Anderson and his pack's help. They are now without their highest-ranking members, and Sebastian wants the remainder of them to disband."

Marcia didn't have the Aufero, nor did Ethos; I'm sure her alliance with him would soon be severed. All the protected objects were now in our possession, but I was sure the Clostra would not be for long. As before, Samuel would be given one. I doubted his assistance wasn't contingent on it. His motives were ruled by his doctrine and delusions of a magicless world. We weren't going to change his path or beliefs any more than he was going to change ours.

CHAPTER 13

*D*r. Jeremy wouldn't release me until my scars were totally gone. Then he came at me with the dreaded jar of hellfire. Of course, he called it by another name, but cream of hellfire seemed apropos. He had used it the day before, and it was like acid on my skin. Having the scars didn't seem so important. Scars built character.

He sat next to me to remove my bandages. Part of me thought they were to keep me from seeing how bad the scars were. But the bandage on my face looked worse to me than any scar. He took the one off my face first and studied me for a while. "I thought you were going to lose the eye," he admitted, "but everything looks good."

"Because you're the best." I gave the preemptive compliment. We often made a point of blandishing him with them or he would go into his soliloquy about being unappreciated. And he wasn't entirely incorrect. We had gotten used to him and probably took him for granted. If Dr. Jeremy couldn't fix you, no one could. When I suggested he hold off on putting the cream on my back, which for some reason hurt worse there than on my face, he simply said, "If I don't do it, you won't be able to wear those bright pink tank tops with the cat on it that you're so fond of." He turned me around. "You do realize you're a wolf, right?"

I was willing to give my Hello Kitty t-shirts up if it meant never feeling the sting again and told Jeremy the same thing.

"You say that now, but I know better," he said as he shushed me.

After ten minutes of excruciating pain, I was re-bandaged and still feeling the dull sting of the medicine that remained on me.

Ethan laughed as he walked through the door. "Some of the things you yelled out aren't even curses. Are we making up languages now?" I had taken a page from Sable, and it kind of felt good. It was a mixed bag of whatever words came to me. So what if *crap-snacks* wasn't a real word, it made me feel better.

"Let me put it on you and see how you like it."

He scooped some into his hand and spread it over his forearm. His jaw clenched tight as he rubbed it into his skin, but he didn't make a sound and let out slow easy breaths, accepting the pain as part of him as the skin started to bubble a little and then melt way to reveal a smoother layer underneath.

"It does hurt," he acknowledged.

"Really? My screaming wasn't a good enough warning? You had to see for yourself."

"You'll be fine," he teased, before kissing me lightly on the lips. Dr. Jeremy was the only person in the room, but it was the first time he'd done anything like that. PDA wasn't Ethan's thing. He remained close, his lips brushing against my cheek as he spoke. "How are you?"

"I feel better than I look."

He nodded and his lips kinked into a half smile. He was still off, and I hated him like this. I didn't always like being inundated by his emotions; but they were him, tightly held to his very being. Without them, it wasn't Ethan.

"We should remove the magic again," I suggested, moving back so I could look at his face.

"I plan to, but I want Josh to do it."

I nodded. It wasn't a slight against me. I found out about Ethan being a dark elf before Josh and it was a source of animosity between them.

"Do you plan on telling him about the Veritas?"

I tried to read the stolid look but as usual I couldn't, and the only thing he offered was a noncommittal "We'll see."

"I stand by what I said. Either you tell him or—"

His finger pressed against my lip, cutting me off. "You know how I feel about threats," he warned.

I bit his finger—hard. Enough to draw blood. He pulled back and brought it to his lips trying to stop the bleeding.

"You know how I feel about people doing that to me." I held back the grin as Ethan scowled. "I understand why some things need to be kept secret, but there shouldn't be any between Josh and you." The one he was keeping from Josh was the only secret we had. They had opened the closet and spilled everything else just to bring down Marcia.

"I'll think about it," he said, before he backed out of the room and left.

He could have just said no, because the amount of time he was there was about as much consideration as he planned to give it.

Dr. Jeremy had moved back to his desk in the corner, looking over papers while scanning his computer. His frowned deepened.

"Did the man say anything else besides Kelly's name?".

He actually didn't say Kelly's name, either, but I had a feeling he needed that to be the case. "No. Did you find something?" I looked over his shoulder. Most of the pages consisted of lab work and photos and comparisons of the differences between a born were-animal, a turned were-animal, and the manimal that died in David's home. Steven was the only turned were-animal that I knew of, but there could be more, it just wasn't discussed.

Changing a person to a were-animal didn't happen often and was usually a final option in trying to save them.

Leaning back in the chair, he scrubbed his hands over his beard before he said, "I hope she isn't going through what he went through." His face was solemn and his voice laden with sorrow and guilt. The sorrow I understood, but not the guilt.

"This isn't your fault, you know that, right?"

"Then whose is it?" Pain reigned over his features, his words tinted with a heartbreaking sadness. His guilt was woven from fraternal love that he had for Kelly. In his mind he was supposed to protect her, and no matter how little control he had over a situation he would find a way to make it his fault that 'he didn't.

"You're positive Liam wasn't involved with it?" I hated referring to the manimal as *it* or even *manimal* but I didn't have a much of a choice.

"No, there isn't any magic present. He was injected with a virus, look at this." Dr. Jeremy went on to explain in the only way he knew how, unnecessarily complicated. In essence he was injected with a virus that replicated all the enhancements of the were-animal, but a binder forced the body not to change. It was definitely science. Someone was creating animals, strong, with enhanced hearing, vision, and speed but in human form.

"So it has to be in a lab or something."

He nodded. "Winter said you saw something like that a few days ago. Where?" He brought up a map. I pointed to a spot close to Kelly's home. He marked it, Kelly's home, and then David's.

"I bet you the lab or wherever it is being done is near David's home," said Sebastian's satin baritone voice. I jerked in his direction, surprised by his presence.

We are going to have to discuss the bell thing. Everyone needs to wear one.

He moved in closer, frowning as he looked at the map. "If she sent him to get help, she would have sent him to the closest pack member's home near where she is," he suggested.

As Sebastian continued to look at the map, he said, "Gavin has been looking for homes, but we should be looking for buildings as well. We'll send a team to look for her. I'll call Joan and ask if she can send some people up to help. She has great hunters and investigators." He took out his phone, then made a face. "We need to get in touch with Chris, too."

"I think she should stay lost," I blurted before I could tame my renegade tongue.

"Any other time I would have to agree, but things like this are her specialty. She will know something about it."

"Are you sure she is actually missing?"

She seemed to be okay with her new role as Seethe Princess and Demetrius's mistress or whatever the kids are calling it these days. Although she adamantly denied a sexual relationship with Demetrius, whatever was going on between them was far from platonic. I would never understand the polyamorous relationship he and Michaela had and Chris was deeply entwined in it.

Jeremy's relief was palatable as Sebastian made a few phone calls, one to the Alpha of the East Coast Pack and one to Joan.

Being around Gavin was one of my least favorite things, but he needed to know what was being worked on. All I had to do was find what corner he had skulked into becoming nearly invisible to anyone who was looking for him. *Here kitty, kitty. I have some information for you.*

No matter how many times I came to the retreat the size of it was always overwhelming. Twelve bedrooms, a multiroom basement with two entrances, two spiral staircases, a huge eat-in kitchen, a formal dining room, living room, sitting room and an ostentatious media room, library, gym, fitness center, infirmary, recovery room and an office, it was quite easy to get lost in the house and that made it even harder to find someone. After looking for Gavin for fifteen minutes, I finally found him coming out of Sebastian's office.

Before I could call his name to get his attention he turned, brushing his midnight hair from his face to reveal deep emotive eyes. His wide mouth pulled into a full line. "Don't call me kitty," he snarled.

Oh you heard that. I guess my bad *isn't going to cut it.*

"What do you want?" he asked in a curt tone.

"I want to discuss Sable."

"There is nothing to discuss, I am done with her."

"I get that. I know you have the fractious, ominous, broody, sexy dominant thing going on. Thumbs-up, you nailed it."

His chuckle was just as dark as his eyes. His vocal cords were probably shocked from producing a sound they hadn't made before.

"You think I'm sexy." A smile reached his eyes but barely curled his lips.

"I said like thirty things before that and twenty more after it, and that's what you took from it? If it weren't for Sable we wouldn't have a lot of the information we have now. She's a very disturbed woman, and the way you ended things with her was cruel. You have to do something about it."

I was speaking quickly because it was only a matter of time before he lost interest and just walked away from me mid-sentence. It wasn't paranoia to be worried about it. It was part of the Gavin package—I had watched him do it to others. He didn't excuse himself; once he was bored enough he simply walked away. Surprisingly, I had his attention and he held my eyes intently as I spoke.

"She helped because of you. I think she's sorry for what she said." I didn't want to have sympathy for her, but somehow it had squirmed its way in. Sebastian was right, she was like Quell, and there was a part of me that needed to help her. Even if helping her was mending whatever the heck was going on with her and

Gavin. "Just give her some closure. Something better than telling her it's over in front of a room full of people."

When I saw the back of his head as he turned and walked away, it was safe to assume the conversation was over. *Gavin, be weirder.*

Before he cleared the corner, he said, "I will talk to her today."

"Thank you."

"I'm not doing it for you."

"You couldn't just give me that one!"

He turned around and smiled.

Did I just get a laugh and a smile from Gavin? I may be a superhero.

Riding high on my conversation with Gavin emboldened me in an odd way. I guess it's the little things for me. I was ready to see Senna. She Tasered me and tried to expunge Maya the first time we met, so pretty much other than assaulting me or trying to kill me, this meeting couldn't be worse.

Senna was being a stubborn pain in the ass. The two days I was sedated, she refused to come out of the room, opening it only to accept clothes and occasionally food. I wasn't surprised that she didn't immediately answer the door when I knocked.

"What!" she snapped when I knocked harder.

"Open the door Senna," I urged softly. "Please."

She was agitated and rightfully so; I doubt she got any more of an explanation other than she needed to stay until they determined she could leave. The pack was very rigid in their tactics and didn't offer a lot of room for disagreement or even explanation. It was their way, period.

She snatched the door open and then immediately went to a spot at the window. The room was one that I had come to consider mine because it was where I stayed when I first came to the retreat. Her long dark curly hair was stacked on top of her head in a messy bun, the white t-shirt was definitely new or borrowed and was a little too big, but her black yoga pants fit, and if it wasn't for the sneer on her face she would have looked like a person just hanging out at home. Just like I had the first time I stayed in the room, she seemed to have an appreciation for the view. The trees that stretched for miles made a blanket of variations of green that was comforting and serene. She moved closer to the window, her face just inches from the glass, her body resting against the frame.

"Believe it or not, we are trying to keep you safe," I said, fighting the urge to move closer. She was on edge, probably scared and definitely angry. If she could, without injury, I imagined she was ready to go out the window, like I had the first time I was brought to the house. But she was a witch with the same limitation as most humans. She couldn't jump from a two-story house without possibly breaking something.

She twisted enough to look at me, her emerald green eyes far more expressive than her face, telling me she didn't believe me.

Information would be more comforting than any platitudes that I could give her, so I told her everything. Mostly everything, it was hard navigating the complex situation, giving her what she really needed to know while protecting sensitive pack information. But in light of everything that had happened, was there any more sensitive information?

"What would have happened to you, if we would have removed her?" she asked softly, looking at me for a brief moment before returning her attention to the window.

"I can only survive as Maya's host." I'd told the story of my birth, or rather death, so many times that I had a spiel. I told it from a dissociated state despite it being a problem that weighed heavily on me. At any given day, if the Tre'ase that created Maya dies, so do I. Or if she is ever expunged from me, I die. It was something I thought about every day. Even if Logan came through and found the Tre'ase that created me, did that really protect me?

Unless we had him under watch at all times, how can we ensure that he continued to live? The only comfort was that it seemed to be very difficult to kill a Tre'ase. Not impossible, just difficult. In the two years that I've known of their existence, I've seen two die.

Senna stared at me for a long time, and the glower that had been fixed on her face since I entered the room wilted. Her features softened and she opened her mouth to say something but decided against it several times. When she finally spoke, it was so low it was barely audible. "We just wanted the other book, nothing more. Your mother left the family, and to me, you weren't family, so I didn't treat you that way." She frowned. "I grew up hearing the stories of your mother's betrayal of the family and the disdain I had for her was naturally transferred to you."

Knowing what I did about the Clostra it was a good thing that she took one. One person shouldn't have them all, including us. They should be separated.

Her eyes dourly downcast, her voice breaking, she asked, "Is my family alive?"

Irritation burned in me. They hadn't told her about her family? How could they not let her know about her family? And then I quickly realized that they might not be alive. She was already in a pretty bad state; the last thing she needed was to learn that she'd be going home to an empty house without her family. My heart ached at the idea. It was hard to hate them despite the fact they had tried to remove Maya from me to get the other books for money. They were still her family and she loved them. I didn't know what it was like to have a big family. Family consisted of me, my mother, and my grandparents. There weren't any cousins, aunts, and uncles in my life, and for the first time in a long time I felt the emptiness of it.

"I'll find out," I assured her, hoping that I wasn't going to have to deliver bad news. *Please don't let them be dead.*

She chewed on her bottom lip, and tears welled at the edge of her eyes. "Even if it's bad, you have to tell me." She turned back to the window. "We shouldn't have done that to you. If I knew what I know now, I don't think we would have. But people are willing to pay so much money for it. Enough money for us to live off for years, and the books aren't that special. Most of the spells in it can't be done without the other protected objects, so they are pretty much willing to pay millions for a book with only a few spells they can use."

"What do you mean?"

Her eyes narrowed and I was treated to a very sharp look of derision.

I don't need that from you, missy. But obviously I had missed something. We all had missed something.

"At the beginning of each spell there's an insignia that tells you which object to use," she said, the look of disbelief at my lack of knowledge of it not changing.

"Show me," I said, leading her out of the room to the library. I thought Josh would be in there, but it was empty. I left her in the room and went to Sebastian's office first before looking for Josh. The door was slightly open so I peeked in; he lifted his head but didn't say anything. Greetings seemed like a bother to him, so he just looked at me, waiting for me to speak.

Closing the door behind me, I asked, "Senna's family, are they still alive?"

"Yes. Her uncle was injured pretty bad, but I was told that he will recover."

"Are there meds you all should be on? Is there a program that we need to enroll you in to help with your social skills?" I snapped. "Why wouldn't you tell her that? She's been up there wondering about her family for two days? How can you do that to someone?"

My outburst didn't seem to affect him. His full lips were set in a thin line, his appearance indiscernible, and if at any point he felt shame or regret he wasn't showing it. He shrugged. "I didn't have clear confirmation. I do now," was his cool response. There was a pause, and when he continued his voice wasn't as cool but was all business. "What is crueler, telling her we didn't know whether or not her family was alive or allowing her to be hopeful until we had verified the information? We have that information now. Please let her know."

Sebastian was pragmatic and rarely let emotions change the way he handled things. That wasn't going to change no matter how much I willed it.

Then he returned to his computer. I waited, and he looked up again. "Did you need something else?" His tone was an invitation for me to leave.

"Just the Clostra. I need to look at them."

"Josh has them." I started to back out, and just as I was about the close the door, he added, "I'm glad that you are okay."

I started to come back in. It just seemed like a hug-it-out moment—which Sebastian quickly squashed. "Please close the door all the way behind you. Thank you."

Guess not.

He'd called me "sweetie." That little display was equivalent to him hugging me and giving me butterfly kisses, and I'm sure it wasn't going to happen again.

When I returned to the library Senna was at the table with Josh on one side and Samuel on the other. Ethan was in the corner, arms crossed, carefully watching Samuel. I didn't blame him; I didn't trust the guy, either, and the way he was salivating over the Clostra only supported my suspicions.

"Have a seat," Josh said, using his feet to push out the chair across from him.

Senna was scrolling over the pages, and when she stopped, she turned the books in my direction. "See this. This symbol here"— she pointed to a small marking at the beginning of the spell in book one and then a different one at the end of the spell in the third book—"I know this means the Gem of Levage and this one is the Fatifer."

We looked over each spell with the symbols; there weren't many, but I assumed that the strongest and most dangerous spells required a protected object. I couldn't help but be concerned that these spells required a booster to work, or perhaps the requirement served as an obstruction, to prevent most people from doing them. The protected objects were separated for a reason. What were the chances that one person would have them all? Although we only had four of the five, Claudia had the fifth one, which was as good as saying we had all the protected objects.

"Some of them are freaking scary," Senna said, frowning as she scanned over the books.

"Which ones?" Samuel asked, nearly jumping over her to look at the page. The moment he did, the words disappeared.

"It doesn't like you," she teased. Samuel smiled, the first one I'd ever seen. I was convinced that instead of a resting bitch face he had a resting glower face. He sat back in his chair, thin wide mouth spread, exposing teeth dimmed from smoking and two deep dimples. His deep cognac eyes were mesmeric and easier to see once he pushed back his disheveled dirty blond hair. Seeing him relaxed interacting with someone instead of spouting his magic-less world rhetoric made me look at him in a different light. His rugged features added years, but his eyes were gentle as they focused on Senna. I placed his age around late twenties; early thirtyish.

As she continued to garner a great deal of his attention, a gentle rose coloring blossomed over her cheeks. He instantly became old. Too old. Creepy old.

"Too bad," he said.

She winked. "You seem okay to me." For a long time they didn't seem to be able to take their eyes off each other.

Stop it!

I was ready to douse them both with cold water. I didn't want to be there for the bourgeoning of whatever it was. She was old enough to take care of herself and definitely discerning and obstinate enough not to become a convert to Team Samuel, or rather Team Magic-less Utopia.

"Will you continue?" Josh asked stiffly, failing to mask his irritation. Hot magic guy was his thing, and I didn't think he liked Samuel sharing the title with him.

She nodded. Perusing over the pages, I remembered that I hated that I was still a novice with Latin. She read through things quickly and didn't have to stop once to ask Josh a word or use Google translate.

"This one is dangerous for anyone who has magic," she said, frowning at the page. "And you need three objects to do it. It's like summoning someone, but once you call they can't decline. With a summons or calling, they don't have to answer. With this spell, they have to. If I wanted to use this against you, I could. That's messed up.".

Ethan and Josh looked at me with the same excitement. Ethos. We could call him. My heart was racing and I was trying not to get ahead of myself. But would it work with the Tre'ase that created Maya? We could find the Tre'ase without involving Logan. I'd forgotten that we wouldn't always have all three books. One was promised to Samuel, and I doubt he was leaving without it. But I pushed that little obstacle aside; I had to deal with one problem at a time.

"What objects do we need?"

"Gem of Levage, Aufero, and Fatifer and blood."

Blood. It's always blood. What I wouldn't give for a spell to ask for a strand of hair or something just as innocuous. But I had Ethos's blood, on a shirt, a knife, and as a stain on my carpet.

The anxiety that no one had acknowledged lifted. Finding the Tre'ase who created Maya wasn't an option, but at least we could get to Ethos. Both Samuel and Senna held the same look of disinterest. Senna was so far removed from this world it was doubtful she cared about Ethos's plans, and Samuel had a single-target agenda and if he could take away magic, Ethos wouldn't be anyone's problem anymore.

"Can I go home to see my mom?" Senna asked. Her large green eyes were hopeful. The absence of her former stern frown reduced her from the agitated, petulant woman she was earlier, to what she really was: a woman who was taken from her home and family by the Creed days ago and was now staying in a home full of strangers, including a cousin whom she had terrible history with. Josh looked at his hands—if it were up to him she would be leaving at that moment.

Her focus was on Ethan, who hadn't spoken: she must have remembered him from their first encounter. After a long moment of consideration, he nodded. "The East Coast Pack will be around a lot until this is handled. If you send them away, try to lose them … or pull any of the crap you pulled before. . ." He let the rest of the sentence linger. He didn't need to finish. She got the gist of it.

CHAPTER 14

A mixture of salt, tannin, and a ground metal that I wasn't familiar with made a large circle in front of me behind the pack's retreat. Just as Senna had instructed, the Fatifer was placed to my right, the Gem of Levage in the middle, and the Aufero to my left. It had returned to the odd coloring since Josh had used it on Ethan, but its magic didn't bother me because Josh's was coursing through me. I enjoyed the familiar aura of a natural source that I was able to control with ease. We weren't going to risk failure by having to do this spell while manipulating the magic in the Aufero. The downfall of the plan was that I borrowed a lot of magic from Josh, which made him weaker and unable to take on Ethos as well as he had in the past. Samuel was there as backup, but I wasn't sure how he would fare against Ethos. We needed this to work.

I double-checked everything: noise-reducing earbuds—they wouldn't drown out the shrill sound he made before but they would definitely help—sword to my right, and the Clostra in front. A couple of feet away Sebastian and Ethan were in animal form with several other pack members near them. Winter as usual had on enough weapons to hold off a small militia.

I ran my hand over the sword again. After constant practice, it had become an extension of me, and I now controlled it with the same ease as I did my body. But the confidence of my skills with it wasn't enough to keep my heart from pounding in my chest. When I exhaled, I realized I'd been holding my breath.

This had to work.

The moment the invocation was spoken magic poured over the area, consuming it until nothing but it could be inhaled. We waited for something to happen. Nothing. For a long stretch of time there was nothing but the feel of my magic wafting through the air, taunting me with my failure. *Dammit.*

I was prepared to try it again when lights swirled around me in variations of orange, red, and blue. A centripetal force of magic slammed hard into me, knocking my breath out with a powerful blow. I struggled for breath, fighting for each one I took, when an angry Ethos manifested himself without his human shell. The shrill angry sound ripped through the air, and I resisted the urge to cover my ears as I went for the sword. His tail whipped out, striking me in the chest. I stumbled back a few feet.

Again, he approached me speaking the same language he had before, but this time I understood. "Maya, wake up.".

Foreign life blossomed, spreading through me, as the unnatural feeling threatened to take over. For a brief moment I no longer felt like I was commander of my thoughts, movements, and feelings. The aching feeling of losing control of my own existence consumed me and I fought it with everything I had. A dense cloud of energy persisted, and she attempted to smother me out. *I can't lose this. I can't let her control me.* I struggled harder, yanking back control, snatching back my volition.

My magic shoved into his chest and he flew back, hitting the ground with a thud. He spread his hands over the area, and fire blazed, blocking me from him. I cast a spell—a shift of wind blew but not strong enough to control the flames. Another one came, stronger than mine, from Samuel's direction, dampening the flames to a small fire. I lunged with the sword, and it slashed through Ethos's arm, severing the limb. Another shrill noise ripped through the air. A ball blasted into my chest and magic wrapped around me binding my arms to my side. He advanced, and the fiery pits of his orange eyes seared into me. Death—he wanted to give it to me slowly and painfully. His tail lashed out, and Steven's fangs latched on to it as his claws dug in, tearing at the thick leathery epidermis.

Ethan and Sebastian attacked from behind, and the band that I had been trying to disable withered into a thick mist of destroyed magic that stuck in the air. The putrid scent of it smelled toxic. Ethos fell back, and as Ethan and Sebastian moved away, I brought down the sword like an axe, splitting his head from his body. He moved: not just the body but the head trying to inch back into position to reattach itself. *What. The. Fuck.*

We watched the bizarre occurrence. That couldn't be happening. Nothing lives without a head. Ethan, who had changed back to human form, moved close to the body; placing his hand on it he leaned down and whispered something. It stopped moving and slowly went through a strange version of the vampire's reversion, the dark scaly skin drying and shriveling before collapsing to dust. The same thing happened to the head, when it touched it. I kept staring at Ethan trying to get him to look at me, but his gaze only swept briefly in my direction, his lips drawn into a tight line as he quickly gathered up all the protected objects. The Aufero continued to build a protective field around itself whenever Ethan neared it.

"What that hell was that?" I hissed in a low whisper, sidling in close to him after grabbing the Aufero.

He was cool and indifferent as he looked at me. His brows drew together as though he wasn't sure what I was talking about.

"What you did—it was like he went through reversion. I thought Josh used the Aufero to fix you—to fix things."

Not even a flicker of interest in the conversation as he behaved as though we were simply discussing the weather as opposed to him touching Ethos and making him turn to dust.

He shrugged. "He did."

I stopped, hoping he would, but instead he kept going, turning briefly. "Sky, don't make this into something it isn't. It was just a spell. If I hadn't done it probably Samuel or Josh would have."

His mom was a witch, his maternal grandmother a dark elf— he had more magic in him than anyone else. He was bound to have some abilities that others didn't, but the cynic in me wanted it to be more. He waited, a light smile lingering on his lips "Everything there is to know about me, you already know."

"You swear."

He nodded. "Everything there is to know about me, you already know," he repeated before going into the house.

I opened the door for Quell, who had knocked so softly I wasn't sure anyone was at the door. He waited outside, slowly looking me up and down taking in the dark jeans and lilac fitted tank, then his attention went to the three-inch heels that were for appearance only. I was sure they weren't going to last most of the night. My tight curls had been tamed into submission and draped over my shoulder in loose waves.

I hadn't been out in so long it felt like I had spent my life fighting Ethos, Michaela, and every possible thing that went bump in the night. We still didn't know where Kelly was and we couldn't find the mystery manimal that Winter and I saw in the woods; but I didn't want to think about any of it. I was joining Josh, Ethan, and the rest of the pack to drink and dance until everything that happened over the past few weeks was just a memory.

He tilted his head. Smiling he touched my hair. "You look beautiful."

"Thanks, we are going out. Do you want to go?"

"No, I want to talk," he said, extending his hand. When I took it, he threaded his fingers through mine and we walked outside toward the back of the house. The heels didn't last long on the uneven surface and eventually I took them off and carried them as Quell led me farther until we were deep in the woods behind the house.

"Do you know what happened to Fiona?"

His grasp tightened; he nodded once but didn't elaborate. I wondered if Michaela was cruel enough to tell him what she did. *Who am I kidding, of course she is.* Michaela didn't see anything wrong with her actions. She was the Mistress of the otherworld, and for some reason she was given a pass on transgressions that would have gotten others punished or worse.

"Michaela asked me to leave the Seethe," he whispered.

My first impulse was to tell him he should have just told her to go to hell, but he would never do that. I had it among other choice words in the chamber of phrases I was ready to lob at her at any given moment.

The moon offered enough light that I could see the sadness on his face. As he looked past me, desolation was a thick presence between us. "I will have to leave."

I felt his sorrow and mine in the pit of my stomach. How could they do this to him? "You don't have to go. Leave the Seethe, that's fine; but don't leave here. Please."

"That isn't an option. When you are exiled from the Seethe it is considered an insult to stay. It will not end well for me. I'm going to go back home.".

I didn't think I knew where *home* was for him. He'd been gone for over seventy-years: how could that be his home? This was his home. Keeping hold of his hand, I walked over to the large oak tree, sat down, and waited for him to take a place next to me.

I couldn't speak for a long time. The idea that he was leaving had rendered me speechless, and all I could do was try to figure out a way to fix it. There was a part of me that wanted him to go because he needed to get away from Michaela, but I wondered what would happen to him. He would need blood; how would he get it? Would it be like the last time? Did she do this to hurt him or me?

"Why did you hang yourself?".

His thumb ran along the side of my hand in a slow, light rhythm before he pressed it to his lips. Coolness lingered long after he'd stopped. "I've killed five people since I've been a vampire. As a human, I lost count of how many. I can remember the women, the way they tasted, the sound of their voices, the way they fought, and the look on their faces before they died. I hate that I did it, and they are my memories—sad memories, but memories nonetheless and they haunt me. I can't picture the faces of those I killed as a human. Not one. There were so many that they merge together into nothing but a collage of my sins. I don't remember the sounds of their screams, their last words, the smell of their pain. Nothing. Shouldn't I remember some of them? Shouldn't they be bad memories, too?"

I couldn't come up with an answer that would give him the closure he needed or absolve him of the feelings. "War isn't pretty, it just isn't, even ours. I've killed people and I will probably kill more." For a brief moment, I thought about the people I'd killed. It didn't make me feel good. Knowing that I wanted to kill Michaela was even more distasteful. "Perhaps it is good that you don't remember, because that was your old life. It and the things you did during it should be put to rest. You owe it to yourself to let it go."

"That is why I did it. I hanged myself because I let it go. The faces, the violence, and all that I did; I had let it go. The memories were leaving me, and they shouldn't have." His grip on my hand tightened.

I rested my head against his shoulder. "During times like that you are forgiven for your actions. What would have happened if you hadn't done the things you had? While you see a monster the people whose lives you saved and those you saved indirectly, don't see that."

Even with the moon illuminating them, his eyes were dark, sullen. Vampirism just allowed him to hide from the things he was feeling, it didn't help. "Why did she ask you to leave?"

"The two of you mean a great deal to me; she created me, you brought me over. My feelings for you two are different but equally true. I don't think I am able to choose between the two of you.".

I wasn't particularly fond of being put in any category with Michaela, but I understood why he was exiled. She wanted him to choose and he was unable to do so. I wanted him away from her but my reasons were selfish. She didn't deserve him and she would miss him. And when I killed her, I wouldn't have to face him afterward. Vigilante justice riled so deep in me that my heart was beating erratically, ready to dish it out. My skin felt tight around me, ready to exact the punishment she deserved. I don't know if there were many I hated more than her. I pushed it aside and dealt with the situation at hand—Quell.

"I think you leaving is going to be good for you. I hate to see you go, but I think it will be good."

"I'll miss her." No matter what I said, I would never untangle his twisted logic. Michaela had saved him from his demons, somehow found a way to absolve him of his sins—or at least masked them temporarily, given him an amnesty from the war crimes he had continued to punish himself for. But she'd really wanted to recreate that person he saw himself as for her own entertainment. I wished I could break the hold she had on him.

"I want you to go. It will be better for you." I returned to my positon next to him, taking his hand as my phone buzzed in my pocket. I was supposed to meet them an hour ago. I sent a quick message to let them know I was running late.

"Will you come with me?"

I couldn't even bring myself to say the words, I simply shook my head no. It took me a while to look over at him, too much of a coward to see the look on his face.

"I will miss you," he finally said after moments of silence.

If someone had pulled out my heart and stomped on it, I don't think it would have felt less painful.

My life had become a series of visiting people I didn't like and, even worse, having to talk to them, which I was reminded of when I knocked on Demetrius's door. I didn't understand why he and Michaela lived separately but I just added that to the many things I didn't comprehend about their dysfunctional relationship.

The palatial neo-Mediterranean stone house stood out in the nondescript land of suburbia. Its manicured lawn looked like it belonged on a magazine; exotic flowers on each side of the stairs produced such a pleasant scent that it almost made me forget I was visiting a vampire's home at night, probably during his feeding time. Large pillars and stucco enclosed the entrance, darkening the area, and I started to count the many things that could go wrong with this visit.

He answered the door before I could knock again, his onyx eyes whetted with curiosity as his brow rose. Supple lips bowed into a deviant simper. Feeling more like I was entering a lion's den than a home, I advanced slowly, pressing my purse with my weapons in it closer to me. I ditched the comb, lipstick, and brush for a knife and stake.

"Well this is a very pleasant surprise," he said in a low salacious drawl. This man could make the word *marshmallow* sound dirty. I'm not sure what I expected Demetrius to be doing on a Friday night, but being dressed in dark jeans and black casual shirt that matched his midnight hair and listening to classical music wasn't it.

But the glass of sanguine liquid that I was sure wasn't wine was definitely what I expected.

"I need to talk to you," I blurted out.

"Of course, come in."

No thank you. Standing at the entryway of the lair of the strongest vampire in the world was as far as I planned to go with tempting fate and potentially becoming a snack.

"Can I get you something to drink?" he asked, his gaze slowly roving over me. I wished I had changed into something different that covered up more and didn't cling so closely to my body. The jeans fit, hugging every curve of my body, when I really wanted to be wearing oversized sweatpants and a turtleneck.

"When Michaela wanted me to come to help Quell, I did without questions. I did because you asked me to." I was playing fast and loose with the story, but I did help; but it was for Quell and not Michaela.

He nodded, taking a drink from his glass as he waited for me to continue. "I need a favor from you, please."

His voice dropped to a deep purr as he started to walk around me, slowly assessing me, and I could feel his eyes boring into me the whole time. When he was back in front of me, he was inches closer. So close, I could smell the metallic scent of blood on his breath. "What is that?"

A lazy smile played at his lips when I stepped back several steps.

"I am sure you know that Michaela asked him to leave your Seethe.".

"Yes, that was an unexpected turn of events. I had long wanted that to be the case but—"

I suspect that Michaela didn't want him to leave and since she got whatever the hell she wanted—Quell was allowed to stay.

"Let me guess, you want him to stay?" Demetrius asked.

I held my place when he moved closer and reached out to touch me. I blocked his hand. "Don't."

Returning back to his position, he took slow draws from his glass, and his body moved with the music as if he was conducting it. "I've been quite curious about his fascination with you. He is quite fond of the pack's unique little member. And you are quite unique, aren't you?" His eyes sparked with thoughtful curiosity. "I might go as far as to admit that his affections for you have surpassed those for Michaela. You understand that if I suspect it, so does she."

I tried not to react when he was in front of me, so close that it was invasive, running his fingers along my neck, slowly. "Is it just about this?" he whispered. Cool lips brushed against my neck. "May I?"

"No." My hand slipped into my purse, grabbing the handle of the knife preparing to engage if he didn't respect my wishes.

"Very well." Within a blink of my eye he was several feet away. "What do you want from me?"

"I want Quell to be able to stay. He doesn't have to be part of your Seethe, I understand that; but allow him to stay here."

"You are asking me to break my own rules. What exactly do I get if I do this?" When he took a final draw from the glass, emptying it, dark rivulets ran down his lips and he allowed them to stay. It was a reminder to me of what he was and that I was coming to him for a favor and I had denied him blood.

Demetrius inspired fear and the reputation that supported it. I tried not to show it; predators are drawn to fear, a fragrance that they enjoy. I stood taller, resisting the temptation to give into it.

"Yeah, that's about right." Things were spiraling out of control. *I might as well ask him for a unicorn, too.*

Demetrius's tongue moved languidly over his lips, removing the trail of blood.

"If I do this for you I will need you to do something for me." The dark intensity of his gaze laid heavily on me.

"No. You owe me," I asserted. I'd be damned if I would make a deal with him.

He chortled. "I voted. My vote saved Ethan's life, and I can assure you there is nothing that I would like to have more than him dead. You have had your favor."

I always assumed that the dissonance between Ethan and Demetrius was about Chris, but now it seemed it existed long before she did and only escalated when she got involved.

That was the favor? All this time I assumed Claudia had her hand in it. But all along it was because of me that the vote went in our favor.

"I don't need to tell you Michaela wasn't pleased with me for siding with you."

"Oh I forgot—we can't dare to have Michaela unhappy. Perhaps you should start a coalition of people whose main job is to make sure Michaela gets her way every single time. They should be there on the job twenty-four seven to make sure everything in the world lines up so that Michaela is happy."

Demetrius just stared at me for a long time as if I'd said the most absurd thing. After all, why shouldn't Michaela be happy? Why shouldn't she get everything she wanted? Why, didn't the world revolve around them? Their narcissism was on steroids.

"Should we discuss this favor?"

He took my silence as consent and continued. "Chris is missing," he said softly, his mood becoming subdued. "I want her back."

"Do you think someone took her?" There was something about his voice that made me feel like there was more to the story.

He shook his head.

"Demetrius, tell me what happened. If I am going to even consider this, I need to know everything." My suspicion was heightened by his evasiveness.

His teeth gripped his lips, and I was impressed with the fact that his fangs didn't cut them. I was always reminded of how sharp mine were seconds after my lips were bleeding. Another oddity about me as a result of a vampire trying to change me in vitro.

When he spoke, his voice was so low I had to strain to hear it. It was as though he was making the confession to himself. "Chris has always been quite recalcitrant." He allowed the silence to settle on his words. "Once she joined the Seethe, it was a hard transition for her to be under my rule. She and I did not always see eye to eye and I had to make my leadership be known."

He wasn't looking at me anymore, and for the first time I saw something I thought I would never see—regret. What the hell did he do to her to let his *leadership* be known? I recounted the statement he made to Sebastian about liking the wild ones, so that he could break them. Apparently he tried to break Chris and it didn't work. She left him.

"Then why aren't you looking for her? You have better resources than I do."

His jaws clenched and his lips pulled into a tight line. He didn't have to voice it; I knew exactly why. Although Michaela allowed their little liaisons or whatever the hell they were calling it, apparently using the Seethe to look for his mistress wasn't going to happen. What a tangled web he had gotten himself into. He needed to look for his mistress or whatever Chris was to him—Ethan stood by the belief that they weren't sleeping together—but she meant something to him and now she was gone. He wasn't able to go look for her, and no one in his Seethe could do it without Michaela finding out.

Demetrius wasn't able to look for his mistress because the Mistress of the Seethe wouldn't be happy with it. And now that she'd exiled Quell she would have more time to focus on him and his extracurricular activities. *Good, they deserve each other.*

"Let me make sure I have this right: you want me to find Chris, who left you after you decided to make your leadership known. I'm not going to ask what that entailed, but I'm sure it wasn't pleasant for her. How audacious of her! You mean she had the nerve to leave you after you tried to break her and demonstrate your authority to get her to behave the way you wanted her to?"

My passing judgment on him meant nothing to him.

His features relaxed and a light smile soon rested over his lips and face. "I saved Chris twice, she is mine. I have as much right to her life as she does."

This conversation was so over. I nodded. "Okay. Let's ask Chris and see how she feels about that. Oh, we can't, because she left you."

I headed for the door, ignoring him as he called my name. Finally, he said, "You know what I want and if you want Quell to stay, then that is the only way he will."

I wasn't a fan of Chris, in fact if there was a group named "Chris is a total bitch" I would quickly put in my membership request, but she deserved better and I wasn't going to be involved with this. Looking over my shoulder, I huffed, "I hope she never comes back."

Before I could get out the door, the dark shadow that accompanied his presence coiled around me. A cold hard grimace crept on his lips as he pulled them back from his fangs. "Do you really want to antagonize the person who can secure Quell's fate? Michaela banished him, I can do worse.".

Ethan was right. I had shown my hand. Quell was a weakness the Seethe kept using against me. Quell was better off away from them.

CHAPTER 15

I was late. Really late. Winter was on the dance floor with Steven. Most of the pack was scattered throughout the club. Some on the dance floor, others around the stage, and others around the bar, testing their alcohol tolerance. When I saw Josh on the stage, my mouth dropped. How many shots had it taken for him to gather the courage to be there? I wondered how long it would take for our club to regain its reputation as the "it" spot after Josh made a fool of himself.

The featured artist was an up-and-coming rapper who was quickly becoming more than a local talent. It wasn't uncommon for Josh to join people on stage, he could sing. No one was giving him a record deal but he had proven that he had an ability to carry a note, yet I thought the cheering he incited had a lot to do with the way he commanded a room more than his singing abilities. He was charismatic, but I often wondered if the same magnetism that drew people to were-animals were the same thing that drew people to him. Were-animals have something carnal, instinctive, that enticed and seduced. People never knew what it was, they were just aware that something captured their interest in a manner so enthralling that they couldn't resist. Josh was magic, period. There was something wondrous about him and even I had a hard time ignoring it, even though I knew it existed. People who didn't have an idea about it didn't stand a chance.

When Josh took the mic, my chest tightened, I could feel the heat of my embarrassment for him creeping up my cheeks. *Poor Josh, this is going to be one of those moments that* will *take a lifetime to live down.* I closed my eyes because I couldn't witness this. It was going to be like watching inebriated patrons who didn't have friends honest enough to tell them they lacked talent to sing karaoke. For some reason, a couple of drinks seem to make people forget that they were going to sound just as bad on stage as they did in their car and bathroom. Josh was about to do the same thing.

How many shots had he tossed back?

He moved to the beat as a woman sang the hook in the background, a light, sultry and upbeat sound, but it wasn't strong enough to drown him out. I looked away when he started rapping —I couldn't watch the train wreck. But I quickly turned back when the lyrics came from him as smoothly as they did from the guy before him as they went back and forth spitting lyrics while the crowd went wild. I continued to wait for the disaster that never happened.

I expected magic to overtake the room. Or a gust of it to shroud me, creep over my skin, pricking at my senses, because clearly we all had been enthralled or something. We had to have been charmed and glamoured by a spell—but there wasn't one. Nothing. It was all Josh and his skills to captivate an audience by being nothing more than Josh, a very charismatic witch. He simply finished, tossed the mic to someone, and left the stage—or rather attempted to. The moment he stepped off he had attracted a small group of fans. After a few minutes of trying to get through the crowd and being bumped and splashed by several drinks, I gave up.

Ethan didn't do crowds, so he would have a table in a corner somewhere. I scanned the club and found him at a small table having a drink with a redhead who was laughing her ass off. I'd known Ethan for a couple of years and he wasn't that damn funny, so I wasn't sure why she kept tossing back her hair and giggling. I doubted anything he said was that funny. When he finally noticed me, he smiled and waved me over. I didn't immediately move. She was beautiful, tall and curvy. Her small black dress hugged her body, making her movements seductive. Who was I kidding, even I found her hot. Holding Ethan's gaze for several minutes, I could hear his voice in my head telling me about his countless infidelities, the trail of broken hearts that he'd left in his past, and his acceptance that he would do it again and often. I was naïve to think what we had was different, that I was different from the other women in his past.

I dropped my gaze from his and turned to leave.

"Sky, where are you going?" Ethan asked, a few feet away.

"Home."

Ethan's gunmetal gaze fixed on me, his brow furrowing as a variety of emotions played across his features, the most profound, confusion. "Why are you going home?"

Sagging against my car, I let the hair that had fallen over my face stay there. Embarrassed, I refused to give Ethan the satisfaction of it. "Because I don't want to spend the evening watching you try to get laid," I snapped. My emotions were getting to me and I wanted—no, I needed—to get it together.

Tension permeated the air. I could see him through the strands of hair and was about to brush them aside, when he did. I lifted my eyes to meet his. He took a while to speak and the words didn't seem to come easily. "I'm sorry."

What the hell was he sorry for? Sorry that he didn't know how to keep it in his pants? Sorry that monogamy gave him the hives? Sorry that he hurt me and would probably keep doing it if I let him? The list of things that he could be sorry for was a loop in my head.

"Sorry for what?"

His tongue moved across his lips and he looked away before returning his attention to me. "My past. I'm sorry that it makes you jealous and insecure. I don't want you to feel that way. You don't have anything to worry about with us. We're good."

At this point I had slipped so far into the rabbit hole of this bizarre world I didn't know what to do. This conversation was making Ethan uncomfortable, which, I wasn't too proud to admit, kind of made my day. Most of the time, I was the one squirming, uncomfortable, and rarely in control of things when Ethan was involved. It was a very good feeling to be on other end of it. No wonder Ethan enjoyed it so much—it was red velvet cake, peppermint bark, key lime pie, and fine wine rolled into one very delicious moment. This was so good it had to be fattening. I wanted it to last.

"What do you mean?" *Yes, Ethan, this conversation is happening in great detail.*

He chuckled, pressing his lips firmly against mine. As his tongue grazed lightly over my lips I could taste a hint of alcohol, but it was the kiss that was intoxicating. He turned to go back to the bar. "I'm going back in, I really hope you join me.".

"It's too loud in there and we have more to discuss." I was unable to let go of the moment. Watching his unease as he discussed feelings was just too amusing. I had the reins and it was fun.

A smirk cruised over his lips, and he kept walking backward to the bar. "We've discussed it enough. This conversation is over, Sky. I'll see you when you decide to come in, okay? I'll order you a French martini, you seem to like those."

That didn't last very long. He just slipped the reins right out of my hands.

. . .

The redhead was still at the table, finding Winter as equally funny as she found Ethan. By the time I got there, her hand was linked with Winter's and she was leading her to the dance floor. And His Smugness didn't let the look falter as it became clear that Ms. Giggles was with Winter as they danced. Dancing that was quickly becoming something not appropriate for a PG-13 audience.

The smug twist in his lips eventually downgraded to an equally annoying smirk. "You could have told me," I eventually said, taking a sip from my martini.

"You could have asked." *Why the smirk—anything but the smirk.* But it was set on his face, and the usually stern and intense eyes had a miscreant glint.

He leaned in. "It's a moot point now, but a better question is, why do you smell like Demetrius?"

His smile disappeared.

How does he smell anything? Alcohol, perfume, and pheromones were the only scents I could detect.

"I don't want to talk about it." I shrugged off the question.

"But we will."

Did I really think that was going to work?

I didn't have anything to hide so I told him everything, and he listened and tried to mask his anger as it filtered through like every emotion that Ethan showed, tempestuous and strong.

"And what did you say to him?"

"I declined. Why would I agree to something like that?"

"It's funny, when it comes to Quell you don't seem to have a lot of boundaries and logic seems to be absent from your decisions."

We sat for minutes in uncomfortable silence as I worked on my second martini and he nursed his Scotch and studied me like he was trying to figure out a complex puzzle. "I want Quell gone, too. I don't like what he does to you and everything you are willing to do to keep him safe."

Why, Mr. Ethan, I do believe you are jealous.

Before I could ask Josh slipped in next to me, two shots in each hand.

"That's six," Ethan said to his brother.

"You're counting my drinks now? You've taken the big brothering to a new level, you control freak."

"I don't care how many drinks you have while you are *working*."

I thought I was the only one who didn't consider what he did most nights—having drinks with half-dressed "it" girls, hanging out with the athletes and their obscene entourages, on the floor dancing with whoever asked—working.

"We are going to see Logan tomorrow and I don't need you hung over," Ethan said.

My night went from bad to worse. I understood the importance of knowing who created Maya, but I would prefer us spending the time and resources on a way to get her out of me and keep me alive.

"I'll be fine," Josh said, taking another sip. He leaned in to me, and the alcohol wafted off his breath as it brushed against my ear. "I will find a way to get her out and keep you.".

Always perceptive, Josh asked me to dance, and I followed. Over the past two days I'd discussed my concerns about Maya with him extensively. He knew that I feared I might not be able to control her or stop her. He didn't seem to be very concerned about it. The problem still remained: I needed her or another spirit shade to live, and it wasn't like you could go to the local department store or Amazon and pick one up.

The music was too loud to really talk and I wanted to dance, to move and not think about all the blood shed over the past few days, Quell leaving, Steven moving out, the Faerie that I hosted and the many more that may still exist, or that Marcia attempted to have the otherworld turn against me and the pack and kill

Ethan. I even tried to dance off Ethan's little stunt today, but that was harder to do.

I pulled Josh closer so he could hear me. "Did you see what your brother did today?"

He stopped dancing, glanced in Ethan's direction, and then returned to me. "Yeah, he said it was an archaic spell that Claudia taught him years ago."

I stopped dancing and looked at Ethan, meeting his gaze. He smiled and I returned it before directing my attention back to Josh. "You don't believe him?"

Shrugging, he sighed and ran his hand several times through his hair, curiosity and concern dulling his eyes. "Claudia said she did." But he didn't seem convinced. "I trust Ethan, I do. But I feel like he and Claudia are hiding something to protect me."

Or just hiding something.

We had stopped pretending to dance and focused on Ethan. Maybe we were driven to our conspiracy theories because of all the secrets in the past, but the secrets were out, exposed for the otherworld to see. I couldn't imagine anything more being out there, but I just couldn't let go of that tinge that there was still something.

Logan never seemed bothered when we arrived at his home, and this time wasn't an exception. The door opened before we could knock. Josh entered first and Logan gave him the same look of disinterest he usually gave him. Logan was drawn to pain, death, and chaos. It intrigued him, which might explain his obsession with Chris. She was all those things mixed with a side order of bitch.

The distinctive scent of cinnamon, mint, and oak met us at the door. It was the typical smell of his home, except there was also a strong scent of tannin and fresh blood that inundated the air. And the smile that settled on his face was far more deviant than usual. His eyes barely glanced in Sebastian's direction, but the moment Ethan walked through the door, his gaze planted on him with interest. The odd art on his arms went spastic, and his eyes narrowed.

Stepping closer, Ethan put his arm out to stop him from getting any closer. He stood just a few inches from Ethan, his hand opening and closing with the anticipation of touching him. "May I?"

"No."

But he was too distracted to care. He took another step closer, panting. His nostrils flared and his eyes glowed as he leaned in closer. "Remarkable," he whispered as he tilted his head, examining Ethan.

"Get away from me," Ethan growled, reaching the apex of his patience.

"We need to talk to you," Sebastian said, stepping between them and trying to refocus the distracted Tre'ase.

Dragging his attention from Ethan he gave it to Sebastian. "Of course you do or you would not be here. You want me to find the Tre'ase that created Maya? Am I correct?"

Sebastian nodded and Logan turned to me for me to answer.

"Yes," I confirmed. Something was off about him. He was unusually confident with a hint of malice and I couldn't put my finger on the changes. I didn't like it. I looked around the room to the door where we found the woman before.

"It's empty, and if it weren't I'm sure you'd just meddle again. It has to be rather exhausting to not only deal with your own problems—and from my understanding there are many—but with those of others." His eyes flew to Ethan, a smirk played at his lips, and he kicked my annoyance level to ultra-high.

"Sorry, if we find your kinks disturbing," I offered.

The smirk twisted into a coy smile. "No need to be judgmental. Some might think your little liaison with Quell ... it is Quell? The Lost One? Is worthy of judgment, too." He couldn't seem to draw his attention from Ethan, which made Josh and me look at Ethan a little more, too. Sebastian was the only one able to fight the curiosity.

"Can you help us find Maya's creator?" I asked, redirecting the Tre'ase, who would stare and touch Ethan all day if we'd let him.

"Of course. Have a seat."

But before I could do it, my curiosity needed to be slaked. "Is Maya a Faerie?"

I held my breath, but I'm not sure why. And when he nodded and said, "Half. Her mother was a witch, but the combination didn't decrease her strength significantly," I didn't realize it would still shock me. There was a large part of me that wanted to be wrong; but at least Emma, Maya's mother, wasn't a Faerie, just a witch. *Just* wasn't appropriate for describing a witch. Marcia wasn't *just* a witch, the Creed weren't *just* witches, and London and Samuel weren't *just* anything. Witches were powerful and could be dangerous, too. There wasn't anything *just* about them.

The desire to get rid of her increased. The power didn't appeal to me if I couldn't control it. Not to mention the idea that I had to live my life constantly trying to keep her in check.

"What about Ravyn, Emmalesse, Leonel, are they still alive?"

"Alive is relative." His gaze slipped toward Ethan, who returned the look with a glare.

"Are they spirit shades?"

"Emmalesse is dead; it was quite violent from the rumors."

"What about the others?"

"Leonel is a spirit shade; Ravyn is still alive, but his whereabouts are unknown."

"Does Leonel have a host?"

Logan moved in closer to me. "I think I've answered many of your questions without requesting anything in return. Would you like me to answer the others?" The patterns started to move, coiling around his fingers. Strong magic flowed from them when he extended his hands to take mine. My hand inched toward them. I was really desperate—too desperate—for answers and this was a strange place to be. Did I want to be indebted to him?

"What are you asking from me?" That wasn't how it worked; I knew that but it was worth a try. Tre'ase were never specific in their requests. You were indebted to them and that is all that mattered. Just as I was about to touch his hand, logic gave me a quick kick in the butt. I yanked back. Being indebted to a Tre'ase was bad; being indebted to someone with Logan's perversions was even worse. I had enough information to go on. I would have to find the rest out without his help.

Logan chortled when I moved several feet away making sure I didn't accidentally touch him. He moved his hand in the direction of the table, inviting me to sit.

After he gathered some items, he took a seat across from me and placed a knife, a small bowl, and resins and a powder that I didn't recognize on the table. He then went to a small box across the room and returned with an odd-looking candle that smelled like blood and honey.

Josh's eyes widened with curiosity as he stepped closer to it. "How did you find one?"

"When I said I needed days to get what I needed, this is why. Would you like it when I'm done?"

Josh couldn't get the yes out fast enough and that made me wonder what the hell was so special about the candle.

"It's the strongest thing you can use to source someone without using their blood. And it can enhance any spell." The way Josh looked at it went past longing, it was taking a one-way trip to creepy-ville. The were-animals had an addiction to violence whether they admitted it or not, but I was starting to think that Josh had an addiction to magic rather than a healthy curiosity.

"If you don't need blood, why do you have a knife?" Blood was powerful and I didn't want him to have mine. I didn't trust that he wouldn't keep some of it.

"It's for me." He poured the resin and powder in the bowl and then lit the candle before closing his hand around the knife. He was in a state of euphoria as the blade sliced across his hand. Only he could find pleasure in something like that.

He took hold of my hand with the uncut one. As soon as he said the invocation and placed a few droplets in the bowl, a foul odor drifted from the bowl, a rainbow of colors hovered over it, and a face appeared, very similar to the one sitting across from me and so was the home that was revealed. Then my face flashed and everything disappeared.

"We do not have time for your games!" Sebastian lashed out, the rage rolling off of him more potent than the magic that remained in the room.

Unaffected by Sebastian's outburst, Logan simpered with the confidence of a man who felt he was untouchable. "*Tsk. Tsk.* We will have none of that." He came to his feet and went to his cabinet. Then he pulled out a cylindrical jar with a pink hunk of flesh the size of a fist submerged in water. An actual heart, still pumping at a steady rate.

"Meet Kalese, Maya's creator." He pulled back his lips in a foreboding grin and although he was still in human form, I could imagine the misshapen maw of his natural form twisting into a terrifying grin.

Ethan reacted, lunging at Logan and hoisting him against the wall by his neck. "What kind of games are you playing?"

Logan could barely speak, only a few words managed their way out as he struggled to breathe through a partially closed throat. "I ... die ... Skylar ... too."

Ethan dropped him and Logan collapsed to the ground sucking in several breaths before he came to his feet. Panting, he said, "As long as I am alive, so is the heart."

Regaining his composure, he stood up and smiled devilishly.

First he directed his attention to Sebastian and then to Ethan, the confidence reasserting itself. "As long as I'm alive so is the heart. It's probably more important than ever to keep me alive." He turned to look at me, and his smile widened.

"Now, let's get down to business. You all have something I *want* and something I *need*, let's make a deal."

MESSAGE TO THE READER

∼

Thank you for choosing *Lunar Marked* from the many titles available to you. My goal is to create an engaging world, compelling characters, and an interesting experience for you. I hope I've accomplished that. Reviews are very important to authors and help other readers discover our books. Please take a moment to leave a review. I'd love to know your thoughts about the book.

For notifications about new releases, *exclusive* contests and giveaways, and cover reveals, please sign up for my newsletter at McKenzieHunter.com.

Made in the USA
Monee, IL
19 March 2025

14240030R00194